The Adventures of
Captain Heman Kenney and Lady Catherine
1833-1917

Catherine Kenney Wilcoxson

Library of Congress Control Number: 2017917453

Publisher's Cataloging-in-Publication Data
Wilcoxson, Catherine Kenney 1952 -
The Adventures Of Captain Heman Kenney and Lady Catherine 1833-1917
Revised Reformatted Edition: First published in-August 21,2009 by AuthorHouse, 1663 Liberty Drive, Bloomington, IN 47403 - www.authorhouse.com -- Phone: 1-800-839-8640
ISBN: 978-1-4490-0212-1 (sc;) ISBN: 978-1-4490-0213-8 (e) – LCN 2009908363
DeQuincy, Louisiana
Watt Light Publishing Company
562p
ISBN-13: 978-0-9966807-5-2 – Paperback
ISBN -13: 978-0-9966807-6-9 -- Ebook

Subjects: 1. Sailing – Ireland -- U.S. -- Canada. 2. Fiction – Romance Novel. 3. Fiction – Literary. – Historical. 4. Slavery – slave trade – Underground Railroad – "Freedom Land". 5. Guilt -- God's forgiveness. 6. U. S. Civil War – Naval Battles – Effect on Nova Scotia, Canada.
Summary: *The Adventures of Captain Heman Godfrey Kenney And Lady Catherine 1833-1917*. The call of the sea sets Heman Kenney, a young captain from hunger-starved Ireland, on a journey across the ocean to the new world. Familiar events of the development of the new country of Canada unfold along side the blossoming love story between Captain Heman Kenney and his beloved Elizabeth. But the deeper emotions come from Heman as he struggles with the dark choices he made in the past. Will Elizabeth forgive Heman from the sins that haunt him? Evading American Civil War ships, the wrath of Queen Victoria and disgruntled natives, join Heman and his crew of misfits as they travel the open seas upon the other love of his life: the *Lady Catherine*.-- Christopher P.E. Wilcoxson .

DEDICATION

I would like to dedicate this book to Paul Wilcoxson, my wonderful husband, for without him, this book would still be in the mires of my imagination. He stood by me and always encouraged me to continue. He spent many late nights on the computer checking out history, making my story more real. Thank you, Dear. I love you.

I would also make mention of my daughter, Jennifer Boyle, and my son, Christopher Wilcoxson. Jennifer was my chief research person. She could find anything I needed. She made sure the history of the times held true. Christopher helped me with my editing and was my best critic. His expertise and his degree in Electronic Media Journalism were invaluable. Both Jennifer and Christopher showed great patience with their mother. Thank you and I love you both.

ACKNOWLEDGMENTS

I am thankful for my readers. These are the people who read chapter after chapter of my unfinished manuscript. Without their encouragement, I would not have made it through the process of writing this book.

Betty Blanton, Danville, Illinois
Carolyn Bowman, Covington, Indiana
Jennifer Boyle, DeQuincy, Louisiana
Lois Brumwell, Dartmouth, Nova Scotia, Canada
Janice K. Elwell, Danville, Illinois
J and Alice Fleming, St. Catharine's, Ontario, Canada
Joan Fleming, St. Catharine's, Ontario, Canada
Ruth Jones, Danville, Illinois
Barry Kenney, St. Peter's, Nova Scotia, Canada
Darren Kenney, Halifax, Nova Scotia, Canada
Jack Macy, Covington, Indiana
Sue Nasser, Danville, Illinois
Linda Sipco, Jena, Louisiana
Geri Spears, DeQuincy, Louisiana
Mary Spears, DeQuincy, Louisiana
Diana Smith, Veedersburg, Indiana
Bill and Linda Thompson, Wallacetown, Ontario, Canada
Joyce Thompson, Jena, Louisiana
Christopher Wilcoxson, Sharonville, Ohio
Paul Wilcoxson, Covington, Indiana
Russell Wilcoxson, Nashville, Tennessee
Sue Wilson, Jena, Louisiana

AUTHOR'S UPDATE
Eight Years Later

It has been eight years since *The Adventures of Captain Heman Kenney and Lady Catherine 1833-1917* was first published by AuthorHouse, August 31, 2009. Since then thousands of my book have been sold. I am thankful to those who have purchased my book and read it. Many have commented about how they enjoyed the book and wished it had not ended. Thank you for your kind words.

I am now reissuing *The Adventures of Captain Heman Kenney and Lady Catherine 1833-1917* through our own publishing company, *Watt Light Publishing*, updated, reformatted, and with corrections. Any book is subject to errors because authors are human. My book is no exception.

I have written two other books. The first is *Open Doors and Open Windows: A Journey with God,* the story of my journey to God and His Son Jesus Christ. It has been reissued as well. The second of my other books is *Don't Forget Maude: The Tale of Two Sisters.* It is the sequel to *The Adventures of Captain Heman Kenney and Lady Catherine 1833-1917,* about the second generation of Kenneys in Sheet Harbour, Nova Scotia, Canada . Information about any of my books can be found at my website: www.theladycatherinecompany.com. If you have questions, I would be happy to correspond with you through email at cawilcoxson@theladycatherinecompany.com.

Contents

CHAPTER ONE

Lady Catherine
1882

The activity on Watt Section Wharf was slowing down on this cold March evening. The sun was sinking into the Atlantic. It looked like a red-hot ball falling from the sky into the frozen ocean. Red and orange streams of light lit up the heavens. The cold made its way through one's coat, and it could be felt in one's bones. It was a sign of another cold winter's night that was just beginning along the coast of Nova Scotia.

All the fishing boats were tied down. Only a few hours before, they made their way up the Straight of Watt Section. It looked like a parade as all the fishing boats passed by the lighthouse. She seemed to smile and welcome them home. Each boat had its own place to tie up to the wharf. When all were secured, the job of unloading the catch of the day began.

It was a good catch, unlike some other days when the men worked hard, only to find the nets sparse with fish. But not today. Everyone was in a grateful mood. Deep-sea fishing was a hard and dangerous job. The ocean can be one's friend one day and a dangerous adversary the next – a Dr. Jekyll and Mr. Hyde complex. There was a feeling of relief, for the fishermen were back on land. The ocean didn't win today.

The Watt Section Wharf was filled to capacity. Horses pulling wagons lined up four deep. The fish peddlers were buzzing around like bees. Since this was wintertime and the bees were deep in their hives waiting for spring, it was a curious sight.

Thomas, a six-foot giant of a man from Cape Breton, was first in line. He was ready. "Hey, Gerald, my man, looks like you had a good one." Thomas could see Gerald standing in his boat up to his knees in fish.

"I thought you moved back to Cape Breton by now." Gerald passed him a friendly smile.

"I keep saying I'm going. But maybe things are beginning to look up here. Looks like you got some fish."

"It's about time, wouldn't you say? I swear they were asleep all winter and today they awoke. We were there to invite them into our boat." Gerald's laugh was light and private.

"Everyone at the fish packing plant will be happy," Thomas added. "We are tired of eating porridge and deer meat all winter."

Gerald was happy. He sold his whole catch to Thomas in five minutes.

As the fishermen unloaded their great catch and peddlers loaded their wagons, a cloud of screaming gulls hovered over their heads. The scraps of fish were thrown over the sides of the wharf, causing a war of the gulls. No table manners here — everyone for himself. The strong got most of it; the old and weak were lucky to get any. No one seemed to notice the great battle going on. The fishermen had seen it daily, and somewhere back in their minds, it was music to their ears. No war meant no fish; no fish meant lean times. The music being played out by the gulls was more than welcomed that day. Every available barrel on the wharf was filled with cod, halibut, and herring. The peddlers went away happily, and the fishermen were left with a sense of accomplishment and a pocket full of money. Life was good.

The fishing boats were cleaned and now it was their turn to rest. Everything around them was quiet. The slapping of the salt water on their bows was a reminder that at sunrise they and their masters would repeat the journey offshore. The ocean would be calling and they would answer that call. The fishing boats always took whatever the ocean threw at them. But on this clear, cool night, they were safe in this small Harbour.

This wharf was home not only to the fishing boats, but a string of dories added to the colourful sight. The various colours of the dories came from leftover paint, which protected them from the salt water. The Harbour also had more than one schooner anchored. These schooners brought trade goods from far off lands daily. The dories were kept busy going to and fro carrying the wares from the schooners to the wharf. That too had stopped for the day.

Gerald and Lloyd were the last to leave the wharf. Gerald looked at Lloyd, "That's a beautiful sunset tonight."

"Yeah," replied Lloyd. "Red sky at night means morning delight; maybe we will have another fair day for fishing tomorrow."

"Yeah." Gerald wasn't much of a talker, but he couldn't help himself from saying, "I never get tired of looking at the sun setting; each time I see it, it gives me great comfort. Like an old friend, you might not see that old friend every day, but you know he will be back. It's something you can count on."

"Go on," Lloyd said. "I didn't know you were a poet," laughing with a laugh that came deep from inside his stomach.

"Get on with ya! You are a narrow person who wouldn't understand," retorted Gerald.

"Didn't mean to get your back up! It was really pretty what you said. Tell me more."

Gerald looked at Lloyd and shook his head. "Enough talking; it never fails to get me nowhere."

Lloyd decided to try and smooth things over, "I know what you mean about the sunset. It's prettier than a picture. Looking out at the Harbour and seeing the schooners rocking up and down is like dancing on the current. I wouldn't want to be anywhere else. Just you and me, Gerald." As he was speaking, Lloyd put his arm around Gerald's shoulders.

"Go on with ya!" Gerald's voice was loud as he jumped back.

Lloyd's laughter returned from the inside of his stomach. "All this laughing is making me hungry. Let's go home to the wives, Gerald. They will have something good cooking. It is good to go home with money in my pocket. The Mrs. will be smiling on me tonight." He winked at Gerald.

Gerald swore his face turned red, and he was too embarrassed to speak. As the men walked along the wharf, they could hear the cries of the gulls, as they made their way to Hen Island to roost for the night. The gulls could hardly fly, being heavy from their great feast. Some distance to their right, the light from the lighthouse was silhouetted as she shone in the dusk of the evening. She began a long night's work, her light searching for a ship in need, while the men's work was finished for the day.

Lloyd cast his arm slightly right towards a schooner and said, "Now, that's the best of them all. Just look at her. She looks like a fine lady. Her name suits her, "*Lady Catherine.*" Sounds like Royalty. Other schooners come and go, but not the *Lady Catherine*; she is queen of the Harbour. This is her home. When other schooners approach, they stop and bow. They ask her for permission to pass by to Sheet Harbour."

"Now who's being a poet?" Gerald chided.

"I must be catching it from you." Walking along in silence, they soon rounded the bend of the road.

"I remember the day she sailed into the Harbour for the first time."

"Yeah, we all do. You ask anyone here in Watt Section and they will tell you what they were doing that afternoon when the Kenneys came sailing in. It changed our lives, it did. And that was for the good, that is. A fine Captain Heman Kenney is," bragged Gerald.

Lloyd nodded as Gerald continued, "He's well respected around these parts. Everyone accepted him as though he was born here, even though he came from Ireland, he did. Brought The *Lady Catherine* with him. He made a name for himself, and one can learn a lot from him, you can."

Gerald broke the rhythm of their stride as he searched for his leather tobacco pouch in his pants pocket. He filled his pipe and struck a wooden match on the bottom of his boot. "His children."

"Mainly lassies, are they not?"Lloyd interrupted. The deep rich earthy fragrance of Gerald's pipe smoke caused him to search in his pants pocket for his own pouch of tobacco.

"Yes, many lassies and one young lad. He had them rowing his dories taking supplies out to *Lady Catherine*. Never saw anything like it. He must be getting ready to sail on a trade trip. People look up to him, they do. He has made a name for himself for sure." For a time they continued their walk in silence, two pipes glowing as dusk turned to darkness.

"His Mrs."

"A fine looking lady she is."

Lloyd was used to Gerald interrupting, that was the kind of friendship they had. "Yes, Elizabeth is a friend to every woman in the Harbour, including my Mrs. and yours.

"Money too," Lloyd added.

"Money. . . ?" Gerald was lost in the moment and Lloyd was always changing the subject in mid-stream.

"Not just a name, but Captain Kenney has made money. Just look over there, a fine house. The biggest house from here to Halifax, it is." As Lloyd and Gerald looked towards the well-known Kenney Show House, they stopped in their tracks. They couldn't move. Unconsciously biting down hard on their pipes, they both saw it at the same moment. Fire. The one thing that brought fear to their inner being. Fire. The side of the great house closest to the water was afire. The fire was small, but it grew larger by the minute.

"Fire!" They finally could speak the word. Gerald and Lloyd yelled, "Fire!" Emptying their pipes and jamming them back into their pockets in unison, they ran as fast as they could towards Captain Kenney's house. The house was still a half mile away as they ran up the road. Lloyd jumped the fence and headed through the field. Gerald was right behind him. They both knew this was the shortest way to the house.

"Fire! Fire!" they both shouted as they desperately tried to close the distance between them and the fire. The snow was not deep, but it was still very slippery and slowed the progress of the two desperate men. Gerald and Lloyd thought they would never reach the house. "Gerald, you bang on the front door. I will meet you at the well."

There were twenty-four steps up to the wrap-around veranda. Gerald only used half of them to get to the top. He ran along the veranda, shouting, "Fire! Fire! Get out! Fire!" Still, there was no response. He banged on the door so hard that he thought it would break. Finally, the door was opened by Captain Kenney himself.

"Your house is on fire!" Captain Kenney, "Your house is on fire!" Gerald watched as Captain Kenney's face turned white and then grey. Then he noticed a tenseness in the man's jaw and the wildness in his dark eyes.

Heman saw that his whole family had gathered in the foyer to see what all the commotion was about, and he turned into the great leader that he was. "Mary Elizabeth and Eliza." His eyes got their attention before his words were even out of his mouth. "Go to the kitchen – anything that will hold water. . ." Before he was finished, they were running to the kitchen. "Meet at the well." "Laura and Sarah, go with your mother and grandmother to the well." As he spoke, he glanced at his sweet wife Elizabeth. There was fear in her eyes. "Be strong, Elizabeth."

He didn't have to say the words. Elizabeth was the strongest woman he had ever known. Heman's mind flashed back to the cholera scare in the Harbour of Halifax. That was the birth of her great strength. Young she was, but he could still see her stamping her foot and clapping her hands, directing Moses, one of his officers on *Lady Catherine*. She had but a short time to clear their living quarters because there was cholera in the Harbour. His memory of her climbing aboard an overloaded carriage in the middle of the night, heading for her parents home was one of pride. Any other woman would have fallen apart. But not his sweet Elizabeth. . .

Alexander's crying jerked him back to the present. Heman looked over at his only son. His mind flashed again. There was another, William, named after his own brother. He died just two years ago. *as it really been that long?* His racing mind returned and he spoke to Alexander, "Be strong my son; be a man. Help your mother." Alexander wiped away his tears with the back of his hand; he had decided to be a man, whatever a man could be at the age of six.

Gerald watched this tide of events happening in front of him as he might watch play-acting on a stage. Heman certainly was the main character and everyone seemed to have a part to play. He was amazed how this man could make people take part and know their jobs without uttering a word. Heman didn't have to use harsh words. No, his words were full of love and concern and loyalty. The family obeyed because of love, not because the master had spoken. Gerald watched this as if it was happening in slow motion although only a few moments had passed.

Heman turned to Gerald. "Show Us." He knew Daniel, his father, would be right behind.

They ran to the east side of the house. On the roof by the chimney, flames danced in and out. "We will need a ladder! In the barn!" As they headed around the corner of the house towards the barn, they almost ran into Lloyd and Wayne carrying the coveted ladder.

"There is water in the rain barrel." Underneath the eaves of the house stood the barrel. The top was iced over but was soon chipped away and the water could be seen. Mary Elizabeth, out of breath, appeared around the same corner carrying a bucket of water. *Just in time,* Heman thought. His oldest child at the age of fifteen was as strong as her mother. He took the bucket from her and said, "Keep the rain barrel filled." She turned and disappeared into the darkness as quickly as she had appeared.

Daniel held the bottom of the ladder while Heman was the first one up. Reaching the top, the smoke stung his eyes. Then he began to cough. "Please, God, not now." Heman was pleading with God himself. His cough cleared and he was able to fill his lungs with the cold salt air. Opening his eyes, he could see the fire spreading along the roof. *It must be inside the attic by now,* he thought. He threw the bucket of water on the flames. Turning around to make his way down, he met the eyes of Gerald. Gerald was over halfway up the ladder. He passed a full bucket of water to Heman.

"Give me your empty bucket," Gerald commanded. A bucket brigade had been started.

A bell was ringing. Gerald and Heman looked at each other. Heman yelled, "That's my Elizabeth!" Elizabeth was on the veranda by the front door. A bell was there, the same bell she used to say, "Welcome home," to Heman when she saw the *Lady Catherine* approach the Harbour. The same bell she used in farewell to Heman as he left her on his many trade trips. Tonight, she rang the bell for help.

"Alexander, come here!" commanded Elizabeth. "Ring the bell and don't stop." She knew the fire was on the other side of the house and Alexander would be in no danger.

Alexander in his best man's voice said, "I will ring it forever."

Lloyd turned to Wayne, "We need another ladder."

"Follow me." Wayne led the way as they entered the barn for the second time The only ladder Lloyd could see was the one to the hayloft. Wayne was already ripping it off the barn wall. This was an amazing feat because Wayne only had one arm. One arm didn't stop Wayne from doing anything, including getting this ladder.

Elizabeth and all the girls kept the bucket brigade supplied with water. They took turns cranking water from the well. Turning, turning, and turning, until the bucket of water was up to the top of the well. They poured the water into buckets, pots, roaster pans and dishpans – anything they could get their hands on that held water. The bucket would be thrown down the well again, and the job of cranking would start all over again. When Elizabeth got tired, Eliza and Laura took their turns. The girls were strong. Their father had taught them to be strong. He knew his girls needed to grow up to be strong women, and he was proud of them all.

Sarah, being eight years old, had the job of filling the empty pots, buckets, and pans that were placed before her. Mary Elizabeth, Eliza, and Alice carried the filled pots and buckets to the rain barrel, trying to keep it filled.

Alexander's ringing of the bell paid off. The first neighbour to arrive was Dan Rood. He made his entrance with a horse and wagon, flying into the laneway. He had his own ladder and buckets with him. He also brought Eric and Cecil, his sons, to help. Dan heard the bell. He thought it strange the bell ringing at this time of night. Everyone knew when they heard the bell that Captain Kenney was either leaving or returning from a trade trip, but he wouldn't be leaving this time of night. Dan went out to his front steps and saw the smoke through the trees. That is when he went into action. Now he and his sons were at the well. He left Cecil to help crank water and said, "Eric, come with me." Dan picked up his ladder, and with Eric's help, ran towards the fire. They met Mary Elizabeth running back to the well with empty buckets. Eric's face felt hot and he was sure his face was turning red. This always happened to him when he saw Mary Elizabeth. He was thankful for the darkness because no one would notice.

Heman threw bucket after bucket of water on the flames. He saw the third ladder going up. His hopes were raised, but his eyes told him the fire was spreading. The road in every direction was full of horses and wagons, all coming his way. Heman was grateful. They definitely needed all the help they could get. The view from the rooftop looked like some kind of race, as the horses raced around the bend and into his laneway. The

Wesdavers, Rutledges, the Mac Kenzies, Lowes, the Mc Clouds and the Codies, and many more he didn't know. They all heard the bell.

"Look there!" Gerald pointed just beyond the Harbour towards Sheet Harbour.

Heman's eyes followed the beam of light circling around from the lighthouse. He wiped the stinging smoke from his eyes with the back of his hand to see clearly. "Are those canoes?"

"I believe so, sir!" Gerald's use of the word sir came naturally. "It's the chief and looks like he has brought the whole Indian Reservation with him."

People were running with buckets of water and ladders, anything they could use to fight this fire. The chaos continued through the still of the night. There was no wind, thank God. Millions of stars looked down on them. The lighthouse continued to shine its light into the darkness.

The men fighting the fire did not have to worry about the cold, not that they had time to think about it. The fire got hotter. Sweat fell from everyone's faces. Mixed with the smoke, everyone's face was dark and unrecognizable.

Sweat fell from Heman's face. His head turned upward to the starry heavens. "God, are you paying me back. You know what I am talking about. I already paid my debt when my son William died two years ago. He was only two years old. Life was just getting started for him. Then he was gone. Am I still paying for the sins I committed years ago? I tried to be a better man. Have my sins caught up with me?"

Gerald heard Captain Kenney's voice. Each bucket of water the Captain threw, his voice got louder and louder. At first, Gerald thought he was speaking to him, but after seeing the Captain's head turn to the heavens, he realized the Captain was having an argument with God. Gerald could see his face in the light of the flames. It was a tortured look that seemed to come from hell. "I know, God, I know it was wrong. The money? I paid the money back three times over. How? By doing good. I can't go back. Oh, God, how I wish I could go back. I see their faces. I know I know You see their faces. The dark brown skin, the black eyes, the tortured look."

"I can't go back.

I can't go back.

I can't go back."

Gerald seeing the Captain's eyes, made his hair stand up on the back of his neck. *Heman might be looking up, but it sounds like an anguished conversation with Satan himself. If I weren't standing on a ladder ten feet off the ground, I would run.*

By this time, a number of neighbours ran inside the great "Show House". They carried anything they could get their hands on and formed a mountain of furniture on the front lawn. They could not help noticing the beauty of the inside of this great house. Mahogany was everywhere. The dark, rich colour of the mahogany staircase was almost breathtaking. If there weren't a fire going on, one would stop to take a closer look. They tried to save the great dining room table more than once. It took six men to move it, but the cause was lost when they couldn't get it through the doorway. As they frantically worked, breaking glass could be heard on the second floor. The fire spread to this part of the house, and the smoke grew thicker. Alexander had to stop ringing the bell, for smoke now came out the front door.

The war against the fire was fought all night. Heman and Gerald had to retreat from the roof. The fire was so hot it burned their eyebrows and eyelashes. Heman was coughing again. The smoke took a toll on his weakened lungs.

Day was breaking. The flames still reached towards the heavens. Flames were no longer needed for lighting up the sky. That would be a job for the sun. The stars left; the sun rose, the lighthouse light grew faint, but it was not extinguished for no one had time to tend to her light. She continued her weary task to shine through the smokey haze of the morning light. The black billowing smoke filled the blue sky as it passed her by, drifting out to sea. Heman thought his life was drifting out to sea with it. The weary neighbours stood around watching the flames. The great house was being eaten up before their eyes. There wasn't a thing they could do. Everything had been done. The faces that watched the flames were blackened. Their shoulders were stooped over. They had lost. The fire had won. As Heman coughed, one by one, his neighbours came up and touched him on the back. There were no words to say.

Over to one side stood a group of Indians. Chief Joseph Paul was standing beside Peter Francis and Lennie Highblood. No words were spoken; they nodded their heads in respect for this great white man as he passed by.

"Thank you, Chief. Your willingness to help has touched me greatly." Heman offered his hand towards the Chief. Awkwardly the two men shook hands.

Wearily he turned to Gerald. "Where is Elizabeth?" he asked. He just realized he didn't hear the bell ringing. When had it stopped? He couldn't remember.

"They are all at the Rood's house." Maude Rood had approached Elizabeth and told her there wasn't anything else she could do. She gathered Elizabeth, your mother, the girls and Alexander and took them to her house.

"How am I going to face her? How am I going to tell her that we have lost everything? How am I going to tell her we have to start all over again?" Heman's coughing interrupted his talking. Daniel put his arm around his son.

Gerald replied, "She already knows that, sir. You don't have to tell her. You just have to be there with her. Women are funny that way you know. They act like they need us men to take care of them. But when a man's down, then the good woman is by your side, stronger than before, this time taking care of the man. I'm sure it won't be any different with Elizabeth."

Heman just nodded his head in agreement. He was too tired to even think about the hard road ahead, the road that Elizabeth and he would have to walk together.

The lane was still completely blocked with horses and wagons. Now carriages were added to the dinge. News had spread fast – all over Sheet Harbour and as far as Mushaboom and the other direction to Port Dufferin. The house was still burning because there was a lot of fuel to keep the fire going for a long time. People from everywhere came to see the end of the great show house.

It was just another day, a good day for fishing, blue skies, and light surf. Yes, it was cold but this was a perfect day living off of the coast of Nova Scotia. Another day had started, but it was far from a normal day. The fishing boats were still tied up at the wharf. There would be no fishing that day. But the fishing boats from Sheet Harbour were making their way to the offshore fishing banks. As they passed by *Lady Catherine*, they blew their foghorn in tribute to the great loss of the night before.

This was far from a perfect day for the Heman Kenney family. He hardly even noticed the sun was shining. It was, and will always be, a black day in March for him. He stood by watching his home beaten away by the flames. *It was such a beautiful house. Elizabeth had a great deal to do with that,* he thought. As he was gazing into the flames, everything was so silent. *I know God still loves me. He told me on the roof last night. Maybe, if I hadn't been a slaver, this would never have happened. God's wrath is not only on me, but a lot of other men are going to pay. We make choices in life – good and bad. I chose the bad. But . . .* As his mind still went round and round with questions, he felt a small hand in his. He turned his head and there stood Mary Elizabeth. Sweet Mary Elizabeth. She had grown up in front of his eyes. *How old is she now? 13? 14? No, amazingly, she is 15.*

She looked into her father's eyes. "Oh, Father, what are we going to do now?" As she spoke, tears fell from her blue-green eyes.

Daniel watched his son talk with his daughter. A tear rolled down his blackened face. He felt deep sorrow for them both.

Heman put his arm around her and drew her close to his heart. "Everything will work out. We have to believe that, Mary Elizabeth. We have to be strong. Do you promise me you will be strong, Mary Elizabeth?" His eyes were pleading. "Do you promise?"

"Yes, Father, I promise."

They both stood there watching the house burn. "It was a beautiful house wasn't it, Father?"

"Yes, Mary Elizabeth, it was a beautiful house."

"I will never forget it. When I am an eighty-year-old woman, I will still remember how beautiful it was."

Heman brought her a little closer to his heart. "Yes, dear, when you are eighty years old, you will still remember how beautiful it was."

Heman's coughing returned. "Father, are you going to be all right? Come, let us join Mother. She is at the Rood's." Mary Elizabeth helped her father walk along the road to the Rood's. The road was still full of people. They stopped and watched, more than just watched. They stared in silence as Heman and Mary Elizabeth passed by. Spells of coughing continued, as Mary Elizabeth helped her father make his way. They reached the stairs to the veranda of the Rood's farmhouse. The house was big compared to other farmhouses, but nothing compared to their show house.

"Sit here, Father, while I get Mother." Heman was too tired to argue. "Now you rest and I will be right back." As Heman sat on the steps, he could see the smoke rising behind the trees. That was his life going up in smoke.

"Are you okay, son?" Daniel was greatly concerned.

"I don't know, Father, I just don't know."

Mary Elizabeth and her mother were by his side. Heman looked up to Elizabeth, his wife. "I'm sorry I couldn't save our home." Then his coughing began stronger this time.

With tears in her eyes, she quickly said, "Mary Elizabeth, help me get him to the kitchen." Mary Elizabeth helped on one side and Elizabeth on the other, while Heman helped the best he could. He felt like he was breathing in cotton batting. He had a hard time breathing.

Maude Rood met them at the kitchen door. She was taken aback when she took one look at Heman. "Here, put him right in the rocking chair." The rocking chair was beside the big cook stove. "Is he frozen?" she asked.

Mary Elizabeth noticed her grandmother, frozen with terror, could only speak the words, "Heman, my son!"

"No, he's not frozen" Elizabeth replied to Maude, "It's his asthma." We need to boil some water!" Elizabeth's voice showed urgency.

"Boil water?" That was easy for Maude. There was always a pot boiling on her stove. She added wood for more fuel. She brought the boiling water over to the kitchen table. Heman quickly put his face over the hot steam, as Elizabeth put a cup towel over his head. They had done this routine many times. In between the coughing, he tried to take in deep breaths of the hot steam. This was easier than breathing in all that smoke for the last fifteen hours. His coughing started to subside; however, he felt an overwhelming weariness come over him. He was tired, but he didn't think he was that tired. Like the fog rolling in, covering everything in its pathway, a fog so thick you couldn't see ten feet in front of you. That was how the weariness was covering his body.

A voice far away could be heard. It was the voice of his sweet wife Elizabeth. She was saying something, something about putting him to bed. Herman laughed a troubled laugh and in between coughing, he said, "I don't have a bed. I have nothing."

Heman barely remembered them leading him to a bed. "A bed – maybe all this was a dream. Maybe I do have a bed." He laid down on the bed. "This is not my bed. It is too small. This reminds me of a book I read to Alexander, Goldilocks, and The Three Bears. I must be in the mother's bed," he laughed. "Maybe I am inside a book. There is not room on this bed for Elizabeth. This is not my bed." The fog from his mind partially cleared, if only for a minute. He remembered that his bed is gone. His bed burned in the fire. It wasn't a dream. His house burned down, his beautiful Show house. "Falling, I am falling. Is the dream back? I am falling. Backwards, I am falling backwards. Falling, falling . . Maybe I'm falling off of the roof? No, I'm still falling. I'm so tired. God, help me." With that, Heman fell into unconsciousness.

The Eric Rood Family
Watt Section
Nova Scotia, Canada
August 2, 1897

Dear Father:

Greetings from your loving daughter, Eric, and your doting grandchildren. We are all well and hope you are the same.

Father, do you remember the words spoken between us just after the great fire many years ago? If my memory serves me right, my words were "I will never forget. When I am an eighty-year-old woman, I will still remember how beautiful this house was."

Those words came back to me this very morning. The children were busy doing their chores, and I was rocking our precious Catherine Elizabeth. She is such a sweet baby. Eric and I are so blessed with our family.

Mind you, I am far from eighty years old, and I look forward to living the years to get there. But, Father, I will always remember the beautiful show house, that is what the older people of Watt Section call it, filled with all the treasures you had brought back from many a trade trip. My whole childhood was spent there. What a childhood it was! I pray I too will give my children, and, of course, Catherine Elizabeth, memories that they will cherish in the future.

We all miss you, especially Mother, but don't you worry we see her every day and make sure every need she may have is taken care of. I am looking forward to you being home soon.

May God keep you safe upon Lady Catherine, and we all will be looking to your return

Your loving daughter,

Mary Elizabeth

CHAPTER TWO

Cork, Ireland
1833 (49 years earlier)

A messenger came running through the Shipyard. "I have a message for Captain Daniel Kenney. A message for Captain Kenney."

He sounded like a town crier, but he wasn't dressed as one. He looked half-starved. If he were trying to make a living as a messenger, it didn't look like it was going well. The jacket he was wearing might have been navy-blue in colour at one time. But now the cloth was worn and threadbare. One could see the shirt worn underneath. His pants came down just below his knee. His stockings had holes, which he had tried to mend more than once. There was a buckle missing on his right shoe. The other had a hole at the end of the toe. No telling what the soles looked like. He might not look like a messenger, but he certainly was diligent in delivering his message.

His name was O'Sullivan and he wasn't a messenger at all. When he raised himself from the February cold that morning, he thought he was frozen. His bed was a handful of straw he had stolen from the horse barn. His blanket was a few pages of the area newspaper. He knew he had to warm himself, so he headed straight up Church Hill Street and turned south on Rose Hill to the Kenney mansion. Ada would give him something. Even if it were a cup of hot water. O'Sullivan made his way to the back kitchen door. He didn't want anyone to notice him. As he rounded the corner, he met George, Ada's husband.

"O'Sullivan, what are you up to? If the Captain sees you mulling about, there will be no good to pay."

"Top of the morning, George. Can you see it in your heart to help a half-frozen bloke this cold morning?"

"I don't have a heart, especially to a no-good bloke like you. I don't know what Ada sees in you. You are worse than an old stray cat."

"Yeah. But Ada has a heart, such a sweet lady."

"Ada has enough work without you adding to her burden. Go on with you – out of here."

"Why, George, you didn't tell me we had company." It was Ada at the door. "Mr. O'Sullivan, haven't seen you in a month of Sundays. Come in and warm yourself by the fireplace. I will get you some Boxty Pancakes and Bairin Bread."[1]

O'Sullivan's vision of a cup of hot water just vanished from his eyes. He whisked his cap from his head, smoothed out his red hair with his hand and answered. "I would be honored, my fair lady."

George's frown was met by the kindness in Ada's eyes. Those eyes melted his heart every time. Maybe he did have a heart after all. If he did, his heart beat for Ada alone.

Ada looked at George. "Stay close. Lady Bridget didn't eat breakfast this morning. You know her time is almost here."

"Aye. I know. I will be in the stable. Send for me if I'm needed."

O'Sullivan was standing close to the stone fireplace. If he weren't careful, he would catch fire. It was so large he could have walked right in. Just think – a room of fire. It reminded him how cold he had been waking up that morning. Now he was warm and getting warmer, and maybe hotter.

Ada's voice brought him back from the edge. "Mr. O'Sullivan, do stand back. I can smell those old clothes burning, not to mention that red hair."

Jumping back, O'Sullivan saw Ada place the Boxty and Bairin Bread on the worktable.

"Bring that stool and sit here and eat. I haven't time to entertain ya. I'm preparing dinner. And when you're finished, the wood box needs filling."

O'Sullivan was so hungry he could have wolfed this food down. He was trying to think of the last time he had such food set before him. And on a plate and with a fork? He ate slowly. Each bite he took he wanted it to last forever. He closed his eyes. His taste buds could send the memory to his brain.

"Are you sleeping, Mr. O'Sullivan?"

His eyes shot open. "No my lady, just tasting this wonderful food you have put before me. You are the best cook this side of Dublin. You need to cook for the Queen of England."

"Go on with ya – don't get me started with the Queen of England. I would cook for Queen Victoria all right. I could stir in a little rat poison, and that would give her a taste she might like."

O'Sullivan hardly noticed the threat made against the English Queen. All he noticed was the wonderful aroma filling his nose. "What smells so good? What are you cooking for dinner?"

"Well, if you must know, it's Creamed Haddock and potatoes, of course." As she stirred in the mustard, O'Sullivan spoke again.

"You and George have a good life here, don't you, Ada?"

"It's not perfect. George works too hard but, yeah, we have a good life here. Captain Daniel Kenney and Lady Bridget are a fine family to work for. The Captain is a hard man, but I believe fair. He is well respected around Cork and we are blessed to work for him."

"Work is hard to find out there, Ada."

"Well, the wood box is still empty, Mr. O'Sullivan."

He jumped to his feet and made a bow. "I'm at your service, Lady Ada." It felt good to have a full stomach.

The door from the main hall came flying open. Ada and O'Sullivan turned to see Honora flying in like a wet hen. "It's time! Oh dear. It's time!"

Ada knew at once, what was happening. O'Sullivan thought someone was dying. She turned to him, "Quickly, go and get George from the stable." O'Sullivan was out the door before she finished her request, running to the stable searching for George. George, hearing the commotion, stepped out of the stall of an Irish draught horse called "Big Red"

"O'Sullivan, is that you?"

"Yes, I think someone is dying!?"

"Dying? Whom?"

"The Lady came flying into the kitchen. I believe her name to be Honora."

"Honora Landers is Lady Bridget's maid. It must be happening."

"What's happening? Isn't someone about to die?"

"No, I believe Captain Daniel's baby is going to be born this day."

"Captain Kenney is going to have a baby?"

"No, you fool, Lady Bridget."

O'Sullivan sat on a bale of hay dumbfounded.

"Well, don't just sit there. Let's go."

When O'Sullivan and George arrived back in the kitchen, they found Ada and Honora filling every pot with water. "We must boil water." Ada then turned to George. "Go for Dr. Garvey." Ada was taking charge, like she always did when something important had to be done. "Honora, go back upstairs with Lady Bridget."

"What will I do? I don't know what to do."

"Be quiet, girl, "Ada demanded, "Use your brains, not your mouth. Just be with her, and be calm."

Honora seemed to become a soldier and Ada was the General. Honora took a deep breath, obeyed the order, and hiked up her dress as she turned and left the room.

Ada then turned to O'Sullivan. "And for you, Mr. O'Sullivan, you must get Captain Kenney."

"Where is he?" as he turned to leave the room.

"Come back here." Ada barked another order. "He is not here. Captain Kenney is at the Ringaskitty Port. She scribbled a note. Here, deliver this to the Captain."

"You mean you want me to go all the way to the Harbour; it's well over a kilometer away?"

"Mr. O'Sullivan, if you ever want to taste Boxty and Bairin again in this lifetime, you will go."

His full stomach gave him a change of heart. He started off on a run. The kilometer might have seemed shorter after all, and he was going to be a messenger. *Me a messenger?* he thought. *Maybe that was what I was born to do. I will think about that tomorrow. Today I have to find Captain Daniel Kenney. No one is going to tell him this news but me.*

O'Sullivan was the messenger running through the Shipyard. He didn't know what a messenger's job was, but he gave it all he had. "A message for Captain Daniel Kenney! A message for Captain Kenney!"

Finally, he got the attention he wanted. Workmen in every direction turned and looked his way.

"Captain Daniel Kenney, I need Captain Daniel Kenney."

Mahoney, a short tough-looking bloke, spoke up, "Why do you need Captain Kenney?"

"A message. I have a message for him." O'Sullivan held up the note that Ada had written.

"Give it to me," growled Mahoney, "I will deliver it."

"No, sir, I am the messenger and I will deliver the message." He held the paper close to his chest.

"Well, follow me." Mahoney was not pleased; He didn't like anyone taking over his turf. O'Sullivan, on the other hand, stood a little straighter. He never had power before and what little he had at the moment set a fire in his heart. "Follow me. Captain Kenney would be in the main building."

They passed through the great yard to a stone building built close to the shoreline and directly in front of the wharf. Climbing the stairs to the second floor, O'Sullivan could not miss the great view of the Harbour in front of him. However, Mahoney didn't even seem to notice. Just as Mahoney knocked on the door to a larger office, O'Sullivan couldn't help notice the sign.

Jeremiah Reilly Darby

and

Captain Daniel Kenney, Esquire

A cross-looking gentleman opened the door. "Why are you disturbing us, Mahoney? You know better than this."

"Sorry, sir, but there is a messenger here with a message for Captain Kenney."

"Surely it can wait until after this meeting. We have clients from Bandon, Mallow, and Kinsale and as far as Dublin. We are talking beef and lots of it."

O'Sullivan spoke up, "Sir, I need to deliver this message to Captain Kenney now. It won't wait."

The man with the angry eyes glared at him. "So be it." He left them standing there.

Mahoney also glared at O'Sullivan. "This best be good."

The door opened. Daniel passed through the door and quietly closed it. "I am Captain Kenney. You have a message for me?"

O'Sullivan handed the Captain the paper that Ada had prepared. The Captain fell back against the door. His face turned grey-white. O'Sullivan wasn't sure if he had just delivered good news or not. The Captain stood straight again. "Is Bridget okay?"

"As far as I know, sir. George went to get Dr. Garvey. I believe he is with her by now."

"I must go to her."

But it didn't look like he was ready to go anywhere. His knees were shaking and again he leaned backwards on the closed door.

"Do you need a chair?" Mahoney didn't know what the bad news was, but he could see the distress on the Captain's face.

"No, Mahoney, get my carriage ready. I will be leaving immediately." He turned and disappeared through the door as it closed behind him. The Captain seemed to be over his weak spell and now was on a mission.

Mahoney turned to O'Sullivan, "What the blazes was that all about?"

"His Mrs. is having a baby."

"Right now? It's not even noon. Heavens preserve us. I thought babies came at night?" Mahoney continued to talk it over to himself as he rushed to the stable to make Captain Kenney's carriage ready. O'Sullivan trailed behind. Now that his job was finished, he didn't know what he was to do. He thought, *Wasn't I supposed to get paid or something? What kind of a job is this? Don't messengers get paid? Maybe this wasn't a good job for me after all.*

Mahoney turned, "Where do you think you are going? Get yourself out of the Shipyards and be quick about it."

That did it. *How ungrateful. See if I do a good deed again.* But then he remembered Ada's Boxty and Bairin and felt his full stomach. A smile came over his face as he made his way home.

He stopped in his tracks. He didn't have a home. *Where should I go now? Back to Captain Kenney's?* He felt he was a small part of all the excitement that was happening that day. He pulled his collar closer to his neck to keep the wind out and quickened his step as he left Ringaskiddy Port and turned left onto Main Street.

Daniel Kenney reentered the meeting room. Talk about cattle trade had stopped. The men were now looking at him. They took one look at Daniel and they knew something was wrong, for Daniel's face was still white.

Jeremiah spoke first. "What is it, Daniel?"

"It's Bridget. It's time. The doctor has been called; the baby will be born soon."

Jeremiah stood up. "Go to Bridget; take my carriage. I will take care of business."

"Yes, I need to go to Bridget. Thank you, but my carriage is being readied now. Yes, I must go to Bridget." He was still saying this as he made his way to the door and disappeared. He didn't remember his feet touching the steps, but he was already outside heading for the stable. Mahoney was harnessing the horses to his carriage and his driver was there. Captain Kenney opened the door of his carriage and as he sat down, he shouted the order, "Home, James, as quick as you can."

O'Sullivan hadn't walked far when he heard a commotion behind him. He turned around and saw a carriage heading his way. The horses were galloping and still, the driver's whip was flying through the air. The horses' nostrils had steam bursting forth. O'Sullivan stepped off the road and gave them lots of leeway to pass. He thought, *Where do they think they are going, to a fire?* As it whizzed by, he caught a glimpse of the passenger. It was Captain Kenney. As he watched them pass, he thought, *Here I am walking freezing myself, and here he is warm in a carriage and both of us going to the same place. Doesn't seem* *like life is very fair.*O'Sullivan kept walking. *That is the way life is,* he thought, *and nothing is going to change it this day.*

Captain Kenney didn't notice if he was warm or cold. He was trying to stay on the seat as he yelled orders to James, "Faster! James, faster!" *I remember how happy Bridget was telling me the news. We were to have a baby. That was five months ago. I am happy, aren't I?* Being a father would be a good thing, a natural thing. But fear replaced the happiness. The fear that every man has. The fear of losing Bridget. *I cannot live without Bridget. I found the only one I want to love, and today I may lose her in childbirth. I would give up the child, but I could not give up my Bridget. Please, God, I can't lose Bridget. Please, God! I will plead, I will beg, I will do anything, God.* He looked around and saw that he was finally in Carrigaline. The horses galloped up Church Hill Street and finally onto Rose Hill and through his gateway and up the wide driveway where they stopped at the front door of his mansion.

The Captain was out of the carriage before it came to a stop. George was there to meet them, and grabbed the bridles, as the horses came to a halt. They were wet with sweat and froth was coming out of their mouths.

"Where is she, George?" He was even afraid to ask the question.

"Why, Captain, she is in your bedroom suite. Dr. Garvey is with her. Don't worry, sir, Ada and Honora are helping the doctor. She is in good hands."

The Captain was already through the front doors and heading for the staircase before George was finished. "Captain, I wouldn't go up there, Sir. Sir."

Daniel didn't even hear him. He was taking the stairs two or more at a time. Out of the corner of his eye, he saw someone sitting in the parlour. *Was that the Vicar? What's he doing here? Things are worse than I thought.*

Hearing the noise Ada opened the bedroom door to see what the racket was. Daniel almost ran into her. Ada, being of good stature, was able to hold her ground. "Captain Kenney, you cannot come in here!"

"Go on with ya. No one keeps me out of my own bedroom."

"Captain, you can't come in here."

Dr. Garvey, hearing the commotion, stepped close to the door. "Daniel." There was an order to the statement. "Go to the parlour and wait for me there."

"But Bridget, I must see Bridget!"

"Go, Daniel." The door closed in front of him.

How dare they? he thought. *This is my house. How dare they?* He turned and there stood Vicar Mc Carthy. The Vicar put his hand on the Captain's shoulder, "Come with me."

Daniel allowed this man who brought a sense of calmness around him to lead him. Daniel was far from calm but could feel the calmness from this man. He thought, *I don't want to be calm; I had to see Bridget.*

"Come with me." He was being led back down the stairs. Panic rose again in his throat. He was going farther away from Bridget.

"Everything will be fine. Just sit here. I will get you a cup of coffee."

Daniel didn't want a cup of coffee. He didn't want to sit there, but he did what he was told. As he sat in the parlour, there were signs of Bridget all through the room. Her decorating style was simple, not fussy, just the way he liked it. Pictures of her parents and his parents were placed on the piano. But no picture of Bridget. Why had he not noticed that before? He would correct that. He wanted a picture of Bridget sitting there so everyone would see it. He wanted more than a picture; he wanted to be with Bridget. He was being denied that request, or demand. It made his blood boil. He was not used to being denied anything.

The Vicar returned from the kitchen, "Here, drink this." It was a cup of coffee. George had taken over the kitchen with Ada busy upstairs.

"I think I need whisky," Daniel demanded.

"It's not even noon! Drink this."

What does noon have anything to do with it? I don't know if it is noon, five o'clock or midnight. The coffee had a hard time going down. Panic was still in his throat. He could feel it.

"Everything will be fine."

"If I hear him say that one more time, I might hang him by the rafters." "How do you know everything will be fine?"

"Women have babies every day. Everything will be fine."

There he goes again. 'Yeah, women die having babies every day."

The Vicar took his seat. He couldn't argue with that. He had seen it happen over and over again. "Bridget is a strong woman; she will make it. And you will be a father."

I don't want to be a father. I want Bridget."

The Vicar had a worried look on his face, but only for a moment. He had to be strong for this man, his friend.

Daniel started to pace; he couldn't sit any longer. He marched by the piano, in front of the fireplace, and to the window. Turned around marched back by the fireplace, by the piano, and to the doorway. Then repeated the process all over again. Now he knew what the tiger felt like at the Cork Zoo. The grandfather clock in the corner struck one in its base tone. Daniel looked up. "One? You mean it's only one?" But his eyes told him the face of the clock read one o'clock.

George entered the room. "Captain, sir, would you like lunch served?" The Vicar quickly said, "Yes, you can set up a small table for the Captain and me to eat here in the parlour."

Daniel looked up. A voice inside of him said, *See, I am no longer the master of this great house. I can't go to my bedroom, and now someone else is making decisions about lunch.* Daniel was past caring. If the Vicar wanted to eat, let him eat. Food was the last thing on his mind. He sat with his head in his hands. Daniel didn't know how long, but the Vicar's voice calling his name brought him back to his senses.

"Daniel, come eat. Look. Food prepared well enough to set before the Queen herself."

"Then the Queen can have it."

"Come, Daniel, eat some of this creamed haddock and potatoes."

Daniel opened his eyes to see the Vicar crossing himself and thanking God for the great food he was about to partake. "Eat what you want, Vicar."

"Are you sure?"

Daniel closed his eyes again, slipping into the hall of terror. As he thought of his sweet Bridget upstairs, he wished he could trade places with his beloved wife and take her pain. In the distance, he heard the Vicar enjoying every mouthful of the food that Ada had prepared earlier that day. *God, let me take her place. I will take the pain.* Daniel felt helpless. The sound of pacing again. Back and forth. Daniel was amazed how the Vicar could stay still hour after hour. In fact, Daniel heard him snore once, but the Vicar tried to remain awake and on duty to comfort the Captain. Finally, there was a sound coming from the bedroom door at the top of the great staircase. The door quietly opened and then closed. The pacing ended and his eyes watched as Dr. Garvey descended the stairs heading straight for him. Daniel met him before he could even enter the parlour. "Doctor, is she okay? Oh, no, she didn't die, did she? Oh, Doctor."

"Get a hold of yourself, Daniel, and step inside the parlour and stop the yelling. That's not going to help Bridget at all." The doctor closed the door of the parlour. He looked straight into Daniel's eyes. "Of course she is not dead. I have come to give you a report. But if you don't get a hold of yourself, I will not return again. Now, Bridget may be halfway into her labour."

"Halfway!" Daniel looked at the clock. It was passed three. "Halfway!"

The doctor looked at the Vicar, "Any food left?" They both looked at the small table.

"Sorry, Doc, it was so good I ate it all."

Doctor Garvey headed for the kitchen.

Daniel again coming to his senses. "Halfway? Where are you going? You can't go to the kitchen. Bridget needs you."

In return, Daniel got a cross look. "Bridget is alright. She is a strong woman. Ada and Honora are with her. Not that Honora is of any help. I am hungry and I am going to eat." He turned around and headed for the kitchen, leaving Daniel just standing there.

Daniel thought, *I have lost control. No one will do what I tell them.* He found a chair and fell into it. His hands were holding his head again.

George and O'Sullivan were sitting at the worktable. No one seemed to notice when O'Sullivan had returned. George had put him to work. They both had finished serving the doctor and the Vicar who ate again. He said he had to keep the doctor company. Now George and O'Sullivan were eating the leftovers. O'Sullivan wasn't used to having two meals a day. He could get used to this. Late afternoon had come upon them. George was wondering what to fix for supper. Ada, if she were there, would be fixing something to be ready by 6 o'clock. But he wasn't a worrier and figured everything would work its way out in good time. It was a long afternoon and even longer for the Captain. He noticed he didn't look very well, and he worried about him.

Raising his head from his hands, Daniel noticed someone walking around the room. It was George. He was tending to the fire and lighting the lamps. He hadn't even noticed it was getting dark. "What time is it, George?" He could have looked at his own pocket watch but felt the need to talk to someone.

"6 p.m., sir."

"How long, how long, George? How long will this take?"

"Everything's going fine, Captain. Why, I was talking to my Mrs. just an hour ago."

Daniel sat up to hear more. "What did you hear? What did she say?"

"Why, Captain, Ada says it won't be long now. Ada's done this before and she knows."

Daniel was on his feet walking the same pathway. Again he marched by the piano, in front of the fireplace and to the window. Turned around marched in front of the fireplace, by the piano to the doorway.

George interrupted, "Captain, can I get you some Irish coffee.[2] You haven't had anything all day."

Daniel found his head nodding, and George was off to the kitchen, happy to be able to do something for the Captain. After a few sips, for it was very hot, Daniel could feel the liquid flow down his throat. It must have been the whisky, because he felt calmer than he had all day. It didn't last for long. He heard a wail, and it came from the direction of the bedroom at the top of the stairs. His hair on the back of his neck stood straight up. He was on his feet so quickly that what was left of the Irish coffee was now on the carpet.

"I will take care of it, Captain." As George was picking up broken glass from the cup, another wail could be heard. Daniel thought he would faint, so he fell back into the chair. "It won't be long now, Captain."

"Pray, George. Where is the Vicar? Bring everyone in here and pray."

The next time Daniel looked up, the Vicar, George, and another man were on their knees praying. Who was that man? He looked familiar. It was O'Sullivan. George had run into the kitchen yelling for the Vicar and pulling O'Sullivan out with him. O'Sullivan wanted to be a part of this history-making moment, but he really didn't think of himself a praying man. But here he was in the parlour on his knees and now the Captain was looking at him. He just closed his eyes and kept praying. Finally, the wailing had stopped. Daniel was on his feet. "She's dead, isn't she?" His eyes were wild as they looked at the other men.

The Vicar jumped up to meet Daniel. "You don't know that." Then another cry was heard. Not wailing this time, a new cry. All the men were on their feet. It was a cry of a baby. All eyes went to the second level. They heard the bedroom door open and close quietly. It was Dr. Garvey making his way down the great staircase. The four men met him before he reached the bottom step.

Again, Dr. Garvey's attention went straight to Daniel. "Your wife is resting."

"Has she had the baby?"

"Yes, of course, I wouldn't be here if she hadn't. You may go and see her now."

Daniel was taking the steps three or four at a time; he didn't take time to count. As he opened the door, Ada was there.

"Shh. Be quiet."

He obeyed immediately. He didn't want to be thrown out of the room again. "The Doc said I . . ."

"Yes, Captain, come in but be quiet."

His gaze went around the room. How tiny Bridget looked in that great bed. Honora was fluffing her pillow. He walked closer and fell to his knees without touching the bed. This brought him closer to her. His hand brushed a dark curl from her brow. She opened her eyes and smiled. "How was your day at work?"

My day? he thought. *I don't care about my day. Bridget, how are you?* He thought, *Words can be so stupid.* "Oh, Bridget, my love, are you okay?"

Bridget opened her eyes and smiled again. "Have you seen him?"

"Seen who?" All he could think of is his Bridget. *God, please make her well.*

She opened her eyes again. She looked so tired. "Your son, you silly man."

"My son?" His eyes opened wide.

Bridget smiling again, "Yes, Dear, your son."

"Of course, the baby. A son?" His eyes went to the end of the bed. Ada was there and it looked like she was preparing bread or something.

"Yes, Captain, your son." Ada lifted a small bundle and handed it to Daniel. He wasn't sure he wanted to take it but didn't have much choice when she let go. He either had to take it or let it drop to the floor. He chose the former. On one end of the bundle, he could see this tiny human being. Dark hair, tiny nose and a line for a mouth. It was sleeping; at least the eyes were closed. He could feel the baby's breathing as he held him in his hands.

"Your son, Daniel, your son."

He looked over to Bridget, "A boy, a son?"

He smiled at Bridget: "Our son. What shall we name him?"

Bridget replied, "It must be a strong name for a strong son."

Daniel announced, "His name will be Heman Godfrey Kenney. Is that strong enough, Bridget?"

"Yes, Daniel, Heman Godfrey Kenney, is a strong name for a strong son."

Daniel looked down at his tiny son. The baby opened his eyes and looked at Daniel. Your name is Heman Godfrey Kenney." The baby seemed to take it in and then closed his eyes for a nap. Bridget also closed her eyes.

Ada quickly said, "All right, Captain, it's time for you to leave and let them both rest." She quickly took the baby and settled him in the cradle, which was placed at the end of the bed. Daniel wasn't sure he was ready to give his son up so quickly.

But like everything else that happened that day, he didn't seem to be in charge of anything. He looked to Bridget and kissed her on the forehead. She smiled but did not open her eyes. Ada was right. They needed rest.

"I will return soon," he whispered to his love. To Ada, he said, "Take care of them both." She nodded her head, and, before he knew it, he was led out of the room. Looking down from the upstairs landing, he saw three men gazing intently his way. He went down the stairs almost as fast as he had come up. This time with a lighter heart.

"I have a son; the baby is a boy!" A cheer went up among the men. Big arms were around his shoulders, and he felt more than one slap on the back.

"Congratulations, a new Kenney has been born."

"Yes, Heman Godfrey Kenney."

Another cheer went up. They headed to the kitchen. All of a sudden, Daniel was starving. "Bridget is tired but doing well." Another cheer – this time for Bridget. "Have you eaten all the food?"

"No, sir," George said, "I made sure we saved some for you. I knew before this day was over, your hunger would return."

Daniel stopped. "What time? Dr. Garvey, what time was my son born?"

Dr. Garvey replied, "7:30 p.m. The clock was striking the half hour." The four men sat at the kitchen table eating, laughing, and talking. Daniel again looked O'Sullivan's way.

"Sir, do I know you? You look familiar?" O'Sullivan's eyes dropped. "Yes, of course, you are the one who delivered the message at the shipyard."

"Yes, sir. Ada sent me. I was eating some breakfast when the need arose."

Daniel remembered something: "Aren't you the one I see at the back gate?"

O'Sullivan's eyes went down again. "Yes, sir, Ada is kind enough to give me a bite to eat now and then."

"Do you work somewhere?"

"Well, I thought I might take up the business of a messenger. It seemed to come quite natural, it did."

"I see." Daniel looked over at George. "George, do you think you could use some help around here? Now that our family is growing, there'll be more work to do."

George raised his eyebrows as he glanced over at O'Sullivan. O'Sullivan's eyes were opened wide. George thought a moment to himself. *If Ada was going to feed this bloke anyway, he may as well work for it.* "Yes, Captain, I could find something to keep him busy."

"Then find him some clothes. I don't want people to think I don't take care of my workers." He turned to O'Sullivan, "I will give you three months to see if you want to be part of this family."

O'Sullivan stood there with his mouth opened. It was the first time he couldn't find any words to speak. He just nodded his head.

"Well, did the cat get your tongue?"

"No, sir. I mean, yes, sir. I mean, thank you, sir. I will do you proud." Now all the men were laughing. What a day it had been.

Daniel was glad it was over. He stood up and said, "I must go to Bridget." He was headed for the stairs. He took them slowly this time. He felt back in control. He had to be the master of this great household.

Rose Hill

Cork, Ireland

1833

To my dearest son Heman:

Only a week ago, we welcomed you into this uncertain world and into our lives. I never want to forget the feelings I experienced, so for that reason, I am putting them down on paper and into words.

Words are hard to find to capture the moment Ada brought you to my side. A tiny perfect face, with dark eyes and a dark curl of hair crowning your head. The pain of labour was gone and replaced with a wave of joy flowing from the depths of my heart. It flooded my soul and body. A feeling only a mother can know.

Your father, Oh you will love your father. He may have caused a scene the day of your birth, not because of weakness, but because of love. Your father would move mountains if that is what it took to care for us.

He asked, "What should we name you?" My answer, It must be a strong name for a strong son. Your name, Heman Godfrey Kenney, you will wear as a strong shield upon your breast for everyone to see. A name that has pride and strength. As you grow, it will make you strong and give you a challenge to live up to.

Someday you may read this letter. For now, I will keep it locked in my hope chest until then. If nothing else, it will show you that you are loved.

Whatever life brings you, my dear son, I will be there cheering you on. We — your father and I— will always be there for you.

You have my heart always.

Your loving Mother

CHAPTER THREE

"The Queer Mist From The Irish Sea"

O'Sullivan stood with his arm around Tera. It was February 12, 1845. He looked around at the festive atmosphere that was taking place at the Kenney mansion. A grand celebration of Heman's birthday. Everyone who was anyone was at the party. Those who were there included Jeremiah Darby, his wife Eileen, and their children. Jeremiah was not only Daniel's partner, but both families were close friends.

Heman was quite a lad. He was a leader like his father. Heman was tearing at the fine wrapping paper of a large box. It was his birthday present from his father. He couldn't get inside fast enough. Tearing the top off of the box, his eyes opened wider as he saw what was in front of him.

"Oh, Father, how beautiful!" He lifted a replication of a fine schooner up for everyone to see. "Will she sail?" Looking up at his father for the answer.

"I hope so, Son. This afternoon we will take her to the lake to try her out."

"Can I go, can I go too?" It was William jumping up and down. "She is such a beautiful schooner. Can I see if she can sail, Heman? Can I go too?"

Heman smiled at his younger brother. "Yes, William, you may go too."

Daniel spoke up, "We shall all go." He looked over inviting Jeremiah and his family. "Your mother too."

"Yes, that would be a lovely thing to do. A perfect day. But let's go early before the sun goes down," Bridget added.

"I will send a picnic lunch." Ada was in on the excitement.

"Well, that's settled." Daniel was pleased with the turn of events. He looked back to Heman. "Take a walk with me, Son. What are you going to name her? We will christen her on her maiden voyage."

It didn't take Heman long to reply. "Father, I have just the name for her. It is from the book I am reading. I love the character, Catherine.

"You love Catherine?" Daniel stopped.

"Father, I am no longer a baby, not like William. Remember, I turned 12 today."

"I forgot that two years makes a difference." He smiled at his older son.

"Two years and six months, Father. But, anyway, Catherine lives on a great schooner. Her father is a fine captain and they travel all over the world."

"All over the world?"

"Yes, places like Africa, West Indies, and even Australia."

Daniel thought how pleased he was to see the joy his son received from reading and being educated. The more education the better. He would need it growing up in this fierce world.

"Father, you're not listening."

Daniel smiled, "Well, Heman, what do you have to say?"

"I am going to christen my new schooner *"Lady Catherine."*

Daniel stopped and replied. *"Lady Catherine*, that is a pleasant name – a fitting name for a fine schooner. Yes, and your mother will like it too." Heman stood proudly; it made him happy that his father approved of the name he had chosen.

O'Sullivan couldn't help overhearing the conversation between the Captain and his son. The Captain was a great father, and he could see the love between the two of them. It was hard for O'Sullivan to believe that twelve years had passed since the day he became part of this family. It was the same day Heman was born. That was the day my life changed. I had a place of belonging. Right after the birth of Heman, George fixed a room for me in the stable. I never had a room before. I had a bed, a chair, a washstand and a mirror. Also, a small stove stood in the corner. I thought I would keep that stove going all the time, because I never wanted to be cold again But I soon found out I didn't need it very often. The horses inside the stable kept my room warm and they kept me company. I never felt alone again.

I became part of the Kenney family. George kept me busy and we grew to admire each other. Ada kept cooking that wonderful food. Shortly after, another person was added to the family, Tera McCarthy. Tera was from Cohb. Her husband was killed in a horse accident. She had no one to turn to. The baby she carried died at birth three months later. Mahoney, being her friend, heard from Captain Daniel and Jeremiah Darby that a wet nurse[3] was needed to help Bridget and her baby, Heman. Before you knew it, Mahoney presented Tera to Captain Kenney.

George and I set up a room on the south side of the attic. It didn't take long for Tera to settle in, for she loved Heman. Bridget and she became friends. She not only was the wet nurse but became the nanny. Every time one saw Heman, Tera was close behind.

Life was good at the Kenney's. Children made a home come alive. Heman had enough energy for several children. They all took care of him. Bridget with her loving, watchful care, and Daniel's strong hand. Ada and Honora loved to see him visit the kitchen. Of course, George and I took him on visits to the stables.

Heman had no fear. The rest of the family had to make sure that he was safe.

Heman was almost three when everyone noticed there was something different around the house. The Captain was bad-tempered and moody. George and I were having a conversation. I asked him, "Do you think things are not well at the shipyard?"

"I don't know for sure, but everything seems to be running smoothly in that direction. And I don't see anything wrong with Heman. I can't put my finger on it, but something is up."

One day Daniel came into the stables. George and I looked up from our work and were surprised to see him there. George asked, "Did you call us, sir? Do you need a carriage ready or are you riding today?"

"No, George, I didn't call and I don't need anything."

We went back to work. Daniel paced back and forth. He looked in at the new pair of Irish Hunter's that just arrived after being purchased. "They look like they will be just right for the fox hunt next month, don't you think, George?"

"Yes, sir, a fine pair of horses, they are. Finest I have seen in Ireland."

Daniel continued with his pacing. "How can I go through this again?"

George and I looked up.

"George, how am I to bear it again?"

"Bear what, Captain?" He was not used to giving advice to the master of the house.

"A baby, George, a baby. Bridget is going to have another baby."

"Congratulations." Both George and I were at his side. We wanted to shake his hand.

Under his breath, Daniel thought, *Yeah, congratulations. I have a son, George. Why do we need any more? Why risk it again? Bridget made it through the first time. Will she make it the second?*

All spring everyone in the household tried to reassure the Captain. Heman was harder to manage than his father. Trying to keep him quiet so his mother could rest was an impossible task. But like George always said, "Everything works out in its own time." Everyone knew that Lady Bridget was a strong lady just like I said. William was born August 1835. Heman was very proud of his little brother. Tera now had her hands full taking care of two children. She loved every moment.

Oh, yes, Tera, let me tell you about Tera. I fell in love with her the day we met. Every time I entered the room where she was present, strange things would happen. Heat would rise to the top of my head. I'm sure my red hair would give off light. And talk – I couldn't. What words would come out sounded like a wild goose, not of a man. I couldn't even walk. I would trip over my own feet. I didn't know what to make of it, so I stayed away.

Ada of course noticed. It wasn't until Ada made the statement, "Tera thinks you don't like her."

Honora said, "You aren't very nice to her."

"Don't like her?" I exclaimed. Then I saw Ada's smiling eyes look my way. "It's not that I don't like her." Ada was still smiling. You couldn't keep anything from Ada. If Ada knew, then it wouldn't be long until everyone in the whole house would know. Swallowing down my fright, I finally got up the nerve to ask Tera to walk with me. Our favourite place to walk was by the river. It was also a good place to ask her to be my wife.

The Captain and I had a meeting. I told him I wanted to marry Tera. The Captain was the only one in the household that didn't notice what was going on. Even though Lady Bridget had mentioned it in passing once or twice, he didn't take notice. Captain Daniel was surprised when I approached him with the request. "I guess that means we need to find better living quarters for you."

"George and I can enlarge the room in the attic. That is all that will be needed."

"Well, O'Sullivan, if Tera says yes, how can I say no?"

So it was settled. Tera said, "Yes," and a Spring wedding was planned. Vicar Mc Carthy came, and he married us right in front of the fireplace in the parlour. Ada made a cake. Captain brought out the whiskey, and we were toasted to a long life of happiness. That was eight years ago.

Life was good. George and I took care of the mansion and stable. Daniel took care of making the money. He and his partner Jeremiah Darby did well. Jeremiah made the deals to trade cheese and salted beef, pork and butter. The Captain loaded the schooners and sailed them to England. The English used it for provisions for the British navy. Captain Kenney also made many trade voyages to the West Indies, but not today. Today was a day of celebrating the 12th birthday of his cherished son Heman.

Heman hated the times his father was away. When Daniel was home, he made up for it by taking Heman to the shipyard often. He was glad that Heman and Mahoney became close buddies. The first time Heman showed up at the shipyards, Mahoney wasn't very happy. All his mates called him "the Nanny." Captain Kenney and Mr. Darby asked Mahoney to show Heman around. Mahoney thought, *What can I show a six-year-old?" Mahoney has had the job for six years, and he got used to being called "the Nanny.*

Heman loved the schooners. He would run and jump swinging a wooden sword. One day he would be the great captain; another he would be the mean pirate. It was Mahoney's job to make sure he didn't fall overboard. Daniel would watch from his office window. What he saw pleased him greatly. He was happy to see his son love the great schooners as much as he did.

William was different. He didn't like the shipyard. He tried to follow his brother, Heman. He wanted to be just like him, but fear would overpower him. Seeing the river rushing by and the sheer size of the schooners made him feel small. He didn't feel at home there at all, not like his brother. He would play pirate for a while, until Heman tied him to the great mast. Prisoner or no prisoner, that did it. He wanted to go home.

William's idea of a good time was to spend the day in the stable with George and O'Sullivan. He loved the horses, and his favourite was the Irish Hunters. The Irish Draughts were okay for every day, but the Irish Hunters were raised especially for the foxhunt. The foxhunt was the only thing that he and his father had in common. For this reason, he wanted to learn everything he could about them. How different these two boys were. Bridget didn't mind. She always knew William would be close at hand, and Heman would take to the sea someday. She loved them both, but in her heart, she was glad to know William was there.

* * * * *

There was a storm brewing. It wasn't just outside the windows of the Kenney Mansion. Ireland was in trouble. The whole family had gathered in the parlour after dinner. While the Autumn storm blew outside, Daniel read from the *Limerick and Clare Examiner*.[4] The newspaper was protesting that even "the good landlords are going to the bad, and the bad are going to the worst extremities of cruelty and tyranny, while both are suffered by a truckling . . ."

Heman piped in, "What's truckling?"

Daniel replied, "Submissive. Now let me finish."

Daniel continued, ". . . And heartless government to make a wilderness of the country and a waste of human life."

"This is boring, and it doesn't affect me," William said restlessly.

"It won't be boring and it will affect you, William, if England destroys Ireland." Daniel's glance at William made William take his place.

"How did this all get started, Daniel?" It was his Bridget joining in on the discussion.

He was glad she was interested in the state of affairs of Ireland. "The British instituted Penal laws, which denied the Irish peasant population freedom. The Irish were forbidden to speak their language, to practice their faith, to attend school, to hold a public office, to hold certain jobs, to own land, or to '. . . own a horse worth more than £10.00.' These Penal laws made everything worse. They were good for you and me, Bridget, not good for our country's peasants."

"You know, Bridget, because Ireland is a colony of England, landlords that live in England have control of 95 % of the land. Every cottage had a garden equal to an acre and a half, and the farmland amounted to five acres. As the families grew, the land was subdivided and living standards declined. Overpopulation caused people to move to less fertile areas where the potato was one of the few sources of food that could be grown. And of course, the landlords living in England didn't care a hoot about the people. All they cared about was to maximize the crops grown for them."[5]

"William, are you falling asleep?"

"No, sir." He sat straighter in his chair.

"I'm listening, Father." Heman was right with Daniel.

Daniel continued, "The English have forced the Irish peasants to pay exorbitant rents and taxes. Because the corn brings in more money, it forced families to sell all the corn crops to pay the rent. They had to rely on potatoes to store over the winter to feed themselves and the livestock, especially the pigs. Potatoes were all they had to eat. A burly farmer could down 15 potatoes at one meal. Only the landlords got the corn."

"Why does England want so much of our corn?" It was Heman's question.

"It all happened after the Napoleonic Wars in 1815."

"Yes, we were talking about that war just yesterday with our tutor," Heman added.

"The British soldiers returned home, which increased unemployment. As Europe transitioned from warfare to a time of peace, there came a depression. The English wanted more and more of our corn.[6] And if we don't look out, Ireland will be in the same depression."

Bridget brought them back to the main topic of the evening. "Daniel, what about the newspaper article? Why are the landlords getting worse?"

Just like Bridget to keep everyone on course, thought Daniel. "Well, it says here that the tenant farmers held short-term leases that were payable each six months in arrears. If the tenants failed to pay their rent, they were jailed or evicted and their homes burned."

"How terrible. I do hope nothing keeps them from paying their rents." Bridget was concerned.

William was having a hard time staying awake. If it wasn't for the storm banging rain on the window beside him, he would have been asleep by now. He stood, "May I be excused?" He was addressing his father, but his mother replied.

"Go to bed, William, we all will be turning in soon."

Daniel smiled at William. "Good night, Son. Heman, you may retire as well."

"Yes, Father. Good night, Father. Good night, Mother."

"Good night, Son."

Daniel and Bridget were alone. "Sometimes I feel I am helping drain this country of its wealth."

"Do you, Daniel?"

"Well, how can I help not think it? Times are getting bad and I fear they will get worse."

"Your trade is not just with England. You make many trips to the West Indies, and places in Europe."

"If I didn't take it abroad, someone else would. It seems like the whole world is sucking Ireland dry."

"I don't think it is all that bad. Come; let us make it a day. Maybe this storm will end by morning."

"Oh, yes, by the way, I have been thinking."

Bridget turned towards her husband as they climbed the great staircase together.

"I want to take Heman on my next trade voyage."

"So soon? Is he old enough?"

"He is 16, Bridget, and it's time he learned about the sea."

The sea, Bridget thought, *It has now begun. The sea, yes, the sea will take Heman away.* She really wasn't ready yet.

* * * * *

There was a buzz in the kitchen early the next morning. Everyone was talking about the storm. "I thought it was never going to end." It was Tera speaking to Ada as she stirred the huge pot of porridge.

Ada was glad to have Tera to talk to in her kitchen. Now that the boys didn't need a nanny any longer, Tera worked beside Ada. Ada missed Honora terribly. Honora had found the love of her life. She and her young husband went off to America. Honora told Ada she was going to seek her fortune, just imagine that. Ada hoped they found it. She was lonely in the kitchen until Tera took over for Honora.

Ada was cooking the eggs in a large skillet. "It was the worst storm I can remember, and I can remember a lot of storms. I know we lost more than one tree on the property. George is out looking now."

"Mr. O'Sullivan. . ." Tera always referred to her husband that way. "is checking the horses. He left me alone in the middle of the night to make sure everything was secure at the stable. I thought the attic window would shatter, the rain was so hard."

George entered through the kitchen door. As he discarded his jacket and made his way to warm himself at the stove, he said, "I was just talking to a bloke walking by the back gate. I asked if he had seen any damage from the storm. He told me there wasn't any damage, but there was a queer mist coming in from the Irish Sea."

"That gives me the creeps. Sit down here at the table. Help yourself to breakfast. Tera, come with me." George was used to taking orders from Ada and naturally went to the cupboard, picked up a plate and filled it with food. Tera and Ada entered the dining room. The whole family was gathered for breakfast. That is, all except William.

"Where is William?"

"I'm sure William will be here soon, Daniel." Before Bridget was finished speaking, in bounced William.

"Good morning, everyone!"

"Good morning, little brother."

"You are late, William."

"You haven't launched without me, have you?"

"Good morning, Son," Bridget said, "Come sit beside me."

Daniel motioned to Heman. "The Blessing, please."

"Thank you, God, for this food. And the rain. Amen."

Daniel motioned to Ada and Tera to begin serving the breakfast. They both quickly began their task.

"That was quite a storm last night, wasn't it?" Bridget looked towards the boys.

"What storm?" William was buttering his toast.

"There was a storm?" Heman passed the juice.

"You mean the two of you slept through that storm?"

Daniel looked towards Bridget, "Those two would sleep through an earthquake."

"Not me," Bridget looked right at Daniel, "I was up more than once."

"Yes, I noticed that you were."

Daniel was waiting to change the subject. "I have news for you, Heman."

That brought Heman awake. "News, what kind of news?"

William stopped eating. He was even interested.

"I've decided that you will accompany me on the next trade voyage to the West Indies."

Heman was out of his chair. "Really, Father, really? When, Father? Now? I will start packing right away."

Daniel was smiling. "Sit down, Heman, and finish your breakfast." We will sail in one week."

"One week!" That seemed like a long time to Heman.

"In the meantime, you will spend the days at the shipyard preparing for the voyage. There will be work for you to do, and I expect you to do that work well."

"Yes, Father, I will do anything to be able to go. I will make you proud."

From this time on Heman spent more time at sea, than he did at home. He loved the sea and the work favored him. Even when Daniel was home, Heman was not. His reputation of a hard worker and a pleasant young man spread. Many Captains asked for young Heman to join them on their voyages.

During one of his trade trips, Heman wrote the following letter to his father:

Somewhere in the Atlantic
This side of the Irish Sea
1852

Dear Father:

Greetings from your eldest son. I am well and hope your health fares well with you also.

The Captain keeps me busy. The crew teaches me daily. They are at least half-civil towards me. As you know being the newest crewman, I'm afraid I suffer the brunt of many of their jokes. But don't fear, that too is an education to itself. I learn quickly.

Greetings to Mother. She may pine over her firstborn leaving her roost. Her, and of course, Ada. Since early childhood, she told the story of the day of my birth. What a story it was. I asked for it over and over again. Now I am a man.

How is William? I miss the shadow of my younger brother.

I must close for now. My watch begins shortly.

Your loving son.

Heman
P.S. I love the Sea

Ever since the night of that September storm, something wasn't right in Ireland. It was said that the day after the storm, tenant farmers went to check their potatoes for harvest. The farmers were shocked at what they found. The potato stalks turned black as soot. The potatoes rotted, giving off an offensive odor. Field after field of rotted potatoes could be smelled for miles.

Daniel and Bridget were sitting alone in the parlour. They seemed to do that more and more now that their boys were older. "The Irish people are being exploited." He was making general conversation. "They were forced to pay high taxes and rents to the English landlords. The people were forced to subsist on potatoes, while other agricultural products were exported to Britain under military escort. The British government believed that it was in the best interests of the people to sell the goods for money so that they could buy food and pay rent and taxes. If tenants were unable to pay rent, the landlords evicted the tenants and burned their homes. Otherwise, the landlord sent the tenants to an overpopulated poor house. They then shipped them to the United States on over-loaded "Coffin ships,[7] or jailed them."

Bridget questioned, "But how can they work in the cornfields if they have no food for themselves or for their families? "How can they buy food? There is no food to buy. All the potatoes are gone. They disappeared overnight. The poor houses are full. I wouldn't send my dog there. Daniel, do they have any potatoes stored up from last year?"

"Yes, they did, Dear. But the same disease that attacked the crops also attacked potatoes that were in storage. This year the potato crop is 100 % ruined, and there is no seed for planting new crops. And worst of all, the British landlords used this opportunity to drive the tenant farmers off their land, so they could now have larger plots of land to grow more crops like corn."

"What can we do, Daniel? I feel so untouched. We may not have potatoes to eat, but we have so much more. I hear Ada has been feeding people outside our back gate. I believe she has been doing that for years, but now they are lining up before sunup. God bless Ada. She has a good heart."

"Bridget, I know Ada has been doing this for years. I have never stopped her, because I believe since we have so much, sharing with the poor is not just our duty but a human thing to do. But now this thing has become bigger than what Ada can manage."

"Daniel, why don't I talk to Eileen? With our friends maybe we can set up some kind of soup kitchen."

"That would be a good idea. I'm sure Jeremiah will want to help his wife and you. Tell me what comes from it."

That very day, Bridget and Eileen, called a meeting in the kitchen. Ada, George, Tera, and O'Sullivan all gathered around the worktable. Everyone had their own story to tell how the famine was affecting them.

"Have you noticed," stated O'Sullivan, "that the hospitals and the poor houses are overflowing? It's because the families who relied on potatoes as their staple food started stealing the corn they were growing for England. The shift in diet from potatoes to corn has been causing dysentery."

George continued, "My friend who leases a farm sent his children to an orphanage, so at least they could be fed."

"The farmers are not able to feed their families," added Tera, "so they are forced to surrender their holdings to the landlord. The Earl of Lucan[8] evicted hundreds of families himself."

Eilene had to speak up, "I must say that not all landlords are alike. My grandfather had a farmer come to pay his rent, and he told him, 'Feed your family first, and then give me what you can afford when times get better.'"[9]

Ada smiled to herself. She knew that was the exception rather than the rule. "These helpless creatures are not only driven off their land," cried Ada, "but they have nowhere to go. Under the new law, we who still have roofs over our heads are not allowed to offer lodging. They do what little they can with materials they have torn from their old homes: propping up broken walls against fences and the like. It is not human I tell you."

"There are hoards of people on the road every day," said Eileen. "Jeremiah and I see them pass by the back gate."

"We have all seen the horror around us. Now is the time to take action. What can we do?"

"Well, the law doesn't say anything about not feeding them," explained Bridget.

Bridget looked at Ada. "We know you have been feeding those lined up in the morning at our back gate."

Ada lowered her eyes.

"Now, we want to help you. If we all work together, we can help more people as they pass our way."

Ada's head was held high now. "Yes, we can do that. The Quakers have set up soup kitchens. They have these heavy cast-iron soup cauldrons. We need one, if not more of them. I will cook the soup. We have to be careful that it's thin enough. These people can't handle food in their stomach. It's been such a long time since they've had any."

"I will help." Tera knew of the hardships of the people. She wanted to do something.

It didn't take long for the public to know that the Kenneys had two heavy cast-iron soup cauldrons running morning and evening. It made Daniel feel better, knowing he was giving something back to Ireland.

* * * * *

Heman had returned to Cork after several months on trade voyages. He was sitting with his father in his office. "I had heard it was bad in Ireland, but, Father, I didn't know it was this bad. I look around and no one is here. Where are all the schooners?"

"Heman, they have left for North America. Their cargo is people. Ireland has lost their best. They are now in the British Colonies and the United States, and no telling where else. They couldn't just stay around here and watch their families starve to death, so they left."

"And you, Father? How are Mother and William?"

"We are fine. Ireland's problems have made our family very wealthy."

"Well, Father, you just happened to be in the right place at the right time. No one will fault you for that. I hear the rest who stayed are starving to death. But I don't understand, Father. We live by the Irish Sea. Fish – there are fish everywhere.[10]

"The peasant farmers don't like fish. It never enters their minds that they could eat fish. Nor do they have the education to get fish."

"I would think that if I were hungry enough, I would teach myself to fish."

"Yes, that is because you are educated. These people have been denied education for generations. Most live on the cliffs with the ocean below them. And those who lived in small harbours tried to fish. There was no fish in the Harbour. They had to go out to the deep ocean. Their crude boats could not hold up to the deep fishing banks. When they did bring fish in, there was no place to take it. It rotted. The British didn't want fish. They wanted corn and grain. Fishing was discouraged."

"Seems to me that Britain is going to have to pay. This whole mess falls back on them."

"I agree, Heman, what a mess they have made of our Ireland."

"Father, because of everything that is going on in Ireland, work for me will be scarce now."

"You have done well, Heman. I am proud. Don't worry. You will always be able to work for me."

"Thank you, Father." But inside Heman knew he would want more. "I think I will go home to see Mother."

"Wait for me, Son. I will finish up here and we will go home together." They agreed to meet at the stable.

Heman took a walk through the shipyard. And who do you think he met but his old friend Mahoney? Mahoney greeted Heman with a bear hug and slaps on the back. "Good to have you back in Ireland, Heman."

"Good to be back, Mahoney. Mahoney, you still working around here?"

"Well, don't you know it? Work's hard to find; people are starving. Your father has been good to me over the years. There is no other job out there for me."

"It's bad, isn't it Mahoney?"

"Ireland is dying, Heman. You've been away too long. I've never seen it so bad."

"What's it really like, Mahoney?"

"Well, you being a man and traveling to Timbuktu and back, maybe it's time to tell you what it is really like around here. I have stories that will give you nightmares. Well, just the other day a cabin a little out of town was seen closed. A man had the curiosity to open it, and in a dark corner, he found a family of a father, mother, and two children, lying in close contact. The father was considerably decomposed; the mother, it appeared, had died last, and probably fastened the door, which was always the custom when all hope was extinguished, to get into the darkest corner and die, where passers-by could not see them."

"Word has it," Mahoney continued, "Six men landed on a pretty island. There was a death-like stillness – nothing of life was seen or heard, except occasionally a dog. One asked, 'How can the dogs look so fat and shining here, where there is no food for the people?' The other answered, 'Shall I tell him?'"

"Then on a cold bleak day, a pitiful old man in hunger and tatters, with a child on his back, almost entirely naked was seen. The child seemed to be in the last stages of starvation. The old man said he lived seven miles off and was afraid the child would die in the cabin, with the two little children he had left starving, and he had come to get the bit of meal, as it was the day he heard food relief was being given out. The officer told him he had no time to enter his name in the book. And he was sent away in that condition. A penny or two was given him, for which he expressed the greatest gratitude."

"The next Saturday the man was seen again. On inquiring where the child was, he said the three were left in the cabin; he was afraid some of them would be dead upon the hearth when he returned. He was sent away again with a promise to wait till next Tuesday, and come and have his name on the books. This poor man had not a penny nor a mouthful of food, and he said trembling, 'I must go home and die on the hearth with the hungry ones.'"[11]

"Mahoney, no more, speak no more." Heman's heart was about to break. What has happened to Ireland? He did not know it anymore. It was a place of death.

* * * * *

Daniel and Heman's carriage took them up Church Street and onto Rose Hill through the front gate and driveway of the mansion, Heman's home. No one was at the front to meet them. He noticed in the back of the property a crowd of people. Daniel noticed where his son was looking. "That is your mother and William. They are feeding the people. We all do what we can."

Heman walked towards the dinge of people. This didn't even seem like home. He wasn't sure of what he expected, but this wasn't it. He felt like an outsider or maybe a visitor. William saw him first. He dropped his ladle at the soup cauldron. "Heman, you are home."

Heman hugged his mother. "Heman, it is so good to see you again, Son. Here, please help feed these people." He was handed a ladle and took his place with his family, helping those who needed help.

He was home. Heman looked to the horizon. He could see far out to the mouth of the Harbour. Even now, you could see the sails of the schooners coming in and those going out. His heart beat faster just glancing at the view before him. The sea was calling him.

He was home, but for how long?

New York City
July 1844

Dear Ada,

I'm glad to be alive after almost two weeks on the crowded ship Oceanie. Though' I got here all right without being sick, many did not.

We slept behind the engines for 12 nights. What a racket. New York Harbour made a big impression on my Ralph. As our ship passed through this great Harbour, everyone was top deck taking in the sights of our new home. Ralph had his cap off his head, and I'm sure I saw tears in his eyes as he realized the great opportunity this country offered.

We all had to wait in a long line to enter Borge Office (official office of immigration). I thought I was going to pass out it was so hot. I thought it may be a glimpse of hell. Ralph assured me it was my double layer of wool I was wearing.

Ralph bought us tickets to Minnesota. Immigrant transport took us to the railroad station. Ralph had a cousin tell him not to stop in New York City. What we saw of the city, we were glad we took the advice. The noise and squalor indescribable. Manners are rough and speech indelicate.

We are on our way. We will cross the great open space of this huge country. Making Chicago is our next destination, where we plan to purchase a wagon and a pair of oxen. After that, God will guide us to Minnesota. I will write when we are settled.

Bye now; you may be sure I remain your,

Dear friend,
Honora

CHAPTER FOUR

The *Lady Catherine* Has a Captain

Activity remained at a low level at the shipyard. The main thing that was being exported was people. Thousands of Irish were leaving; they didn't have much choice. It either was leave or watch their families starve to death. Food riots were breaking out everywhere. What little food that was around, people fought over it like they were dogs. If one had a little money left to spend, he would take the voyages to the British Colonies or the United States, even New Zealand, and Australia. A quarter million people left. The less well-off emigrated to Liverpool, Clyde, Swansea, Cardiff, and Newport from Cork and Skibbereen. They swarmed across Britain seeking food and spreading disease.

The great cauldron was never empty at the Kenney mansion. The line of wretched people continued daily. Ada thought the line would never end. George made sure there would be no fighting over the food. More than once he and O'Sullivan had to break up fights of those trying to break in the front of the line. No one had mercy for anyone else. Between broth and what little the soil produced and even seafood or weeds, the people were kept alive, but barely so.[12]

Everyone helped. It was common to see Daniel there himself. His Bridget worked every day. He worried about her. Disease was spreading rapidly. He also knew there was no stopping her. Bridget's fellow Irishmen were in need and she was going to be there. Daniel was glad that Ada, George, O'Sullivan, and Tera were here to help, not to mention Heman and William. They were there daily, carrying large pots of gruel from Ada's kitchen to the back gate.

"Day after day we carry these pots. Ireland is dying. Why don't we just leave like everyone else?" William was complaining to Heman. "This is not what I call the best of life."

"Father is not going anywhere. He will be in this until the end."

"That's what I'm afraid of. There isn't going to be anything left of me either. If I have to look at those pitiful wretched people . . ."

"William, just be thankful you aren't one of them. I don't see you missing any meals or sleeping by a fence. You and I have it very good considering what's going on in Ireland. The English – it's those bloody English that I grow to hate more each day."

"What can we do? It's between us and them. How can one family fix politics?" William didn't like politics. "I'm just tired of it, that's all. I'm tired of it all."

"I know, little brother; this can't last forever. It's got to get better. I tell you what; let's go visit the racetrack and stables. I hear they just opened and are operating at least once a week. Let's go see the Irish Hunters."

William's head and shoulders straightened. "Let's go. I need to get away from this."

Heman knew that would cheer up William. All one had to do was mention Irish Hunters and William would be right there. "All right, William, let's go." Before leaving, Heman made sure the supply of gruel was in place by the back gate, and then he sought out his mother. "Mother, I'm taking William away for a while. We will be back later." Bridget looked up. She was going to protest but noticed Heman wasn't asking permission. He gave his mother a hug. "Promise me you won't work too hard."

"Yes, dear, you sound like your father. Well, you take care of William."

"Yes, Mother. Aren't you forgetting he can take care of himself?"

"Of course he can. Just watch that he doesn't get into trouble."

Heman raised his eyebrows. "Trouble? What kind of trouble?"

"Oh, never mind." Bridget turned to Ada. "Are we ready? George, open the gate."

Heman took his leave. He met William dressed like an Irish gentleman top hat and all, waiting by the front door. "You certainly are dressing the part." Heman looked down at his own clothes.

"Don't worry, big brother, I have everything you will need." William pointed to the jacket and top hat sitting on the chair waiting for Heman. "I have played sailor with you. Now it is your turn to play the role of the Irish gentleman."

It didn't look like Heman had much choice. "Thank you, little brother. I put myself in your hands this afternoon."

William saw to it that a carriage was waiting for them. They stepped inside as William directed the driver, "Cork Park Racecourse."[13] They were traveling through the countryside. The signs of spring were everywhere. Birds were singing and the heather was blooming on the Moores. Heman was out of his element. The call of the sea gave him excitement. But looking at William and his happy mood even made him happy about seeing horses.

"You know, William, horses are not my thing. Don't get me wrong; they are useful, and I know we need them, but that is as far as it goes with me."

"I know, big brother. Schooners are your thing, but today I am going to show you what it feels like to be in the world of horses."

There was a silence between them as they took in the scenery as it passed. Heman ended the silence. "Mother asked me to keep you out of trouble. Are you in trouble, William?"

"Mother worries too much. Here we are, Heman – Cork Park Racecourse." William gave orders to the driver. "Take us to the regular place."

"Sounds like you have been here before."

"You know schooners; I know Cork Park Racecourse. This is my second home."

As they stepped out of the carriage, a flock of servants came forward. "Welcome, Mr. Kenney. Good day to you, sir. Would you like drinks served?"

"Yes, bring them to my box."

As they walked through the throng of people, many continued to close in around them.

"William, good to see you." Heman's little brother would just nod his head.

"Haven't seen you in a while." It was a short man wearing a green derby hat. He put his arm around William's shoulders. "Are you ready to make your wagers?"

"When is the first race?"

"30 minutes from now."

"Soon as my brother Heman and I take a walk to the stables. Come to my box in about 20 minutes."

Heman was taking this all in. "You do seem to know your way around this place."

"Yes, I love to come here, but today is even better. You are with me – my brother Heman." They walked around the great stable, William pointing out the good points of each horse. Heman just nodded and continued to walk with William. "Now, are you ready to make your wager?"

"How would I know who is going to win?"

"That's the fun of it. You must have seen a favorite horse. Start there."

"I don't know about this."

"Come on, big brother, this is going to be fun." They were now in William's box. Wagers were made. Heman thought too much money was bet. William assured him everything was just fine. The bugle was sounding, and the horses made their way onto the track. Heman noticed that they had the best view of the whole place. The finish line was right in front of them. There would be no problem seeing who won.

They were "Off." The horses thundered around the track. Dirt was flying upward, causing a cloud. William turned into a different person. He didn't know anything was happening except horseflesh flying around the circle track. William was yelling and directing his favorite horse around the turn, into the last stretch, and towards the finish line. Heman was watching William more than he was watching the race.

"You won! You won!" William was banging Heman on the back.

"I did?!" To Heman everything happened so fast, he missed most of it.

Heman came home £50 richer; William lost £500.

* * * * *

There was much to talk about during dinner that evening. William told both their mother and father how Heman had won at the horse race.

"And what about you, William?" It was Daniel asking.

"I didn't have as good a day as big brother. But that's okay; there will always be another day."

"Another day? Oh, William." Bridget looked down at her soup.

Daniel sat in silence as William continued the exciting story his sons had during their day. Daniel refused to argue with his youngest son. He was enjoying the fact that Heman was dining with the family. It didn't happen as much as he wished it would. Daniel ended the conversation at dinner by giving Heman an order. "Heman, Mr. Darby and I would like to meet with you at the office tomorrow morning at 8:00 a.m. sharp."

Heman's eyebrows quickly rose and brought his gaze towards his father. He had his attention. "What's going on at the shipyard? Business picking up? I will be glad to get back to work."

"I think you will be quite interested in our meeting with you." Daniel looked towards his Bridget and smiled.

"It's not your birthday and Christmas is a long way off. So what's all the commotion?" William was trying to figure out what was going on.

"I'm sure your brother will tell you all about it tomorrow," replied Daniel.

"Big brother, it seems like something big is going to happen tomorrow."

Heman remained quiet for the rest of the evening. He was deep in thought as he contemplated the meeting the next morning. What kind of trip did they want him to go on? It didn't matter. He was ready to go anywhere. The sea was calling again. He excused himself and retired early.

* * * * *

The next thing he knew it was William banging on his bed. "Big brother, aren't you going to your meeting this morning?"

Heman was out of bed before the end of the question. "What time is it?"

7:15 a.m., and it looks like you are going to be late. Father has been gone for an hour now."

"Good grief. I can't believe I overslept!" As he put one leg into his pants and was working on the other, "Quickly, throw my boots this way."

William kicked Heman's boots in his direction. "Perfect, brother, I believe you are going to be late."

Heman threw his brother a questionable look. "What does that mean? I don't have time for this." He was out the door and heading down the grand staircase. Entering the kitchen, he asked for a biscuit. Ada stopped her work and just looked at Heman. "I'm sorry I'm late. All I need is a biscuit." Heman took two biscuits off the worktable as he left the kitchen. Ada with a smile just shook her head.

Heman arrived at the shipyard with three minutes to spare. It was Mahoney, who met his carriage. "They have been asking for you."

As Heman sprinted towards the office, he turned, "I know, Mahoney, are they waiting for me?" Heman didn't wait for the answer. As his practice, he took the stairs two at a time and came to the door with the sign:

Jeremiah Reilly Darby
and
Captain Daniel Kenney
Esquire

He had seen it many times. He stopped and took two large breaths, breathing in the cool, fresh air and knocked on the door.

"Enter." He opened the door.

"I thought you would be here before now." Daniel looked at his son.

"Sorry, Father, I was running a little late this morning. Good morning, Mr. Darby."

"Good morning, Heman."

Heman was still catching his breath. *How stupid to be late of all days,* he thought. He took another deep breath and looked around the room. There were three other men at the table. All were staring at him. He was surprised to see Captain Collins and Captain Buckley. His head nodded in recognition, "Good morning." The identity of the last man was unknown. Heman also acknowledged him with a nod of his head.

Both Captain Collins and Buckley had been there for Heman. They taught him everything he knew – how to master a vessel, how to navigate by the stars, how to read the fast-rising currents, and how to charter. They were by his side when he took his oral exam and received a service certificate and supported him in his many hours in navigation school. Heman remembered the party Captain Collins threw with the crew when he passed his mate's license exam. He was with this captain for the next two years gaining experience before he could take his Masters.

Mr. Darby brought the meeting to order, "Gentlemen. Captain Kenney. Captain Collins. Captain Buckley. Mr. Walsh, I would like to introduce you to Heman, the son of Captain Kenney."

Heman thought this was a strange state of affairs. He had already worked closely with Captain Collins and Captain Buckley many times. There really wasn't any introducing that had to be done, except for the fifth man sitting at the table, a Mr. Walsh.

Mr. Darby continued. "This is a very proud day for *Jeremiah Reilly Darby and Captain Daniel Kenney, Esquire*. It's like passing the baton onto the next generation." Hearing those words, Heman began to squirm in his seat. "I will turn it over to you now, Daniel."

Daniel took his place at the head of the table. "Most of you know my son." His eyes turned towards Heman. Heman didn't know what to do so he just smiled. "Heman has worked hard for everyone sitting at this table." All the men nodded in agreement. "My dream for my son is to be a great captain someday." He looked straight at Heman. Heman felt very uncomfortable seeing those dark eyes, even if it was his father looking at him. When his father's glance turned into a broad smile, Heman relaxed a little. "We all have hopes and dreams of our children doing well. Heman has proven himself over and over again as a worthy seaman. Anyone who he has worked for has reported that he does his work well, and is a natural leader among those he works with. My partner Jeremiah Darby and I have invited you here today to witness history taking place."

Heman looked around the room, and thought, *Maybe the stranger, Mr. Walsh, is about to get hired for a special job. But why would I be here and why does Father keep mentioning me?*

"We are going to have a new captain in our midst."

I knew it, thought Heman. *It must be that gentleman, Walsh.* Their eyes met and they both were smiling.

Daniel continued, "I have the greatest pleasure to introduce for the first time, Captain Heman Godfrey Kenney." At that Daniel started to present the captain's insignia and uniform to Heman.

Heman actually jerked forward. He thought he might come out of his chair. Everything turned to slow motion. First, he realized his mouth was hanging open. He managed to close it. Surely, his ears were playing tricks on him. But his father was staring at him with a big grin on his face. Heman looked over at Mr. Walsh, then back to his father. Everyone was looking and grinning at him. If he didn't know better, he would think he was dreaming. His mind played back the order of events that happened that morning. He couldn't be dreaming; William woke him up. Mahoney told him they were waiting for him. He was awake when he entered the room. How could he be a captain? He didn't have a schooner. Heman was on his feet and both Captain Collins and Captain Buckley were shaking his hand and beating him on the back. He couldn't be dreaming; he felt each blow as their hands hit his back. Looking back at his father and turning to Mr. Darby, "Have I heard you correctly. Is it really true, Mr. Darby?"

"Yes, Heman, it is true," replied Mr. Darby.

Heman felt weak in the knees. But if he was a captain, he had better get over that quick. He chose to fall back into his chair.

Daniel was leading the meeting again. "Captains, would you like to have a word?"

"Yes, Sir!" Captain Collins stood. "I watched this lad grow from being a runny nose kid as he joined my crew the first time, to a well-educated seaman. I was lucky enough to know at least one of his teachers, and he commented to me that he had never met a student with a keener grasp of the subject presented in the courses. He not only took a three-hour exam made up of math problems, graphs and sightings, he answered oral and written questions for two days. Heman reads eddies, whirlpools, rocks, and cloud formations like most people read books. But he didn't stop there; he continually checked his readings and impressions with his navigational officers and me his Captain. I am honored to be here today. I wish him the best as he now becomes a Captain." At that, he took his seat.

Heman was still sitting low in his chair, trying to figure out what was happening around him.

Daniel was speaking again. "Mr. Walsh, it is your turn to take the floor. We know you have information for us all."

Mr. Walsh slowly went to the head of the table. Heman wondered, *Who is this man?*

Mr. Walsh looked towards Heman. "Congratulations, Captain Heman Kenney."

How that sounded strange to Heman's ears.

"Congratulations, Captain Daniel Kenney and Mr. Darby, you have a fine business here, and you must be proud to be able to pass part of it onto your son, Captain. I'm sure there are many questions going through your mind, Heman."

He doesn't know the half of it, thought Heman.

"I'm here today to answer one of those questions. First, let me introduce myself. My name is David Walsh, the owner of the Victoria Shipbuilding Company at Victoria Docks, West passage, Cork. For the last eighteen months, we have been under contract with your company to build a schooner. Mind you we have built schooners for you in the past, but this one is special. Captain Daniel Kenney and Mr. Darby have been at the shipyard many times overseeing the building process of this great Lady. Captain Heman, the day is near when you will christen the *Lady Catherine.*"

Heman put his hands on the top of his head. The room was spinning, and he wanted to make sure his head didn't spin off with it. His eyes closed momentarily, trying to clear his mind. When they opened again, he was still sitting in his chair. He was watching these men around him. Everything was moving slowly again – a feeling of being in the clouds watching down upon the drama that was playing in front of him.

"*Lady Catherine*?"

"Yes, Heman. A pleasant name – a fitting name for a fine schooner. Yes, and your mother will like it too."

Where had he heard that before? His brain searched his memory bank. Well, of course, on his 12th birthday. A knock at the door brought Heman back to the present.

"Come in, "instructed Mr. Darby. Mahoney entered the room carrying a large platter. You couldn't tell what it was, for it was covered in a silk cloth.

"Place it here, Mahoney," Daniel gestured in front of him. "Thank you, Mahoney." As Mahoney took his leave, he winked at Heman. The silk cloth was removed, and Heman saw it was his *Lady Catherine*. The fine schooner she was, the best present he ever received.

"Did you miss her from your bedroom?"

Heman looked at his father. "I guess not. I've, we've been so busy feeding people gruel ever since I came home, I guess I didn't notice she was gone."

"I'm glad the secret was kept."

Mr. Walsh again got everyone's attention. "So are we, Captain Daniel. So are we glad the secret was kept? My company was given the task of building *Lady Catherine*. We believe we have built her to a 'T.'"

Heman still couldn't believe what was happening. His life had changed completely in the last hour. It was a life-changing moment he would remember for the rest of his life.

"Now the Victoria Ship Building Company[14] requests your presence at a luncheon held on The *Lady Catherine* today at

The Victoria Docks, West Passage, Cork at 12:30 p.m. We will celebrate Heman's becoming a captain and introduce the captain to his first charge. This will be a lifetime relationship, even better than a woman."

A roar of laughter went through the room.

"Thank you, Mr. Darby," said Mr. Walsh as he took his seat.

Mr. Darby took the lead in saying, "One more item of business before we adjourn this meeting. Heman, being our newest captain, I would also welcome him to a partnership in the company. If he accepts, we will change our name to *Jeremiah Reilly Darby and Captain Daniel Kenney and Son, Captain Heman Godfrey Kenney, Esquire.* May history repeat itself when my son becomes of age. Now I call this meeting adjourned."

"I second it." Daniel was smiling at his son.

After handshakes were given all around, Daniel and Jeremiah approached Heman. "Do you accept?"

Heman was only hoping he had a voice to answer. "How can I not accept? It would be an honor to be a partner in the family company. I have grown up around here. It feels a part of me. Yes, I will accept. Thank you. Thank you for today and everything you have done. Thank you for the confidence you have in me. I will serve to the best of my ability. And for *Lady Catherine,* there are no words." His eyes began to mist. Not now; a captain does not shed tears. He swallowed hard and reached out his hand for a handshake that would be the beginning of his manhood. The strong handshakes in return lasted momentarily. He was embraced by his father. This hug felt good, and his childhood flashed before him. It was a hug only felt between a father and son, reassurance only a father can communicate to his son that everything was fine and all would go well. Daniel was proud of his firstborn. Heman was delighted to make his father proud. The hug between the two men went on for a long time, but only seconds in reality.

"Heman, take your uniform and dress in there." Daniel pointed to his office.

Heman found himself alone in his father's office holding onto a Captain's navy blue uniform with yellow braid. He couldn't help look out the window and see the activity of the shipyard, the same window through which his father watched him playing pirate on the schooners. He couldn't help but smile. *Well, Heman, you are on your way; dreams do come true. Today was proof of that.*

The only mirror was the faint reflection of the window, showing him dressed as a captain. He liked what he saw. *But can I live up to it? Anywhere I go now, I'm not just along for the adventure. Now, everyone will look to me. Am I ready?* Sometimes it's better not to think about a subject too hard. He decided he would just be himself, act the way he always did. His actions got him this far, and it would carry him into history. What mark would he make in this world? His head started to swim. He shook it and reminded himself to take one day at a time. *Right now I need to take one moment at a time. That's what William always said, 'Enjoy the moment.'* And that is what he intended to do. He clicked his heels together and took a better look out the window. Everyone was gathering at the bottom of the stairs.

There was a knock at the door. It was his father. "Are you ready? Step back and see if you pass my inspection." Daniel straightened Heman's yellow braids. "Your cap?" Heman gestured towards the desk. "Let me be the first to place it on your head. You might play captain as a child, but as an adult, only captains wear this on their heads. It is like a crown. It shows you are king over a kingdom. Your kingdom is anyone on your schooner. Are you ready?"

"I hope so."

"You will be just fine." With a smile towards his son, he said, "Follow me." As they went through the hallway from the office, Heman noticed a workman painting the door. They were adding, "and Son, Captain Heman Godfrey Kenney." Daniel slapped Heman on his back. "Proud of you, Son." Heman didn't have any words, and his father didn't expect any. As they arrived at the landing of the staircase, a loud cheer rose up from the shipyard. When they reached them, a natural pathway opened up.

Mahoney slapped Heman on his back, "Let me lead the way," and he did. Through the crowd, Heman and his proud father walked following Mahoney. At the stables a line of carriages was ready. Heman and Daniel stepped into one. "To Victoria Ship Building Company," Daniel ordered before he closed the door.

"Father, I don't know what to say." Heman was alone with his father.

"That is natural, Heman. The words will come when you need them. In the meantime, just sit back and take it all in. The next few days will be the days you will remember forever. I remember the day I became a captain. Remind me someday to tell you all about it. But this is your time. I am so proud to be a part of it."

Heman watched the scenery pass by as they made their way to the Victoria Docks. "How did you keep such a secret?"

"You made it easy by being away on trade trips. But I must say it was quite difficult these past few weeks since you have been home."

"Did William know?"

"No." Daniel's eyes went down. "I didn't think he could keep such a secret. "That boy can't do anything."

It was Heman's turn to lower his eyes. He wondered what was going on with William.

"Today is your day, Heman. We will figure out what to do with William another day."

Heman's carriage lead the way through the gates of the Victoria Ship Building Company. There were green streamers hung, and banners were everywhere. Heman took a wide glance towards the water's edge. Several schooners were in different stages of being built. But his focus stopped at one schooner, and he recognized her at once. "Is that her?" He pointed for his father to see.

"You're good, Heman." Daniel was impressed.

"I would recognize *Lady Catherine* anywhere. She is beautiful. All my dreams have come to life. Look at her."

Daniel watched his son with delight. "Let's take a closer look."

It didn't take long for Heman to leave the carriage. If he had his way, he would run as fast as he could to the gangplank. But the uniform he was wearing brought him to his senses. He patiently waited for the others to exit their carriages. Captains Collins and Buckley were by his side. They all were following Daniel and Jeremiah, and they were following Mr. Walsh. Mr. Walsh was strutting like a peacock. You could tell he was proud of what he was about to show everyone.

A special gangplank was set up. Irish flags, banners, and streamers added to the festive occasion. Mr. Walsh stopped the procession. In a loud voice, he made the command, "Captain Kenney," then paused, "Captain Heman Godfrey Kenney, front and center." All eyes were on Heman as he answered the order. "Before you cross the gangplank for the first time, your first mate, Henry, will do his duty."

I have a first mate? though Heman. He heard the whistle sound. It wasn't new to him; he had heard it many times. Every time the Captain crossed the gangplank to his domain, the whistle sounded. Everyone working on board knew when the Captain came aboard and went ashore. The whistle would sound its special sound.

This time the whistle sounded for him. "Now you must go first!" Mr. Walsh was directing Heman. Heman could see everyone at attention, as he crossed the plank. A flood of emotion came over him. He was home.

On the main deck, tables were set with the best white linen and Royal China. Heman had so much to take in that he failed to notice the people. There were people standing at the back of their chairs, waiting for the Captain to start the procedures. All the faces were familiar, and all were smiling at him.

The Captain's table was set for Heman. His mother and William were there waiting for him to arrive. He didn't realize until this very moment how beautiful his mother was. She was dressed in her finest, her hair braided, pulling her hair back from her face. Her eyes were shining, and a hint of a tear gathered under her eyelashes, and she smiled at him. Since he has been home, he saw his mother only in a work dress and her hair covered with a scarf. Today she looked like a queen. If Ireland had its own queen, his mother would be Queen of Ireland. Heman went to his mother and hugged her.

"Congratulations, Son. I love you," she whispered.

"You are a good secret keeper," he smiled back at her. "And I love you, too." As he made his way to the head of the table, the eyes of his little brother were searching for his. Heman acknowledged his brother with a nod and a smile.

William answered, shaking his head and smiling back. *The whole world falls at big brother's feet,* thought William.

Heman could see that William was as surprised as he was at the turn of events of this day. He turned and made eye contact with the others sitting at the Captain's table – Mr. Darby and his wife, Eileen; the Captains Collins and Buckley and their wives; Mr. Walsh and his wife.

Before he sat in the Captain's chair, his father came forward. Taking a silver spoon, he gently tapped it to the crystal goblet. The musical sound brought everyone to attention. "Thank you for coming. My partner, Jeremiah Darby, everyone in our company thanks you for coming. Our company: *Jeremiah Reilly Darby and Captain Daniel Kenney, and Son Captain Heman Godfrey Kenney, Esquire.*

William's ears picked up on the announcement. The hair on the back of his head rose slightly. The air emptied his lungs like hot air out of a balloon, when he heard his father's statement. A murmur went through the audience, as the news was first released of Heman's being added as a partner to their company.

"We, and of course along with my sweet wife Bridget, would like to welcome you on board this beautiful schooner. At this time, lunch will be served." At that, a line of waiters appeared. The first several in line walked crisply towards the Captain's table. The others seemed to float around the deck of the schooner, taking care of tables as they went. Daniel was now sitting beside Heman. He leaned closer. "Well, Son, what do you think?"

Heman didn't know what to think. "I'm afraid to take the next breath in fear that I might wake up from a dream, and this will be over."

Daniel laughed, "No dream, my Son." He looked to Bridget, and they both laughed. Daniel raised his glass to acknowledge William. William seemed to be in shock.

Colonial Mock Goose[15] was placed on the end of each table. The waiters served it individually.

William leaned over to Heman. "This sure beats that gruel we carry to the back gate."

It was the first time he could address his little brother. "William, are you sure you woke me up this morning?"

William laughed, "I believe you are as shocked as I am, big brother. Nice suit."

Heman looked down at his suit, and sure enough, it was a captain's uniform. He was glad to see William enjoying the food. One mouthful was all Heman managed, and it felt stuck in his throat.

"What's wrong, Heman?" William was laughing again. "Mock Goose is your favorite." William could be mad about this whole affair, but the reaction of Heman became a form of entertainment. Someone had dropped his brother in the ocean, if only figuratively speaking, and he was having a hard time swimming. Maybe William would be the one to throw him a life preserver. He continued to laugh.

All the handshaking was over. Even his father and mother had gone ashore. Heman thought he was alone.

"Come on, brother, let me show you around. Here is your sword. I will be the pirate and you be the captain. But this time I will tie you to the main mast, Heman." It was William. Heman met William's eyes. A flood of emotions came over him. He held them in all day. But it wasn't a flood of tears, which he fully expected, but a flood of laughter. Both were laughing until they were crying. What a picture they made.

"Is all this true, William? Or are we just children playing on this schooner?"

"No, my brother, we are not children, and this is your very own schooner. It didn't surprise me at all that they called her *Lady Catherine*."

"Come on, little brother. I can't take any more in. Let's go home." He put his arm around William's shoulders, and William did likewise, and they both went down the gangplank together. Neither of them noticed the sound of the whistle, as they stepped onshore. The Captain was leaving his ship.

* * * * *

There were many celebrations, one being the christening of his beautiful schooner. What a day it was. The noon sun was shimmering, and enough breeze was in the air to keep the flags waving, but not strong enough to blow the hats from the heads of the ladies. Heman chose his mother to do the honors. She let fly the ribbon holding the bottle of champagne that hit the side of the great schooner, christening her *Lady Catherine*. She was everything Heman could ever ask or hope for in a schooner. She sailed like the wind. He was getting used to hearing the whistle call when he came aboard. It made him feel important, and he took this "captaining" seriously. Men were counting on him. It

78

came naturally to Heman, and he was good at it. Life was good, and he was thankful to his father.

* * * * *

Heman was home, and this was a rare occasion. The pot of gruel was no more. Finally, the line of people stopped coming. New crops were planted and doing well. Ireland had survived this famine, but just barely.

Heman entered the kitchen to hear Ada talking, "She wouldn't dare come. If I had my way, William, I would meet her with my largest frying pan. There would be no food in it. I would need it to hit her over the head."

"Who's coming? And that doesn't sound very hospitable to me, Ms. Ada."

"If I had my way, there would be more done to her than that," she said as she gazed towards Heman taking a place at the worktable.

"Guess who's coming to visit." William directed the question to Heman.

"I give up, but I wouldn't want to be whoever it is. Doesn't sound like they would leave this place in one piece."

"Queen Victoria herself," Ada spoke as she peeled potatoes.

"No kidding. What are you cooking, Ms. Ada?"

"I wish I were kidding. Dublin Coddle – I'm fixing Dublin Coddle."[16]

"You're an angel. I can see William's tongue drooling now. Why would the Queen of England want to visit you, Ms. Ada?"

"Not me – Cork – she's coming to Cork. Where have you been, Heman, living under a rock? Everyone is talking about it."

"He lives on a schooner, Ms. Ada." William looked at his brother.

"Why is she coming here?"

"To make history."

"What kind of history?"

"She's coming to mark 1849, the year she helped end the famine."

"Help end the famine? She's one of the main causes."

"Isn't that the truth?"

"Because of her, we had to make that dreadful gruel daily. I thought I would lose my mind."

"William, it didn't hurt you to help those poor people." Ada still mothered him.

"Ms. Ada, I'm on your side."

"It's not the poor people I'm mad at. It's that Famine Queen. It's been told she promised £5000 to help the Irish people. All we saw was £5."[17]

The kitchen door opened, and Daniel himself walked into the kitchen. "These boys bothering you, Ada?"

"No, sir." Ada worked a little harder on the potatoes.

"Father, they have been telling me about the Queen's visit."

"That's why I am here – looking for you. We have been asked to have every available schooner at the mouth of Cork Harbour welcoming the Royal Yacht. We want *Lady Catherine* to lead the Queen into Cork."

"I'm not sure I'm happy about that idea."

"None of us are. Sometimes you have to do distasteful tasks in your lifetime."

"You can take Ada's frying pan." It was William commenting.

Daniel looked at Ada, "Your frying pan?"

"No, sir. Sorry, sir." Ada was turning red. William was laughing.

"I believe it is one of William's jokes." Heman was looking at his Father. "And when does all this take place?"

"This weekend."

"It seems I just came home in time."

"How are those two young colts doing?" Daniel's attention had changed to William.

"Doing fine, sir, fine. Expect a lot from them."

"Don't get in Ada's way. You two may not want to eat dinner on time, but your mother and I do." With that, he left the kitchen.

"What's with the horses, William?"

"Oh, I forgot, dear brother. You are never home long enough to know what goes on in the Kenney family. You get a schooner; I get a horse barn."

"A horse barn?"

"Racing horses – Father and I are breeding them. Amazing, isn't it big brother? And guess what – I happen to be good at it. I quit losing money and started making it big time. Father's proud." You get to lead the Queen of England into Cork. I get to give her the tour of my breeding stock. Go figure!"

* * * * *

The great day came. Everyone who could sail was in Cork Harbour. Heman was kept busy making sure no one had a shipwreck. The Royal Yacht was sighted. The *Lady Catherine* took her place to lead her into Cork. As he entered the Harbour, he wasn't sure whether all the boats were there to welcome the Queen or to do her harm. He told his first mate, Henry, to keep watch for trouble. "The Famine Queen wants to make history today, but it may not be the kind of history she wants."

"Aye, aye, sir!"

Heman knew his father had to put out more than one fire in the preparations for this visit. The Queen's people arrived early to make sure everything would be just right for the Queen's visit. The Duke of Leinster, one of the better Irish-English landowners and landlord over the area, was disgusted with the overspending. At one banquet £5,000 was spent on food and wine alone. He wondered how in this land where hundreds of thousands were starving, where a family of six could be kept alive for a week for less that £1.00, the Queen's government could justify spending thousands of pounds to entertain a privileged few for one night.[18] Heman was invited to that very banquet. He didn't know how he was going to eat the food without choking.

Lady Catherine sailed further into the Harbour. Heman looked back at The Royal Yacht following. On land, you could see the great variety of troops and bands playing as the Queen approached. Heman saw that the course they were taking would lead them under a huge Union Jack flag, which was just before they entered the docking area. It was with a sigh of relief when *Lady Catherine* passed under it. Her main mast had only inches to spare. He turned back to see if the Queen would follow. *Looks like there is plenty of room,* thought Heman. Out of the corner of his eye, he saw a man shimmying up the pole that held the Union Jack. "What in the world is he doing, Henry?"

Just as the Royal Yacht came under the flag, a cheer arose from the crowd. The flag was falling and as it fell, the cheers grew louder. It's resting place was the whole front bow of the Royal Yacht. The cheers grew even louder. The Queen and the Queen's party ran for cover. Luckily it seems that no one was hurt.

Heman looked up at the flagpole. A man was waving in victory. The people were cheering him on. This man was not just waving at the people; he was waving at Heman. Heman's jaw dropped open. "It couldn't be." The man was waving and yelling at him.

"Big brother." He yelled. It was William himself.

"He's gone and done it now." As Heman spoke all the English troops came alive. The Irish troops followed. They were all after William. Heman looked up at the pole, and William was gone, disappeared. "I hope you can run fast, my little brother." But now it was his job to get *Lady Catherine* into dock, not to mention the Royal Yacht, and to make sure that no one was hurt.

There was total chaos on the dock. Troops were running in every direction. Heman hurried to the docking birth next to him. The Union Jack flag had been commandeered. Heman quickly headed towards the Royal Yacht. Before he could board he was stopped. "Halt, you cannot come aboard." With that command, two muskets crossed in front of him.

"My name is Captain Heman Kenney. I was aboard the schooner *Lady Catherine* as she lead you into to Cork Harbour. I must see if anyone is injured."

The Captain of the Royal Yacht approached the guards and waved his arm with authority. The muskets rose in front of him. "Follow me." They entered into a great room where a man seemingly in charge of the Queen's affairs was upon Heman like a wild dog.

"This is outrageous! This is outrageous! The Queen will have his head. I've never seen anything so outrageous!"

Heman bowed and then came to attention. "We are terribly sorry for such an unfortunate set of affairs. Accept my apologies from me and the City of Cork."

"You planned it. It was planned. Did you hear the people? They cheered. It was planned."

"I assure you, sir, that this was not planned. No expense was spared to make the Queen's visit a welcoming experience for Her Majesty Queen Victoria and her entourage. Has the Queen been hurt?"

"Lucky for you, she wasn't. If she had been, it would have been war – between England and Ireland."

"Anyone else hurt?"

"I'm not sure. The Queen is with her ladies in waiting and cannot be disturbed."

"If anything can be done for Her Majesty, do not hesitate to inform me or anyone from Cork Government, and it will be taken care of immediately. Unless otherwise informed, we will continue the planned activities and public appearances that have been scheduled for the rest of the Queen's visit. You can be assured that security will be heightened and no more unfortunate incidents will occur."

Heman brought himself to attention and even clicked his heels before leaving the room. He was escorted off the Royal

Yacht. There to meet him was a throng of high dignitaries waiting at the gangplank. No one had been allowed on the Royal Yacht. Speaking above the dinge, Heman spoke, "Follow me; we will have a meeting." He was walking straight ahead, looking for a meeting place, when he heard his name.

"Heman?" It was his father walking along by his side. "Did you see who did this?"

He looked at his father. "You don't want to know."

The meeting with the dignitaries of the City of Cork went well. Everyone was assigned duties to make the Queen as comfortable as possible. Everyone was trying to make up for the ordeal she had experienced. The Royal Tour was going to continue.

Finally, Heman was alone with his father. "Father, you aren't going to be very pleased, but we need to work together to get through this."

"Is there something about the Queen you didn't reveal at the meeting?"

"No Father, it's William. He is in trouble and he is going to need our help. That's if they didn't catch him by now."

"What trouble?"

"He did it."

"Did what?"

"The flag that fell on the Queen. He did it."

Daniel stopped, "Heman, how do you know?"

"I saw him."

Daniel was quiet again. "They will hang him."

"I know. That's why we have to help him and quickly."

"Where is he?"

"I don't know."

"Then how can we help him?"

"If I were William, I would go to your shipyard. He knows he has friends there. Father, go to the shipyard. I will meet you as soon as I can." They went their separate ways. Heman headed for home.

* * * * *

George and O'Sullivan were tending to the horses, when Heman rushed through the double doors of the barn. "Mr. George, Mr. O'Sullivan, I need your help." Both men dropped their pitchforks and were at Heman's side. "William is in trouble."

"What kind of trouble?" It was George. He had tried to keep William out of trouble for years.

"I don't have time to explain. Have a carriage ready for Mother and then the wagon for you." Heman headed for the back door of the kitchen. As he entered, Ada was standing there.

"We saw the *Lady Catherine* leading the Royal Yacht and the Queen right into the Harbour. We were watching and we were so proud."

"Did you also hear that someone cut the Union Jack, and it practically fell on the Queen's head?"

"No." Ada had a smile on her face.

"Did you hear who did it? William."

"No!" Ada no longer had a smile on her face. "They will hang him. It's all my fault. If I didn't tell him about the frying pan. It's all my fault."

"They won't hang him if I can help it, Ms. Ada. Now listen, I need food. Just pack me some food."

George and O'Sullivan arrived in the kitchen to Ada's wailing as she threw food into a basket. "It's all my fault. It's all my fault. They're going to hang him."

Heman didn't wait to calm Ada down. He was going up the grand staircase as fast as his legs would take him. "Mother, Mother, are you there?"

Bridget came out of her bedroom. "Heman, must you be so loud?" But one look into her son's eyes told her something was wrong. "What is it? Heman, tell me."

"William is in trouble. Come, we must go to the shipyard."

Bridget was turning white. "Is he dead?"

"No, I don't think so. Not unless they caught him. Come, I will explain on the way."

The carriage lead the way into the shipyard's gate. The wagon wasn't far behind. George and O'Sullivan were informed by Ada that the English were going to hang William, and it was all Ada's fault. For sure something serious was up, but it couldn't be what Ada said, and what the blazes did she have to do with it?

Daniel's carriage was already there. "Let's all go to the office." It was Heman taking charge.

O'Sullivan hadn't been back to the shipyard since the day he played the part of a messenger. Many years had passed, but he remembered the way to the office. He confidently headed that direction with George following him. They came to the door:

Jeremiah Reilly Darby

and

Captain Daniel Kenney and Son,
Captain Heman Godfrey Kenney

Esquire

Heman passed by the two men and opened the door for his mother. Daniel and Mahoney were sitting at the table talking.

"Bridget, my Bridget, are you alright? Come, sit down here."

Mahoney nodded his head in acknowledgment to Heman. He wasn't sure of the other two men, even though one looked oddly familiar.

"Where is he, Daniel? Where is William?"

"He is safe, Bridget. Mahoney has him safe." Heman was relieved to know that.

"You were right, Heman. He came here to the shipyard. Mahoney took care of him."

"Everyone, sit down." It was Heman and he was taking over the meeting. "This is what we have to do next. We need to get William on the *Lady Catherine* and then out of Cork and out of Ireland."

"Oh, no, Heman, not out of Ireland." Bridget couldn't see living without William.

"Yes, Mother, out of Ireland. That's the only way."

"But, *Lady Catherine* is right next to the Royal Yacht." It was Daniel who wasn't sure of this plan.

"That's what makes it perfect. They won't be searching her."

"But how?" It was Mahoney.

"I need supplies on *Lady Catherine*. You, George and O'Sullivan, can get William on board, while you stow the supplies below deck. No one else is to know about this."

O'Sullivan gave a look towards Mahoney. "Looks like we will be working together again, bloke."

"You know him?" George was questioning O'Sullivan.

"Many years ago, my friend."

Mahoney nodded his head, "Many years ago." Then Mahoney looking at Heman, "Count it done. Come on, men, follow me."

Heman turned his attention to his father. "Now we need to make plans to sail."

"When?"

"Tonight during the big banquet. No one will notice us leaving."

"But you are supposed to be there. William too."

"I'm sorry, Mother, you will have to count William out. Tell people he was kicked by one of his horses and won't be dancing for a while. Father and I will be there and I will slip out early."

"Where will you go, Heman?"

"West Indies, Father. It will just be a regular trade trip to the West Indies."

"When will you bring William back?"

"I don't know, Mother, not for a long time."

Bridget was about to break down, but she willed herself to stay on her feet. "I want to see him?"

Daniel looked at Bridget, "I will take you. Heman, are you coming?"

Heman thought for a moment. "No, Father, it's best I don't know. Just in case something goes wrong."

Daniel nodded as he lead his wife out of the room. They entered a back room in the stables. Bridget wasn't used to being in such an environment, but she didn't care. She lifted her skirt and stepped carefully forward. Daniel lifted a trap door. "It's safe, William, you can come out." William full of straw emerged from the hole.

"Father, I'm sure you're not proud of me now?"

"It doesn't matter, Son. I brought your mother."

William turned. Bridget took one look at her son and her heart started breaking. "Oh, William."

William was at his mother's side, and they clung together. "Don't worry, Mother, everything will turn out fine."

Daniel looked at his son. "Be ready, George, O'Sullivan and Mahoney are coming for you."

"Where are we going?"

"Do everything they say. They will take you to the *Lady Catherine*."

"The *Lady Catherine*?"

"Yes, your brother will take you out of Ireland this very day."

"Out of Ireland? I don't want to leave Ireland. Mother, tell him, I don't need to leave Ireland."

Tears rolled down Bridget's face. "They will hang you, William."

"No, the English can't be that mad. It was a big joke."

"They are not laughing, Son. Your mother is right. They will hang you. Heman is making plans right now. You will sail tonight."

"Tonight? Where will we go?"

"The West Indies, William, the West Indies."

Dear Mother and Father:

Just a note before we set sail.

Thank you for the brave front you put on this evening. I am sure having dinner with Queen Victoria would have been more enjoyable to both of you, if you didn't have such a burden to carry. You carried it well. No one, not even I would have guessed.

William is safe and stored away from harm's way. We will make him more comfortable tomorrow morning.

I apologize for my brother's actions. Do not concern yourself for his well-being, for I will take care of him. It distresses me to leave you, when hearts may be broken.

It may be wise to dispose of this note. We wouldn't want it to fall into the wrong hands. However, since William is now considered a hero in Cork, the English authorities will have a difficult time finding anyone who will be willing to betray him.

Farewell for now. May God keep you in His care.

Your loving Son
Heman

CHAPTER FIVE

Fugitive Onboard

The sun was shining, and the sea breeze was a brisk one. All sails were full of wind, including the jib. This is when *Lady Catherine* was at her best. She skimmed through the water as easily as flat stones skipped over the surface of a small lake, only faster. She was clocking 11 knots. It seemed *Lady Catherine* knew where she was going and was in a hurry to get there. There was no holding her back. Why would you want to hold her back? She was making good time, and time was money.

No sound was heard but the spray of water off the bow, not even the sound of a seagull. Even they were left behind the night before. There was no land in sight. The rolling of the schooner was in tune with the beating of Heman's heart. This was his favorite time of any journey. All the frantic preparations for loading the cargo and preparing for sail were done. The first morning at sea was calm. His crew was resting, and a well-deserved one it was. The life of the sea was a hard one. One's guard could never be let down, and the men knew it. The opportunity for rest was rare, and they were going to take advantage of it.

Heman was leaving his Captain's cabin and headed for the top deck. His cabin boy came to attention and asked, "When would you have breakfast served, sir?"

"Give me an hour, Tom. I want to stretch my legs this fine morning."

"Yes, sir."

Heman climbed the ladder and opened the hatch. A breeze of cool, fresh salt air met him in the face. He filled his lungs; nothing revitalized him more than this salty air. He walked confidently with his hands clasped together at his back. He enjoyed his daily walk to listen to *Lady Catherine*. She would tell him if something were wrong. They were one in spirit. Even his crewmates saw it. If one were superstitious, it could unnerve a man.

But today was a fine weather day at sea and Heman could sense no trouble, unlike the day before. He was thankful when he was out of Cork Harbour. He had a cargo filled with supplies, including salted beef and butter to trade in the British West Indies.[19] He also had the special cargo, a fugitive. Mahoney, George, and O'Sullivan did a good job of getting his little brother aboard. They made him a special berth at the front of the bow. No one would find him, even if they did do a search of the ship. The fugitive was not too happy about his living quarters, and Heman had to place a guard to make sure he didn't move.

There he was, the fugitive himself, looking over the rail. "Good morning, William. Little brother, are you looking for something?"

"Very funny." William straightened up and wiped his mouth with the back of his sleeve.

"Your dinner not settle well?"

"What dinner? You call that dinner? I was forced to sit in that hole in a pile of straw, while you ate with Royalty. Do you see something wrong with that picture?" William was gagging again, leaning over the rail.

"Don't fall overboard."

"Maybe that is what I should do. Jump and then it would end this agony."

"You always were melodramatic, little brother. Don't worry; you will get your sea legs soon. *Lady Catherine* is now your home." Heman raised his hand towards the whole schooner.

William looked. "I'd rather be in a barn."

"Sorry about that, little brother. It's not going to happen, not after what you did yesterday."

"It wasn't that bad. I don't understand why everyone is making a big deal out of it."

"You're right, William. You wouldn't understand. No one, especially an Irishman, would treat Queen Victoria that way and get away with it. What made you do it?"

William looked at Heman, "You wouldn't understand."

"Try me."

"O'Brien bet me £1000 if I did it."

Heman shaking his head, "Did you get the money?"

"I haven't had a lot of spare time to go and collect it."

"I didn't think so."

"O'Brien is good for it; he'll pay up."

"Yeah, sure. And when do you plan to ask about it? If you haven't noticed, Ireland is back that way," Heman swinging his arm back the way they came. "And we are going this way," his arm changing direction 180 degrees. "I don't think you understand, little brother. You aren't going back to Ireland, not for a long time."

William had his head over the side again. This time Heman didn't think it was seasickness.

The heaving finally subsided. William looked at Heman, "So what do I do now?"

Heman actually saw fear in William's eyes. This may be the day – the day William becomes a man.

"One day at a time, little brother. Who knows what will become of you. But you can be assured of one thing: I will be there until you don't need me any longer. Let's begin by showing you your apartment. I don't think we will make you sleep in the hole again. Are you up to it?" Heman asked William.

William nodded, "I believe so. My stomach has stopped heaving."

"That's a beginning. Your sea legs will follow." Heman led the way, while William staggered behind him.

"What to do with William?" That was on Heman's mind all night. William would not be comfortable bunking with the crew. Nor would they be happy having the Captain's brother around. Heman decided to take a kitchen storage room and turn it into William's bedroom. There was room for a bed and a small desk. An old rusty lantern was added.

William was trying to keep up with his big brother, as they went below deck. They were headed for the crew quarters. William was aghast at what he saw. He thought his stomach was going to roll again. But he managed to keep his dignity, as he was introduced to the crew. There was not enough space. At least that is what William thought. However, the crewmembers were quite at home. Each crewmember had 18 inches of deck for his hammock, with men to either side of him.[20] Heman looked at William, "Considering that the First watch is working, and the Second watch is at ease, this is not as crowded as it might at first seem, but certainly not luxurious. The crew eats sitting on sea chests or boxes, which are on planks placed on trestles. The midshipman has a locker." William noticed that the size of the locker was no larger than the bunks or hammock.

"Now, let me show you your living quarters."

William had a sigh of relief. "Anything has to be better than this."

"Voila," Heman opened the door. "Little brother, your castle."

William smiled when he saw the desk and bed. Now he knew why Heman showed him the crew quarters first.

"What do you think, brother?"

"Just fine, brother. I don't have much luggage anyway."

"Oh, but you do." Heman pulled a wooden chest from under the bed. "Mother still loves you. Everything you can possibly need."

"What have I done to poor Mother?"

"Don't worry; she will get over it. Just remember to write her and thank her for packing for you. By the way, you will be eating your meals with me and the officers. Breakfast will be ready in five minutes." Heman left William sitting on his bunk.

* * * * *

Several days passed before William got his sea legs. Now that he was feeling more like himself, he was no longer satisfied to lie on his bunk. He wondered what he was going to do now. But Heman had it all planned and was waiting for William to leave his bed.

"Nice to see you up and walking about, little brother."

"Thanks, I thought I would watch the scenery go by, but there is nothing to see but water."

"Ocean you mean."

"Whatever you want to call it. It looks like water to me."

"You'd better get used to it; we won't see land for another month or so."

"You must be kidding!"

"No, little brother."

"That just made my day. I think I will go back to bed."

"No, you won't, William, if your life is to be on this schooner, you need to earn your keep. You don't want the crew to think you're soft."

"What are you going to make me do? Swab the deck?"

"Not unless you want to. I have something better in mind. We have a meeting with the officers at Two bells."

"That's another thing. What's with all the bells ringing? You trying to wake the dead?"

Heman was being patient with William. All of a sudden his world of horses has turned into a world at sea – with a set of rules only a sailor would use.

Heman turned to William. "Lesson #one: Ship bells. The bell is used to note the passage of time during the watch, and the bell was struck each time the watch glass (Half-hour glass) was turned. For example, the day starts at noon. The bell was struck eight times.[21] You can be sure, every time the bell rings, something is taking place."

"What time is Two bells?"

"1300 hours."

"What?"

"1:00 p.m., William. Be at the meeting."

The meeting took place at the table where meals were served. It was a small room with a table that sat four. They made it sit six. There was a lantern swinging from the wood ceiling. It was not needed, for sunshine was coming in the porthole. William took one look out the porthole, and again, all he could see was water, or rather, "ocean" as Heman put it. William hadn't spent much time here. The little food he did manage to eat was eaten in his bunkroom. But now that he had his sea legs, he planned to be here more often.

Heman was a natural leader. He made eye contact with everyone around the table. "You all have met William, my brother. He has been incapacitated lately and has not had the privilege of meeting you. Please introduce yourselves."

"I am Henry, First Mate. Welcome aboard."

"Patrick is the name and my job is Watch leader one."

"Watch leader two, and you can call me Moses."

Heman taking it upon himself, pointed to John. "This is John Charles, and he is our navigation specialist and supply officer."

"Thank you, Patrick and Moses, for coming. Moses, this is your sleep time, and Patrick is on watch, so you may be dismissed. Henry, I will meet with you at Four bells."

After the officers managed to leave the crowded room, Heman turned to William. "John Charles and I have discussed the matter, and from this day on, you are to be his apprentice. He will teach you his trade of navigation and keeping up with supplies. Is that agreeable, William?"

"Well, I have nothing else to do for the next month. So be it."

"John Charles stared at William, "Be here at Six bells in the morning." He looked at Heman.

"You are dismissed." John Charles left the room.

Heman looked straight into William's eyes. "I don't like your attitude. This is no joke. John Charles is one of the finest navigators in Ireland. You will learn everything he knows, and you will learn it well. Now that you will be living with me, you will tow your weight. Do I make myself clear?"

"Sure, Heman."

"From now on it will be, 'Aye, aye, sir!' I am your Captain, not your brother, during working hours. Do you understand? You will be treated like the other officers, not any better, not any worse. I expect you to work hard. If any bad reports come to me, there will be consequences to pay. Do I make myself clear, little brother?"

William looked into Heman's dark eyes, "Aye, aye, sir!"

"You may be dismissed." And with that William left the room.

Except for evening dining, Heman had not seen William in more than ten days. He was giving John Charles the leadership role concerning his brother. William seemed well enough at dinner. Heman noticed his appetite was getting better. *Maybe I will turn him into a sailor yet,* he thought. Heman had a good report from John Charles, and he was anxious to meet with William alone, brother to brother, to see how he was doing.

A few days later, there was no ocean breeze. The sun was beating down on *Lady Catherine*, and she was sitting still in the water. All Heman could do was pray for a little wind, not a stormy gale, just a little wind. The crew was lying under any shade they could find. Most were sleeping. Heman took the opportunity to speak to William. They met in the Captain's cabin. The two portholes were open. It was as cool there as any other part of the ship.

"Is it hot enough for you, Captain? Not like Ireland, is it?"

"Okay, William. Now it is brother to brother. How are things going?"

"Swell."

Heman lowered his eyes.

"No, really. I'm getting into this supply thing. I didn't know everything was so organized. Well, look here." William placed a paper in front of Heman.

Food Rations

Sunday – Bread, one pound, Beer, one gallon, Pork 1 pound, Pease 1 Pin

Monday – Bread, one pound, Beer, one gallon, Oatmeal 1 Pint, Butter 2 Ounces, Cheese 4 Ounce

Tuesday – Bread, one pound, Beer, one gallon, Beef 2 Pound

Wednesday – Bread, one pound, Beer, one gallon, Oatmeal 1 Pint, Butter 2 Ounces, Cheese 4 Ounces

Thursday – Bread, one pound, Beer, one gallon, Pork 1 Pound, Pease, a Pin

Friday – Bread, one pound, Beer, one gallon, Oatmeal 1 Pint, Butter 2 Ounces, Cheese 4 Ounces

Saturday – Bread, one pound, Beer, one gallon, Beef 2 Pound[22]

"All the food for a week written down neat and tidy. I even get to pass it out."

Heman read in front of him.

"And that's not counting the fruit and sauerkraut. And, brother, did you know the meat we eat daily – the cook has to soak that stuff in water for hours before he can cook it. Water is even measured out for the steep-tub? Brother, did you know we stow 103 tons of water, which lasts eleven weeks and six days?"[23]

Heman smiled at William. He was pleased that William was taking interest in his work.

"I didn't know when they handed me water the first week I was here, that it was measured and written down. Now I do that. Also, I know Two bells I eat. Eight bells the crew receives first half of grog. The next Eight bells I have to blow my lantern out. Six bells I'm late for John Charles and the beat of a drum is – second grog or beer rations. The other bells I just ignore. And what's amazing, this happens every day rain or shine."

"This has been an easy voyage so far," Heman was informing William. "Sometimes things happen out here that turns schedules upside down. I'm happy you can learn when everything is calm around you. What does John Charles have in mind for you next week?"

"I begin navigating. It's fascinating to watch him. He's always watching the sun and then at night the stars. I believe he knows where he is going."

Heman laughed, "I hope someone knows. *Lady Catherine* will find her way."

William joined his brother in laughter. It felt good. If there was any tension between them, it was gone now.

* * * * *

Six bells and William wasn't late. He might even like this navigation.

"Ah, navigation." It was John Charles beginning his first lesson. He could talk all day about navigation; it was in his blood. Not too many people would listen, mind you, but here he had a student, and now he could share his years of knowledge. "Ah, navigation, the stars, the sun, the shiny brass tools, complex mathematical calculations, playing with timing glasses, throwing logs, counting knots, pricking charts, squinting at the moons of Jupiter. Staring directly into the sun (going blind in one eye), squinting at the moons of Jupiter. Staring directly into the sun (going blind in one eye).[24] Everything you think you would ever need aboard to navigate a great schooner as this, but forget all those, William. All you really need are these." He dropped a book and an instrument on William's lap.

William picked up the book: The New American Practical Navigator.[25] "Sure is thick."

"That is the latest addition to navigation. Anything you ever want to know and how to get there is found in this here book. A book every captain like Captain Kenney and navigators rely on. And of course, the sextant. You need to learn how to use that. Navigation is very simple. I use two methods most all the time. One," John Charles pointed one finger up. "Stars – they are always there. Well, except for stormy nights. But they are still there. Stars are constant, and with them, you can find out where you are, or you'll never know where you are going. Number two," his second finger went up, "dead reckoning."[26]

William had no idea what that meant.

"Dead reckoning – simple. If you know where you were yesterday, and what direction you have been sailing in, and how the tides have affected your course, and the winds, and how fast you have been going, you can reckon where you should approximately be now. By using the log to check your speed each hour, and accurate tidal information and a good compass, you should be able to do well enough at finding the West Indies."

William just realized that navigation was going to be harder to learn than the supply roster.

"Come with me and bring the sextant." William followed as they went on deck. It was a sunny, hot day. The ocean breezes were strong enough to fill the three sails. *Lady Catherine* was making good time.

"Where's the sun?"

William looked confused, but John Charles was looking at him, waiting for an answer. William refused to say, "In the sky." He knew that wasn't the answer to the question. He didn't want to look stupid. He shaded his hand over his eyes and looked straight up.

"Is it east or west?" John Charles was getting impatient.

"Well, I believe it's more in the middle."

"Right on!" He slapped William on the back, knocking William off balance. "You mean straight up or its highest point."

"Yes, I believe so."

"On clear days, just before the hour of noon, you will measure the angle of the sun at its highest point above the horizon with your sextant. This measurement calculates the latitude position of the ship. And from these calculations, and use of either an accurate chronometer, or the lunar observations taken as well, and consulting the Almanacs and your book, which may warrant a correction of the chronometers – then your readings are recorded and delivered to the Captain."

William had a blank look on his face. "Never mind, we will just start with measuring with your sextant. This is how you do it." John Charles finished his lesson and left William to figure it out.

If it were left to me, thought William, *we would be going in circles, and we would never reach the West Indies.* He was amazed at the knowledge of John Charles, and he was determined to learn from the man. John Charles pointed out how important navigation was. William will always remember well the story John Charles told: 'Now, if you are in the middle of the ocean, are running out of fresh water, and the crew is dropping from scurvy, because they haven't had any fruit or sour kraut in weeks, and the closest island should be nearby, being 60 miles off in your position means you might miss the island and then, die. So a navigator keeps watch around him all the time. Even in his sleep.[27]

John Charles noticed he finally got William's attention and laughed an eerie laugh that made William's hair stand on the back of his neck.

William thought, *What have I done? It was a lot easier timing a horse running around a track. Nobody was relying on me for life and death decisions.* It was the first time he thought about his brother being a captain and the awesome responsibility that brought. His respect for his brother just grew.

* * * * *

Heman's comment about a calm voyage was short lived. A week later, William was accompanying his brother on his morning walk. Heman was preoccupied in thought. His brother brought him back to the present by asking him a question. "What's your favorite time of the day, Heman?"

"Morning, and yours?"

"Definitely sunset. To see the sun dip into the ocean like a ball of fire. The red sky is breathtaking. Heman, I notice the sky is red this morning, is that usual?"

"No, William it is not. All sailors know: 'Red sky at night, sailor delight. Red sky in the morning, sailor, take warning.' Watch the crew."

"They do look a little edgy."

"They have a right to be. Before this day ends we will run into bad weather. There's a storm brewing. John Charles had better make his calculations early and often this day. Looks like we are all in for a hard day's work. Report to Watch leader one. He will tell you what to do."

"That's Patrick?"

"Yes, William, and be careful. You are about to get educated on the dark side of this mighty ocean. You will see her angry today." William wasn't sure, but he thought he saw a look of excitement in Heman's eyes.

"Batten down the hatches," Patrick was bellowing orders to his crew as William appeared.

"Sir, reporting for duty."

"Son, have you ever been in a storm on this here ocean?"

"No, sir."

"I didn't think so, and Captain wants me to babysit you, is that right?"

"No, sir! a babysitter I do not need. I'm willing to do my share, and strong enough to do anything you ask of me."

"Strong – you don't know the meaning of strength. My mother has more muscles on her arm than your puny muscles." Throwing a look at one of the crew as he went below deck, he gave them an order, "Tie him aboard."

"Don't worry, Sir William, this will keep you safe enough." Dick was tying a rope around his waist and pulling it tight.

"I'm not Sir William. How in blazes am I to help when I am tied up?"

"Don't worry, Sir William, all I'm doing is tying you to the side. You will be able to work just fine. But when you fall overboard, we can just pull you back in." As he was hooked up, William was amazed he could walk the whole starboard side of the ship. The rope just came with him.

It wasn't just the hatches they tied down, but anything that could move. There seemed to be more crewmen hustling around deck than normal. William noticed Moses among them.

"Moses, I thought you would be sleeping?"

"No sleep for anyone for who knows how long. It's time to ask the Almighty to be merciful." At that, Moses crossed himself and went back to work.

The sky was no longer blue but grey. The blue ocean, which welcomed *Lady Catherine* and gently pushed the schooner along, now was very angry. What had she done to cause her wrath? The waves were now green and ugly. Each wave got larger and tried to toss spray and foam over the side and onto the deck of the schooner.

It was just after sunset, not that you could see the sun disappear in the West. But you knew darkness was spreading a curtain over the angry sea. Increasingly high waves battered the *Lady Catherine*, and the wind had risen to an eerie whine. The ship's sails flapped and billowed in the gale, and sea spray filled the air, soaking everything in the open. William managed to crawl his way towards the bow, his rope following. Heman, the First Mate, and John Charles were at the wheel.

"Why didn't we sail around this?" William questioned John Charles more so then Heman.

"We are," John Charles grinned at William. "Hang on tight. You are in for a wild ride."

"How long will this last?"

"Your guess is as good as ours." Heman looked at William, "You'd better go below deck."

"And miss all the excitement?" William was gaining respect from the crew. If he was afraid, he was not showing it.

Hours had passed, the motion of the vast ocean waves and clouds mixed with torrential rain was unspeakable. The wind was fierce. The waves now seemed like they were a hundred feet high, as they swept across the schooner from fo'c'sle to the fantail. She rocked from starboard to port, shaking ferociously as they encountered wave after wave after wave crashing and smashing against *Lady Catherine*. The boarding and exiting ladder was viciously torn from its place and carried off into the depths of the ocean. Shipmates were tossed to and fro as well as the ship's cargo. William appreciated his rope, for, on more than one occasion, he rolled to one side of the deck and then to the other, the rope keeping him from going overboard. The schooner rushed up one mountain of water and down the other end, as she dipped deep into an ocean valley.

The thunder and lightning were enough to unnerve a man. The lightning would light up the sky, revealing men scrambling to do what it took to keep the ship under control. The storm was right above them. A deafening bang and a flash of lightning that singed one's hair came upon them. The First Mate, Henry, appeared to those around as in a blaze of fire. He was knocked down and laid still on the deck.

"Quick, get him below deck. I will take over for him." Heman grabbed the wheel.

William and three other shipmates managed to bundle Henry up and start for the main hatch leading to the lower deck. William fumbled to get rid of his rope. They barely managed to keep Henry in one piece as they fell down the ladder, closing the hatch behind them. There was water raining in from the deck. William thought, *"Are we going to sink?*

Dick reading his mind, "Don't worry, Sir William, we are not sinking yet."

William was grateful for the information. "Here, put him on my bunk."

Dick actually tied Henry in place. "He seems to be breathing. He will be okay in a few days." It amazed William how tough these men were.

The screech of the wind continued, mixed with the sound of pots and pans, spoons, wisps and other galley utensils flying through the air as the ship sunk into one of these vast ocean valleys.

"You stay with him. We will return to help the Captain." With that Dick and his shipmates were gone. William had had enough of this storm and began praying for it to stop. The Lord answered his prayer twelve hours later.

* * * * *

After one month and four days at sea, a sound was heard that was music to everyone's ears, "Land Ho." Dick was on duty in the

Eagle's Nest. Through his spyglass a welcoming sight indeed – Land Ho. Everyone strained his eyes in the direction that Dick pointed. Off to the horizon, a brown and green colour could be seen.

West Indies. John Charles had brought them safely through the long journey. No one doubted his ability. Three cheers went up almost like they were toasting him. He nodded his head in appreciation.

William was glad to see land. As soon as they got on the beach, he looked forward to dropping to his knees and kissing the ground. He didn't care who would be watching.

It had taken more than a week to clean up after the great storm. Sails had to be mended and everything put back in place. He hoped he would never see a storm like it again. The First Mate, Henry, was still in William's bunk. It took him two days to wake up, if you call it waking up. He didn't know where he was; he couldn't see and he couldn't hear. His crewmates were nursing him back to health. Dick was the head nurse. He took that position, because he felt he saved Henry's life by dragging him below deck at the time of the incident. Dick made it known that he thought illnesses were an imbalance of the body. All Henry needed was to be placed back in balance.[28] He sat with him daily, feeding him specially made soup. Only yesterday, two weeks after the storm, his sight returned just in time to see land.

William was with Heman. They too were straining their eyes to see land. "One more day, William. We will be moored in Cinnamon Bay in the morning."

"I will be glad to be on land." William was holding his back as he spoke.

"What's wrong with your back, William?" Heman knew the answer before asking the question.

"You know very well, Henry's hammock is less to be desired. Tonight I get my bunk back. Henry can see his way to his hammock."

Heman laughed, "It was good of you to help the sick."

"What else was I to do? When I told them to put him on my bunk, I didn't know it was going to be for two weeks."

"You can look forward to lying on the sandy beach of Cinnamon Bay, not a care in the world. You've earned it. You proved yourself during the storm. The crew has accepted you as a sailor and has added you to the crew. You should be proud."

"Yeah, I noticed a change since the storm. Dick quit calling me, Sir William."

Sailing into Cinnamon Bay reminded Heman of the day he led the Queen of England into Cork Harbour. Life sure can change in one month. Cinnamon Bay was the prettiest harbour he can remember going to. The warm breeze off the ocean was pleasant. The blue-green water was contrasted by the green tropical plant life that flourished in this part of the world. The palm trees stood guard everywhere, but today they opened their palm leaves welcoming the *Lady Catherine* into the Bay.

"Cast anchor."

"Did you see that village on the edge of the bay, Heman? Did you also notice they were all Negro?"

"Cinnamon Bay Plantation is one of the largest plantations in this area. They raise sugar cane and, yes, they have slaves. I believe more than 100 slaves work this plantation. They have a three-acre "village" on the bay side. They have the opportunity to fish and easily harvest seafood, such as conch and welk, and they can grow what they need to feed themselves. My paperwork informs me that the plantation produces sugar and rum.[29] That is why Father likes to trade with them. They seem to be doing well."

"Where do the slaves come from, Heman?"

"The slaves here on this plantation came from Africa. But other plantations have slaves from Ireland."

"Ireland?"

"Yes, Ireland! During the potato famine, many were sold as slaves. They ended up here in the West Indies."

"Take a look around the Bay. We are not alone; many countries come here to trade. Usually, there are more ships here than what you see."

"Look. A boat is coming our way."

"Yes, it's called a Pram.[30] This is a very well-run port. We will now receive instructions on when our cargo will be disembarked and who will do it. As soon as we have everything in ship shape, I will have schedules made up for shore duty. But first I must see my instructions."

William continued to take in the view. The crew was coming up through the hatch from below deck. They sure looked different. Hair was slicked back, and they were actually dressed up. They wore green vests and jackets and canvas-coloured trousers, and a neckcloth that matched the ribbon on the green vest. Embroidered on the ribbon were the words: *Lady Catherine.*[31]

"Moses, you're looking mighty fine. Come let me see you close up."

"William, I thought you would be first in line, to go ashore, I mean."

"Looks like you beat me to it."

A whistle sounded. "Landlubbers on deck." They watched as two men boarded the schooner. Heman lead the way to his cabin.

"It won't be long now. In fact, some of us have to go ashore with those blokes to get a Pram to use for transport, while we are in the Bay. Moses planned to be one of that party.

The bell started ringing. Everyone turned in surprise. "Why is the bell ringing? Eight bells? It certainly is past 8:00 a.m."

Captain Heman appeared, "All crew on deck." The order was passed one by one. In 10 minutes everyone on board was present. The Captain was on the upper deck with his back towards the wheel and began to address his crew, "Until further notice, all shore duty has been cancelled."

A loud murmur was heard from his crew. William also wondered what was going on. After all, no one on this ship had stepped upon dry land in more than a month. Captain Heman was not going to be very popular.

"Settle down and give me your attention, Heman ordered. "I have just received a very disturbing letter. It reads as follows:

Cinnamon Bay,
January 3, 1854

My Dear Captain Kenney,
I am sorry to inform you that a woman has just died of cholera on this estate. She was taken at 1 o'clock this morning and died at 3:30. A little boy about 5 years is also very bad who was taken at the same time, and I am afraid will not be alive when you receive this.
We are in need of a bottle of Bitters and a vial of Camphor Drops - everything has been done that has been recommended: particularly rubbings to cause a perspiration, but is no avail.
I remain my dear sir.
Yours truly
Thomas Ivinson [32]

Now there was dead silence. No one uttered a word. The word "cholera" sent fear into the toughest men. "Until further notice, follow your daily routine. Dismissed."

Heman was not finished. He turned to his First Mate, "Henry."After the cargo is unloaded, take *Lady Catherine* farther out into the Bay."

"Aye, aye, sir."

William was alone with Heman in his cabin. "What is your next move?"

"I'm not sure. We need supplies, but it's too dangerous to get them here."

The next two weeks the crew upon The *Lady Catherine* was filled with tension. The days of easy sailing at sea were over. No one had work to do, which gave them too much time to think. Even though The *Lady Catherine* was moored at the mouth of Cinnamon Bay, the crew could see the sandy beaches. Tired of being aboard ship, they weren't too happy being stuck on board. But cholera was the only thing keeping them there.

Heman knew if he didn't keep control, nasty events would follow. He gave orders that every day at One Bell, the new watch had the crew bring their bags and chests on deck. The lower decks were cleaned with lime and then whitewashed. This not only made work for his crew but would be a defense in the fight against cholera. This routine was repeated for two weeks.

Moses and Patrick had a meeting with the Captain. "Sir, we have the cleanest and prettiest quarters a crew could ever live in. The crewmen are calling it 'the Royal Yacht.' "

Heman appreciated Moses' attempt for humor. The Captain was in a pacing mood, except the room was too small. He drummed his finger on the table as he spoke. "I know it's not easy for you both; it's not easy for anyone aboard this ship. We all know we are running low on supplies. I've been in constant communication with Mr. Thomas Ivinson. I was hoping the cholera epidemic would subside, but after receiving this letter today, it doesn't give much hope. Let me share it with you." Heman took a letter out of a brown envelope covered with white powder and begins to read:

Cinnamon Bay, January 15, 1854

Dear Captain Kenney,

We have to date 21 deaths from cholera, and 3 very ill. We are now using some medicine I think is doing a great deal of good . . . All of the people are living in my house, not one in the Negro Houses. I hope you and crew are all well. Believe me.

Yours truly,

Thomas Ivinson

"How do you know that their letter is not full of cholera?" Patrick was concerned. "Don't worry, I had them bury it in a bucket of lime and didn't touch it for two hours."

Both Patrick and Moses were satisfied with the Captain's vigilance to make sure cholera didn't make its way on board. "Now what? they asked.

The Captain turned the question towards the two men. "How are your crews fairing?"

"The men's tempers flare every day there is a shore breeze. It is believed the cholera could come towards us in the wind."

Moses added, "Tempers are our biggest problem. I have a report here for you, Captain, of four fights. If we don't stop it, it will spread like the cholera."

"Pass the word. All crew on deck at Six Bells and rig a grating for a flogging. Have the accused there."

* * * * *

Having seen what happened, William wasn't too pleased with his older brother. Captain or no Captain, to flog his crewmen was going too far. He couldn't believe it as he watched Heman give eight lashes to those eight men. It was over now. The crewmen always took care of their own. The victims had the welts on their backs rubbed down with oil.

Heman was at his desk looking over paperwork and was trying to make plans for what to do next. He wished his father was closer to ask advice, but he knew he was on his own.

William, barging through the door, brought him to attention, "What kind of show was that? Did that make you feel good, brother? I never thought I would see you be a tyrant." William's eyes were glassy with fire, as he vented his anger.

"William, it wasn't a show, and I had to do it. The fighting had to stop, and I had to make an example of them. There was no other way."

"Find one." William's anger was not spent yet.

"When you work with horses, do you ever use a whip – a whip to remind them who is boss?"

William let himself fall into a chair.

"I know it wasn't pretty. But being a Captain, there are things that go with the position that no one can do but me. The crewmen would disrespect me if, for example, I got you or my First Mate to do the flogging. It was my job, and everyone knew it. It's my job to keep these men safe, and I intend to do it."

"We will sail tomorrow."

"Tomorrow?" William stood up. "Where to?

"Up the Caribbean to San Juan, Puerto Rico. Word has it the cholera hasn't reached them. They won't let us come ashore until we are inspected, but because no one from this crew was ashore here, I think we will be okay. The crew, including you, will be able to go ashore and we will have to re-supply. After that, I don't know yet."

The crew was happy to have wind in their sails again. *Lady Catherine* sailed closer to the coastline of the islands. This made William happy there was more to look at than ocean. The combination of lush green tropical plants and the white sandy beaches lying on a blue-green ocean, and topped with blue sky, had a soothing effect on all who were aboard the ship.

John Charles said, "With a good wind, we should make it to San Juan in three days." William's navigation lessons continued.

"We need the log." Magically a crewman appeared with this lengthy rope.

"Take notice, William, there is a knot tied every ten fathoms or 50 feet." He yelled an order, "All ready at the stern?"

"Yes, sir!" came the reply.

At that, John Charles heaved the logline overboard. The crewmen were stationed along the side with the last man at the stern. As John Charles kept time for 30 seconds, the men called out numbers as the knots passed: 1, 2, 3, 4. As the rope made it to the stern, the number was11. John Charles ordered, "Stop." He looked at William "We are going at 11 knots. That's good time. If the wind keeps up, 11 knots is great speed." He turned to Dick, "Deliver the message to the Captain."[33]

The whole crew took notice as they entered the harbour of San Juan. There were many ships of all kinds moored there. There were Sloops, Cutters, Frigates, and Brigs, and between them were Lighters and Prams. This was a very busy harbour. There were other schooners as well, but *Lady Catherine* sailed by them all with dignity and pride. She made an impression, as she slowly sailed into port.[34]

After the Harbour Master and his inspectors were satisfied that no cholera was aboard the ship, they quarantined the crew for one week. If no cholera outbreak occurred, they were welcomed to come ashore. That explained the large number of ships in the harbour. They were waiting for their quarantine to expire.

In anticipation of shore duty, Heman planned for the two watches to draw straws to see which watch would have the first shore duty. This would take place at Eight Bells, after which dinner would be served on deck. The Harbour Master had delivered food, a gesture of goodwill he called it, a feast set for a king. William remembered the last royal feast he missed out on. He shook his head; he didn't want to think of that. Fruit of every kind was set on the upper deck by the schooner's wheel. Bananas, many varieties of melons, grapes, coconuts and many fruits that William had never seen before. Fish and meat were cooking on open coals. The aroma made your taste buds stand to attention. The atmosphere was light and lively. A fiddle and an accordion added to the festive feeling.

Patrick and Moses took their places. Heman held the straws. A cheer went up as Moses picked the longest one. Patrick and his crew took defeat with a sportsman's attitude. Just knowing their turn would come to go ashore was enough to take the sting out of their defeat.

Two weeks had passed. A Pram had made countless trips to *Lady Catherine*, taking crew ashore and bringing them back to do their duty onboard ship. Heman and William were sitting around the dining table, which was now permanently placed on deck.

"Heman, why is that old schooner moored off to herself?" Heman's gaze followed William's arm pointed to an old two-masted schooner.

"She looks old, doesn't she? There usually is a good reason that they isolated her. I've been invited to a Captain's reception onshore day after tomorrow. I'll find out about her."

"How do you like San Juan? I know you have been ashore on more than one occasion. Did you kiss the ground?"

"Surprisingly I did not. Never crossed my mind."

"Making a sailor out of you, aren't we?"

"I didn't have much choice. Being a sailor doesn't seem to be as dreadful as it was at the beginning. And San Juan is a nice place to visit, but I wouldn't want to settle there."

"Didn't find any horses, huh?"

"Not close by, that's for sure. What's our next plan, big brother?"

"Maybe I will get some ideas after I meet with some of the Captains that are here."

A few days after his meeting, Heman was in his cabin looking for something to do. "Everything taken care of, Henry?" Heman asked his First Mate.

"Everything is shipshape, sir."

Heman was anxious; he had the feeling before. The sea was calling, and he was ready to go. Stretching his legs might calm him and he went in search of his brother.

"There you are." William was sitting gazing out to sea. "Don't tell me you are ready to set sail again?"

"Don't know what I feel. Heman, did you find out about the old schooner over there?"

"All I heard was it is Captain Cook's schooner, who, like us, could not go ashore in Cinnamon Bay and ended up here too."

"I made Captain Cook's acquaintance at the Wharf's Sea Biscuit yesterday."

Heman broke in, "They have great fish chowder there."

"Captain Cook has a problem." William ignored Heman's statement about chowder.

"What kind of problem?"

"He couldn't deliver his cargo at Cinnamon Bay, and no one wants it here."

"Where is his cargo from?"

"Africa."

"That explains it. That is why they have that schooner isolated. And did you notice no one is downwind of her? Slaves. Isn't it, William? Slaves? And that is why they don't want them here. They abolished slavery here in 1817. It was not until 1831 that the Law was effectively enforced. People of Colour obtained the same rights as whites."[35]

"Well, it's not the best cargo to transport. But look at all the people around here; they are all descended from slaves. The slaves are still here, but they call them Mulattos and pay them to work in the gold mines and sugarcane fields, not to mention the making of rum business."

"I've been figuring, Heman. Captain Cook wants them off his hands. He is willing to make a deal, a deal that one cannot just ignore."

"You've got to be kidding me, William. That cargo you speak about is human beings. They are not cows, lumber, or salted beef. Even if we take what you call 'a great deal,' what would we do with them?"

"Massachusetts."

"Where?"

"Massachusetts, America. They are willing to pay nicely for this kind of cargo."

"You're serious about this, aren't you? Well, I will have nothing to do with it. You hear me, nothing to do with it." Heman walked away, "Just the idea gives me nightmares."

Cinnamon Bay
West Indies
January 1854

My Dear Parents:

Heman informed me of our landing in Cinnamon Bay would take place in the morning. Lying on my bunk, thoughts of you entered my mind more than The West Indies. I lit my lamp and sat at my small desk to write this before the coming of dawn.

I have had time on my hands this past month. Time to think. Not that I stay in my bunkroom often. Heman has made sure of that. He is trying to turn me into a sailor. Not by choice mind you, I miss the stables and our horses. Heman insists, rather strongly, that I take care of the supplies and learn all there is to know about navigation. Father, you will be pleased to hear that I am learning quickly.

But that is not what I want to get off my heart. I would still be there in Ireland with you both, if I hadn't acted so out of control. Even if I still think Queen Victoria deserved what she got. I realize now that the joke got way out of hand.

When will I return to Ireland? Someday. For I love Ireland and think of her daily. I miss you, Mother. Thank you for my trunk. That is all I have to remember you by.

Your Loving Son,
William

P.S. There have been moments, I believe, Heman would have liked your presence, Father. However, he is a great Captain, greater than I ever thought.

CHAPTER SIX

Black Gold - The Great Lie

Heman couldn't believe it. But here he was sitting at a table on his ship on his deck with Captain Cook and William. The subject: slave cargo. It was obvious that the Captain and William had been planning this meeting for days.

Captain Cook bowed forward to Heman. "Thank you for welcoming me aboard your great schooner. I am privileged to be here."

Heman scanned the squinting eyes of this Captain Cook. A shiver went through him and he felt his skin crawl. This man had evil written all over him. Heman met William's eyes, questioning everything, but William missed the concern his brother had. He guided Heman towards the table and they all took their places. "Captain Cook has a business offer for you and me, Heman."

In the next hour, Captain Cook educated the two brothers about the slave trade. He numbered the males, the females, and children that were in his cargo. They were all healthy enough to make the trip to America. He even had a diagram of how to house the slaves for the journey. The Captain said he would send his crew to take care of the preparations that were needed. The meeting ended with William telling the Captain they would get back to him.

William knew that because of the cholera epidemic, the trading business was nil. Heman was sitting on a schooner with an empty cargo bay, and it didn't look like that would change for a long time. "Heman, it's not like we are slave traders. We didn't go to Africa, and we didn't plan to have slaves for cargo. But these are difficult times. What are we going to do? One trip with slaves, that's all I ask. One trip and I swear, just one trip."

A week later the cargo bay was being prepared for the arrival of the cargo. Heman assembled his crew and gave them the plan. *Lady Catherine* will sail to Massachusetts, America. Every one of the crew cheered. Heman had to tell them the cargo. They had to know. It would affect their daily lives, working this great schooner with people living below as the main cargo. "The cargo we will deliver will be slaves."

Silence, stark silence, no cheers. The good news of America just went overboard. The crew was not happy. Moses looked at Patrick. John Charles sent disturbed looks at the First Mate Henry, *Slaves? Has the Captain lost his mind?*

Heman was speaking again, "A roster of job assignments will be forthcoming promptly." He turned to William. "William will be in charge of this project."

"Sir William's idea?" It was Dick passing on his opinion. "I tell you, lads, this isn't going to be a pretty voyage, no sirree. May Heaven preserve us."

The only one happy as *Lady Catherine* sailed slowly out of San Juan was Captain Cook. He dumped his problem and didn't lose all his investment, most of it but not all. He was getting out of the slave business. Cook would rather transport bananas than have the problems with slaves.

William hired five of Captain Cook's crew just to take care of the cargo. Heman sat in on the last meeting before the cargo arrived. William tried to introduce the new men. Heman waved his hand and stopped it. "I don't want to know who they are. I don't want to remember them for the rest of my life." You could tell they were mean men. Shaking his head, he again thought, *How did I get myself into such a mess?*

"I am the Captain of this ship. We will do things my way. Is that understood?"

A growl passed through the men, but they agreed.

"Our cargo will be treated humanely. Twice a day they will be allowed deck side to wash and exercise. They will be fed food, real food once a day. That includes fruit."

"Captain, sir, you can't spoil them, sir. If you fatten them up, they will turn on you, sir. You have to crack the whip and keep them weak."

"Compromise, sir?" It was the leader of the five. "Food daily, fruit weekly." He was being patient with Captain Kenney.

"Agreed." Heman knew he wouldn't get everything he wanted. "A blanket for every member of the cargo, including the children, and no use of the whip without my approval."

William stood up. "Heman, that will eat into our profits."

Heman sent a look at his brother that would melt ice.

William sat down. "I will take care of it."

Heman was glad the meeting was over. The leader of the five handed him a package. "A gift from Captain Cook."

Heman unwrapped a handsome wooden box. It was engraved and must have come from India. He opened the lid, and there were several fine silk handkerchiefs with bottles of smelling salts and perfumes.

"Captain Cook says you will appreciate these after a few days at sea."

Heman made no reply. He closed the box and left the room, carrying the box with him. Entering his cabin, he threw it on his shelf as he closed the door.

The six-week journey was a long one. No longer did Heman take his morning walks to converse with *Lady Catherine*. She was angry and he knew it. Only once did he make his appearance known, when the slaves were on deck to wash and exercise. It unnerved him so badly he never did it again. Or, at least, if he could help it. The dark brown eyes of the male slaves met him eye to eye, a haunted look that pierced your mind. The look that reappeared nightly in your dreams. Two days into the journey, Heman was asking God to forgive him, but God was nowhere to be found.

The sound – it never stopped – the clanging of the shackles that bound their wrist and the chains that held them together by their feet. Their movements sounded like skeletons marching together . . . and the smell. He cursed Captain Cook every time he opened the box of smelling salts.

Heman called a meeting of the five and William. "I want you to free the women and children."

"Is that wise, sir?"

"Wise or not, I want it done."

"Compromise, sir?" It was the leader speaking again. "All children male and female age seven and younger will be freed. All women 40 and older will be freed. These same women will make sure the freed children stay out of trouble, or we will use the whip on them."

"Agreed. No whipping. Dismissed."

Heman spent most of his time in his cabin. He ate there alone, unless he was needed to sail *Lady Catherine*. He allowed the crew to do their work freely. First Mate Henry did most of Heman's work. John Charles seemed to know where he was going. Patrick and Moses took care of their crews, making sure everything was ship shape. And William, Heman didn't care what he did, as long as he kept those five scoundrels in control.

The crew respected the Captain's solitude. They also respected him on how he handled a difficult situation. They were glad they weren't responsible for what was known as the cargo. Hauling slaves aboard affected everyone.

A six-week journey in late spring 1854 was a good time to travel to America. The winter storms had passed, and most of the time the weather was kind to them. However, it was cold. Heman felt better, if only a little better, knowing that in the cargo bay everyone had blankets.

There was another storm that had to be endured before reaching America. It was particularly fierce. Heman and the crew fought the 50-foot waves and brought *Lady Catherine* through the storm safely. The cargo didn't fare as well. Whoever's idea it was to remove the hatches and replace them with metal grills was very shortsighted. Heman was told it was for ventilation needed for the slaves to breathe. That being true, no thought was given to passing through a storm.

The waves that thundered over the deck ran right into the cargo bay. William and his five men had a time of it, keeping the slaves from drowning. Canvas was quickly used to cover the grated hatches, but it was too late for three children. Two girls and a boy perished during that storm.

Heman had never presided over a funeral at sea.[36] That changed the next day. He gave the three children a proper Christian ceremony. The Captain began by reading from the Gospel of Matthew in the Bible: *"But Jesus said, Suffer little children, and forbid them not, to come unto me: for of such is the kingdom of heaven."*[37] It may not have made the mothers feel any better, but it felt good for Heman's soul. There was an imprint already seared in his mind, three small bodies wrapped in canvas given as sacrifices to the Ocean. The ceremony ended with everyone, including the crew, reciting the Lord's Prayer.[38] The ceremony touched his crew as well, but not the five. The leader came up to Heman and slapped him on the back. "Only three so far; we are doing good. You should be proud. This here is the best slave ship I've ever worked. You should be proud, Captain."

Heman was not proud. His shoulders stooped, and he lost the spring in his steps. He walked slowly away. He was heard saying, "I know, *Lady Catherine*, I know."

William, hearing the last part of what Heman said, came up beside him, "Are you all right? And you know what, Heman?"

"God will never forgive me. " *Vengeance is mine; I will repay, saith the Lord.'"* [39] There is going to be payback time, William, you watch and see." William guided Heman back to his cabin and ordered him a drink. "What would Father say? Promise me something, William."

"Sure, Heman."

"Let this whole journey be a secret between the two of us. Once we reach America, may we never speak of this again. Promise me, William."

William seeing Heman's haunted eyes, "I promise you, big brother, not to utter a word of this journey to anyone. It is between you and me."

"And Father, never tell, Father."

"No, Heman, I will never tell Father."

"I wrote him you know – before leaving San Jan I had it dispatched by a Captain Reed on the Sloop *Fair Lady*. She was headed back to Ireland. I told Father we were headed to America with a cargo of gold – gold mind you taken from the gold mines." Heman followed with a haunted laugh, "Black gold."

William didn't laugh. He left his brother muttering to himself, "Father didn't know it was black gold."

* * * * *

"Land Ho," a cheer went up.

John Charles was knocking at the Captain's cabin.

"Enter."

"Reporting navigation information, sir." He hoped his shock of seeing the condition of the Captain wasn't so apparent. The Captain was breathing hard. His face was white with dark circles under his eyes.

"Well, John Charles, what do you have to report?"

"Sir, working out my calculations, I do believe we are close to Boston Harbour. Seeing other ships heading the same direction, I do believe I am right. Sir, we should be in Boston Harbour tomorrow sundown."

"Good work. Have William sent to my cabin at once. You are dismissed."

It troubled John Charles to see his Captain ill. He was glad this journey was ending. It couldn't end fast enough for him.

"William, I want this cargo off my ship as fast as you can get it off."

"Brother, I will take care of everything. A Mr. Rice Carter Ballard will meet us in Kingston Harbour. He will be waiting for us when we are moored."

"I thought we were going to Boston Harbour?'

William answered, "Mr. Ballard does not do business in Boston. Kingston is more secluded. There is less chance of others knowing our cargo. Mr. Ballard and his cronies will meet us there."

"Call John Charles back to meet us now. He will have to change our course to Kingston. As they waited for him to appear, Heman got William's attention, "Not us, brother. You said Mr. Ballard and his cronies would meet us. Not us, but you will meet with Mr. Ballard. I don't want any more to do with it. If I have to pay to have them leave my ship, so be it."

"Heman, I will take care of it. Mr. Ballard will pay us to take them off. He will pay handsomely."

"I don't care about the money, William. You may think this is a fine day for our family's company. I don't share it. Shame and more shame, William. Take this cancer out of the bowels of *Lady Catherine*. She will take a long time to heal, if healing is even possible."

"For shame and more shame will remain with the Kenney family forever. We will have to make up for it somehow. God will expect no less. I pray He will forgive our souls."

San Jan
West Indies
February 1854

Dear Father,

The Lady Catherine and her crew have been stranded here in San Jan. After two weeks we left Cinnamon Bay because of Cholera. Don't worry, no one went ashore. We are not alone here in San Jan. Many Captains are waiting with empty cargo bays and no trade in sight.

However, William has been ashore and has stumbled upon a trade deal that he tells me we cannot turn down. Since William has no idea about trade, I am skeptical of the deal. But what choice do I have? It's a gold deal and we are on our way to America.

I will send more details later.

Your loving son,

Heman

CHAPTER SEVEN

New Beginnings

Heman was sitting on the side of his bed, when he heard his First Mate Henry, "Cast the anchor." The Captain knew he was not well, but he couldn't decide whether it was mental or physical. He knew one thing: his lungs felt like they were full of cotton. He couldn't breathe, at least not very well. Heman spent most of the last two days sitting on the side of his bed, forcing his lungs to take in air. His chest would heave as he sucked in the air through his mouth. Then there was a creaking sound, as his chest relaxed, pushing out the used air. Then the process would repeat itself. His shoulders ached, and a cloud of weariness enveloped his whole being.

Henry was knocking at the Captain's door. He heard a weak sound coming from the inside of the Captain's cabin. "Did that mean enter?" Henry questioned himself. There was no other sound, so he took it upon himself to open the door. "Captain, sir, reporting navigation information into Kingston Bay. Sir, are you alright? Do you need some assistance?"

Heman couldn't even reply.

"I will get help, sir!" Henry turned with urgency and left the room. "Where is William? Get William. Also, get Dick and

John Charles. The Captain is in distress and needs our assistance immediately."

It didn't take long for John Charles and William to be at Heman's side. One on either side of him, they were making the Captain walk. Dick arrived, hearing the Captain cough. "I've seen it before. Quickly, bring him deck side; he needs fresh air." It certainly wasn't easy carrying Heman up the ladder. William, Henry, John Charles, and Dick managed it. "Tell the cook to boil water and bring it."

Dick was still in charge. He began making a place for his Captain to sit. The fresh sea breeze hit Heman in the face. His lungs took in the clean air. The heaving in his chest eased to heavy breathing. The boiling water arrived. "I need a towel, a bandana, something." William ripped off his shirt. Dick placed the shirt over the Captain's head. The steam filled his lungs, and his breathing slowed down.

"How long has he been like this?" Dick was asking anyone who might know the answer.

Henry spoke up, "I found him like that just after casting the anchor."

"So no one knows how long." William held Heman in a sitting position.

"Well, considering he's not conscious, it's been a long time," Dick added. "It's a good thing he was found."

William still holding Heman over the steam asked, "What's wrong with him?"

"Looks to me like asthma," Dick replied.

"Heman doesn't have asthma."

"He does now." Dick checked his breathing. "I believe the worst is over."

"How can that be? He's not even conscious," John Charles questioned Dick.

"A good place for him to be," Dick answered. "He needs rest and plenty of it. Let's get him back to his bed, this time more gently." When the Captain was brought into his bed, Dick was waiting. He had everything prepared. Both portholes were open, and fresh salty sea air filled the room. Close to the bed were two pots of boiling water, sending steam in the direction where they laid Heman.

"Open his shirt." Dick placed a mustard poultice on his chest.

"What's that for?" William could smell mustard and vinegar.

"I don't know," said Dick, "but it works."

William wasn't so sure, but he felt it couldn't hurt.

Heman seemed to be in a restful sleep. "Go on with ya's. I will sit here with him." Dick dismissed everyone in the room.

William looked at Henry and John Charles, "We do have to make plans for the cargo. As soon as he wakes, send for me, Dick."

Lady Catherine had been moored in Kingston Bay for four hours. Moses cried, "Landlubbers approaching starboard side."

William, Henry, and John Charles took charge. Moses came to William, "Welcome to America." William was so anxious about Heman and the meeting with Mr. Rice Ballard that he forgot he just landed on a new continent.

"Thank you, Moses. Maybe we can find time to celebrate later."

"Under the circumstances, I don't believe anyone is in a partying mood. We need to thank the Great Almighty we made it here." Moses crossed himself.

William asked Henry and John Charles to join him in meeting Ballard. Ballard was a short, heavyset man, but light on his feet and didn't have any trouble coming aboard. He had long, grey sideburns that met in the middle of his face just below his chin. He met them with a great smile and shining eyes – like they were long lost, friends.

"Captain Kenney, it's a delight to make your acquaintance. We've been anticipating your arrival for days." Ballard searched the three men to see who would own up to the greeting.

William stepped forward, "William Kenney at your service. My brother Captain Kenney is not well and is unable to make your acquaintance at this time."

"I hope it is nothing serious." Ballard showed genuine concern.

"We hope it isn't. Thank you for your concern. This is the First Mate Henry and navigator John Charles. Your men may wait here, and we will have a meeting on the upper deck," William moving his arm in the direction of the bow of the ship.

"That would be splendid, but may I take a peek at the cargo first? You have no idea how hard it is to find first quality cargo these days. Government isn't making it easy either. But as long as we don't advertise, they seem to leave us alone."

William dismissed Henry and John Charles. "We will meet on the upper deck in 15 minutes." He led Ballard away.

Twenty minutes later they were sitting around a table on the upper deck. "I have seen fine healthy specimens of the Negro race in my day, but your cargo beats them all. I must commend you for a job well done on your ocean voyage. They will bring top dollar. Gentlemen, you are going to make money today. By the way, how many did you lose on the journey?"

William broke the silence, "Three – three children."

"That's all?! That's remarkable. Are you planning another trip? I will pay you up front with a bonus on return to Kingston Bay."

"No, Mr. Ballard, there will be no other trips."

"What a pity!"

Ballard informed them how the cargo would be collected. After the deal was final, William had a request. "Before you begin the task of collecting the cargo, I need a place to take my brother Captain Kenney."

"He doesn't have the cholera, does he?"

"No, sir. Captain Kenney's sickness is asthma and weariness."

"Well, then, yes, William, I have just the place. Kingston is small, but I have a friend, and he owes me a favor. Drew is his name. C. Drew and Company make tool and iron products. I will make the arrangements. Your brother the Captain will be the first to leave the ship."

"Thank you," William replied.

The meeting was over. William turned to Henry, "Will you see that Mr. Ballard and his men are seen safely off the ship? I need to see to Heman."

William entered the Captain's cabin. Dick was still sitting at the Captain's bedside. "How is he doing?"

"I believe he is doing better," answered Dick in a low whisper. "His colouring is coming back in his face."

"How long are you going to let him sleep?"

"Another six hours at least. Then I will give him my soup."

"You like doing this, don't you Dick?"

"Yeah. I've always wanted to be a doctor, but this is as far as I got."

"Well, we are moving the Captain to Kingston. We have a place set up for him."

"Where is Tom his cabin boy? He needs to prepare for the Captain's journey."

"Let me go with him?" Dick was questioning William.

"I was going to send Tom."

"Tom doesn't know anything. Let me go."

"I think that would be a good thing. Dick, you go, and take good care of him."

"I will give him the best of care."

* * * * *

Dick miscalculated how long the Captain would sleep. It was not six hours, nor 12, but 18 hours later that Heman opened his eyes.

His eyes and mind tried to take in his surroundings. Maybe he was dreaming. He shook his head, but that didn't change his surroundings, but it sure did hurt his head. He closed his eyes again. Maybe he would wake up soon and be in his cabin onboard *Lady Catherine*. He didn't feel like sleeping and he opened his eyes. If he was still dreaming, he was doing a good job of it. He was dreaming in colour. The room he was in was blue with white trim. Two large windows had curtains with large yellow and blue flowers. The windows were open, and a cool breeze was causing the curtains to flutter inward. On one wall was a chest of drawers with a mirror hanging above it. On the other wall were three family portraits. The problem was he had no idea who they were.

His head was clearing as he became fully awake. This is no dream. He slowly sat up to the side of the bed. Looking down, he was horrified to see he had frilly white pajamas and wondered how they got there. He managed to make it to the window. Gazing out he saw other houses neatly placed in a row along a street. In the distance he saw a river, its blue water running somewhere. To where he did not know.

How in blazes did I get here? he thought. *And who brought me here?* Questions and no answers. He was afraid to open the bedroom door to see where it led. No telling what he might find. He wasn't ready for it. Lying back on the bed, he thought, *This bed is so comfortable. Beats my bunk on the ship. White sheets, with a goose down comforter.*

Okay, Heman," he was talking to himself, "what was the last thing you remember? Dropping the anchor – that's right. Henry was dropping anchor. That's it – that's all I remember."

The bedroom door opened quietly. Heman was afraid to look. He couldn't believe his eyes. It was Dick, at least it looked like Dick. "Why would Dick be here? If I am losing my mind, I didn't think it would be Dick who would accompany me. At least I know him. I know Dick."

"Good morning, or rather good afternoon, Captain. It's good to see you with your eyes opened. You've given us quite a scare, but I knew you would come through. Had to get your body back in balance, but we did it."

Heman was in shock and speechless. Finally, he was able to make his tongue work. "What the blazes is going on? Where am I and why of all people are you here, Dick?" Heman began to get out of bed, until he saw his frilly pajamas, and he covered himself up again.

"Nice pajamas, aren't they, Captain? Madame Caroline said they were the finest in Kingston."

"Madame who?"

"Madam Caroline Drew, Captain. She has been taking really good care of us. She made me take a bath, but other than that she's alright."

Heman jumped out of bed. "Where are my clothes?" He was searching the room.

"Take it easy, Captain, we have orders to keep you in bed for another day at least."

"By whose orders?" demanded Heman.

"The doctor, sir. He told Madame Caroline to keep you in bed. I wouldn't cross Madame Caroline, if I were you."

"You're not me. Where are my clothes?"

"Madame Caroline took them. She's a smart lady. She knew if they weren't here, you couldn't go anywhere."

Heman was getting angry. "All I hear is Madam Caroline this and Madam Caroline that."

"Take my advice, Captain. Calm down or you will have her in here."

Heman fell back on the bed and covered up.

"There you go, sir, and I have some soup for you. You've got to be hungry?"

All of a sudden the talk of food made Heman very hungry. "How long have I been here?"

Dick, passing the Captain his soup answered, "Two days."

"Two days?" Heman almost spilled the soup.

"Be careful, sir, you wouldn't want to mess up this pretty bed, now would you? You eat and I will tell you everything, starting with carrying you off your ship."

It took a while, but Dick brought the Captain up to date and how he got to be in this house and in this bedroom.

"Where's William?"

"You'd be mighty proud of your brother, Captain. He has taken over. He, Henry, and John Charles have done a fine job. Your ship *Lady Catherine* is almost back to her old self. I'm to send word when you opened your eyes."

"How far away is my ship?"

"Down-river about a mile. Do you want more soup? Madame Caroline made it. Says it's Boston Clam Chowder. I hear we are close to Boston. I think you need to rest, Captain."

Heman did feel tired. Now that he had a full stomach he was feeling better, but his weariness had not yet disappeared. "Yes, I do think I will rest. Thank you, Dick. Thank you for everything you have done for me. I am grateful."

"No problem, Captain. You need to get your strength back; we have a new world to explore." With that Dick left the room.

Heman, being alone, thought over all the events that Dick shared with him. Asthma? That explained why he couldn't breathe. Why asthma? Then he remembered the slaves, his cargo. God would not allow him to forget. God marked him with asthma. He deserved it, and it could be worse. God could have killed him. "I will make up for it." He was talking to God as he fell asleep.

* * * * *

The last two days for William were a test of manhood. Knowing his brother was in good care allowed him to focus fully on the job before him: get rid of the slaves and put *Lady Catherine* back together again. He knew his brother wasn't up to it. William always looked to Heman for strength. After all, he was his big brother. Heman always came through, but not this time. William watched his brother fall apart, and it was all his fault. He meant to make it up to him by putting things back the way they were before leaving San Juan.

Henry and John Charles were right there with him. While William dealt with Ballard, they prepared the crew for work detail. Ballard, a misguided man, thought of slavery as a sport or game. The Negroes were put upon this earth for people like Ballard to use and make money. Ballard and his cronies arrived early the following day ready to take his paid property. William noticed immediately they were carrying whips.

He remembers looking at Ballard, "These people have not had a whip used upon them since arriving on this ship, and that's the way it's going to stay."

"So that's why they are in such good condition. You're right, Mr. Kenney, we must not damage the cargo. Leave your whip on the Pram," he directed the order to his men.

William looked into Ballard's eyes, "I want you to take good care of these people."

"Agreed. They will have the best of care until their day at the market."

William was glad to see the last of Ballard. And he was especially glad that Heman didn't have to deal with him and witness the cargo leaving his ship. *At least I could keep him from that dreadful memory,* thought William

Moses and Patrick came upon William just as the last of the slaves was taken ashore. "William, now it's our turn." It was Moses speaking. "We will give The *Lady Catherine* such a cleaning we will have to christen her all over again."

"Thank you, both. I want both watches to work together until it is completed. I will work as well. I want it done before Captain Kenney ever sets his feet back on this ship."

"Aye. Agreed. We know our men on each watch," said Patrick. "They will want it that way. Don't you agree, Moses?"

"Agreed, and may God be with us," and crossed himself. To Moses' surprise, William and Patrick crossed themselves as they walked away.

For William, that was two days ago. He didn't even allow himself time for sleep. He was in a hurry to get this cancer cut out of the bowels of *Lady Catherine*. The crew noticed how hard he worked and maybe a feeling of forgiveness to William was forming in their hearts. For without William, slaves would never have set forth on Heman's *Lady Catherine*.

Word of the Captain's recovery was good news indeed. It made them want to work harder. Another day passed before William allowed himself to stop his work and see to his brother.

"Before you go into Kingston, you need to sleep." Moses was talking to William. "You have worked hard, and it won't help your brother any to see you with black circles under your eyes."

"I will take the time to bathe and clean myself up. Tomorrow I will go to Kingston. Send a message to Mr. Drew that I would like to dine with him and my brother tomorrow at 7:00 p.m.

When the message arrived at the Drew's residence, Heman was sitting in the kitchen enjoying coffee and conversation with Madame Caroline.

"How wonderful, I will get to meet your brother, Captain."

"Just like my brother to barge in without an invitation. I do hope you will pardon him."

"Not at all, Captain. I believe that Charles, my husband, told him to make it known when he could dine with us."

"You have already done so much for me. I will never be able to thank you enough."

"Leaving here well is more than enough. When you first arrived, I thought we might have to add you to the family cemetery. I would think you would want to see more of America than our family cemetery." She smiled at Heman.

"Yes, indeed, Madame Caroline. Yes, indeed."

A knock at the kitchen door and it was Dick. "Excuse me, sir. I heard Sir William is coming tomorrow. May I ask, sir, to take my leave? I would like to be aboard that Pram that would bring your brother here."

"You getting tired of shore duty?"

"No, sir. I mean, yes, sir. I mean Madame Caroline is doing a splendid job of taking care of you, sir."

"Well, thank you, Dick."

"You're welcome, ma'am. I just like to get back to my crew, sir."

"I'll see to it Charles sends you back tomorrow. Is that okay, Captain?"

"That will be fine, Madame Caroline."

"I'll make sure Sir William has everything ship shape. Thank you, Captain." And Dick left to prepare for his departure.

"Is your brother a Captain or a knight or something?"

"No, ma'am. Why do you ask?"

"Dick only refers to him as 'Sir William.' "

" That is only something William has to live up to, and at that time, when that time comes, Dick will drop the 'Sir'"

"So, Captain, what are your plans?"

"I believe we will go to Boston and set up some kind of business."

"How delightful. That means our paths are bound to cross one time or other."

The dinner was a welcome event for both William and Heman. The dining room was not large, but adequate for dining of four. Just to see a tablecloth set with china cheered the mood of the brothers.

Mr. and Mrs. Drew were charming hosts. Heman and William gleaned helpful information about the new land they were to call home. Madame Caroline served more Clam Chowder and beans that were sweet and cod baked to perfection. Heman had noticed the fine vegetable garden that was at its peak.

He was not surprised to see green beans but was curious to see a red fruit known as 'tomatoes.' He might just fit in with regards to this America.

"The Captain says he will settle in Boston. Did you know that, Charles?"

Charles nodded to his wife and then directing to Heman, "With your schooner, you will find many opportunities for trade runs."

"That's what I'm counting on. We hear that Boston is a great harbour with trade entering daily."

"You're right. Fate seems to be smiling your direction. And there are many Irishmen there to make you feel at home. We wish you good fortune. When do you think you will sail?"

"Don't hurry them, Charles. It's not like we get company every day," added Caroline. "Especially such fine company."

William spoke up, "You have been so kind. Looks to me you have worked a miracle. I haven't seen my brother looking so well in a long time. If you're well enough, Heman, we will sail in two days."

"Two days? Will *Lady Catherine* be ready? Heman asked in surprise.

"Yes, brother, *Lady Catherine* will be ready. She will be ready for her Captain to take his place on the upper deck of his ship. I have also made inquiries for temporary housing for us when we reach Boston."

"You have been busy, haven't you, brother?"

"Making sure everything is just right for you, Captain. Your crew awaits."

The morning of departure came in late June. Heman with Madame Caroline at his side, walked slowly to the front gate. A carriage, more like a wagon, was waiting to take him to the river that lead to Kingston Bay.

"What a glorious morning," Caroline was smiling at Heman. "I have enjoyed your company, and I will miss you. I will not say goodbye for, I believe our paths will cross again. I look forward to that meeting."

Heman bowed toward Caroline, "Thank you again for all you have done. You are right. It is a glorious morning. I feel a crispness in the air," sending a questioning look toward Caroline.

"Wait until it's fall. Then you will really feel the crispness in the air."

"Fall?"

"Yes, fall or autumn, and what a surprise awaits you. It's the most beautiful time of the year. God shows you His glory. You just wait and see."

"I look forward to it. Let me leave you an Irish blessing until we meet again. He took her hand in his, and began with:

Whenever there is happiness
Hope you'll be there too,
Wherever there are friendly smiles
Hope they'll smile on you,
Whenever there is sunshine,
Hope it shines especially
For you to make each day for you
As bright as it can be.

With that Heman was on his way down the road toward the river. The Pram was waiting, thanks to Mr. Drew.

"I hope you don't mind, but I would like to see you safely upon your schooner."

"Not at all, Charles. I would appreciate the company. You can be my guide. I seem to have missed the trip coming."

Charles laughed, "That you did."

Heman couldn't help noticing the vastness of this new world. Wilderness – virgin wilderness untouched by man. This was 1854. What would it have looked like when the pioneers saw it for the first time? Fewer people, perhaps, but the beauty remained.

The river opened into Kingston Bay. It was not a large Bay, but you could see it was home to a community of people. They built their houses at the bottom of hills that ran right into the Bay. But what took your eye this day was not the blue water and blue sky. Not the neatly built houses at the edge of the forest. Not the wooden wharfs that dotted the shoreline of the Bay. It was *Lady Catherine*.

"I've never seen anything like it." Charles was looking at Heman.

"It's a surprise to me also."

"Look. The whole village has turned out to see your schooner."

Heman took his eyes off *Lady Catherine* long enough to see hundreds of people standing on the shore waving.

William really has been busy, thought Heman.

It wasn't just his brother, but the whole crew was responsible for the sight before Heman's eyes. *Lady Catherine* was back to her glory. She looked wonderful. Flags! She must have been flying 20 flags. Every colour of the navy and more. Human eyes went to the Irish flag – Green, White and Orange. A flag was being raised right above her. It was "Old Glory." William wanted to show Heman a new start – a new world – a new flag.

As the American flag was raised, a cheer was heard. From the banks of the Bay, people were cheering and waving. The Pram came alongside the schooner. Heman saw the whole crew dressed in their offshore best. They were standing at attention in a row facing him as he approached. The gangplank was already lowered. Streamers fluttered in the breeze. Then he heard the whistle. It was calling him aboard *Lady Catherine*. As he crossed over and stepped on his deck, another cheer went up. It was his crew welcoming him back, not just his crew but his family.

William was front and center, the first one to shake his hand. "It's time to play Pirates again, Heman."

He answered his brother with a smile. Then turning to his crew, he saluted them all. Another cheer. When the chaos grew quite again, he spoke, "Thank you. Thank you all. It is good to be back; it feels good to be home. It looks like we are ready to sail?"

"Yes, sir!" his First Mate Henry replied.

Heman turned back to the Pram. Waving at Charles, he yelled, "May our paths cross again, and may it be soon."

Charles waved, "Godspeed, Captain Kenney."

Heman then delivered an order to Patrick: "Cat the anchor.[40] Henry, you have the wheel. Crew, to your posts. Let's set sail."

A cheer rang through the crew as they took their positions. It didn't take long before *Lady Catherine* was skimming through the water.

John Charles was beside Henry. The Captain turned to him. "I take it you know where you are going?"

"Aye, aye, sir! Welcome back, Captain."

Heman nodded his head in reply.

"William, meet me in my cabin."

Taking his seat at his desk, Heman motioned for William to sit in the only remaining chair in the room. "Have a seat, William. It's plain to see you took the leadership role while I was away. You've got the crew eating out of the palm of your hand."

William just smiled.

"Have I got a mutiny on my hand? Do you want to be in control? You look like a Captain."

"Heavens no." William was on the edge of his seat now. "You have got to be kidding, brother. Have you forgotten I like barns?"

It was Heman's turn to smile.

"Big Brother, I did all this for you. Can't you see I've tried to make it up to you?"

"Then it wasn't a bad dream, having slaves in the bowels of this ship really happened. Stepping onboard an hour ago, I thought it might have been a nightmare. There is no sign of then, not a sign."

"Thanks to your crew, we removed the cancer from *Lady Catherine*. No one will ever know what kind of cargo we had."

"God will know. I will know."

"Yes, brother, but God forgives, and you must put it behind you and move forward. *Lady Catherine* is ready to move forward. I've seen to that. Let's agree to not speak of it again. Do you agree?"

Heman looked into the begging eyes of his brother. "I will try."

"That's a beginning." William accepted what his brother could offer.

Heman sat straighter in his chair. "Well, if you are giving up being Captain, you'd better fill me in with the details of where we are going and how long it will take us."

"I give you back your job of Captain," with a sigh of relief. "Now, let me tell you the plan that Henry, John Charles, and I came up with. I hope you approve. We are only around 30 miles away from Boston. We should arrive there this very afternoon. The Harbour Master knows we are coming and will meet us to guide us to our new home."

"New home?"

"Yes, our new home, well at least *Lady Catherine*'s new home – Lincoln Wharf. They had a birth opening, and I grabbed it quickly. It's paid for the next six months. I've been told that our neighbor will be the *Alma*, a ship larger than *Lady Catherine*. Mr. Drew knows her Captain, a Reuben Freeman. He speaks highly of him and says the *Alma*[41] is a very beautiful ship. Time will tell."

"I have more to tell, but that's enough for now. Come, let us pick up your tradition of walking with *Lady Catherine*. I will join you."

"That does sound like something I would like to do." Heman got up from his seat and joined William as they climbed up the upper deck. Take a look around, William, at the wilderness of this land. If you look hard enough, I think you may see Indians."

"What I have seen so far, Heman, this is a wonderful land, with great opportunities. Excitement around each turn. Come look at the cargo bay."

Heman stopped, "Are you sure?"

"Yes, Brother, I am sure."

"The whole cargo bay was rebuilt. There's no sign of them, brother."

"No, and you have made it better than what it was in the beginning."

"Yes, it is ready to pick up trade from all up and down the East Coast to as far as New Orleans and even as far as Bermuda. I made different compartments to hold different trade goods. This area is for rolled up rugs and this compartment for glassware. But I left a large area for cotton, or lumber, or whatever you guys trade." He smiled at Heman, "Do you think it will work?"

"You've made *Lady Catherine* ready for all of our future adventures."

"It's new beginnings, Heman, for you and me."

They were walking the starboard side when Heman stopped in his tracks. He was like a statue. "What is it? Are you ill again?"

Heman pointed to a large wooden compartment where sails were stored. Just under the lip of the trap door was a metal ring – a ring big enough to place on a man's wrist. William was devastated. He had ordered all rings removed. This one was missed. "I'm sorry, Heman, I will have it removed at once."

After a moment Heman replied, "No, William, let it remain. Let it be a reminder of the past. Once a man's arm was chained to it. A black man, a slave. I promise from this day forward I will help every Negro man to get his freedom. I will not sit back and pretend I don't see slavery. I don't know what I will do, nor do I know what I can do. But I know my life has been changed forever. I will fight for their freedom."

From that moment, William knew his brother would be alright. Heman was changed, but so was he. He was not the same boy who had to run from Ireland. He was going to enter Boston a new man.

Enter Boston they did. Every crewman was on deck, as they were guided into Boston Harbour by the Harbour Master. "You're the first Irishmen to dock at Lincoln Wharf. Most of you are in the North End. You are the first Irishmen I would like to get to know."

William, the Captain, and the crew weren't sure what to make of the Harbour Master's words, but they would think of them later. Now they were entering a new world, and they didn't want to miss any of it. Mr. Drew was correct when he said the *Alma* was a fine ship. *Lady Catherine* felt very comfortable gliding in beside her.

That very evening Heman was finished with all the paperwork necessary for him and his crew to be legally in the United States of America. Heman heard the whistle announcing a visiting Captain onboard *Lady Catherine*. He hurried on deck to welcome a Captain aboard.

"Welcome to Lincoln Wharf and to Boston."

"Thank you, sir. I am Captain Heman Kenney.

"I am Captain Reuben Freeman. The *Alma* is to your starboard.

"A wonderful looking ship, sir. You are to be congratulated."

"I didn't expect an Irishman. But am delighted to see one with culture."

"You're the second to state that, sir, and as for my culture, I have to thank my mother, Bridget Kenney, of Cork, Ireland."

Captain Freeman extended his hand and Heman did likewise. The handshake went on longer than normal. It was a beginning of a friendship that would last years. William arrived during the handshake. He bowed toward Captain Freeman. "I'm sorry I was detained."

"Let me introduce you to my brother, William."

"The *Alma* is a wonderful looking ship, sir."

"Thank you but don't let me take up any more of your valuable time. I know you have just landed. I would like to invite you both to dinner Thursday on the *Alma*."

"Thank you. We accept." Heman was answering for William.

"7:00 O'clock." Captain Freeman turned and walked in the direction of his ship

* * * * *

William knocked at the door of the Captain's Cabin.

"Enter."

Standing in front of his small mirror, Heman was finishing his tie.

"Are you ready? It's 6:40 p.m. It's not good for a Captain to be late."

"I'm looking forward to this evening."

"I thought you would be. The *Alma* is a fine looking ship."

"You're about to see the top of the line, William. Everything about that ship is state of the art. She was built here."

"In Boston?"

"No. Sullivan, Maine. Impressive this new world. No money was spared. She's owned by the company, Messrs., Ingalls and Shepard.[42] Those who inspected her, when in the course of construction, say that she is as good a vessel ever built at Sullivan, and we can add that she looks as well as any freighting ship of her size belonging to Boston."

"You've done your homework."

"I'd tried to find a little information. I didn't like the idea of having dinner with Captain Freeman, not knowing anything about his ship."

"Well, I will let you take the lead when it comes to ships."

"I know. And when the subject of horses comes up, I will take the back seat."

"That will be the day when Captains talk about horses."

They walked swiftly down the wharf reaching the gangplank of the *Alma*. William heard the whistle announcing another Captain. He always wondered if Heman ever got tired of it.

Captain Freeman arrived to welcome them aboard. "Come before the sun goes down. I will give you a tour of my ship."

William could tell Captain Freeman was in the habit of doing this often. What he could see as he stepped aboard, the Captain had every reason to be proud.

"The *Alma* is registered at 826 tons. She is designed to stow a large cargo and sail fast. She is 153 feet long between perpendiculars on deck, has 34 ½ feet breadths of beam, and 20 ½ feet depths of hold, including 7 ½ feet height of between decks."

Heman whistled. He was impressed.

William had no idea what Freeman had just said.

Freeman lead them into what was called a house, which contained spacious quarters for the crew and galley.

William thought, *Our crew better not see this; they will jump ship.*

They came to another quarterdeck that had another house 38 feet long. This house contained two cabins and an anteroom. The after cabin was the whole width of the house and was splendidly wainscoted[43] with mahogany. It was set off into Gothic-arched panels, relieved with pilasters and gilding. Everywhere was well lighted and ventilated, and elegantly furnished.

William managed to get up behind his brother. He gave him an elbow in his ribs. "This is what you need, brother."

Heman gave William a look – that look; William knew it. He had better obey it and fell back into good manners mode.

They weren't finished yet. Above it, were two staterooms, and another apartment. In between was a mahogany staircase, which led to the poop.[44] The forward cabin was also tastefully wainscoted and painted, containing a fitted dining saloon.

William noticed the table ready for them to dine. But they didn't stop yet. On the starboard side, they entered what was called the Anteroom that had a pantry. Here also was the First Mate's stateroom.

"Henry would love this." William couldn't help himself.

Heman ignoring his brother, "Thank you for the tour of this great ship."

Captain Freeman nodded his head in reply. "Gentlemen, let's return to the dining saloon." As they entered the room, four waiters were standing guard two-by-two. They were actually waiting for their Captain to be seated. Their Captain signaled for the dinner to begin.

Platters of food were served to the men individually. You had to make a choice, and the waiters placed it on your plate. Clams, oysters, salmon, cod were displayed like art on the first platter. Beef, lamb, and pork were on the second platter. The third had every kind of vegetable you could think of.

Choosing what to have placed on your plate was not easy. However, Captain Freeman made choices easily; he was accustomed to doing this.

Heman thought, *Wish we had some of this food back in Ireland two years ago.*

William wondered if there was a garden onboard. This ship had everything else.

After the dessert tray of blueberry pie, strawberry shortcake, and chocolate cake, the brothers were surprised when Irish Coffee was served.

"I thought I would make you feel at home. I hope the Irish Coffee is made well."

"Yes." It was William tasting the coffee. "As good as Ada and George made it in our kitchen back in Ireland."

"Tell me, gentlemen, if I'm not getting too personal. Well, most of the Irishmen, and there are many of them, are not like you. They came here because of some potato disease."

"You speak of the Potato Famine. Bad time for Ireland. We lost over half of our population. All Irish peasants were forced to work in fields and denied education. Our mother, bless her soul, tried to help those people. Starvation was rampant, because the potato crop failed. Everyone left. My father would not leave. He was an Irishman, and he would stay and help those who were left behind and starving."

"For a year we had a soup cauldron twice a day outside our back fence." It was William talking to Freeman. "I thought I would lose my mind. But Father and Mother never quit. The people knew there would be food for them at the Kenney Mansion."

"Your father?"

"Captain Daniel Kenney has a shipping business with a partner. *Lady Catherine* is part of his fleet. He is still there in Cork, Ireland."

"Well, there are thousands of Irishmen living in the North End. I'm not sure you could call it living. They have no trades. The people of Boston are not too pleased that they are here. Don't get me wrong, the Boston people wanted to help and they did. Great amounts of money were sent to Ireland for relief, but they preferred them to stay there. It's a different thing when they are on their doorstep."

"So that explains the signs I've seen the past few days," William added.

"You've seen them? 'No Irish apply.' "

"I thought they were odd."

"Don't worry. Boston will accept them before long. And I'm sure you being here will help."

Changing the subject, Captain Freeman asked, "Did you arrive in Boston with no cargo? I'd heard ships coming from San Juan had no cargo to bring?"

William noticing Heman's haunted look spoke up, "You're correct in saying there was no cargo to bring out of San Juan."

"Now tell me, what are your plans? If I can be of help, I am at your service."

Heman with a sigh of relief addressed Captain Freeman, "William has done some scouting around Boston in the last three days. Share with him, William, what you told me."

"I've been up to Summer Street. I like what I see there. We want to open a store and I noticed a block of stores there."

"Yes, The Webster Buildings.[45] I know them well. If you would like, I will make inquiries for you."

"Thank you, that would be helpful. They were interested until I opened my mouth. Then they asked, 'Do you have money?' I assured them I did."

"Let me look into it for you. Is there anything else?"

"I saw a row of houses on Franklin Street. One had a sign 'To Let.'"

"Tontine Crescent. Good choice. The *Alma* doesn't sail for a week. I will look into that also and get back to you. When does *Lady Catherine* sail?"

Heman answered, "I haven't had time to set up my business as yet."

"Well, I understand of course. Why don't you meet with me and Messrs, Ingalls and Shepard? That is the company I am with. They are always looking for schooners for trade."

"Can you meet with us at 2:00 p.m. tomorrow?"

"2:00 p.m.?" William was amazed to hear those words.

"Is something wrong with 2:00 p.m.?"

"No, sir. It's music to my ears. Or at least a different music. I've just learned to do the bells."

Captain Freeman looked confused.

Heman explained, "William has learned a lot about the sailing world in the last few months, including Bell Time while at sea."

Freeman laughed, "I see. While docked in Boston, I try to use regular timing. It's easier for the public to understand."

The evening was ended with handshakes and words of appreciation for what Captain Freeman planned to do for the Kenney brothers. To be successful in this world, they both knew they needed friends like the Captain.

"I believe we are on our way, Heman." William slapped his brother on the back. They both were enjoying their walk back to the *Lady Catherine*. "My head is overflowing with ideas. This America is an open opportunity for a successful life. It's all around us. Don't you see it? Don't you feel it, Heman?"

Heman was happy to see William so enthusiastic.

"I can't wait to get started. Heman, it begins tomorrow. That meeting with the good Captain Freeman. What a stroke of luck. We need someone like him to be on our side."

"Tomorrow is the beginning."

"New Beginnings, Heman. A new chapter in our lives."

Heman remained quiet, but also thought, *Yes, William, New Beginnings.*

Cork, Ireland
August 21, 1884

Dear Heman and William,
Greetings from Ireland. We, the country, are healing, thank God.
Your first letter brought concern for your Mother and me. America is quite a journey away. Now we hear of your plans for settlement in Boston. We wish you well.
Your friendship with Captain Freeman pleases me. I am sure it is good to have someone to help you as one sets up a business.
Keep me abreast of your sailing adventures.
Your Mother sends her love, as does the rest of the household.
Yours always,

Father
P.S. The English have given up hope finding the perpetrator, letting the Union Jack fall on Queen Victoria's head.

CHAPTER EIGHT

The Irish Coffee Company

Autumn 1854. Heman couldn't believe how the world around him could change so drastically. It was almost like he woke up one day and everything had changed. He was always amazed at the green colours around him. Being Irish, the colour green was his favourite. There were so many trees – fir, spruce, and pine, and of course, maples of every kind were all around him, and in the distance, he could see forest – light green to dark green and every shade of green in between.

But now he couldn't help remembering the words of Madame Caroline, "You are going to be surprised." Surprised, delighted, breathtaking – all these words described his feelings. There were not enough words to describe what he saw.

He was sure someone up above lost his cargo of paint, and it spilled over all the trees of the land. The colours of the leaves on the trees took his breath away. He had never seen a red tree, but there was one in front of his house. It was not just red, but it looked like it was on fire. Just standing on the sidewalk, colour fell before his eyes. Red, orange, yellow, rust, brown, all mixed in with the dark green of the evergreen trees. There was even the colour purple. He didn't know what the plant was, but it had changed from green to purple.

One couldn't help being happy. How could one be sad? You would have to keep your eyes closed. Opening your eyes, you could see a free gift given by God.

William made good choices about where to set up business and finding a place to live. With Captain Freeman's help, things fell together quickly. They had moved into the house on Franklin Street three weeks ago. Heman was grateful that William took the lead. It turned out he was very good at it. He was even able to rent a store on Summer Street. They were known as the Webster Buildings, and many people gathered there to shop. The store wouldn't be ready for them until January. That was good timing because *Lady Catherine* didn't begin her trade runs until the first of the year.

This gave time for Heman to rest and regain his health. He didn't believe he would ever be 100% again, but he was learning to live with asthma.

Heman was still on the sidewalk when William came out of the front door. "I've found her. I don't have to put up with you trying to poison me."

"Found who?"

"Peggy and Duncan O' Donovan and their daughter, Faye. She looks just like Ada, and I'm told she can cook."

"Where did you find them?"

"Went to the North End. I've been spending time over there playing cards."

"You're not gambling, William?"

"No, brother, I have made some friends. I feel at home with the Irish. So many are out of work. I made mention we needed an Irish cook."

"You needed an Irish cook?"

"Believe me, you need one too."

"If Peggy is going to cook, what is Duncan going to do? Plus a daughter how old?"

"Faye is 16. We'll find something for Duncan to do. Maybe sweep our sidewalk. Obviously, it is filled with leaves.

And Faye can keep house. You are awfully messy you know. I've got to go. I have to prepare the third floor for them. I will make it into a family apartment. It sure will be better than what they have now."

* * * * *

Peggy had tears in her eyes as William showed the O' Donovan's their new home. He prepared three rooms for them – two bedrooms and a reading room. Peggy had her arm around Faye, "Just look, Faye. We have never had a home such as this. A bedroom of your own."

Duncan was a quiet man but managed to say, "Thank you, Mr. Kenney. I will work hard for you and your brother." Duncan was grateful for a job after the Potato Famine. He was thankful to be alive, and now his family can work together for the Kenney brothers. He felt blessed indeed. He wasn't sure it was the right decision to come to America, but now looking around at his family he knew the journey had saved their lives.

It was nice to hear the Irish accent being spoken in the Kenney home. Faye became the little sister the brothers never had. Peggy made sure they didn't spoil her. Hearing them speak was a reminder of Ireland, but just one look out the window would tell them they were not in Ireland.

Boston was a fascinating place, a little strange at times, but fascinating nonetheless. Both Heman and William were busy working on weekdays. Sundays were, in their minds, a day of rest and recreation, but not in Boston. Sunday became a ghost town. Heman wasn't sure where everyone was, but it didn't take him long to learn that there was a Sunday Observance Law[46] Heman found out it was profaning the Lord's Day by walking or standing in the streets. He was told that if one were caught doing so, one might expect the execution of the law.

Sunday in Boston was a sleepy quietude with comparatively few people stirring about. The Sabbath began on Saturday at sunset, and upon no pretense whatsoever was any man on horseback or with a wagon to pass into or out of the town until the time of Sabbath observance was over. Heman joked with William, "You should be happy that your beloved horses get a day of rest."

Sundays passed slowly. Heman tried to find newspapers from Ireland, England, and of course, Boston to read. Boston newspapers included the Boston Herald and The Liberator, put out by William Garrison, an anti-slavery paper. William used Sundays as a planning day. Strategy was mapped out for making money in the next week.

Christmas holidays would soon be upon them. They heard of social gatherings of the high society of Boston. They were not invited. This Irish thing was an obstacle they weren't able to conquer as yet. William was more concerned than Heman. He preferred the quiet life.

But they did get two invitations. One was for a holiday party given by Captain Freeman and his wife. The other was a Christmas party given at the Omni Parker House Hotel" [47] here in Boston by Mr. and Mrs. Drew on behalf of their company. The tool and iron business was thriving.

Heman and William enjoyed the Drew party. As soon as they entered, Madame Caroline gave them a grand welcome. "Delighted to see you again. I knew our paths would meet." Taking them by the arms, she gracefully moved them throughout her guests. The brothers felt welcomed by these working class people. Here people helped each other, as they all tried to make a living.

The party at the Freeman's did not go as well. The brothers felt shunned. It didn't matter how hard Captain Freeman tried to include them. As soon as they opened their mouths, the people would walk away. This was high society, and they weren't ready for any Irish.

"Don't take it personally, Captain Freeman. It's not your fault. You did everything you could."

"Insulting, the whole affair is insulting to me. How dare they be rude to you, my guests?!"

"Don't let it spoil your party. Go and join your sweet wife. We will see one another again."

"Soon I hope."

"Yes, soon."

* * * * *

It was the Sunday before Christmas. Heman was reading the Liberator. William was teaching Faye to play chess.

"Faye, I need you in the kitchen." Peggy was in the middle of cooking dinner. William's nose was the witness to that. The smell of food cooking had reached him an hour earlier.

William encouraged Faye towards the kitchen. "We will finish the game after supper. Let me guide you." He took her by the arms, and they were doing an Irish Jig as they entered the kitchen.

"What's cooking, Peggy?"

She looked towards William. "A Dublin Coddle.[48] Does that sound good to you, sir?"

"One of my favorites, dear lady. One of my favorites."

Almost from the beginning, Heman and William invited the O' Donovan's to eat with them at the table. It was more like a family for everyone.

"See if the Captain is ready."

William entered the living room. His brother was standing at the window. "Supper's ready."

Heman turned towards William. "Looks like a storm's brewing. Take a look at those clouds." Darkness was almost upon them, but William could see the clouds forming.

"You're right, and it's too cold to rain. This may be our first real snowstorm. I've heard they can be wild ones." They had seen snow flurries for weeks, and one morning there was a skiff of snow on the ground.

William noticed that look in Heman's eyes. "Oh, I see, big brother, now I know what's wrong. It's not the snow at all. The sea is calling, isn't it? It's almost been four months since *Lady Catherine* has been on a voyage."

161

"You know me well, don't you?"

"Come eat supper. We will talk about your first voyage in this new land afterward."

The wind was howling. All one could see was white. Duncan had the three fireplaces burning trying to keep the house warm. William was setting up a small table close to the fire.

"Heman, come sit down. Let us talk about your trade trip."

"It won't happen for at least five weeks. Looking out the window, it may not happen then. I'm not used to watching for good weather. Except for the North Sea, Ireland didn't have such severe storms."

William went to the window. "It does look bad out there. Do you think *Lady Catherine* will be okay?"

"I think so. I don't worry much. Henry, Moses, and John Charles are living aboard her."

"What about the crew?"

"They were welcome to live there as well. Some did and some didn't. But when the call to sail comes, they will all be there."

"Where is your first trip to take you?"

New York, Charleston, and Bermuda. We will be gone at least six weeks."

"I'm not going, Heman. Did you know that?"

Heman looked at William. "I never really thought about it. I just assumed you would go."

"The sea isn't calling me yet. It may never call again. I have projects in mind. I can work on them and get them ready for the spring. I plan to work out of the store. Is that okay with you, Heman?"

"What kind of projects?"

"Boston wants more land. They are planning to fill in parts of the Harbour area. It will take manpower and lots of it – cheap manpower, which they can't seem to find. But they have it right under their noses. The Irish in the North End – I plan to organize them, turn them into manpower, train them and send them to work.”

“Isn’t that a large undertaking for one man?”

“O’ Donovan – Duncan is going to work with me. After your first trip, I will take care of the store. You find the stuff, bring it back to Boston, and I will sell it.”

The deal was set, during the first snowstorm of the season. Heman would sail *Lady Catherine* to ports along the east coast, buy trade goods, bring them back to Boston and William would sell them. They were happy to have work to do, and it satisfied them both.

“What should we name the store?” Heman asked William.

“The Irish Coffee Company. What else?”

Heman agreed. “What else?”

Before they knew it, the end of January arrived and temperatures had been below zero Fahrenheit for weeks. Both William and Heman thought they would freeze. Duncan was kept busy keeping the fireplaces going.

“We need warmer clothes,” Heman said to William. “We should have been better prepared. Madame Caroline even warned us. Find us a Taylor and have him come to the house.”

“Thanks, brother, you mean I will have to venture out in this freezing weather to find you a Taylor.”

“Us a Taylor. Look out! You are sitting so close to the fire, your shoes are about to burn.”

A knocking was heard at the front door. “Who can that be? They will be frozen before we open the door.”

“I will get it, sir.” Duncan headed that direction. Before he could open the door, he had to remove the quilts that were piled up in front of it to keep the cold draft from coming in.

“Delivery for the Kenney brothers.” The deliveryman was stamping both feet. Duncan looked towards the road, and clouds of steam were rising as the two horses breathed in the cold air.

"Come in, man, before you freeze to death." Duncan didn't have to ask twice. The man was in closing the door behind him. Little pools of melted snow were forming on his feet.

The deliveryman looked down, "Sorry, sir," as he watched the puddle of melted snow grow larger.

"Peggy. Peggy, we need something hot for this man to drink."

"Thank you, sir, but that's not necessary. I'm here to deliver two packages for the Kenney brothers."

By this time, William and Heman had left the warmth of the fireplace. Their curiosity overcame both of them. In their foyer stood a man wrapped in wool scarves and anything else he could get hold of. "We are the Kenney brothers," Heman addressed the man.

"Nice to meet you both. I have packages for you. Let me return to the sleigh, and I will bring them in." Duncan, William, and Heman watched as the man went towards the sleigh. You could hear his feet crunch, as they walked over the snow. He slipped twice but managed to stay on his feet. Returning, he carried two very large boxes. Duncan helped him in through the doorway and closed the door.

"Who are they from?" William asked.

"I do not know, sir. But there is a card here." He handed the card to Heman, who was closest to him.

Peggy arrived. "You poor man. Take this. It will warm you." The deliveryman reached out for the mug and took it to his cold hands.

"Be careful, it's hot." Peggy thought he might burn his hands. But his hands looked red and frozen. The heat didn't seem to faze the man.

He swallowed the hot liquid with two big gulps. "What is this?"

"Irish Coffee," Peggy answered. "Is it not good?"

"Not good, it's the best thing I have ever tasted. It has warmed me right to my toes."

"That Irish Whiskey will do it for you every time," Duncan told the man. But there was no reply; he was busy finishing the hot drink.

"Do you want more?"

"Oh, if I could!"

Faye took the empty cup back to the kitchen to make more.

In the meantime, Heman opened the card. "It's from Captain Freeman. He says he was thinking of us and thought we could use these. He hopes to see us soon."

The deliveryman was drinking his second mug of Irish Coffee. "You need to sell this stuff; you'd make a fortune."

"Maybe we will," declared William. "We are opening an Irish Coffee Company soon, and maybe we will sell mugs of Irish Coffee."

"Where?"

"Along Summer Street. The Webster Buildings."

"I know it well. I will be watching for it. I'll even spread the word."

"Thank you, sir."

"Now I'll be going."

"Stay warm." Peggy was worried about the man.

"I'm warmer than I have ever been, thanks to you, Madame." He closed the door behind him.

Everyone moved closer to the fireplace, carrying the large boxes with them.

"You go first, William."

"It's almost like Christmas, isn't it Heman? Faye, come and help me open it."

Opening the box, Heman blurted out, "Holy cow!"

"No, brother, I don't think it is a holy cow. Holy buffalo maybe, but not holy cow." At that William lifted a fur coat up and around his shoulders.

"You feel soft." Faye was rubbing the coat while William was waltzing around the room.

"Now I can go find you a Taylor, brother. I will never be cold again. Your turn, Heman."

Heman, too, had a buffalo fur coat. "William, there is something else in this box." He lifted up a fur hat.

William rushed back to his box, and sure enough, he had one too.

"What a delightful gift. Captain Freeman is such a nice man," said Peggy.

"How do you know? You have never met the man."

"William, you don't have to meet a man to know if he is nice. His actions preceded him."

"You're right," Heman agreed. "He is a nice man, and he has a wonderful wife."

"A wonderful wife – that explains the way he is." Peggy knew the answer now. "We need to have them over for dinner."

"Peggy, it's not your position to say such a thing," Duncan trying to put Peggy in her place.

"Not at all, Duncan, I was thinking the same thing. It's time they came to our house. I will write them a note immediately." Heman left to do so.

Heman had never seen such cold. Now that he had his buffalo coat, he ventured out into this new world. One of his first trips was to visit *Lady Catherine* and see how she was faring. He told Duncan to order a taxi and was surprised when a sleigh with two horses pulled up in front of his house. The driver helped him aboard.

"Nice to see you dressed well. Half the people I pick up, I fear they will freeze to death. Here I have another Buffalo rug to put over you. Put your feet over the bricks. I baked them in the fireplace all night."

Heman was amazed how warm his feet and legs were. People really do know how to live in these cold temperatures. He enjoyed the ride; he enjoyed the sound. Bells – every sleigh they met, and there were a number of them, all had bells. The sun was shining, but it was hard to open his eyes. He squinted. The sun shone so brightly on the snow it was blinding. He adjusted and only opened his eyes enough to see around him.

Traveling down Franklin Street, they made a right onto Oliver Street and then a left onto Atlantic Avenue. It wasn't even a mile down Atlantic Avenue when he could see the tall masts and spars of Brigs and schooners. He strained his eyes looking for *Lady Catherine*. Heman felt off balance and disoriented. Something was out of place, but he couldn't put his finger on it.

The sleigh stopped. "Lincoln Wharf, sir."

There they were – *Lady Catherine* and the *Alma* – but everything looked so strange. Heman's jaw dropped open. "Where is the water?"

"The water, sir?"

"Yes, the water, the ocean, the sea, whatever you want to call it. Where is it?"

"Sir, did you not know that the Harbour is frozen?"

"The whole Harbour, the whole Harbour is frozen?"

"Yes, sir." The driver was laughing now. "You've never seen it, have you, sir? Look. There are horses out there pulling wagons on sleighs. They are unloading the ships that can't make it into the Harbour. See all those people out there. They are ice skating."

Heman couldn't believe his eyes. People walking on water. No one prepared him for this, not even Madame Caroline.

"Can I help you find your way, sir?"

"The *Lady Catherine*," Heman pointed to her. "She is mine. Thank you. I will find my way from here." Paying the driver, he began to slip and slide towards his ship. He didn't notice the taxi driver leaving laughing up a storm. Heman's mind was so out of kilter that he had given the man a $20.00 tip.

There was no whistle sounding as Heman walked the gangplank to board the schooner. *Lady Catherine* was wrapped in a two-inch thick layer of ice. From the masts to the upper deck, everything sparkled as the sun shone on the ice. Heman was thankful that there was a pathway cleared to the hatchway leading towards the lower deck. He thought, *I might have skated my way right overboard,"* but laughed, "No water to fall into."

Opening the hatch warm air escaped. "Well, they weren't freezing to death anyway." At the bottom of the ladder he heard, "Captain onboard," and the scurrying of men to try to come to attention was apparent to Heman.

"Welcome aboard, Captain." Henry was in charge, so he thought he should be the first to speak.

"*Lady Catherine* damaged?"

"*Lady Catherine* damaged, sir? No, sir. You must be referring to the ice. No, sir, everything has been taken care of, thanks to Captain Freeman and her crew. They helped us greenhorns, but we are learning, sir."

"How so, Henry?"

"We were given a boon, sir. It's logs chained together, and they circle the whole ship. It keeps the ice from hurting us, sir."

"Nice coat and hat, Captain. I thought a bear was visiting, sir. I almost ran for the gun. Then I saw it was you." Moses was smiling.

"Nice, isn't it? Thanks to Captain Freeman, he seems to be taking care of all of us. Where did you get your wool shirts and pants?"

"Captain Freeman's crew, sir. They have been real nice neighbours."

"Can you believe it, sir? Ice two feet thick and thicker in places." John Charles addressed the Captain. "We're not going anywhere, not for a long time."

"I didn't know it was this bad, until just a little while ago. The taxi driver thought I was mad. I asked him where the water went. We are supposed to sail in a week. Is that going to be possible?"

After the laughter died down, John Charles answered, "I can't see how, sir. Nothing is moving out or into this Harbour."

Moses broke in, "You've got to give it to these people who live here. They take a bad thing and make it into a money-making thing."

"What do you mean, Moses?"

"I hear they are going to have a party."

"A party?"

"An Ice Holiday Party."

"Appropriately named."

"Captain, really, it's going to take place this weekend. Booths are going to be set up right out there." Moses pointed to the Harbour. "They are going to sell food and drink and make lots of money."

Patrick had a question. "How are they going to sell drink? Boston has a stringent liquor law?"

Moses was laughing. "Wait, till I tell you. There will be a tent set up with the placard reading, 'The Striped Pig on Exhibition.'[49] They will be exhibiting him in the form of drinks to suit."

Everyone laughed. "Are you going, sir?"

"May do that, and bring Duncan, Peggy, and Faye, along with me."

"Who?"

"My new family. Well, our new family. William found them in the North End. We needed a cook, and it turned into a family."

"North End is bad, sir. The Irish are freezing to death. Came out of the Potato Famine into a frozen hell."

"I will speak to William. We will see what we can do for them."

* * * * *

At dinner that evening, Heman spoke to William about helping the Irish. "I'm already a step ahead of you, brother." William had taken action the day before. "Duncan and I carried food, firewood, and blankets. I've made plans for Duncan to make a run every day until this weather breaks."

169

"Have you also heard about the Ice Festival that will take place this weekend?"

"Ice Festival?" Faye was listening the whole time. "Where?" she asked.

"The Harbour."

"Down by the Harbour?" William asked.

"No, on the Harbour."

"How can that be? It's too cold to be on the water this time of year."

"When was the last time you were down by the Harbour, brother?"

"It's been a while."

"I thought so."

"Why?"

"There's no Harbour."

"What do you mean 'no Harbour'?"

"Well, no water. It's frozen."

"The whole Harbour is frozen?"

"My words exactly."

"They're walking on it, actually skating on it. They have horses pulling wagon sleighs on it."

"Horses walking on the Harbour?"

"Amazing, isn't it?"

"Are you going?" Faye's eyes were big with excitement.

"Of course," William said, "This I've got to see."

Heman was able to contact the same taxi driver that took him to the Harbour a few days earlier. In fact, Heman couldn't understand why the man remembered him so well. But arrangements were made to hire him and a larger sleigh.

The Saturday of the Ice Festival, Fred the taxi driver had safely stowed his passengers on the sleigh. Heman made sure that Peggy and Faye had warm fur coats to wear as well. Duncan insisted he was warm enough wearing two wool coats and a sweater, shirt, and long underwear. It didn't take him long to snuggle under the buffalo rug with those on the sleigh.

As Fred guided the horses onto the Harbour, Peggy cried, "Are you sure it's safe?"

Fred, sensing her fear, stopped. "Ma'am, the ice has been tested at two and one-half feet thick just yesterday. The temperatures have been well below freezing. If anything, the ice is thicker by now. The Harbour is frozen all the way down to the lighthouse. Take a look out there, and what do you see?"

They all looked in the direction of the Harbour. Where normally they would see sailboats, they saw people skating, coasting, sledding, and sleighing. They would be sleighing.

"It's still not natural." William was more nervous than Peggy. He had never had a love for the ocean. Now, a feeling of fear was about to overtake him.

"I will let you off at my favorite booth, and you will be fine, William. Tell them Fred McCloud sent you."

The horses stopped outside a tent. A sign read: "The Striped Pig on Exhibition." Heman was laughing. William asked, "Why would I want to see a striped pig?"

"Oh, but you will," answered Fred. "Have a 'striped pig' on me. We will be back in half an hour or so to pick you up."

"A half hour! Duncan, you come with me. I may need protection from the striped pig."

"See you, brother, you will be fine."

Heman, Peggy, and Faye continued on. They enjoyed watching the crowd.

"Do you want to skate, Peggy?"

"I'm staying put. I don't want to walk on any water." Even Faye was content sitting in the warm sleigh watching the events play out around them.

"Food," Fred eyes lit up, "If you don't want to skate, we can eat." He led the horses over to a booth. Steam was rising, and the smell of food cooking seemed to float in the cold air. Fred threw blankets over the horses and a feeding bag over their heads. They were content to eat their oats.

"Now that the horses are happy, come with me," Heman directed Fred. "We will see about food for us. The ladies can stay put where it's warm."

The men returned with a tray full of food. Faye exclaimed, "This is fun. I've never had a picnic in the middle of a Harbour before."

"Don't forget to say on a horse-drawn sleigh," Peggy added. "They would think I had lost my mind, if I spoke it in Ireland."

"Well, here we are, Peggy. I brought you and Faye something special to eat. This was one of my first meals in America – Boston Baked Beans. Try them."

Peggy exclaimed, "They're sweet."

"Just a little, aren't they?" Heman was glad Peggy was having a good time.

The sun was going down, for it went down early these days. Four o'clock and the sun was almost set. Fred had the horses ready, "I believe it's time to leave."

Heman noticed they weren't the only ones to leave. Everyone was making their way to shore. Picking up William and Duncan, Heman asked, "Well, are you happy now?"

With smiles like a fox, they answered, "Oh, yes, very happy. We enjoyed those striped pigs." Both Heman and Fred laughed. However, Peggy and Faye didn't understand the joke.

* * * * *

Three days later, Heman and William were discussing the first trade voyage. "We are already a week late," Heman complained to William. "We are paying rent on an empty store." Just then a message arrived calling the Captain to come to the *Lady Catherine* as quickly as possible.

"What do you think the problem is, Heman?"

"Who knows? Come with me. We will find out."

Henry and John Charles were waiting for them, as the brothers boarded the ship.

"Is there trouble, Henry?" Heman went right to the subject.

"No, sir, not trouble but opportunity. Come, we need to talk about this."

Before they were all seated, Henry had started. "Did you know that the Cunard[50] steamship is icebound in this Harbour?"

Before Heman could answer, "She is overdue in England. The Queen isn't very happy."

William interrupted with a snide remark, "The Queen is never happy."

Henry gave William a dirty look that made him squirm in his seat.

"Go on, Henry." Heman was interested in the subject at hand.

"Well she, the Queen, said she would make it worthwhile for Boston to get the Cunard out of her Harbour. The Boston merchants, aided by the Fresh Pond Ice Cutters Company[51], have been cutting a channel to begin her voyage to England. And did you know that the Cunard is a rock throwing distance from us?"

"How far have they got with the channel?"

"I heard six miles, Captain."

"How far do they need to go?"

"Seven. Seven miles."

"Good work, Henry."

"What's that got to do with us?" William didn't know about this good work Henry did.

"Don't you see, William? If the Cunard can get out, there's a good chance we can get out with her."

Heman turned to Henry and John Charles, "Get the word out. Be ready to sail in two days." And they did.

* * * * *

Heman and William were sitting on wooden lawn chairs outside their store. Heman couldn't help glancing at the sign above the entrance: Irish Coffee Company. The store wasn't opened, for it was Sunday afternoon. "It's hard to believe it's 1859, William. The end of the 50's. I wonder what the 60's will bring."

"If the last five years are any indication, we will continue to do well, Heman. The Irish Coffee Company has become a very popular meeting place for many people in Boston. The men bring their wives in to look at the beautiful things you have found to sell. The men drink Irish Coffee, and the ladies drink iced tea."

"Remember that delivery man the first winter we were here?"

"Delivered our fur coats, didn't he?"

"Yes, that's the one. He was right suggesting we sell Irish Coffee. That brings them through the door, and then they buy the other stuff."

"I always thought there was a hard liquor law here in Boston."

"There is. The inspectors have been through. Duncan and Peggy told them the Irish Coffee was a secret recipe passed down from their grandparents."

"And they bought that?"

"Yes, they did."

"I believe the inspectors like Irish Coffee," William gave a wink in Heman's direction. "The women don't seem to know the secret ingredient."

Heman laughed, "So that's how we are getting away with it?"

"That, and Peggy is very careful how much Irish Coffee she sells to one person."

"I've kept the store filled, thanks to *Lady Catherine*'s voyages to New York, Charleston, and even Bermuda."

"But your business has grown too, William. You have made a name for yourself around here. Whenever the government needs workers, they are at your door."

"It's not me, Heman. The Irishmen want to work and make a life for their families. They are good workers and dependable. There is a great pride in what they are doing. The landscape of Boston is changing, thanks to them."

"Yes, I heard people talking," Heman replied. "They were saying how things have changed. So, I went to look. Mount Vernon and Pemberton Hill were leveled, also Beacon Hill. Where are they putting all the earth?"[52]

"Much of the earth removed from those sites went into filling the coves along Boston's coast. We have created a new South End and two new neighbourhoods – the Black Bay and South Boston. The job won't be finished for 20 years. The Irishmen will have secure jobs for a long time to come."

"Enough about Boston, bring me up to date on your voyages."

"Except for two, most ports are about the same. New York is the largest. I would like you to see Charleston and Bermuda. Cotton is the largest cargo. I could fill *Lady Catherine* twice over with cotton. Of course, we pick that up in Charleston. However, I always leave room for silks, whale oil, coffee, molasses, and tea. In Bermuda, we made a contract for rugs. I can buy as many as I want, but I limited them to 50."

"This last trip I made a run to Charleston, loaded *Lady Catherine* with lumber and shingles, headed back to New York, sold it all in one day. Returned to Charleston, loaded cotton plus candles, brandy, butter, nails, onions, flour, and cheese. *Lady Catherine* was full, and I didn't even make it to Bermuda."

"Don't forget the smoked and pickled tongues. Don't care for them myself, but they sell like hotcakes."

Heman laughed, "I bought 18,000 oranges from W. Robinson and Company. He threw in those cases of smoked and pickled tongues for free."

"Well, then, what does the future hold, Heman?"

"I've been thinking about that. I would like to add a new port to our repertoire."

"You can hardly keep up with what you have."

"Charleston is too hot in the summer. The hot, muggy nights spent there makes me dream of Ireland."

"You mean the cool summer nights of Ireland? What new port do you speak of?"

"I met a man in New York, Tom Finley. He was in the textile business. I knew he wasn't a New Yorker, nor from Boston. He sounded slightly British. I asked him where he was from. He turns out to be from Halifax, Nova Scotia. It is just north of here, on the other side of the border."

"British territory?"

"Yes, and a fine Harbour I'm told. His whole family is in the textile business and would be interested in the *Lady Catherine* to import cotton to them."

"How do you figure to make it work?"

"Like I said, it's too hot going south in the summer. I would like to try a run north. It wouldn't hurt anything to go see."

"And the cotton, where would you get it?"

"Make a few extra runs south to Charleston in the winter. Bring it back here and store it until spring. Then make the trip to Halifax."

"Looks like it's a worthwhile plan. Go for it, brother."

"I will send the paperwork to Tom Finley. Let's see if a business agreement can be made."

"Speaking of Charleston, you would like Charleston, William. They don't care if you are Irish."

"Charleston? Oh, we are back to Charleston." William was confused about the subject change.

"In fact, I was invited to more social events on one trip there than I have in Boston for five years. The ladies would gather around me, just to hear me speak. Of course, when that happened, I had nothing to say."

William laughing, "Women tend to do that to you, don't they?"

Heman blushed slightly, "I don't have time for women."

"I did do something else there, William. Can I confide in you?"

Those words brought William out of his Sunday afternoon laid-back attitude. He sat up on the edge of the lawn chair. "You don't trust me, brother?'

"It's not that, but you have to promise me you won't accidentally tell anyone."

"Sounds serious." William was almost sliding out of his chair.

"Heman looked to make sure no one was around. "I've joined the Underground Railroad. There, I've said it."

"You've what?"

"Shhh, quiet. The Underground Railroad," Heman repeated in a lower voice.

"That's what I thought you said. Are you crazy? That could ruin both of us."

"Remember the promise I made, that I would do what I could to stop or help slaves? Nothing you say is going to stop me. That's another reason to go north."

"Now I see, brother. It's not because of the heat in the south."

"Partially, and I'm checking out a route for the Railroad."

"Are you sure you want to do this?"

"Yes, William, I am sure. But I wanted your blessing. "I've never done anything behind your back."

"Looks like to me you need someone to watch your back."

Heman smiled. William shook his head, "And Father thought I would be the one to get into trouble."

Heman quickly stated, "But this is trouble for 'good.' Remember the less people know about this the better."

"The family? William asked.

"They are not to know. You, and soon my crew, will be the only ones who know in Boston."

"Are you afraid?"

"Yes, brother, I will always be afraid."

After a period of silence, William made a decision. "I will stand by you, brother."

November 1859

Dear William,

Ireland sends her greetings. My heart grieves each day knowing the distance there is between us. Your letters are of great comfort. I read them often and share them with those of our household. Ada believes she is to blame for you being in America and asks my forgiveness daily. I assure her you were on your own and should have known better than dropping a flag on the Queen. But let's not talk about that. All is forgiven.

You write of the leaves turning to red, orange and yellow. I wish I could be there to see them with you. And your new family, the O'Donavans, and your townhouse and your store. Everything seems so exciting for you.

Your Father is proud of the company you have built. And helping all those fellow Irishmen. We are all proud of you. But, Father said you need to stop telling stories. Having a picnic on the frozen Harbour, really, William, who would believe such a thing?

O'Sullivan and George maintain the stables. Father has lost interest and rarely visits the horses. Without you, the foxhunt is not as exciting. We both try to keep busy, for life moves forward.

Take care of yourself, and be sure to listen to your brother. I will always love you, no matter how many miles may separate us.

Your loving Mother

CHAPTER NINE

A Fort on a Hill 1860

The date was July 9, 1860. *Lady Catherine* was making her way into Halifax Harbour for the first time. The journey from Boston had taken five days. Not that they pushed it, Heman took it slow and steady. He was in no hurry and enjoyed the time at sea. The sea breeze was not hot, as it was traveling south. Heman breathed in the cool sea breeze easily. He believed his lungs liked breathing in the British air. The whole crew was top deck taking in the beautiful sight before them.

Henry was standing beside Heman. "Wow! I don't believe I've seen such blue water."

"Beautiful, isn't it? That's the sign of deep water," replied Heman.

John Charles was taking the beauty in around him. "I don't believe I've seen a better Harbour than this."

"And we've been in many harbours," Moses added. "I have a good feeling about this place, Captain."

"We can all rest easy, now that we have your blessing," chided Henry.

Moses cuffed Henry on the back of the head. "You mind my words."

John Charles was fascinated by what he was seeing. "That small island over there is in just the right place. It doesn't prevent ships from entering the Harbour but protects the inner Harbour from winds coming in off the ocean. And look, hills on three sides protect it from storms."[53]

"Talking about your island, did you see that?" Henry was pointing to an elevated area of the island.

Heman whistled, "Whoeee!" It was a whistle of amazement that he couldn't believe his own eyes. "Do you see what I see?"

Moses in an urging voice, "Take a look to your left." He pointed to the first of three hills that John Charles spoke of.

Heman whistled again, "Another one."

"Captain, do you have a feeling someone's watching us? Look, by the gun battery there are soldiers."

"I wouldn't want to get them mad at us," added Henry.

"Are they trying to give a message?"

"Cannons pointed at you from two directions are certainly a message."

"Maybe we should raise a white flag."

"I don't think that will be necessary."

"Not unless we fire first." Patrick was watching the soldiers practice their drills.

"Yeah, that would be really smart," added Moses, "We have 10 muskets. Our range would be 300 yards. They would blast us out of the water."

Heman interrupted, "Whoa, boys, let's not start a war with England."

As they entered the inner Harbour, Henry was in agreement with his Captain. "Look up there. You think those two cannons would be trouble? Take a look at that."

Off in the distance, they could see a huge fort. It was on a hill overlooking the town.

"Beautiful sight." John Charles couldn't keep his eyes off it. "A diamond shape, no, more like a star."

Moses laughed, "It's a good thing Sir William is not with us. The British may still be after him."

They all laughed, but Heman did not. Seeing their Captain not partaking of the joke, they quickly changed the subject.

"Landlubbers approaching starboard side." It was the Harbour Master.

"Welcome to Halifax. Where are you coming from?"

"I'm Captain Heman Kenney," Heman replied. "Boston, sir."

"Your matter of business, sir?"

"I have business with a James Finley. He is in the textile business. My cargo is cotton and silk, etc."

"Captain Kenney, I believe the Queen's Wharf will accommodate you nicely. How long will you be in Halifax?"

"At this time I do not know."

"Your first visit?"

"Yes, sir. I'm not sure the welcome is a warm one or sending a warning message."

The Harbour Master laughed. "Oh, you're talking about the cannons. You will get used to them after a while. Between you and me, they haven't shot those cannons in 20 years. Halifax has been a garrison town for more than 150 years."

"I noticed I came into the Harbour several Royal Navy ships. What role do they play here?"

"There are six of them here at the moment. Their role you ask. Well, let me see – first to show the flag. You didn't notice all the Union Jacks?"

"It was hard not to notice."

"The Royal Navy patrols the fishing grounds and keeps a suspicious eye on the United States. Word has it they want continental expansion.[54] Haligonians regard . . ."

"Who?"

"Haligonians, people who live in Halifax, and the people who live over there," he pointed across the Harbour, "are called Dartmouthians."

"Dartmouthians?"

"People who live in Dartmouth."

"Haligonians regarded the squadron as their own. They have been good for Halifax's prosperity."

Heman could see his visit to Halifax was going to be interesting indeed. He looked forward to it. The next day Heman was preparing for his meeting with James Finley. Henry was with him discussing prices. "Halifax, not being in the United States, is there not some kind of tariff or tax?"

"That's what makes Halifax so prosperous. There isn't one."

BOOM! – Heman's hair stood up on the back of his neck.

Henry thought about hiding under the table, but in a nick of time, his cowardice turned to bravery. "I thought they hadn't shot cannons for 200 years."

The time it took for the men to arrive top deck was measured in seconds. Heman's eyes scanned the deck, the wharf, and the hill straight above him. This too only took a second. His crew also scurrying around the deck, were searching for danger. "It's from up there." Heman pointed to the top of the hill where the fort was. The smoke had not cleared from the blast of the cannon. He didn't hear another blast, but he did hear laughter reaching his ears. Laughter and lots of it. His gaze now scanned the wharf area. Everyone was watching The *Lady Catherine*. It was like they were on a stage of a theatre, and the audience was enjoying the entertainment. The audience began to clap and whistle in delight. Heman and his crew froze.

"Bravo, bravo" was heard as the audience broke up and went back to their work duties on the wharf. A young boy who was also part of the audience said, "Hey, mate, you must be new here?" He was directing his question to Heman.

Heman's hair was standing on the back of his neck again. This time for a different reason – embarrassment. But he didn't know why. This boy might be able to give him a few answers to his many questions. "Young man."

The boy was taking his leave and turned back. "Who me?"

"Yes, you, come aboard. I would like to meet you." That was all it took. The boy was now standing beside Heman.

"Great looking schooner you have here. Are you the Captain?"

"Yes, I am Captain Heman Kenney."

"Ian Schaeffer." The boy reached out his hand. They shook on it.

"Do you live around here, son?"

"I guess you could say that. They call me the wharf rat. I work here and there, and I get by. Do you have any work I can do?" Ian looked around the deck. Most of the crew had gotten on with their chores. They figured the Captain would get to the bottom of it. When that happened, he would share the cannon shot with the rest.

"I work hard, I do and I'm strong, I am."

Heman smiled. The boy was answering his own statements. "I'm sure we can find something for you to do around here. But before that, I need to ask you man to man. Who shot that cannon?"

A smile came across Ian's face. He was remembering the entertainment that was witnessed by all just a short time before. "Will it make you feel any better to know that you weren't the first to give such a show? It happens every once in a while. I've seen it twice myself. You see up there – that's the Citadel, also known as Citadel Hill. What you heard was the noonday gun.[55] The soldiers shoot a cannon twice a day: one at noon and one in the evening."

Heman now realized what a sight he and his crew must have made. They made it look like a war was just beginning. No wonder they laughed.

"My Papa said the noonday gun started back in 1749. He told me the gun was timed for vessels in the Harbour to set their chronometers by the sight of the puff of smoke, rather than the noise of the report, which took time to carry."

"I will make sure my navigator gets this information. What about the evening gun?"

"Eight o'clock during the winter season, and nine o'clock in the summer. This told the off-duty soldiers they had half an hour to return to barracks."[56]

"Thank you, Ian, and for payment for your information, you can eat lunch with my crew, after which, they will find you work to do."

"Thank you, sir. You won't regret it. Captain, thank you."

* * * * *

James Finley lived on Argyle Street with his family. His father and grandfather settled in this area in the 1700's. Even though he was proud of his three-story house, there were many grander homes around him. Newer, of course, and the city's high society – such as it was – referred to them as mansions. Anyone who was able to live on Argyle and Barrington Street was known to have made a name for themselves. Somehow living on Argyle Street made James walk a little taller. He had a right to do so. His father and grandfather started a textile business. He followed in their footsteps, and the business was prosperous. He owned the Textile Mill (factory) on the corner of Cornwallis and Water Street. Both his father and grandfather, may they rest in peace, would be proud of how he had added to the small empire. James' success had given him other benefits. He was always invited to attend all the banquets and balls put on by the Royal Navy Admiral and the British Army General, who entertained lavishly. James and his wife Janet had been to the Admiralty House on Gottingen Street and Bellevue at the corner of Spring Garden Road and Queen Street. James' sons often accompanied them. It wouldn't hurt James Jr, Charles, and George to mingle with the city's best families. Who knows, they may find a good catch when it comes to wives. Tom did. He found a very good wife. His father-in-law sent him to New York to work for him there. The last he heard, which was just this week, he was doing fine.

James didn't forget his daughter. Oh, how could he forget his Elizabeth Janet? Named, of course, after his sweet wife. James had two women in his life whom he loved dearly. He was a lucky man. Years had passed quickly, and just yesterday his wife Janet told him it was time for Elizabeth to find a special man. Time? It would never be time. How could he ever let her go? Fathers are not able to hold back the wave of time, and she, too, was attending the social events of Halifax. Elizabeth and her mother attended the tea and garden parties of the area.

Elizabeth was not a plain looking girl, to the contrary. Dark hair reflected diamonds as the sunlight shone upon it. Blue-green eyes like the ocean. Fair skin, which required her to wear a large-brimmed bonnet to protect her from the sun. She had access to the most beautiful clothes in the city. James was always amazed that she chose the simple, classical look. Showy clothes did not interest her. As long as she looked well dressed, she did not care for the frills. Her father noticed that many heads turned, whenever she was out in public.

Elizabeth had worked alongside her mother at the Textile Mill. She, like her mother, had a keen sense of design and fashion. James knew his daughter didn't have to marry just to have someone to take care of her. Elizabeth could take care of herself. Maybe attending all these functions, she would find a British officer to her liking. It would be up to her. Time would tell.

The Finley family was gathered in the dining room. James insisted the whole family dine together once a week. Everyone was present, at least almost everyone. Tom and his wife Laura now lived in New York. However, a letter just arrived that day, and the letter was passed around, taking turns to read aloud:

June 1, 1860

Dear Father and Mother, James, Charles, George, and of course, sweet Elizabeth,

A murmur went through the room. It was a good feeling their brother remembered each one of them. Mother, looking down, hoped no one saw the tear she wiped out of the corner of her eye with her silk-embroidered handkerchief.

We have good news. Laura is to have a baby sometime before Christmas.

Excited congratulations were passed along the table. Even the maid had a smile to offer.

"Congratulations, Father, soon you will have to get used to 'Papa,' and what will we call you, Mother? Nana would be good." James Jr took the lead, since Tom was away. "And you, Elizabeth, 'Auntie.'" There was a gay atmosphere throughout the room.

James passed the letter to Charles, "Your turn. I got to read the good stuff; everything else must be boring."

Mother encouraged Charles, "Go on, Charles. I must hear more."

Charles began to read:

There is a wonderful hospital here just for having babies.

Charles stopped, for he was blushing.

So, don't worry, Laura will have great care.

Charles passed the letter to George:

We do miss Halifax and especially all of you. But New York City is a wonderful place to live. It never rests. It doesn't matter if it is night or day, the city is growing.

"Elizabeth, now it's your turn." George handed the letter to her.

Father, three months ago, or thereabout, I met a Captain of a schooner. Fine man, he is. He does trade all along the east coast. Picks up a lot of cotton in Charleston, South Carolina. We spoke of how much cotton you need. Just this week I heard from him. We made a business deal that he would try a new run to Halifax. He is coming there with a cargo of cotton just for you. In his letter, he wrote that he would arrive in Halifax, July 9, 1860, if all goes well.

James interrupted, "Why July 9 was yesterday. A load of cotton is here in Halifax for me, and I did not know it. What's the Captain's name?"

Elizabeth continued reading:

Captain Heman Kenney, and his schooner is Lady Catherine. He is from Ireland. I sent him your name, and where the Textile Mill is located.

"Captain Kenney must be wondering where James Finley is. What a welcome I have given him. Janet, I must leave at once."

"We haven't finished reading the letter, James."

"Can't be helped. James Jr., you come with me."

"Can we come also?" George was speaking for his brother Charles.

"Yes, let's all go."

"What about me?" Elizabeth asked.

"Sorry, dear, the docks are no place for a beautiful girl like you. We would never talk business." As they left the room, James winked and smiled at Elizabeth, and threw a kiss toward Janet. "See you soon," and they were gone.

"Life isn't fair, Mother. I can't go just because I'm a girl. I wish I were born a boy."

"Four sons are plenty, Elizabeth. What would we do without our favourite daughter? Your father's heart would be broken." Elizabeth smiled a little.

"Come, let's decide what to wear at the garden party tomorrow. I do hope it doesn't rain."

* * * * *

BOOM! The nine o'clock cannon sounded. "Oh dear, I hate doing business so late in the evening, but it can't be helped."

"Father, calm yourself; everything will be fine." James Jr. was trying to help his father. "Besides, where is the schooner going to go this time of night? She will be there."

"Where should we begin looking, James?"

"My guess is to start at the Queen's Wharf. What do you think, Father?"

"Yes, that's where I instruct the Harbour Master to bring our imports for the Textile Mill."

The carriage stopped alongside a schooner. "That's her," Charles cried. "Look, The *Lady Catherine*."

Moses was on first-night watch. His nerves were still on edge. It was that blimey cannon they shoot. He jumped two feet every time he heard that boom. Looking at his pocket watch, he noticed it was 10 minutes after 9:00 p.m. Maybe things would quiet down for the rest of the night. Night – it wasn't even dark yet. Not long ago, he watched the sun setting with red and orange and yellow colours, racing across the horizon. God had put on another show. Moses thanked God for everything He gave him. At that, he crossed himself.

Moses noticed a carriage pull up and stop on the wharf beside the *Lady Catherine*. Four gentlemen climbed out and headed for her gangplank. Moses turned to a crew member, "Sound the whistle – land lubbers on board." He then met the gentlemen to inquire their business.

"James Finley and my sons, James Jr., Charles, and George. I know this is a terrible hour, but we have business with Captain Heman Kenney."

So this is the James Finley the Captain's been waiting for these past two days, thought Moses. "Come aboard, sir. The Captain has been expecting you. If you wait here, I will summon the Captain."

"That would be fine. Thank you, sir."

Moses knocked on the door to the Captain's cabin.

"Enter."

"Captain, sir, a James Finley and sons to see you."

"Now?" Heman was eating a late dinner. "Quick, help me clear my desk." Moses took the half-eaten dinner away to the galley. Heman quickly refreshed himself and put on his jacket. Moses was back. "Show them in, Moses."

"Yes, sir."

It was crowded in the cabin, but three stools were brought in for the sons to sit on.

"Welcome aboard The *Lady Catherine*," Heman began. "I'm sorry for the cramped quarters, but I believe we will be more comfortable here than out there with the mosquitoes."

"Not at all, Captain. No apologies are necessary. It is I who need to apologize. I didn't even know you were coming until an hour ago."

Heman had a questioning look on his face.

"My son Tom, Tom Finley, from New York. His letter of June 1st just arrived today. We were reading it at dinner, when we got to the part of your coming. I'm sorry, sir, I would have been here yesterday to greet you. Knowing you were here, I didn't want to wait until tomorrow. These are my sons, Tom's brothers, James Jr., Charles, and George."

"That explains it." Heman had wondered why no one had met him. "I was going to send a messenger tomorrow."

"I'm glad I did not wait for tomorrow. Tom tells great things about you."

"Your son, Tom, is a bright young man. I am sure he will make you proud."

"Makes the whole family proud, he does."

"Your cargo of cotton is secure. I will arrange to have it unloaded first thing tomorrow. We can talk business at that time."

"Tom told me I would like you, and I can see he was right. You must come meet the family."

Heman turned to James' sons, "And what interests you, lads?"

"Your schooner, sir." They all agreed.

"Have you sailed on a schooner?"

"No, sir."

"You live on a great Harbour as this, and you've never sailed on a schooner?"

"My fault alone," James said. "I have them completely involved in the textile business."

"Your wife, sir?"

"Janet. She is home. We live on Argyle Street."

"You have four sons?"

"And a daughter, Elizabeth."

Charles spoke up, "She wanted to come, but Father said the docks were no place for her."

"Your father is wise. But there are times when ladies are welcomed on The *Lady Catherine*. In fact, why don't we plan one of those events? Sunday, if the weather holds, *Lady Catherine* will take your whole family sailing. Would you like that?"

"Elizabeth sure would. What do you say, boys?"

The brothers hated it when their father referred to them as "boys." They were men, and they wanted Heman to recognize them as such. "As men, we would love to see the art of sailing, sir." James Jr. did the talking. The other brothers agreed.

"Then it's settled. Sunday 1:00 p.m. Sailing for six, is that correct?"

"Yes, sir," George answered, "six."

* * * * *

Elizabeth was dancing across the floor. "How marvelous. I can't wait for Sunday, Father."

Janet was not so sure. "James, you know I don't like boats. I prefer to stay on land, thank you."

"You don't want Elizabeth to be the only lady amongst so many men, do you?" Janet looked at Elizabeth.

"Mother, you've got to go. A schooner is not a rowboat, you know. You won't even know it's a boat."

"I'm sure," Janet replied. She saw how excited Elizabeth was. How could she disappoint her? "I guess I will go."

"How wonderful?! I do hope it doesn't rain. Come, Mother, let's decide what to wear."

As Elizabeth led her mother away, Janet was heard to say, "I wouldn't mind rain at all."

"Oh, Mother," Elizabeth chided her.

* * * * *

"Landlubbers on board." Heman and Henry were top side. They could see several wagons lined up on the Queen's Wharf. "Early aren't they, Captain?"

"I believe they are making up for lost time. I see Ian amongst them. Take care of our wharf rat, Henry. I will let you take care of the lot. I'm going to eat breakfast."

"Aye, aye, sir. I will find work for the wharf rat."

* * * * *

That same day Elizabeth didn't get much work done at the Textile Mill. She fretted to her mother. "I don't have anything to wear. Sunday will be here in four days."

"You must have something to wear." Her mother was surprised her daughter was fretting over clothes. It was so unlike her.

"Not sailing clothes. I've never been sailing. It should be wonderful, Mother."

James entered the workroom, the sound of his steps echoed from the hardwood floors. This room was the size of a barn and was filled with long, large, wooden tables. Here is where the large bolts of cloth of many colours stood like soldiers against the wall. Ladies of every age were busy cutting out cloth laid on patterns. He noticed Elizabeth's table was idle. "What's wrong, Elizabeth, are you not well?"

"No, Father, I am well enough."

"Your daughter has nothing to wear for sailing on Sunday?"

James laughed. "Dear daughter, you will have to make yourself something."

"Can I, Father?"

"Anything in this room is yours." His arm rose and outlined the wall of the workroom. "I have hundreds of bolts of material. If my daughter can't choose what she wants, then I say why have this business?"

"James, you spoil her."

Looking with a gleam in his eye at Janet, "Since when has she made anything for herself?"

To that Janet agreed. Elizabeth only sewed for herself when her mother made it an order. And with that did so reluctantly.

"Thank you, Father." Elizabeth hugged him. "But I only have four days."

"Take some of the ladies." He pointed to the women working at the tables. "They can help you."

Elizabeth knew exactly what she wanted. Walking by the table she grabbed an arm. "Linda, come with me." Linda loved

Elizabeth, and the two girls giggled as they began their task together.

* * * * *

There was not a sight of rain on Sunday. A beautiful summer day in Nova Scotia. In the afternoon a breeze would come up – perfect for sailing. Elizabeth stood before her mirror. She was satisfied with her reflection. Her special outfit had turned out perfectly. The final touches were finished the night before. Linda and she had worked hard the past three days, but it was worth it. Elizabeth had chosen a long culotte in navy blue. A white blouse with short puffed sleeves. *"A little daring,* thought Elizabeth, *but in the peak of style.* She made a sailor's collar outlined with bricker bracket of navy and red. Linda gave her the idea, taking it from the soldier's dress uniform. Her bonnet – she had to have a bonnet to keep her hair from flying everywhere. It was also navy blue with ribbons of red, blue and white hanging down the back. Shoes, she decided to wear sturdy shoes, not her normal slippers she customarily wore with her dresses. After all, she was practical and had plans to be able to move about the schooner without sliding.

"Elizabeth, are you ready?" George was eager to leave. "We are waiting for you."

"Be right there, dear brother." One more glance in the mirror, she pinched her cheeks to make them red and headed for the staircase. The whole family watched as she ascended the stairs. "You look marvelous." James Jr. was very proud of his sister. "Father, you'd better bring a whip or a stick to beat the gentlemen off."

James with a happy heart directed his family to the waiting coach. "Queen's Wharf," they directed to the driver. They were on their way for a day of sailing.

Sailing they did, and how Elizabeth loved it. She loved the speed. Land travel was so awkward when riding in a coach or a carriage. Any small hole in the road was very noticeable, as one was bounced about in the carriage. But not on the ocean. One glided over the water like a huge bird. Freedom, that's what it was, and she stood up on the bow watching the shoreline pass with the feeling she could fly. Her enthusiasm was contagious. The crew stumbled over each other trying to be the first to lend a helping hand. Elizabeth never stayed in one place, which gave plenty of opportunities to hold her delicate hand, as she moved from the upper and lower decks.

Heman watched Elizabeth as he entertained his other guests, her father, and mother. She was the centre of attention and had been since she walked the gangplank landing on the deck with a little hop. As he was introduced to her, he took her hand and kissed her small knuckles. He didn't know how, but he felt sparks enter through his lips surging through his body right to his feet.

"So you are Captain Heman. I expected someone older. Tom wrote that I should get to know you." With a little grin, Elizabeth said, "I do believe I agree."

"Welcome aboard *Lady Catherine*. She longs for a woman's touch since her company is only men journey after journey. She welcomes you; I can feel it." Heman looked up as far as the crow's nest.

"Drop sail."

A crewman beside him repeated the command, **"Drop sail"** echoed down the line and with a whoosh, a white sail dropped from the mast and fell into place.

Elizabeth clapped her hands in delight.

"Look, Elizabeth, *Lady Catherine* is as well dressed as you are," James Jr. exclaimed.

"Cast Ho."

The ropes securing the schooner to the wharf were thrown to the crew, who were ready to stow them in their place. "*Lady Catherine* is eager to sail. Please follow me." Heman took James's daughter by the elbow and led the way.

James guided Janet who held on tight. "What do you think?" he whispered close to her ear.

Janet with her eyebrows raised, "Very romantic. That's all I have to say. Captain Kenney knows how to get a woman's attention." Janet sat down on one of two deck chairs that were provided. She was grateful they were sitting in the middle of the deck.

Heman turned to the brothers who were taking in the recent tide of events. "Feel free to go as you please. Explore, ask questions, have fun and be safe."

"Me too?" Elizabeth exclaimed.

"I don't know," quivered her mother with a look of fear in her eyes. James looked concerned as well.

Heman motioned to Henry, and he stepped forward. "This is Henry, my First Mate. I will assign him to follow your daughter. He will keep her safe." Heman thought, "I'd do it myself if I could." He didn't know what was coming over him. James and Janet Finley were satisfied with the arrangements. Henry was delighted. Heman added, "I grew up as a small child playing on schooners. She will be safe enough." From that moment Elizabeth was flying free as a seabird on the decks of *Lady Catherine*.

The schooner was soon passing a small island. "We noticed two islands in the Harbour."

"Yes, George's Island and McNabs. McNabs being the larger." James was pointing down the Harbour.

"The one with the cannon?"

James laughed, "I'd forgotten about that. If we are lucky, we will see something else on McNabs Island."

"What's that?"

"Wild horses.[57] Yes, look over there. The herd is moving across the sandy beach now."

Sure enough, Heman saw about twenty horses. "How did they get there?"

"Been there for as long as I can remember. My grandfather told his grandchildren that the horses were brought to the island in the 1700s."

James' attention was turned to his daughter. She was jumping from one side of the boat to the other. "I believe she is keeping your crew busy."

"Don't worry, sir, they need exercise." It was very entertaining to Heman to see his crew running around the deck. *Lady Catherine* sailed to the mouth of Halifax Harbour and beyond. She tacked straight into the wind. The offshore breeze would be behind her on the return journey, gently pushing the schooner back to the Queen's Wharf.

Heman had another surprise for the Finley family. He had tables set up on deck, and they ate an early supper together in the late afternoon.

Elizabeth was hungry and ate heartily. "I could get used to this sailing business. Maybe I will become a sailor." Of course, everyone laughed.

Heman said to himself, *You could sail with me any day. There I go again. What's come over me? I've never felt this way toward a woman before.*

"I have a great idea." It was Elizabeth, "Why don't we go to the "Public Gardens?"[58] I would love to have ice cream. We can finish this wonderful day with ice cream."

"There is a military band playing at the gazebo at 6:00 p.m.," Janet interjected, looking toward James.

"Well, Heman, looks like the ladies are ready for another adventure."

Heman wasn't ready for them to leave yet. But what could he do? "Thank you for being my guests today. Elizabeth, I am glad you have taken to sailing. We must do it again soon."

"No, Captain, we are not leaving without you." Elizabeth was horrified to think Heman wasn't going with them. The second adventure began.

Heman enjoyed his evening immensely. In fact, he couldn't remember the last time he enjoyed himself so well. Walking on the Queen's Wharf, he seemed to glide aboard *Lady Catherine*. The sound of the whistle announcing his arrival back on board seemed to dance around the ship. Patrick was on duty. "Did you have a good evening, sir?"

"Immensely, Patrick, you don't know the depths of it. I think I will take a walk with *Lady Catherine* before turning in."

"Yes, sir, beautiful night for a stroll. Sea breeze is keeping those mosquitoes at bay."

Heman wouldn't have noticed a mosquito if it was there. He was in a state of mind, where he had never been before. "You liked her didn't you, *Lady Catherine*. I know. Perfect isn't she? Perfect in every way. So silly, isn't it? I just met the lady, but I feel like I have known her all my life. Well, of course, I'm going to see her again. When? I don't know, *Lady Catherine*, but I'm working on that." Heman stood looking over the Harbour for a long time. He liked this Halifax. Off on the horizon, he saw a star fall into the ocean. *A falling star, isn't that a sign of good luck?* thought Heman. He turned and slowly walked to his cabin. *I do believe I will have good dreams tonight.*

The Captain was up early the next morning. His life had changed. He didn't know how exactly, but he felt different somehow. His officers were already at breakfast when he arrived. Patrick had filled them in on the strange behaviour of the Captain the night before.

"Top of the morning to you."

The men at the table froze. "See what I mean," whispered Patrick. "Morning, Captain."

"Sleep well, Patrick?"

"Like a baby, sir. And you?"

"Wonderful dreams, just wonderful."

The Captain's new personality didn't last long. Only two days had passed but Heman was miserable. No sign of any member of the Finley family. He had to do something. He did not know what, but something had to be done.

The crew wished he would do something as well. They never saw the Captain so jumpy. His temper was short, more than one of them had experienced it. "Someone is going to have to talk to him."

"Who?"

"Not me." Patrick was the first to decline the job.

"I think it should be between you two." Moses pointed at Henry and John Charles.

"Why us?"

"If we had Sir William here, we wouldn't be in this predicament. You two are higher up than us. So who is it going to be? "

"Draw straws," piped in Patrick.

John Charles pulled the long straw. "Wonderful, I didn't even get a turn to help Miss Elizabeth off the upper deck."

Henry shook his head. "I'll do it. As you know, I spent most of the day with her. At least until the Captain took her away to some garden."

"Looks like Miss Elizabeth has turned your head as well," laughed Moses. "This gets more interesting all the time. Are you going to have a duel with the Captain over this young lady?"

"Very funny, she may have turned my head, for she is a wonderful lady, but it looks like she has the Captain's heart."

"Aye, to that we agree."

"ENTER." Heman didn't realize his voice was so loud until it was out of his mouth.

"Captain."

Heman looked up, "Henry, what do you want? I'm busy."

"We need to talk, sir."

"Talk about what, Henry? Did they leave cotton some place on board or something?"

"No, sir."

"What then?"

"Well, we need to talk."

"You said that already."

"Yes, sir. I mean, sir, man to man or friend to friend, that kind of talk, sir."

"What the blazes are you talking about, Henry?"

"Elizabeth, sir. We need to talk about Elizabeth, sir."

Hearing her name, Heman dropped his pencil and fell back into his chair. "Has she sent a message?" sitting straight up in his chair again.

"No, sir."

"Then why do we need to talk about Elizabeth? Heman thought for a moment. "Oh, I see, now I see. Henry, you have fallen in love with her, and you want permission to see her?" Heman's jaw tightening in his face.

"No, sir, Captain. You have."

"I have what, Henry?"

"Fallen in love with Elizabeth, sir. It's obvious, sir, you have all the signs. Can't eat, sleep and all you can think of is her. And a little cranky too, sir."

Heman fell back in his chair again. "Is it that obvious, Henry?"

"Yes, sir, the crew has noticed."

"I can't keep anything from you, can I?"

"Why would you want to, sir? The crew is happy, and they will be rooting for you. Elizabeth is a fine woman."

"She is, isn't she?"

"Yes, sir, and, sir, what are you going to do about it?"

"I don't know. I have been waiting for a message or something."

"That is not going to happen, sir. That's not the way it's done. Ladies do not send messages. It's up to you to make something happen, sir."

"Right, Henry, and, since we are talking man to man as you put it, what should I do?"

"I'm sure you will think of something, sir. Now that I've got you going down the right road."

"Not a word to the crew."

"No, sir, but, sir, they already know. They will help any way they can."

"Oh great, that's all I need. Thank you, Henry, you may go."

"You're welcome, Captain, sometimes it's helpful to have someone to talk to, than just the *Lady Catherine*, sir." Henry left the cabin. Moses, Patrick and John Charles were waiting for a report.

"How did it go? Tell us."

"Everything went just fine," Henry answered as he walked past his comrades. "Just fine."

"Action. I have to take action." Heman wasn't sure if he was talking to *Lady Catherine* or himself. "Henry. . . . Henry." At the doorway, he met Henry coming, and Henry met his Captain going. "A carriage, order me a carriage, Henry."

"Yes, sir. May I ask where the Captain is going?"

"To the Textile Mill and I don't know when I will be back."

"Yes, sir."

The Textile Mill was not a mill at all. Heman's carriage pulled up in front of a three or four-story red brick building. The driver knew where to go, the corner of Cornwallis and Water Street. He was well aware of The Textile Mill. Heman climbed up the stairs to the front entrance. Letting himself in through the double doors, he entered a room crowded with spinning wheels of all kinds. Weaving machines turned the newly made thread into yards of material. It was clear to Heman they were working with wool. The material coming off the weaving machines was high-quality wool in black and navy blue. He stood for a moment, taking it all in. No one noticed his entering the room. This was understandable, for the noise was deafening with the clacking of the machines. Finally, a man of middle age came toward him.

"Sir, may I help you?"

"I would like to see James Finley."

"I'm sorry you will have to speak up."

"I would like to see James Finley. And if you could direct me I'd be obliged." Heman spoke directly into his ear.

"Mr. Finley's office is on the third floor. The staircase is at the other end of this room. Follow me and I will guide you." He spoke loud enough for Heman to hear.

"Thank you," Heman yelled as he followed the gentleman. "What will this material be made into?" He asked as they passed by weaving machines.

"Suits, men's suits."

The men climbed up a wide staircase. There were large windows along this wall to let in the natural light. Heman could see the city around them, right out to the Harbour. The farther they got from all the machines the easier it was to hear. "Second floor is the sewing department." A door was opened for Heman to view through. The noise changed to silence. Ladies sitting around a table of material were busy sewing garments together. Continuing to the third floor, Heman commented, "A lot of people work here, don't they?"

"Yes, sir, every person, including me feels a debt of gratitude towards the Finley family. Jobs are hard to find, and we are all thankful we can say we work for Mr. Finley. He's a good boss. Opening the door on the third-floor landing, Heman could see work being done on the great wooden tables. "This is our cutting room. Also, all the design work is done here. Mr. Finley's office is here to your left." A knock was made on the door. "Mr. Finley a. . ."

Heman volunteered; "Captain Kenney."

". . . A Captain Kenney is here to see you."

James Finley left his desk to meet the Captain. "Welcome, Heman, what a pleasant surprise."

"Hello, James, I thought I would come see for myself how a Textile Mill is run. Impressive, I might add. Your worker here has taken the time to show me around."

"A pleasure, sir. I will leave you two gentlemen to your business."

"Come in and sit down. How are you and your crew doing?"

"Waiting for a deal on exporting lumber back to Boston. That should take another three or four days."

"The cotton you brought us is top grade. The best we have ever seen."

"Thank you. I noticed downstairs you are using wool."

"Just changed over. Wool material will be needed for fall and winter. It gets mighty cold around these parts in the winter. I'm sure it is the same in Boston?"

"Like you said, mighty cold. When do you start working cotton?"

"January, February."

"The woolen material coming off the weaving machines is also top quality. Making men's suits, I'm told."

"Can't find a better suit in all of British North America."

"Why don't I take some back to Boston to sell in our store? My brother and I run the 'Irish Coffee Co.' William always says, 'You find it and I will sell it.'"

"Finley suits exported to the United States of America. My father and grandfather would be proud."

Heman kept looking out to the working area through a large plate glass window. He was hoping to see Elizabeth. "Are Mrs. Finley and your daughter working today?"

"Yes, would you like to see them?"

"Since I am here, I would like to say hello."

"Come with me. We will tell them the good news. Our suits being exported to Boston."

Heman's heart jumped, as his eyes finally tracked down Elizabeth. She was sitting at a smaller table working.

"Captain Kenney, how delightful. . . " Elizabeth began to leave her seat.

"Please don't let me disturb you." Heman was at her side.

"Not at all, how nice to see you again."

Heman was looking at her table. "What are you making?"

"Bonnets, of course. Don't you think they are the best bonnets you have ever seen?" Heman agreed they were. In fact, he was sure he hadn't seen anything like them before.

"Darling daughter, I have great news. Our men's suits are to be exported to Boston. Captain Kenney is going to take a shipment himself."

"That is wonderful, Father." *What about my bonnets?"*

"I will take as many as you can give me." Heman eagerly offered.

Elizabeth was clapping her hands. "Wonderful, how long do I have?"

"A week."

"Oh dear, just a week?"

"Yes, I'm afraid *Lady Catherine* will be on her way home to Boston at that time."

James hugged his daughter. "We will have to work overtime, won't we?"

"Yes indeed, Father, we will."

"I wouldn't want you to work too hard." Heman was worried that he wasn't handling this situation very well. His main interest was to see Elizabeth, and now she will be working the whole time. "Well, at least take Sunday off. We could have a picnic or something."

"Point Pleasant Park."[59] Elizabeth exclaimed, "Perfect for a picnic."

"Your mother can plan it," James added. "Captain, we will get back to you when the plans are made."

Heman felt that he was being dismissed. What else could he say? "See you Sunday, Elizabeth."

"Yes, of course." Elizabeth was already making plans, but not plans for a picnic. *How many bonnets do you think we can make in one week?* She turned to see her father and the Captain walking away. "But wait." Heman turned. Elizabeth was questioning, "How much?"

"How much?" Heman was confused.

"How much are you going to pay for my bonnets?"

"Heman laughed, "I'm sure we can come to a fair deal."

"Yes, of course." Elizabeth paused for a moment, "See you Sunday."

Only one more day, then *Lady Catherine* would be on her way back to Boston. Heman had already stayed longer than planned. But he couldn't help it. He wanted to be with Elizabeth. The thought of leaving and not seeing her was torture. Sitting on the storage compartment on deck, he was pondering what to do.

Cannon fire cut through the silence. Heman never failed to jump. Nine o'clock, I wonder what Elizabeth is doing right now? I am in bad shape, aren't I, *Lady Catherine*? I've decided one thing we are coming back. I thought you would be in agreement." 'BANG.' There are so many 'Booms' and 'Bangs' around here, how is a man to think?" He looked down to where his legs were swinging. Panic rose from inside him, and his breathing ended. Well, almost ended. The cotton was coming back, stuck in his throat. "Relax Heman." He was ordering himself to be calm. "Breath slow and easy. Take in the cool salt air. That's right, relax."

"Don't worry, I saw it. You wanted me to see it, didn't you, *Lady Catherine*? You will never let me forget, will you?" The ring, his foot hit the ring. "I know God, I really didn't forget. The bang, is that a message? I hear it. I will do something about it tomorrow. Yes, I will do it before we leave."

* * * * *

Heman was walking through Point Pleasant Park. Thanks to Elizabeth he learned the pathways well enough to find his way to the meeting place. There was some kind of mini fort. It was locked up and had not been used for years. It was round in shape. The walls, at least three feet thick, were made out of stone. He was meeting Thomas H. Jones.[60]

Today, being a Thursday morning, there were very few people in the park. In fact, Heman had seen one other person, and he was walking the opposite direction in which Heman was

206

going. This was a good place for a secret meeting. He placed himself on a park bench, where he could see anyone coming from the three different paths that led towards him. Heman was only there a moment, when he almost fell off the bench. A hand had touched him on the back. Turning around, he saw a Negro man standing right behind him.

"Sorry I startled you, Captain, but I had to make sure you were alone."

"How did you know I was a Captain?"

"I know everything, Captain Kenney. Been expecting a message from you for two weeks now. A letter from William Garrison[61] informed me you would be in my area."

"Then you must know when I arrived in Halifax, and what my business is while I am here."

"Yes, sir." Mr. Jones smiled, "She is a very beautiful lady, and I did worry that she may be a distraction to our cause."

Heman was almost angry. "I don't appreciate being spied upon. I am volunteering for this service. No one will make me do it. This business is between me and God, and no one else."

"I appreciate your concern, and I assure you, Captain, everything, including this meeting, is done in absolute secrecy. I also want to assure you that we appreciate your involvement in the Underground Rail Road. I hear you want to be a conductor?"

"I believe that is what they call it. I have an opportunity to help free these people. My schooner will be making more trade trips to Halifax from Boston. I'm willing."

"Can your crew be trusted?"

"When I tell them, Yes."

"Arrangements will be made for your passengers. Stations[62] will be contacted. You will be notified in Boston. Your code message will be the old Negro spiritual 'Steal Away, Steal Away.' Do you know of it?

"No."

Jones started to sing:

"Steal away, steal away.

Steal away to Jesus.
Steal away, steal away
I ain't got long to stay here.[63]

"That's a beautiful song, Mr. Jones. Very easy to remember. How many passengers will I have?"

"Up to twenty-five, no more. Larger groups are too high a risk. We don't want anyone to get caught."

"Will you meet me when I arrive in Halifax?"

"No, a white man will board your schooner. He will be using my name. Keep your passengers hidden until that time."

The meeting ended with a handshake. The Captain tightened his grip and began to speak:

May you be poor in miss fortunes
And rich in blessings.

May you know nothing but happiness
From this day forward.

May good luck be your friend.
In whatever you do.
And may trouble be always
A stranger to you.[64]

You speak in poetry?"
"More than a poem, Mr. Jones. An Irish blessing, sir."
"I've never been blessed by an Irishmen before. Thank you. I will remember the words."

* * * * *

Lady Catherine was leaving the Harbour. Heman was on deck as they passed George's Island. Looking over his shoulder, he could see the great Citadel on the hill. "Take care of her while I am gone." They passed McNabs Island, no wild horses could be seen, but Heman knew they were there. Just as he knew Elizabeth had taken his heart.

Farewell to Nova Scotia, the sea-bound coast
Let your mountains dark and dreary be
When I am far away on the briny ocean tossed
Will you ever heave a sigh or a wish for me?[65]

July 12, 1860

Dear Captain Kenney,

God's Speed on your journey back to Boston, may it be a safe one.

As a businessman, I would like to thank you for a shipment of cotton of such great Quality. May we do business again in the future. Also, your interest in exporting our suits has guaranteed my employees work over the winter.

I hope your visit to Halifax has been a pleasant one. May you return often.

Your kindness towards my family will not be soon forgotten. They still speak of the day of sailing and our get together in the park. How right Tom was, saying we would get along just fine. If you see my son in your travels, send my greetings.

It has been a pleasure meeting you. May our paths cross again.

Sincerely yours,

James Finley

CHAPTER TEN

Elizabeth, My Sweet Elizabeth

The excitement was rising to a fever pitch. A messenger had just delivered a letter to the Kenney residence on Franklin Street, in Boston from the Captain. He was expected to be back home around August 18. That being the day after tomorrow, Peggy was figuring, "We have just enough time to plan something special for his arrival. What should we do, Faye?"

"We have to do something! I feel like I have been cooped up in this house all summer." Faye felt she had been neglected. She was used to having lavish attention given to her by William and the Captain, but not this summer. William was so engrossed in his building projects with his Irishmen that he didn't have time for her. When he did come home, it was very late, and he was too tired to play Chess or do anything else. Even with Faye's encouragement, he only managed to eat and then find his bed and sleep.

Every morning he would pat Faye on the head and say, "Maybe Saturday we can make plans for an outing," but it never happened. And Sundays, because of the Sabbath law, one couldn't do anything but sit in the lawn chairs, where, again, William would fall asleep. He didn't seem to mind at all, but to

Faye, it was very frustrating. She thought she would burst if something didn't change.

Faye couldn't count on the Captain for that change. He was away all June and July. His chair remained empty, and she wasn't sure he lived there anymore. But maybe she was wrong about the Captain. Her mother's enthusiasm was catching. Yes, they needed to plan something special.

Duncan walked into the kitchen, "What's all the excitement?"

"Captain is coming home. We need to do something special. Do you have any ideas?"

Duncan was happy to see his daughter interested in life again. The Kenney brothers had spoiled her, making her life difficult when they weren't available to her. "Just having everyone together at dinner would be special enough to me. And you don't know the Captain's plans, nor do you know if Mr. William can take time off. We are very busy filling in another cove. He has a hundred men depending on him for work. Daughter, you forget these are working men."

Faye hung her head, her lip came out, and she felt tears sting the corners of her eyes.

"I understand what you are trying to do, Duncan," Peggy replied, "but you don't have to be so hard on your daughter."

"I'm just trying to show her the real world."

"Father, you are right. I will try not to mope around and find something useful to do." Faye couldn't stand for her father to be upset with her.

"That's my girl."

"Come with me to the kitchen, Faye, we will begin planning that special meal." Peggy was trying to protect her daughter from the harsh reality of life. Their family had it easy since coming to work for the Kenneys. Duncan had not forgotten the hard times they had in Ireland. It was with God's grace they survived at all.

The hard times were not remembered the evening when all the chairs were filled around the dining table. William made a toast to his brother, "Welcome home, and may your chair not be empty for a long time."

"I will drink to that." Duncan raised his glass to the centre of the table. Everyone followed.

Faye raised her ice tea, "Welcome home, Captain."

"Thank you for welcoming me home. Peggy, this is a feast to remember, I will think of it when I eat my rations at sea. And my favourite food, Mock Goose, and it's not even Christmas. Irish Taffy[66] – I haven't had any since I was home in Ireland."

"I made it." Faye wanted everyone to know. This was the changed Faye. Her father's words awakened something inside. It was time she grew up. She was trying to be useful. Faye definitely thought Irish Taffy was useful.

"Tell me, Faye, what have you been doing this summer?"

"Nothing," she blurted out.

"Faye," scolded her father.

"I mean, I've tried to be useful," and she ended that with a huge smile, the same kind of smile a famous person would use when having her picture taken for the newspaper.

Duncan changed the subject, "Tell us about your trade route to Halifax."

"Yes, brother, tell us about Halifax." This was the first time William had the chance to talk to Heman since he arrived home.

"I do believe the British air was good for me."

"Tell us an adventure you had, Captain. I like real stories rather than reading books." Faye was still having a problem projecting a positive attitude, but she was trying.

Heman thought for a moment. "I have just the story."

"Is it real?" Faye excitedly inquired.

"It's real, 'for real,'" answered Heman. This made everyone laugh, including Faye. He began his story: "The *Lady*

Catherine was sailing into Halifax Harbour. On an island at the mouth of the Harbour was a gun battery. Henry saw it first."

"What's a gun battery?" Faye didn't want to interrupt, but couldn't help it.

"A platform for a cannon."

William was grateful for Faye's question. He did not know what a gun battery was either. "Was there a cannon on it?"

"Yes, now can I get back to the story?"

"Oh, yes, go on!" Faye was already pulled into the story and wanted to know more about the cannon.

Heman continued, "Then Moses cried, 'Take a look to our left.' Upon a hill was not only another gun battery but soldiers practicing their drills."

"What kind of soldiers?"

"They were British soldiers straight from England, William." Heman threw his brother a sheepish grin. "Moses made mention of you at the time. He said it was a good thing Sir William wasn't here." Heman laughed. William did not think it was funny. Duncan, Peggy, and Faye didn't know what he was talking about.

"Back to the story, Heman," urged William who didn't want to get into his past.

"Now, where was I? Oh, yes, two cannons. Well, Moses wanted to raise a white flag, and Patrick thought we should shoot first until he remembered we only had ten muskets on board. He figured if we used them, our range would be 300 yards. In the meantime, the cannons would blast us out of the water. That was when I stepped in like a Captain should. I said, 'Whoa, boys, let's not start a war with England.'"

There was laughter from all seats at the table.

"The story doesn't end there. Henry was glad we didn't shoot first, because he cried, 'Look up there!' Upon the hill overlooking the town of Halifax was a huge fort, Citadel Hill, crawling with British soldiers. When the Harbour Master came aboard, I asked him about those cannons. He assured me that the cannons had not been used for twenty years."

"What a nice story." Faye was well satisfied.

"No, wait. There is still more. The next day Henry and I were in my cabin going over the accounts for our cargo. When 'BOOM.' We thought a war had started. I was not sure if the cannon was shooting at us or not. . . . ." The story continued.

They were still laughing. "I've never seen you embarrassed, brother. What a sight that would have been."

"And a wharf rat?" Faye seemed interested.

"His name was Ian Schaeffer, a young man who does not have much in life. Moses made sure he was well fed while we were there. Worked hard for it too."

"What will happen to him now?" Faye looked concerned.

"I don't think you have to worry so. He told us he got by."

This growing up thing was hard for Faye. She looked around her and could see how God had blessed her whole family. She barely remembered the hard times, but hearing about the wharf rat made her determined not to act like a spoiled girl.

"Heman, I hope you brought something for us to sell at the Irish Coffee Company. Inventory is down. All we are selling is Irish Coffee."

"Lumber – lots and lots of lumber. *Lady Catherine* is full of it.""Great, I can use all the lumber you can give me. Duncan and I are building for the City of Boston now. We cannot get enough lumber. They can't cut it fast enough for us. We will get a great price for your lumber. Duncan, we are going to be busy making money now, aren't we?"

"That means we can hire more Irishmen," Duncan added.

"Yes, we can."

"That's it?" William was questioning Heman. "Just lumber?"

"I have men's suits, men's work clothes, and lady's bonnets."

Peggy finally found something of interest to her. "Bonnets? Ladies bonnets?"

"Best bonnets I've ever seen. And, Peggy, for cooking me such a great Irish meal as this, you can pick one as a gift. You too, Faye. The whole lot will be delivered to the Irish Coffee Company in about two days."

"Speaking of Irish Coffee," William added, "why don't we have some out on the front stoop? Heman, we have a lot of catching up to do."

There was a briskness in the air, as they sat watching life playing out in front of them on Franklin Street. Heman saw a couple walking. They probably didn't have a destination; they were just walking, just like he did with Elizabeth. He loved to walk with Elizabeth. That was the only time they had to themselves. It had been a week since he saw her. It felt like a year. Heman thought, *I must write her a letter. Yes, that is what I will do, before the day is over.*

"I think you have changed, big brother. There is something different about you somehow." These statements brought Heman back to the present. "Your health? Are you breathing well these days?"

"Breathing just fine, William."

"I thought so. You look healthy. You have more colour in your face. There is something different in those eyes."

"William, have you lost your mind? Maybe you have been working too hard."

"You look calmer, in a more confident calmness and a spring in your step. I saw it this evening. Heman, walk for me, just to the sidewalk and back."

"Now for sure, I know you have lost your mind. No, I will not walk for you. If people were to look, they would think we both had lost our minds. I'm not sure about you, but I know I have not lost mine."

"See, that's what I mean. You're confident. You have a mission, a life-changing mission. Is it the Underground Rail Road?"

"Shh! Someone might hear you. I may be involved in what you just mentioned, but I don't believe I would call it a life's mission."

"Well, it is something," William retorted. "You are keeping something from me. I can feel it. See, those eyes are doing it again."

Heman quickly turned his head. William was quiet for a time. Heman was grateful for it. He sat back in his chair and looked up into the sky watching great white clouds passing by and thinking of Elizabeth.

"I know it!" cried William in a loud voice.

Heman jumped, "Know what? And do you have to be so loud? People are beginning to stare."

"I knew it; I should have gotten it sooner. All the signs, well, most of them." William sat up and looked right into Heman's eyes. "A Woman. You met a Woman!" Heman turned red.

"I knew it; it took me a while, but I figured it out. You stayed longer in Halifax because of a woman."

Heman closed his eyes and willed his face to return to a normal colour. Before he reopened his eyes, words were coming out of his mouth. "She's wonderful, William. I've never met anyone so special."

"Congratulations," smacking his brother on the back. That opened Heman's eyes and almost knocked him to the ground.

"She's wonderful; I fell in love with her the moment I met her."

"Isn't that kind of soon?"

"Those are the same words I spoke to *Lady Catherine.* 'How can I fall in love in one day?'"

"Are you still talking to that schooner? And you think I have lost my mind. You have it bad. What's her name?"

"Elizabeth, Elizabeth Finley. Elizabeth, my sweet Elizabeth. Just speaking her name makes me swoon."

"Heman, men do not swoon, ladies do."

"I have to go back. I must make a trip before winter."

"What are you going to take to trade? You do not have any cotton. Cotton will not be ready for another two months."

"I know, I haven't figured it out yet. But mind my words, I am going back before winter." Heman was grateful to have someone to talk to, at least someone who talked back. He emptied his heart to his brother, telling everything he knew about his sweet Elizabeth.

William was happy for his brother. He listened quietly while Heman spoke of his true love. At the end of the story, William felt a little nervous. He had one question for his brother. "Heman, you spoke of your great love for this Elizabeth, but not once have you mentioned her love for you. Can you explain?"

Heman was quiet for some time. William was actually patient with him and figured he would speak when he was ready. "She doesn't know."

"Do you mean to tell me that you have found the women of your dreams and she doesn't know?"

"That is why I have to go back – I need to tell her. I think she could learn to love me. I would give her all the time she would need."

"You don't know much about this do you, big brother?"

"About this, what do you mean?"

"It won't just happen. You have to make it happen."

"That is exactly what Henry said."

"Henry – you have had help from Henry?"

"And the crew."

"Don't tell me – *Lady Catherine* too?"

Heman had a hopeless look come over him. "Don't worry, big brother, it is a good thing you have friends, and me. Everything is going to work out just fine."

Heman didn't sleep well that night. He had tried to write a letter to Elizabeth. There was so much he wanted to tell her, but he was afraid. Maybe she would think he was crazy and maybe he was losing his mind. He wasn't sure himself.

The next morning he was looking for coffee. His head hurt, and he didn't seem to be feeling well. *Maybe Irish Coffee is what I need,* he thought. *It is only 7:00 a.m. Peggy will not be serving Irish Coffee at this time. Maybe it's my asthma?* He took two large breaths of air into his lungs. It did not hurt and the air came back out just fine.

"Good morning, Captain, sit right down here and have some coffee." Peggy was singing a tune. He did not remember Peggy being a singer. In fact the longer he listened, he knew why she didn't sing very often. Every other note came out flat as a pancake.

"Peggy, please, my head." Heman couldn't stand it any longer.

"Sorry, sir. What you need is a good breakfast."

"Coffee will be fine, Peggy, at least until my head stops spinning."

The kitchen door swung open and in marched William. "Good morning, brother. Oh, dear you do not look so good." Turning to Peggy, "I told you he had it bad."

Heman looked at them both. "Oh, Oh." And let his head fall into his hands on the top of the table.

"That is okay, Captain, I already knew. Women always know. Soon as you stepped through the front door last evening I knew."

Heman moaned again. "Everyone in the whole world knows, all except sweet Elizabeth."

"Don't worry, Captain, we are going to teach you all we know."

"That is what I am afraid of," groaned Heman.

"Not to worry; everything is going to be just fine." Peggy held to her promise, and to Heman's amazement, it made sense. Peggy helped him write his first letter to Elizabeth.

"We have to start at the beginning, Captain. I hear she does not know of your love. Tell her about your trip to Boston. No pirates got you. Then, tell her the weather in Boston. Tell a little about your family and the special dinner they had for you. Not too much, you don't want to bore her. Then speak of her bonnets – how all the ladies of Boston are wearing them."

"We only sold two, Peggy."

"She does not know that; give it time, they will catch on. Faye and I love our bonnets and everywhere we go, the ladies ask where we got them. Captain, let us get back to the letter. End your letter with, 'I miss you,' nothing more. Now that I have you wound up, you are on your own. You will not need any more help from me."

How right Peggy was. That was four letters ago. Three received from Elizabeth. Heman read them nightly. It felt like a part of Elizabeth was with him. Heman was working hard to make plans for a return trip to Halifax before winter. Two days after arriving back in Boston, he set up a dinner for Charles and Caroline Drew. Heman was happy when a message was returned from Madame Caroline.

Dear Captain Kenney:

What a surprise to hear from you. Much too long of a time since we have seen each other. Charles and I accept your invitation for dinner at the Kenney residence on Franklin Street. We will see you on Friday, September 1 at 6:00 p.m.

Until then,

Madame Caroline

Heman sent another message to Captain Freeman and his wife. He requested their presence at a dinner held at the Kenney residence on Saturday, September 2 at 6:00 p.m. He was thrilled when an answer returned. They would see him at his residence on the evening of September 2 at 6:00 p.m.

Peggy was far from high society. Anyone from the Irish community in Boston would tell you. Even back in Ireland – what pretty things she had were passed down from grandparents and great-grandparents. Such as the candlesticks her Granny May had given her when she married Duncan. They only used them for special occasions like Christmas. The candlesticks along with everything else they owned were sold during the potato famine to make passage to Boston. She sighed as she walked through the Kenney brother's dining room for the second time. "This just won't do," she was talking to herself. "The mismatched plates and silverware did not bother the Kenney brothers, but for a dinner party?" Peggy had taken it upon herself to buy a piece of green material with tiny white flowers to cover the table that William had hauled in from no telling where. The small tablecloth reminded her of the heather growing on the moors back in Ireland. She was standing in the middle of the room with her hands on her hips, stamping one foot, still thinking out loud, when she heard a voice at the doorway behind her.

"Looks like you are catching flies and one is avoiding you?" Heman questioned. "Can I be of service?" He began looking around the room as Peggy was."

"Oh, no, Captain, no flies. If I should be so bold, Captain, does this room look like a place for a business dinner?"

"Never gave it much thought," Heman continued to look around.

"We do not have dishes, silverware, table linens." Peggy was just getting started. "Not to mention pictures on the wall, and look over there, five mismatched chairs."

"Where is William?" Heman thought he had better have a meeting with his brother.

"He and Duncan left for work two hours ago."

Heman stood there thinking for some time. "Well, thank you, Peggy, sometimes it takes a woman to point out the many flaws of a man. You are right. I believe our company would not be comfortable in this room. Looks like we need to do some shopping. If you will help me, Peggy, also Faye, let's make a day of it right after breakfast."

* * * * *

"Wow!" William was rubbing his eyes. "This doesn't look like my house. Duncan, do you think we are in the wrong house?"

Duncan did not say a word; he just looked at the new dining room.

William turned around, "Must be the right house, there is brother reading his mail by the window."

Heman put down his mail, "Good afternoon, brother, have you lost your way?"

"It sure looks different around here!"

"Peggy, Faye and I have been shopping."

"We have had a wonderful day! Come look, William." Faye was tugging his arm drawing him into the new dining room. "Doesn't it look wonderful?"

"That it does, Peggy, did you have your hand in any of this?"

"Only a little; now it is ready for our dinner guests."

"We couldn't have company in if we didn't have a chair for them to sit on." Heman was standing at the entryway to the new room.

"I guess we couldn't, dear brother, I guess we couldn't."

Faye's summer days of boredom ended. Peggy needed her help in the kitchen. She never saw her kitchen so busy. Heman, not wanting to stress Peggy, hired two girls to help for the business dinners. Heman had to find cargo, and he had to find it quickly. He was determined to go to Halifax before winter.

Dinner with Charles and Madame Caroline was like seeing family again. Peggy outdid herself; all the preparations

224

were perfect. Heman insisted that Peggy, Faye, and Duncan sit at the table with his guests. The two hired girls served. They were all proud to sit in their new dining room. The dinner began with Leek and Potato Soup.[67]

"Charles, how is your Tool Company fairing?" Heman inquired.

"Interesting you should ask. We could make twice as many tools, but my trade route south has slowed down. I have too much inventory, just sitting in my warehouse. I may have to really slow down come winter. My men will be out of work, making it a hard winter for them."

"Charles, do not burden the Captain with our problems. We are guests at his table with his new family." Madame Caroline was eager to change the subject and very interested in his new family. "What do you do, Duncan?"

Duncan was not used to being the centre of attention, but working with William, he had learned to work with the public. "I work with Mr. William Kenney. Boston keeps us busy filling in the coves. William regrets he could not be here this evening. He had a meeting with the city council."

Charles was very interested in the Boston Project. "I have noticed you have changed the landscape around here."

"The Irishmen have built three new residential areas around Boston. More people are moving in every day." Duncan was always proud to point out the hard work the Irish did for Boston.

"What about you, Captain, what adventures have you been up to?" Madame Caroline took the role of keeping the conversation lively.

"Added another trade route, this time north to Halifax, Nova Scotia.

"British Territory?"

"Yes!" Faye interrupted, he has great adventures. Captain, tell her the story of the cannon."Meanwhile, the Dublin Coddle[68] was being served. Peggy was proud of her Irish cooking and made sure the girls served it properly.

"Maybe another time, Faye. I am sure Madame Caroline is not interested in cannons."

"Oh, but do tell, I am tired of stories from the factory."

Heman grinned at Faye. "Looks like you are going to hear it again."

"It is a great story and I love to hear it."

After the story, Heman brought the factory subject back up to Charles. "I believe I have a solution for your inventory problems."

"I am listening." Charles put his fork down.

Madame Caroline was enjoying the Irish food and asked, "Peggy, what did you say this was? It is delicious." While Peggy quickly told her the history of the popular dish called Dublin Coddle, the men continued to talk business.

"What did you have in mind, Heman?" Charles asked.

"The *Lady Catherine* is making another trade trip to Halifax, before winter. Why don't I take your extra inventory with me and sell it there?"

"Would you have a buyer?"

"I have a contact there, James Finley. I am sure he could find a buyer, and if not right away, he has a Textile Factory, where we could store tools in his basement."

"Did you hear that, Caroline? I do believe the Captain has saved the day. I will not have to lay my men off for the winter." Heman was happy as well. One step closer to sweet Elizabeth, but he had to find more cargo.

The next night Peggy prepared Colcannon and Creamed Haddock.[69] Heman and Captain Freeman took up their friendship as if they had only seen each other the day before. Peggy made sure that Captain Freeman's wife, Marie, felt welcomed. Even William was able to join them. After a delightful evening of conversation, and as the double layer chocolate cake was being served for dessert, Heman asked his friend for a favor.

"What can I do for you, Heman? Just ask and it is yours."

"So kind of you, Captain, but maybe you need to wait until you know what it is I desire." Both men were laughing. "Captain, I need cargo."

Freeman looking concerned, "Is your business having difficulties?" That was hard for him to believe.

"No, we are doing well. I want to make one more trade trip north before winter. There is no time to go south to pick up cotton. I need something from Boston to take to British North America."

"Well, that is a relief. I would not want to see my friend having financial problems."

William was taking this all in. He smiled under his breath. His dear brother was working hard to get back to Nova Scotia. "I have an idea, gentlemen."

Heman looked to William, "And your idea is?"

"Boots, and lots of them. This is the time of the year to sell boots."

Heman and Freeman laughed together. "He is right, everyone in Nova Scotia needs boots in the winter. Let me look into it. I will see if we have a supplier."

A few days later a message was delivered to Heman from Captain Freeman. "I have found your boots! Walton Shoe Factory has boots and shoes of every kind and size. When do you want them delivered?"

Heman's return message was: *Lady Catherine* sailing Tuesday the 19th of September. Heman was a happy man. He wrote Elizabeth he was coming. Also, he wrote her father James, but this letter spoke of business.

Heman thought he would sleep well that night, but he was wrong. He ended up in the kitchen with Peggy holding a cup towel over his head. He was trying to breathe in the hot steam. The cotton was back in his lungs. Heman knew why; "I know, God, I promised."

"Are you speaking to me?" asked Peggy. She could not make out what he was saying.

Heman pulled the cup towel from his head, "No Peggy, I was talking to God. Thanks, I will be fine now." He went back to bed.

Heman took all the next morning to figure out what to do. He walked up and down the living room with his hands clasped behind his back. More than once he entered the kitchen. Peggy and Faye watched with concern. "Can we do anything for you, Captain?"

"No thank you, Faye, I am the only one who can solve this problem." He sat down at his desk and picked up his pen, addressing it to "Dear Mr. Garrison."

April 20, 1862

My Dearest Captain,

Every time I pass the Harbour I look for Lady Catherine. Not seeing the tops of her masts brings sadness to my heart, for it also means you too are far away.

I try to stay busy, Mother will not allow me to sit around and mope,(as she puts it). She insists I attend all events high society can offer. But I have no interest.

My interest lies with you and your adventures with Lady Catherine. I delight in every detail you write, telling me about the many cities you visit. I could grow jealous of Lady Catherine, she gets to share your days, where I only see you in my dreams. But I can't grow jealous, never, for she keeps you safe and one day will bring you back to me. I love the Lady Catherine, almost as much as you do.

I gaze out towards the mouth of the Harbour and beyond. Looking, searching for a schooner to appear out of the mist. I long for the day of your return.

May God keep you safe and may the ocean be calm and may your many voyages be full of adventure. Heman, I care greatly for you.

With Love,

Elizabeth

CHAPTER ELEVEN

Steal Away, Steal Away To Jesus

Heman was sitting at his desk by the window. His pen flew across the page. He finally had a plan. Heman sent for a messenger and his message went like this:

Dear Mr. Garrison:

I need passengers by September 19th. The price of passage is a steal. We go away towards the horizon for a great adventure. Please join me.
Yours Truly

Captain Heman Kenney

Now all I have to do is wait, thought Heman. *"Okay, God I cannot just wait. Preparations need to be made. I'm on my way to Lincoln Wharf."*

The whistle sounded as he crossed the gangplank to *Lady Catherine*. She was beckoning him along. "I know, I am taking care of it."

Henry was quickly at the Captain's side. "I want a meeting of the officers in ten minutes, Henry."

"Aye, aye, sir."

Heman entered his cabin. "See, God, I am doing it. I cannot back out now." Leaving his cabin, he entered the dining area. Henry, John Charles, Patrick, and Moses were sitting around the table waiting for him. "Close the door and shut the portholes."

Something was up; the men had never seen their Captain so serious. They thought trouble was brewing as they closed the door and shut the portholes. "The *Lady Catherine* will sail Tuesday, September 19th. Our cargo will be tools, boots, and slaves."

After an eerie silence, Moses shook his head. "I don't believe I heard you right. The cargo I mean, tools and what?"

"Did you hear?" The Captain questioned Henry.

"I believe so, sir."

"Repeat it to Moses."

Henry turned to Moses, "I believe the Captain said, 'tools, boots,' and if I am not mistaken, 'slaves.'"

"That's right, Henry." The Captain continued, "Now this is what has to be done." Heman was going to explain the plan.

Moses did not let him say another word. "Sir, we have done that once, and once was too many. It almost killed you. If you continue on with this, I will head up a mutiny. I am saying so right now, either a mutiny or I quit."

Heman could tell his officers were not with him. "Moses, before you jump ship, hear the plan. We are not going to sell slaves; we are going to free slaves."

"God, have mercy," Moses replied. His mates could see he was about to cross himself. Watching Moses carefully, and in unison, they all crossed themselves with Moses.

"*Lady Catherine* would never have allowed selling slaves, Moses. She would have scuttled herself first. This is her idea; maybe she is helping to cleanse our souls. We have an opportunity to free slaves, and we are going to take it. The

Underground Rail Road, have you heard of it? There was just silence. Let's start there. . ."

After the plan was revealed, the Captain asked for a vote. "Those who are in agreement, raise your hands. If anyone does not agree, they can sit this voyage out." Everyone raised their hands.

"Remember one thing: secrecy is of the utmost importance. Absolutely no one is to know. Do I make myself perfectly clear? Can we trust the crew?"

"Do you even have to ask?" Patrick was speaking up for his comrades.

"I had to ask, but I already knew the answer." Heman glanced at Henry, "Call a meeting of the crew. We will meet below deck in fifteen minutes."

"Aye, aye, sir."

This time when Heman told of the slaves coming aboard The *Lady Catherine*, he was careful to inform them it was to free slaves, not to sell slaves. The preparations began. A secret room was made right in the middle of the cargo bay. Crates of boots and shoes would have to be moved to open the door. The ventilation holes were still there. Proper hatches were made on deck to cover them. Bunk beds were erected, enough for twenty-five people. Mattresses of straw and colourful quilts were added for warmth, and they gave it a homey feeling. A table large enough for all to eat together was placed in the middle of the room. In the corner, a privacy closet was made. Two lanterns were hung from the ceiling. To top it off, a shelf of books was ready for those who could read.

"What do you think, Moses?" Heman was inspecting the work.

"Looks like a hotel. Much better than the poor creatures had the first time, Captain."

"We have to look to the future, Moses. We cannot do anything about the past." Heman raising his eyes, "God, we are ready. The rest is up to you; keep our passengers safe." Heman looked at Moses, "Now, we wait."

That night while reading Elizabeth's letters, his mind was never far from his passengers. This was dangerous business, and he realized if caught he and his crew would go to prison. Not only that, they might take *Lady Catherine*. Heman was not afraid. He felt a sense of calmness that even he thought was a little eerie, but he knew he was doing the right thing. After eating dinner that evening, he told William about the plan. William was surprised that part of Heman's cargo was to hide and free slaves. He would stand by him. Now all Heman could do was wait.

Turned out the wait was not very long. The next day a message arrived:

Dear Captain Kenney:
Passengers delighted for a great steal. They are ready to go away with you on the day of departure. You will hear again from them soon.
Yours Truly,

William Garrison

* * * * *

William Garrison was very surprised to get a message from Captain Kenney. He was told to expect to hear from him, but he didn't think it would happen until spring. He was delighted with the plan and got to work on preparing for a number of passengers. Traffic in the Under Ground Rail Road was at its peak for this year. Everyone made a run for freedom before winter set in. He had to communicate with stations and other conductors. Fifteen days was short notice, but knowing he had a backlog of passengers, he could easily fill the quota of twenty-five. It was dangerous keeping passengers in one station for too long, and he was happy he could move them. Nothing was kept in writing; that is why the Underground Rail Road was so successful. Information was passed on by word of mouth only.

William Garrison had a very good memory, but even he had to make a list once in a while. This was one of those times. The first passenger to come to mind was James Banks.[70] He wrote down initials only. J. B., Anthony Burns, A.B., and Iskar Istroyer, I.R. They all had a story to tell, always amazing Garrison how they ever survived the journey. When he met James Banks for the first time, he took the half-starved man to the side of the room and asked him if he would tell his story.

The weary dark brown sunken eyes looked straight at Garrison, "It's a long story; you have time Master Garrison?"

Garrison had to correct Banks. "I am not your master, and you will be free soon."

James Banks lowered his head, "My tongue won't quit saying, Master. Thank you, Mr. Garrison, for helping me get free, but I'm not free yet."

"I have time, James, as long as it takes. But if you don't want to tell me, you are free to say 'no'."

"Never been free to say 'no' before. Every time I say 'no,' I get a hit across my head. But knowing I am free to say 'no,' I choose to say 'yes.' I will tell you my story, and, Mr. Garrison, you tell my story to the whole world. Maybe it will help some other poor Negro that is still a slave down there in the south."

"It started when I was tired, so tired of being whipped for no reason. No reason. The overseer made his move towards me and said, "Lay down that pick, and cross your hands." I said, "I have done nothing, and I do not mean to let you whip me for nothing." He then called to the other men to come and assist him. The men gathered around me, but they all remembered what I had said the day before, that I would kill any man of them who should assist in overpowering me, and they were very shy. The overseer shouted them on and yet they did not take hold of me. M'Kalpin came with his large bully stick, which he leveled at my head, but he missed. I seized hold of his club as he struck at my head, and as quick as thought snatched it from his grasp, and sent him down to the dust. I must truly and freely confess to you that I was a desperate man. So I left my master M'Kalpin and his overseer literally crawling about on the ground like a pair of rickety boys. . . .

"The first point I made for was the cane break swamp. This was a very extensive tract of land, mostly underwater and overgrown by the common reeds of which canes are made. On my way to this break, I took my way into a small stream of water. This stream varied from four to twelve inches in depth. This would be the means of defeating the bloodhounds, as they cannot scent in the water. About two or three o'clock in the afternoon, I heard the sound of the horns, and the yelping of the hounds; but from the sound, I knew they were not on my track, so I took encouragement for the night. When the night came on I took again to the road; and having remembered the direction in which I heard the running of the (railroad) cars, and watching the north star, I set out for my journey."

Garrison remembers looking into the dark eyes of this giant of a man as he continued his story. You could tell he was reliving every moment. The nightmare played on.

"My journey lay through a very large track of the cotton country. Many a day I lay in the hot broiling sun watching the movements of the cotton gangs at work. One day I saw a gang of about forty cotton pickers under their overseer, coming in the direction where I was; and such was my location, that had I remained still, they would have come right upon me, so I had to crawl crosswise the rows of cotton so as to clear them. I could not stand on my feet, as they would see my head; and in crawling on my hands and knees, I could not help making a track by breaking down the cotton, and thus tracking them after me. It was a critical moment for me. When the gang came up, I was all of a tremble, expecting every moment to hear the overseer say -- "Who has been in this cotton, breaking it down in this way?"

Banks was now sweating and his eyes looked past Garrison. Garrison was living the experience with him. "Go on Banks," he encouraged.

"On the 15th of the month, while lying in ambush in a thickly shaded place, I espied (saw) a colored man passing near to me. He remained with me that day and night, and we traveled together. The next day we encamped in a place where we found a great many hazelnuts; of these, we ate freely and filled our pockets. But by this time such kind of food did not nourish me, and I found my strength failing me daily. We started out early that night with a determination that we would stop at some farmhouse and ask for food.

"My friend went first quietly up and looked about the cabins. He returned and reported to me that he saw no one but two colored women. I then went myself: but before I got to the cabin door I met an Irishman, whom I asked for a piece of bread. He told me to go into the cabin, and the women would give me bread. I went in; and while they were getting the bread, I found the cabin door blocked up by some twenty or thirty men. The principal man came up to me with a pistol, which he presented at my breast, and ordered me to surrender on pain of death. I was taken and put in irons; a blacksmith was called to fasten them on my limbs. We were required to tell from whom we had escaped, and all about ourselves. Both of us were locked up in a room and watched that night, and the next morning we were placed in a jail to await our owners. Here we were to be kept twelve days.

"Was it comforting having a traveling companion?" Garrison brought Banks back to the present.

"Maybe a little, but I had to lead; I didn't lean on anyone. And that is why on the night of the eleventh day of our imprisonment, there being six others with me in the same cell, I gave directions to each man to take his shoes in his hand and follow me. The order was to creep barefooted down the steps. The jailer lived below, and he had a watch of several men in the backyard, so that the thing had to be done very stealthily. I then lifted the old door off the hinges. I looked out and saw the watches sitting on a pile of wood. Just as we were about to descend the stairs an Irishman, who was in the next cell, gave the alarm upon us. We ran scattering for about half a mile, till we got to a small wood on the road, when we came together. About midnight we made the railroad again, and laid our course once more to the north.

"I heard the sound of a person walking and secreted myself in some bushes close to the road, so as to see whether the person was white or black. I soon discovered that it was a black man. He was a slave in the neighborhood going four miles on that road to visit his wife, who belonged to a different master. We gained valuable information from him in regard to our whereabouts, and the proper way to conduct ourselves. He informed us that we were about forty miles from the river; and when we crossed he warned us that we would be in danger of being taken, nearly as much as in the Slave States. He stated that he himself had once escaped from his master, and after crossing the river he was arrested and taken back, only after three days.

"The river rolled her sullen waters along in nature's own majestic style. I placed the men in a position where they would not be easily seen, and with my heavy stick, I went some distance up the shore, where I found a boat locked in a quiet place. With the use of my stick, I loosed the boat. Returning quietly back, I assured my men that I was ready to take them over. Having been reared on the banks of the old Shenandoah river, I was at home in a small boat, and a pair of oars in my hands.

"The part of the country we were in is inhabited a good deal by Kentuckians and Tennesseans, or settlers from those States, who watch for and catch escaping slaves, mainly to get the rewards offered for them. Feeling very much the need of food, and coming to a house, which we found to be occupied by a free colored man, we made application to him for food. He welcomed us in with the greatest apparent cordiality, and he said he knew our condition and sympathized with us. He ordered his wife to get us something to eat, and he went out, saying he was going to get some whiskey for us, that we must be cold and in need of it. After being gone awhile he came back and said he could not get the whiskey, as they had shut up. Supper being ready we sat down and were eating when there came a knock at the door. The door was pushed open, and, behold, a gang of enemies stood before us. The number I could not be certain about, but it was large, and they were all armed with guns. I knew at once that we had been betrayed by our black host."

"A freed coloured man actually betrayed you?" Garrison couldn't help but say.

"Couldn't even count on our own kind." Banks with angry eyes was shaking his head.

"We were confined in the Smithland jail, in Kentucky, seven months and two days. The life in this jail was more like a place of punishment than a place of detention, for it seemed to them that the worse we were treated the more likely we would be to tell where we came from. Our seat was the floor. Our bed was one blanket each and the floor. When we entered the Smithland jail our only hope was in strict secrecy in regard to our owners, not to tell their real names or place of abode. We might just as well turn and go back home ourselves, and better, because it would save the masters expense and would be likely to save us severer punishment.

"I came to the conclusion that my only hope was to get out of the jail, and that as soon as possible. So I set about examining every part of our cell with this view. The structure of the jail was a log cabin interspiked, and the whole enclosed by a brick wall, some eighteen inches in thickness. The plan was first to burn through the log a space large enough to admit a man's body, and then to make use of the spikes in working through the brick wall. One night the jailer left a candle burning in the entry at the head of the stairs. We had a pole in the cell used for cleaning a vent; attaching a piece of cotton to the end of this, and extending it through the door to the candle, I got fire, and I now felt more confident than ever of success. We were allowed water in the jail, and in burning through the logs I could manage to keep the fire in bounds by occasionally applying water just where

I wanted to restrict its progress. To prevent it blazing up, or smoking too much, I would let the ashes accumulate so as to suppress both smoke and blaze, something after the manner of burning charred or pit coal. On the third night, about eleven o'clock, in a pouring rain, we came out of Smithland goal, leaving the jailer and his family sound asleep. Being near the River, after looking along the shore for some time, we found a boat in which we crossed to the other side. Then I just kept coming north until your friend Mr. Smith found me half dead."

Garrison's memories were lost as his eyes focused on the candle burning and the pen in his hand wrote Garrison's name on the paper. *He has earned a chance at freedom,* Garrison thought as he continued the list. He looked at the name Ismary Introyer.

It was not just men who had a story. Garrison's mind took him from the present again. Ismary Introyer told her story as well. He remembered her quiet voice beginning, "It were so hard to travel, all by myself." She looked towards this white man William Garrison. She was told he could be trusted, but she was told that before. But she had heard the name at stations along the way.

"Go on," Garrison gently encouraged, "You do not have to be afraid."

With a quiet voice, she continued. "It took 89 long tiring days. I traveled through 23 swamps, and had nothing to eat, but grass, leaves, and the rare food I would get at a stationers house."

Garrison shook his head. "I must keep focused." Then kept making his list until late in the night. The Underground Rail Road was rolling, rolling along.

* * * * *

Finally, Heman received a message two days before time to sail. "Steal Rail Road arriving September 17, 1:00 a.m. Away they will be delivered is every two hours."

Heman told Duncan and Peggy he would be spending the night aboard *Lady Catherine* on Sunday. He assured them there was a lot of preparing to do before sailing the following Tuesday.

Mostly paperwork, but he did want a family farewell dinner on that Monday night. He did not want to surprise anyone by running to the dock in the middle of the night Sunday. Everything needed to run smoothly.

Sunday was a moonless night. There was no activity at the Lincoln Wharf. The *Alma* was at sea on a trade run. The crew was ready for the passengers. Heman gave orders not to whistle anyone aboard. When they arrived, the crew was to quickly and quietly take them below deck. He doubled the night watch to assist. They were to keep out of sight until they were needed. The activities on board the schooner had to look normal. Too much activity might cause suspicion.

Finally, at 1.15 a.m. a carriage pulled up beside *Lady Catherine*. Two men and a lady quietly stepped out and looked wildly around them. Moses was first in line for duty. He quickly crossed the gangplank. "May I be of service?" Those were the words he was instructed to say.

A large man with dark skin and even darker eyes in a low voice answered, "Steal Away; Steal Away to Jesus."

That is all Moses needed to hear. "Come this way quickly. Be quiet and do not talk." He led them across the gangplank. Each carried a bundle wrapped in cloth. It was everything they owned. Two crewmen appeared to help the three passengers with their positions. They were guided towards the hatchway leading towards the cargo bay. "Watch your step and be careful on the ladder." It was evident they had never been on a schooner before. The crewmen were very patient with them, as they cautiously made their way down the ladder. After the hatch was closed, they were then informed they could talk. But no one said a word.

"Welcome aboard The *Lady Catherine*. Accommodations have been prepared for you." He opened the door, James Banks, Anthony Burns, and Ismary Istrayer stood in silence taking in the room around them. They were speechless.

After a time James was the first to find words. "Anthony, I do believe we are in paradise and on our way to the Freedom Land." Anthony still had no words.

"You are the first of the passengers, so pick a place to your liking.

"You." They pointed towards the large man.

"Who me?"

"Yes, you."

"James Banks the name."

"Mr. Banks, you look like a leader. Be obliged if you organize them as we deliver the passengers to you."

"Yes, sir, we can do that."

"The Captain will give you instructions after everyone arrives. But in the meantime, please be quiet. The ventilation holes are open and sound may travel down the Harbour this time of night."

It was more than two hours later, 3.30 a.m. when another carriage arrived on the wharf. This time six passengers arrived: a family of four and two men. Heman was worried. The sun was going to rise in another two hours. Would the rest of the passengers arrive in time? Ten minutes later a wagon pulled up. Eleven people jumped off. This certainly was a mixed group. Children were guided by parents. Quiet was ordered, and not a peep could be heard as they were guided over the gangplank. Two were elderly and Heman wondered how they made the journey. It was quite evident the family was not going to leave them behind. Before the wagon was gone, a carriage pulled up behind it. Five more exited. That was twenty-five; Heman breathed a sigh of relief. "Quickly, get them settled and get that wagon and carriage out of here."

The crew had worked together and managed to get all twenty-five people stowed away in cargo. This was one of the happiest jobs they had ever done. The people were very grateful. It was 4.30 a.m. when the Captain stepped into the secret room. As he gazed around, he silently prayed, "Thank you, God, for the safe journey of these people. I need your help to get them to freedom."

The quiet whispers of these people went silent when they were aware of the Captain's presence. They were staring at each other for quite some time. Heman was taking in the energy within the room. Some were sitting at the table. Others, mostly children, were sitting on bunks. *These poor weary people,* he thought. Through their weariness, he could see the look of hope written on their faces. Happiness was also there, but not joy, not yet. These people were afraid to feel joy; they were not yet free.

"I am Captain Kenney. Thank God you have made the journey safely so far."

"Amens rang throughout the whole room."

"Welcome aboard *Lady Catherine*; she welcomes you. I and my crew welcome you. Before I let you rest from your journey, I need to share with you what will take place in the next two days. We need to work together for this to be successful. The next two days will be the most dangerous of the journey to Nova Scotia."

"Freedom Land" gently echoed through the room.

"We sail on Tuesday morning. You must stay hidden until Tuesday night. Boston is full of slave hunters. They would love to catch every one of you and send you back to your masters in the south. Believe me, we are not going to let that happen. For that reason, you must stay in this room. No one will enter or leave. You will be on your own. Everything you need is here. The air ventilation leads to the deck of this ship, which means sound can travel to the deck as well. In less than one hour, the wharf will come alive with workers. You have to make sure they do not hear you. After we make our way to sea, we will come and open the door. Do you understand?" Heman searched the eyes of the men present. His stare required each man to answer 'yes,' they understood. We must leave; the sun will be coming up any time now. When I close this door, crates of boots and shoes will be stacked four or five rows deep, hiding this secret room."

Before he left, Heman turned to the children. "Children, I look forward to getting to know you on the journey. I have a business deal for you." He waited until all the large brown eyes were staring at him. "You must be quiet and listen to the grownups. If you do this, when we get to the Freedom Land, I will give each of you a new pair of shoes." The brown eyes lit up like candles. Heman smiled at the adults. "Good luck," and he closed the door. The crew artfully placed the crates of shoes in rows right up to the ceiling. There was no sign of a room amongst the cargo.

Heman gathered around his officers. "Good job, boys. Do you think anyone was aware of what took place this night?"

"I placed watchmen on every corner of the ship. Out of sight, of course, and two on the wharf," Henry reported. "Everything was clear, sir."

"Good, now we will return to the regular night watch. All the other crew, including you, get a few hours of sleep. We will have a meeting at 8:00 a.m."

Heman was in his bunk watching the light cut through the darkness, finding its way in through the portholes. Monday morning he thought, *God, we made it through Sunday night, let us see what today brings. Keep us safe.* Of course, he did not sleep. How could he? His mind was racing, like one of William's racehorses. He planned to win this race. There was no coming second or third.

Not one of his officers looked tired. Heman was sure they had not slept any more than he did. They were ready to be informed about the next step of the plan. No one doubted the Captain had one, and they were eager to carry it out.

"Any sound from our passengers?"

"Not a peep," answered Patrick. "I have been walking back and forth by the ventilation hatch, testing to see how much I could hear. Not a sound I tell you. They must be used to hiding. No one is going to know they are here."

"Just to be safe, let's have four watchmen on duty at all times today. And pass the word to the crew to have a watchful eye. Anyone else have anything to report?"

"There is something." It was John Charles.

"What is bothering you?" the Captain wanted to know.

"One of the women is pregnant. Not that I know much about it, but it seems to me her baby is coming soon."

"I did not see a pregnant woman last night."

"Neither did we." Everyone was listening to John Charles.

"They did not want you to see."

"Who did not want me to see?"

"The other women; they were hiding her, or standing around her, so no one would notice."

"How do you know?"

"I helped her down the ladder."

"The room is sealed and has to stay that way. If anything happens, they will have to deal with it. I have to go back to my house. I will not be back until morning. Henry, you are in charge."

"Aye, Aye, sir."

* * * * *

The whole family was together for the Captain's going away dinner that evening. Heman thought he was a very good actor, because he did not feel like being there.

"How is your cargo?" William asked.

Heman jumped in his chair, but recovered and stared at William. "The cargo is stowed aboard ready to sail tomorrow."

Peggy noticed Heman was a little edgy. *Maybe he is nervous about seeing Elizabeth again,* she thought. "When do you see Elizabeth?"

"Yes, tell us when?" Faye added to her mother's question.

"All I know is I sent a letter telling her I was coming. I guess I will have to wait until I get there. Here, I will help you ladies clear the table." It only took two trips from the dining room to the kitchen. "Can I do anything else for you?"

245

"No, Captain, Faye will help me wash up. Faye, you start. Captain, can I have a word with you?"

"Of course, Peggy."

"Why don't we sit on the lawn chairs?" Peggy was leading the way. Heman just followed.

"Is there something bothering you, Peggy?"

"Not at all, Captain. But do you remember needing help writing your first letter to Elizabeth?"

"Of course." Heman squirmed in his chair a little.

"It may not be any of my business. But I do not think you know things, and if your mother were here, maybe she would tell you, or maybe she would not, but . . ."

"Whoa, Peggy. What are you trying to say?" Heman was nervous.

"Women, Captain, there is a proper way. And your loving this girl like you do, you need to do it the proper way."

"I am not sure I understand."

"Captain, you need to talk to her father."

"What about?"

"For permission to court her, of course."

That never even entered Heman's mind. Not that he had time to think of Elizabeth these last few days. "Are you sure?"

"Yes, you do not want to lose her, do you? You are in Boston most of the time, and she is in Halifax. You need to speak with her father. There I have said it." Peggy fell back into her chair fanning herself.

"Are you warm, Peggy?" Heman felt the coolness of the night. "Thank you, Peggy, I will think hard about what you said."

"I must get back to Faye," leaving her lawn chair as she spoke.

Heman sat there for a time. Summer was gone. The trees were just giving a hint of the magic they planned to reveal. *My life, what has become of it? More like a three-ringed circus. The show is about to begin in ring number three.*

* * * * *

The whistle sounded; everyone knew the Captain was on board. "Henry, meet me in my cabin. I need a report. How was it last night?"

"The watchmen report nothing out of the ordinary. As you can see, The *Alma* came in late, and it made us a little nervous. We have not heard any sound from below deck. Have you talked to Captain Freemen? He was asking about you."

"Was he on board?"

"Yes, an hour ago, but only as far as the gangplank. I told him you were expected anytime this morning, for we were sailing this afternoon. Should I send a message telling him you are here?"

"No, that will not be necessary. I met him on the wharf just before coming on board. He wanted to know if I heard the rumor of slaves being taken out of the Boston Harbour. The Harbour Master spoke of it when he docked. The Harbour Master was ordered to search every ship leaving port starting today."

"What are you going to do, Captain?"

"Nothing. We go on with the plan. However, spread the word to the crew that there might be a search of the ship. I want everyone to act normal, no surprises. Also, before the Harbour Master boards, close the hatch on the air ventilation."

"That is going to be hot for our passengers."

"It cannot be helped. We will open them again as soon as the Harbour Master leaves.

* * * * *

As soon as Heman closed the door to the secret room, James Banks took charge. "You heard the Captain. We are here for two days. Let us get prepared. Anthony, help organize where everyone will sleep. Ismary, you help the ladies. We need something to eat before the workers come to the wharf."

"Who made you the 'Master?'" A tall, dark man came forward from the corner. James could tell he was somewhere in his twenties. Dark eyes stared at him, and they were filled with hate.

"Nobody's Master, son. Especially not yours. How long you been on this journey, boy?"

"80 days and I do not trust you nor that white Captain."

"You know how to swim, boy?"

"I manage."

"Swimming in those swamps, not the same as swimming in the ocean. You do not have to trust me, but if I was you, I would trust the Captain. Captain put me, Anthony and Ismary in charge cause we got here first. If you got here first, you would be in charge. We all afraid here, every one of us. Didn't count, but I figure there is 20 or 25 of us. We work together, 25 of us will get to the Freedom Land. What is your name?"

"Jim."

"Where you from?"

"Don't matter where I'm from; it's where I'm going, all that matters."

"Well, Jim, from Freedom Land, come with me. We have work to do." James put his arm around the boy's stiff shoulders. "You been by yourself for a long time?"

"All I need is me."

"Me is kind of lonely, but I understand, Jim. It is hard enough to take care of me, without having to worry about anyone else. Your day of just 'me' is about to end. Freedom will see to that." James could feel the tension in Jim's shoulders relax, if only a little. "Come, let's see what kind of food we get to eat for the next two days."

Less than an hour later everyone was on a bed. James did not think it was going to be difficult to keep these people quiet. They were exhausted. Never had two days to rest in their whole lives. They would sleep most of the time. "Anthony, I believe we need to keep watch. You sleep first. I will watch a while." One lantern was left lit but only dimly. Everything was quiet. A few rays of sunlight made its way through the air ventilation, not enough to light the room but enough for James to know morning was here. He could hear horses pulling wagons, and men's voices greeting each other for another day's work. James knew if he could hear them, then they would be able to hear him. They had to be quiet. So far so good.

James noticed movement on the right side of the room. A man was tending to his wife and there seemed to be a problem. Ismary was on to it. A few moments later Ismary came towards James and whispered, "Mr. Banks."

"Do we have a problem, Ismary?"

"Yes, Mr. Banks. Over there." She pointed to the corner. Carl and Betsy Jones; his wife Betsy is in labour."

"She is in what?

"She's having a baby!"

"But no pregnant women are allowed to travel the Rail Road."

"I know, Mr. Banks, but I do not think that is going to keep this baby from coming. What are we going to do?"

"Have you delivered babies, Ismary?"

"No, sir."

"Go talk to all the women; there must be someone who can. Start with the mothers."

James made his way to the corner. "Mr. Banks, I am sorry, we could not just leave her behind. She is my wife, sir." Carl was pleading to James.

"Everything will be all right, Mr. Jones. We will figure something out. First thing we have to do is move you. Mrs. Jones, you do know you cannot scream? You do know that?" Betsy had her teeth clenched, so she answered by nodding her head.

Ismary arrived leading Jane, the oldest woman in the group. She and her husband were the elderly couple that wouldn't be left behind. "This is Jane; I hope she can help us."

"Seen a lot of babies born in my time. They just pop out. All you have to do is catch them."

James was not so sure, but Jane was all he had. "Ismary, we need to move them to the other side of the room. See who will trade with them. No children, Ismary, the vent is right above us."

Word spread quickly of a baby being born. All the ladies flocked around Betsy, hanging two new quilts for privacy.

Jim approached James. "What are you going to do about this? We cannot have a baby born. We will be caught for sure. I say kill her; that is the only way."

James stepped very close to Jim. His face was only inches from his. He whispered but it was more of a low growl. "There will be no killing. If you kill her, you will have to kill me first. Now you get on your knees and ask God to forgive you. You cause any more trouble and I will have you tied and gagged."

"I gave up on God a long time ago," replied Jim.

"That is why your eyes and heart are filled with hatred. It is time to give it up, Jim. You get free and you still be a slave. A slave to hate. If you are not going to help, you stay out of the way. From now on I will make sure you are watched every minute."

Groans were coming out of the corner from behind the quilts. Jane ordered, "Get me a wooden spoon."

"A wooden spoon?" questioned James.

"On the table, I saw a wooden spoon. Get it."

"Why?"

"She needs to bite on it, you fool. Quick before someone hears her." The spoon helped a little, but not much.

James turning to Anthony, "Quickly, we have to cover the air vent." A new quilt was stuffed inside the air ventilation.

"Are we going to die?" James was startled to hear the question. It came from a small boy.

"What is your name, son?"

"Eddie. Eddie Randle."

"How old are you?"

"Don't know for sure? Sold my mother when I was a baby. I tell everybody I am seven."

"Who are you traveling with?"

"Auntie Jane and George."

"No, Eddie, we are not going to die. You want to work for me? I do not have anything to pay you, but I need your help."

"George told me I had to do anything you say."

"Good then, if the children are not sleeping, I want you to gather them together on your bunk and quietly, very quietly, tell them stories about their new shoes. Can you do that for me?"

The day passed slowly. So did the labour. The air was hot and muggy. It could not be helped. No sound could travel to the upper deck. James could not tell for sure, but he thought the day had turned to night. Books were passed out. Amazingly, several could read. This helped pass the time. All of a sudden the boat started to rock. They were used to the subtle swaying, but this was a definite rock.

"What is happening?" Anthony was alarmed, "Are we leaving early?"

"Listen." They could hear shouting. "Throw the line." "I've got it." "Rope secured." Rope secured was called out four times. "The *Alma* is docked, Captain." "Call the night watch; the rest of the crew can stand down. . ." "Aye, aye, sir."

"Another ship has docked beside us. Stuff the quilt back," James spoke in a low voice. "They must not hear us."

* * * * *

"All crew on deck. Are we ready to sail?" Heman was calling the orders.

"Yes, sir, just waiting for the Harbour Master," Henry informed the Captain.

"Is he late?"

"No, I believe he has another ten minutes."

The Harbour Master arrived in five and he was not alone. "Captain Kenney, request permission to search your schooner?"

Heman was there taking charge. "Why do you wish to search my schooner? You have never searched my ship before. Is there something you know that I do not?"

"No, sir, only a rumor. Slaves are rumored to be in the Harbour. They are being assisted to run to freedom."

"Slaves, you say? I would think you a man who would be happy to assist anyone to freedom. Tell me more."

"That is not for me to say, Captain. My job is to stop it."

"A nasty job you have, isn't it?"

"Are you saying I cannot search your schooner?"

"No, sir, not at all. Be my guest. How long will this take? We hoped to sail on the high tide."

"Not long, sir."

"Henry, Moses, assist these gentlemen." Turning to the Harbour Master, "Do you require more assistance?"

"These two will be sufficient, thank you, Captain."

A search was made in the crew's quarters, galley, and even the Captain's cabin. When they returned, Heman asked, "Have you finished? Did you find any slaves?"

"No, Captain, but what about your cargo?"

"Tools and shoes. The cargo bay is full."

"Where is your destination?"

"Halifax, Nova Scotia. We hope to be there in a week. I am in no hurry. This will be our last trade trip before winter."

"Can we see?"

"See?"

"The cargo, Captain."

"Open the Cargo Bay hatch, Patrick."

The Harbour Master and two guards descended the ladder. All they saw were rows and rows of crated shoes. "Where are your tools?"

"To the back, sir." Patrick was leading them away from the shoes.

Heman held steady and stood in place waiting for the Harbour Master to return from the cargo bay. The crew remained poker-faced. But he knew inside, they were nervous as a long-tailed cat in a room full of rocking chairs. Thinking of cats, Heman was surprised when Patrick emerged from the cargo bay yelling to Moses, "Have you not fed the cat yet, Moses? Heard him down there. Maybe there are no rats to catch."

"That is a lazy cat. I have not fed him on purpose, and, yes there are rats down there."

"Rats?" The Captain thought he had better say something.

"Yes, rats, Captain, saw one yesterday morning. Hate rats, sir. I will shoot them 'rats' if I see them again."

"Moses, I do not think that will be necessary. The cat will do its duty. I am sure the Harbour Master and his friends have better things to do than chase rats. Am I right, sir? Have you gentlemen seen any slaves?"

"Captain, you are cleared to sail. We will escort you midway through the Harbour. There a tugboat will pick me and my men up."

"Drop sail," Heman ordered.

"Drop sail," echoed down the line.

"Cast Ho." The ropes from the wharf were thrown to the crew. The *Lady Catherine* slowly made her way out of Boston Harbour.

"Tugboat approaching starboard side."

"We will take our leave now, Captain. Sorry for the inconvenience."

"Not at all, sir, you are just doing your job."

The tugboat was 300 feet away from *Lady Catherine*, heading back into Boston Harbour. Knowing they were downwind, the Captain cried his order. "Open the hatches to the air ventilation." The crew was waiting for the order and the hatches were quickly opened.

Henry came up beside Heman. "Captain, I do believe we have done it. A little iffy there for a while. You handled it very well, sir."

"We are not out of the woods yet, Henry. I will be glad when we are farther north." Heman felt if he was going to err, he would err on the side of caution. He waited until 8:00 p.m. and no land in sight when he gave the order to unseal the door of the secret room. It was Henry, Moses, Patrick and two other crewmen who made a safe pathway to the door.

"Well, open it!" Moses was addressing Henry.

"Should I knock?" Henry was not used to opening doors to secret rooms.

"I do not think they will care," Patrick informed Henry. "Just open it."

Henry opened the door, and there in front of them stood all the men ready to jump whoever came through. Henry for his own safety quickly asked. "Are you okay? You are safe now. Everyone is safe. We are at sea. The next port of call is Nova Scotia."

"Freedom land!" The men lowered their weapons of wooden spoons, books, and even a few knives. They turned to each other and a roar of celebration rose up from the room. Women came out from the corners and children from under beds. They joined the men in celebrating.

"Now we can hear them," Patrick spoke in Moses' ear.

"Yes, and let them yell as much as they want. They have a right."

It did not take long for the officers and the two crewmen to be dragged in amidst the celebrating. They were in the middle of a circle, and the people with dark faces and dark eyes danced around them. And then a silence fell among them. At first, the men in the middle did not know why, then they saw their Captain standing in the doorway. He had a smile on his face, and when the noise died down, he said he came to see if his crew needed to be rescued. The crew was left and the Captain was now in the centre. Patrick thought they might worship him. But before that could happen, the Captain raised his hand for silence. "Now, bow with me as we thank our Heavenly Father for bringing us through this journey thus far." Some were on their knees. Others just bowed in respect. James could not help but notice that Jim was on his knees.

After the prayer, Ismary approached the Captain. She was carrying a baby, a very tiny baby. "Captain, I would like you to meet a new passenger. Number 26, James Kenney Jones. He was born free, sir."

Heman took the tiny bundle and carefully held him up high. "Born free, God. May all children be born free." Amens echoed throughout the room. Spontaneous singing broke out.

Steal Away, Steal Away

Steal Away to Jesus

Steal Away home.

Heman gently returned the baby to his mother. "How kind to name him Kenney."

"Never heard a better name," replied Betsy.

As the singing echoed out over the ocean and could be heard no more, the Captain got everyone's attention. "There is information you need to know. Depending on the wind, we will arrive in Halifax in five or six days. During the journey, you are free to be top deck anytime you please. Watch the children; we wouldn't want any accidents. If for any reason we need you to go back into hiding, the bell will ring three times, twice. Ring, ring, ring. Ring, ring, ring. When entering Halifax Harbour, you must be back into the secret room, until you are collected and taken to Africville,[71] where there is a thriving community willing to take you in and make your transition to freedom an easier one. For the safety of me, my crew, my ship, and the Underground Railroad, you will forget you knew us. You will remain in my heart forever; I hope you will do the same for me."

The journey continued, and it turned out to be an unusual one at that. There was a community on board. The crew tripped over children, as they carried out their daily chores. The Captain found a pretty curly headed girl no more than five sitting in his chair at his desk and in his cabin. All he could do was smile. The cook wasn't so patient. He swore if he caught any more boys searching for something to eat in his galley, he would cut them up and make soup out of them. The little boys believed him. John

Charles taught the men or whoever would listen all about navigation. And James Banks taught reading down in the secret room in the cargo bay. His table was always full.

Heman was on deck as they entered Halifax Harbour. The trees were changing colour, but everything else was the same, including the blue sky and blue water. The cannons were still in their place, and the great fort on the hill was guarding Halifax. It felt like he was coming home. This journey didn't give him time to sit around thinking of Elizabeth. Knowing he would see her soon made his heart beat faster.

The Harbour Master guided them towards the Queen's Wharf. *Lady Catherine* seemed to know the way. "Your cargo, Captain?"

"Tools and shoes. Mr. Finley will be meeting me."

"Fine, sir, have a happy visit to Halifax."

Lady Catherine had not been docked an hour when a man approached the gangplank. "Thomas H. Jones to meet with Captain Kenney."

Heman was impressed; the real Thomas Jones knew his business. "Follow me, Mr. Jones, we will meet in my cabin."

Before Heman could sit down, Mr. Jones inquired, "Your code word. I haven't heard your word, sir."

"Oh, I'm sorry, new at this you know. Steal away."

"I take it you had a safe journey?"

"We did – hairy at times, but we made it safely."

"Your passengers?"

"They are waiting to depart this ship."

"We will begin collecting at dark. Twenty-five is the number, correct?"

No, sir, 26."

Mr. Jones seemed rattled. Looking at his paperwork he replied, "I have 25 written here. Our figures are always correct. The numbers, unfortunately at times might go down, but never up."

"You tell Thomas Jones that this time he does not know everything. A baby was born on the *Lady Catherine* the first day out."

"A baby?"

"A baby – born free, James Kenney Jones."

Heman stood by the gangplank as every passenger left for freedom, each carrying a new quilt and their bundle of belongings. Inside the bundle, everyone, not just the children, were carrying a new pair of shoes. Heman suggested they wear them, but they wanted to wait until their feet touched the ground of their new home, and they were truly free.

After everyone had gone, Heman looked out at the Harbour. "We did it, *Lady Catherine*, we really did it." To God, he added, "It's not enough yet, is it?"

It was Sunday night, and Heman had a message from James Finley. They would meet tomorrow at the Textile Mill. Heman wondered what Elizabeth was doing. Maybe he would see her soon. He would find out tomorrow.

* * * * *

James Finley was surprised to get a letter from Captain Kenney telling him he would be in Halifax September 24-25. He was even more surprised to learn that Heman was bringing tools and shoes. What was he going to do with a warehouse full of such items? Had Heman forgotten he was in the textile business? Elizabeth had been running around the house like a chicken with her head cut off for more than a week. Something was going on here, and even James was smart enough to know what it was. He would not even think about it, until Heman made the first move. For that was the way things were done, wasn't it? He was questioning himself.

A knock at the office door and Heman entered at once, walking towards James with his hand outstretched. "James, it's good to see you again."

"And you, Heman. I was surprised to hear of your coming. I thought I wouldn't see you until spring at the earliest."

"Couldn't keep away." Heman hoped he didn't sound too crazy. "You get my letter?"

"Yes, of course. You brought tools and shoes?"

"That's right. I know you are not in the tool business, but shoes go right along with the suits you make. There must be somewhere we can sell those tools."

"Somewhere, I'm sure," agreed James.

"Is Elizabeth here?" Heman was looking out through the window again. "Your wife, Janet?"

"Not today, they are at home." Heman looked like air came out of a balloon. "But that's okay, Heman, they are at home preparing a meal for you this very evening."

Heman came to life again. "You must know, James."

"Know what, Heman?" James wasn't going to make it easy for the Captain. He was not ready to give away his daughter.

This is going to be harder than Peggy said, thought Heman. "Mr. Finley, I would like your permission to court your daughter."

James was relieved; he thought the Captain might ask for marriage. He could handle courting. Elizabeth's mother would be at his daughter's side at all times. He knew Janet.

"It makes me happy to hear of your interest in my daughter, Captain." James also added, "That explains your quick return to Halifax. Also, explains the tools and shoes."

"Yes, James, I mean, Mr. Finley. I have fallen in love with Elizabeth."

"More serious than I thought." James then asked, "How does Elizabeth feel?"

"I don't know, sir. I will do everything it takes for as long as it takes for her to return my love."

"I want you to know one thing up front, Captain. You can't say you hadn't been warned."

"What's that?"

"I have a love for my wife that any other man might envy. I also have a love for my daughter, a different kind of love but no weaker. A love only a father would understand. A love only a father and daughter could have. Captain, I will not let you take her away. Tom is in New York. I cannot live; I will not live without Elizabeth being near. Do you understand, Captain? You have my blessing to court my daughter, as long as you understand what I just said. You must promise me you will never take her away."

Heman could only think of crossing one bridge at a time, that was to see Elizabeth. He would agree to anything. He just hoped he wasn't burning bridges behind him.

Lady Catherine stayed in the Queen's Wharf for three weeks. She didn't seem to mind, but the crew started to worry they might be there all winter. Halifax wasn't a bad place to live, but they knew they were expected back in Boston. The question was: when?

Heman knew he had to leave soon. The coloured leaves were falling all around him. There was frost in the mornings. He worried the Atlantic would be stormy for his return to Boston. He spent every moment he could with Elizabeth. Between her and working and his looking for cargo to take back to Boston, they only saw each other in the evenings. He spent a lot of time at the Finley home. He was getting to know more about Elizabeth, but more important, she was getting to know him.

* * * * *

There was a cold rain falling with blustery winds when the Harbour Master guided *Lady Catherine* into Boston Harbour. It was Saturday, November 1, the day before Boston's Sabbath. Heman looked forward to resting with the family. He was happy to be back, but he knew part of him was missing. He had a lot of thinking and soul-searching to do. How was he going to make Elizabeth part of his life, when she was in Halifax, and he in Boston?

"Did you have a good trip?" The Harbour Master got Heman's attention.

"Tell you the truth, we ran into bad weather the 2nd day out, and it followed us all the way home. So the crew is tired and will be happy to have a few days of rest. By the way, did you find your slaves?"

"Slaves?

"Yes, remember you were looking for them on my ship."

"Oh, yeah, never found any. Must have been just a rumour."

"Yes, just a rumour," replied Heman.

After the welcome dinner that Peggy fixed, they all gathered in the living room. It was too cold to sit on lawn chairs. Duncan had stored them away for the winter. They were replaced by the fire in the fireplace. William was nodding off from the welcomed warmth of the room.

"So that's what you do when I'm away – sleep?"

William opening his eyes, "Better than chasing women. How's Elizabeth?"

"It was difficult to leave."

"Figured it must have been. You were in Halifax over a month. When are you going back? Next week?"

"Very funny."

Faye joined them sitting down in her favourite chair. "Kitchen work all done?" William was teasing her.

"No, thanks to you, William. At least the Captain has been known to lift a finger once in a while."

"Brother, talking about work, what did you bring us? Always like something interesting to sell at the Irish Coffee Company."

"Bonnets."

"Bonnets, you brought bonnets last time. We still have two shelves full," added Faye.

"Well, make room for more. The *Lady Catherine* is full of them."

"Where do you get them?" William asked. Then quickly answered his own question. "Don't tell me. I know, it's Elizabeth, isn't it? She makes them."

Heman smiled, "Best bonnets I've ever seen. I told her I would buy as many as she could make, and she took my word for it."

"What else did you bring?" Peggy was interested.

"This time Elizabeth made a line of ladies' clothes. It will not help until spring, though. They are ladies' sailing clothes."

"Do many ladies sail in Boston?" William had no idea, and neither did Heman.

"It's a good thing one of us is making money," William chided his brother.

"Don't worry, William, I did bring back a few things that might sell. But I like your idea better. You make the money, and I will go back to Elizabeth. What a dream that would be."

* * * * *

Time passed and before they knew it, both Thanksgiving and Christmas holidays were over. Heman knew the mail carrier very well, for he met him on the sidewalk daily.

"Nothing today, sir. Nothing from British North America."

Heman hadn't heard from Elizabeth in over a week. He knew the mail had slowed because of the harsh winter weather. That didn't stop him from sending a letter every day. The words he received from her were words of love. She was free to speak her feelings on paper. She didn't have to worry about her mother sitting beside her and Heman. All Heman knew was that he was falling deeper and deeper in love.

March found the *Lady Catherine* in Charleston, South Carolina. Heman was interested in cotton. That was his ticket back to Nova Scotia. He sent daily letters there, and he could send himself soon. In the meantime, he enjoyed the warm spring air of the South. The crew was enjoying the warm climate. Henry was having a lively conversation with the Captain. "Since we are

261

this far south, we might as well go to New Orleans. We have room for more cargo than cotton. We can pick up anything we want there." The officers agreed New Orleans sounded like a good place to visit before going north.

Heman knew that Cargo wasn't on the minds of his crew. It was a good time. New Orleans was a party town. However, Henry was right, one could buy things from all over the world. It would be good to have a new inventory for the Irish Coffee Company in Boston. The crew was in a festive mood, when the Captain announced that *Lady Catherine* would stay in New Orleans two days.

New Orleans was a party town, but Heman noticed trying to do business was more difficult than his last visit to the city. He had always had problems being accepted, because of his Irish background. He had found ways to overcome that. But now he was being called "a Yankee," and once was suspected of being a spy. Heman knew there were dissensions in this country between the South and the North. He read the newspapers, but he didn't know it was that bad, until being in the South. Even in South Carolina, he felt the tension, but it was worse the farther South he traveled. The Federal government in Washington was not making the Southern States very happy. Eleven Southern States were threatening to pull out of the Union. They figured they would just form their own government and call themselves the Confederate States of America.

The main reason was money. There were more rich men in the South than anywhere in the United States. The plan the Federal government in Washington was about to propose would ruin them. Their money was tied up in their business. Their business was cotton, and the cotton trade was dependent on labourers. These labourers were slaves. The North wanted the same kind of labourers, but they couldn't afford to buy slaves. Of course, they wouldn't admit that, but that was the main problem.

Slaves were expensive. A young black man could be worth more than $1000 in 1861. By this time, the South was raising their own. The abolitionists in the North were pressuring President Abraham Lincoln to abolish slavery and to declare emancipation.

Heman knew how he stood on slavery, not that he could freely express his feelings in New Orleans. But he could see that this great country was going to be torn apart over slavery. He didn't know when, but he could see it coming. The Captain cut short shore leave and left a half-day earlier than planned. He wanted to get back to Boston and fast.

He wasn't home two days when it happened. William entered the front door of their house, banging the door behind him. "Heman, Heman, where are you?"

"Brother, I am right here in the living room. He was reading a stack of Elizabeth's letters, which arrived while he was away. "Why are you in such a hurry?"

Duncan and Peggy hearing the banging of the front door, arrived in the living room. "Is there something wrong?"

"I don't know yet," Heman replied. "William, what is it?"

"They did it; the South seceded from the Union. Yesterday, April 12, the Confederate forces attacked a Federal fort, Fort Sumpter. It's all over the wires and in the papers. War has begun. Abraham Lincoln is ordering a Naval Blockade."

Peggy with her knuckles to her lips, "Where is Faye?"

"Working at the Irish Coffee Company." Duncan held his wife.

Heman was on his feet. "What will this mean, William?"

"I don't know, brother, but I do know it will change our lives. People are starting to gather in the streets.

"Come, let's go to the Irish Coffee Company. Faye will need our help."

Dear Captain,

I can't write letters very good. (Ismary is writing this). You the only good thing that came to my life. I know you said to forget you, and before you forget me — I just got to tell you how much I thank the Great Lord up above for making a man like you. You a man angel.

Anything I can do for you — I here.
Now I free

James

CHAPTER TWELVE

The Great Escape

The opening of the Civil War in 1861 found Boston in a state of patriotic fervor. Great outdoor meetings were held, and recruiting was early begun and carried on vigorously. The Irish were more than willing to sign up. They had adopted America as their new country and were willing to fight for the North.

William and Duncan were worried about losing their workers, but there seemed to be enough workers to go around for the construction of neighbourhood housing. They didn't have to worry; their work continued on the South End of Boston and the Back Bay.

Heman had his own worries. The Federal government implemented a Naval blockade to prevent southerners from earning revenue, by exporting their staple products and to prevent them from freely exporting needed manufactured goods and provisions. He managed several trade trips to Charleston before the laws were enforced. With the help of William, they found warehouses in which to store the cotton to be brought back from Charleston.

Boston was booming. The cotton textiles and its woolen industry enjoyed a 100% production rise during the early days of the conflict. Shoes and leather industry also enjoyed tremendous growth, thanks to Army contracts. Other war-related industries, especially firearms, gunpowder, and wagon manufacturing, grew rapidly on the strength of military contracts.[72]

William and Heman took advantage of the trade that was coming their way. By 1863, Heman's trade business and William's construction business had grown threefold. It wasn't just the Kenney brothers who were doing well, but Captain Freeman and the Drews were kept busy during this conflict between the North and South. During this time, Heman had made several trips to Halifax. He couldn't bring himself to stay away from Elizabeth any longer than he had to.

One wouldn't think the War would affect Halifax, it being British Territory and all, but it did. Warships from both the North and the South entered Halifax Harbour. The law stated that ships entering the Harbour from the United States could only stay 24 hours. That gave them time only to refuel. There were to be no engagements between ships from the North and the South while in the Harbour. This was strictly enforced, but just outside the Harbour, it was fair game for either side. There was more than one occasion when the citizens of Halifax gathered on Citadel Hill to watch a naval battle taking place. War might have been brewing just offshore, but in Halifax, there was a love affair burning strongly.

William and Duncan were left in Boston to take care of business there. That's how the new business in Halifax started. The Irish Coffee Company II opened in Halifax the Spring of 1863. Its location was the corner of Brunswick and Cornwallis Street, just a block from the Textile Factory. All the crew took turns manning the store.

It was hard to imagine, but the Civil War brought changes to the Finley family as well. With the help of Heman, their Textile Mill had upgraded to the newest technology in sewing machines. In Boston, Heman was right in the middle of production of new inventions.[73] As Heman brought sewing machines into Boston, he saved several in his warehouse and brought them to James Finley in Halifax for his Textile Factory.

He also set up a contract for Union Soldier uniforms. The Finley's Textile Factory sent more than one shipment by *Lady Catherine* to Boston.

The Irish Coffee Company II was prospering in Halifax. Heman spent most of his time making sure there were plenty of trade goods to fill the storerooms of his new company. Since the Civil War, his trade trips were limited to Boston and back to Halifax. He was more interested in cotton. That is where the money was. But how was he to trade cotton when President Lincoln had a blockade along the eastern coast?[74] Any ship found with cotton was confiscated for the government. But Heman knew cotton was getting through and he wanted a part of it. Letters from Tom Finley in New York informed him that President Lincoln was personally recommending applicants for trade permits.

As the war continued, requests for Lincoln to approve permits or issue executive orders regarding trade accelerated. Heman also knew that Lincoln gave the necessary passes to go through Union lines to Richmond and to return with Southern goods.[75] Heman wanted one of those passes. But there was one problem: Lincoln only approved all of the requests made by friends and family including several in-laws. How was he to overcome this problem? He certainly was not related to the President of the United States. The answer came from a telegram from Tom Finley in New York.[76]

Heman replied with his own telegram.

It turned out Tom knew a brother of a Georgia clergyman. This Georgia clergyman knew President Lincoln well. In fact, both President Lincoln and this Georgia clergyman were handing out permits. That is how Heman received a permit to bring out 250,000 bales of cotton from four states in 1864.[77] *Lady Catherine* was not big enough to take on such a deal. But that didn't stop Heman. He sent another telegram.

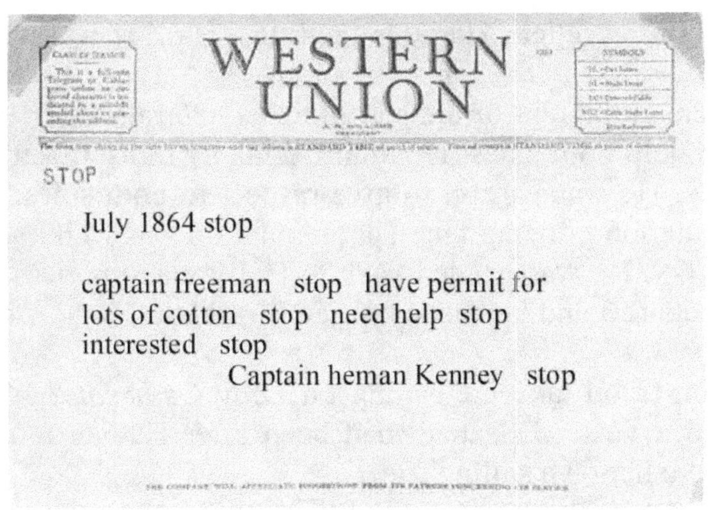

Heman now had all the ships he needed, thanks to Captain Freeman and the Messrs. Ingalls and Shepard Co. Cotton was delivered to all the textile mills in New York, Boston, and, of course, he saved some for Halifax. That is where he was headed now. *Lady Catherine* was loaded with cotton on her way to Halifax. Heman was on his way to see Elizabeth. It was a slow voyage. The *Lady Catherine* had been stopped twice. The blockade runners stopped all ships. It did not matter if the ship were large or small. But each time Heman had his permit. It was signed by the President himself.

Heman never had strong feelings for either side of this terrible conflict. He read the newspapers telling the terrible events of the many battles. But being Irish, he considered himself an outsider. Naturally, he was completely against slavery and always would be. He felt bad that the South's entire economy depended upon the slave worker. Cotton was their gold; however, he also knew if the North could get cheap labour, they would be in the same boat as the South.

Also being in Halifax during most of the war, he saw both sides of the conflict. For the blockade runners for the South and the North were using the Port of Halifax on a fairly regular basis. Because of the close proximity to the theatre of war on the high seas, and the excellent Harbour facilities, Halifax was a natural choice.

Heman thought of himself more as neutral. When needed, he would help both sides. He didn't think of himself a traitor to either side. He was careful to give respect to both sides, and he had a reputation of being fair. That reputation was well known all over Halifax. He was headed back to Halifax and he was happy. He needed a rest and he needed to see Elizabeth.

* * * * *

"Why won't you take me sailing on *Lady Catherine*? It's been more than a year." Elizabeth had been after Heman more than once to take her on a sailing trip.

Heman never said "no" to Elizabeth. But this time it was a firm 'no.' "No, my dear, it is too dangerous. Halifax Harbour and Bedford Basin are full of warships."

"Warships? They don't look like warships to me," Elizabeth stated.

"Any sailing vessel from the United States, South or North, are considered warships. You know how busy the Harbour has been."

"Yes, but they can't start fighting one another until they are out of the Harbour."

"That is the law, but laws could be broken, and I do not want you anywhere near cannon fire."

James, entering the room joined in, "I could not help overhearing your conversation. Elizabeth, he is right. Did you know the *Tallahassee* is in port?" James was talking to Heman.

"Yes, I met Captain Wood just yesterday."

"You mean John Taylor Wood?"James asked. "You know he is a grandson of Zachary Taylor, the 12th President of the United States."

"So I hear, and also a nephew of Jefferson Davis, the President of the Secessionist State."

"The whole town is talking about him. I'm surprised he isn't on the front page of the newspaper."

"Give it a few days and he will be. He told me he didn't have time to talk to the newspaper men."

Elizabeth looked at both Heman and her father. "So what is so special about this grandson and nephew of two presidents?"

"Word has it, before arriving here in Halifax, he had a brilliant 19-day raid. The *Tallahassee* has been busy from her home port of Wilmington, North Carolina. She has created absolute havoc with Union Commerce along the Atlantic Seaboard. In this short period, she destroyed 26 vessels and captured seven others."[78]

As they were speaking, Charles and George came through the front door. "Father, have you heard?"

"Heard what, son?" James was on his feet and halfway to Charles.

"The *Tallahassee* is stuck; she is cornered."

This brought Heman to his feet. "How do you know this?"

"In the paper, look."

Charles passed the paper to Heman, "The Nansemond and Huron, two Federal warships have dropped anchors in the main shipping channel at the mouth of the Harbour. They are waiting for the *Tallahassee* to make her move."

"See, everyone is talking about it."

"Not only that," George added, "everyone is headed for Citadel Hill. They are excited at the prospects of watching a naval battle on our own doorstep. They expect this to be the end of the *Tallahassee*."

"I have to leave." Heman was headed towards the door.

"What does this mean, Heman?"

He stopped as he saw the worried look on Elizabeth's face. "Don't worry, my dear. Under the terms of Queen Victoria herself, Captain Wood has about 24 hours before the *Tallahassee* has to leave. The problem is the Union warships also know she can't stay here long. They will be patiently waiting for her, fully expecting to engage the cruiser and blast her out of the water."

"How dreadful, Heman, but what are you going to do?"

"Captain Woods and I only met yesterday, but it was one of those meetings in which one knows that a friendship had begun that would last a lifetime. I need to go help him. I surely wouldn't want to see him get hurt."

"But you are not for the South," James pointed out as Heman went through the door.

"I'm not for the North either," Heman shouted behind him. "To the Dockyard," he shouted, as he climbed into his waiting carriage. "To the *Tallahassee*."

The *Tallahassee* was not the greatest looking ship Heman had ever seen, but her design was one that enabled the vessel to move in any direction and quickly at that. She had twin screws[79] run by separate 100 horsepower. Steam drove the ship at 17 knots, by reversing one screw, the ship could turn about her centre. She was 220 feet in length, with a 24-foot beam. Given her speed and low profile, broken up by two funnels and two sparsely rigged masts, the ship was ideal for running blockades but left a lot to be desired as a raiding cruiser. Coal was necessary to drive the ship, and her design was suitable for journeys of only 1,000 miles.[80] Captain Wood had sailed the *Tallahassee* into Halifax Harbour to take on bunker coal and water.

Heman was dockside of the *Tallahassee* asking permission to board. The *Tallahassee* was well-guarded. No one was getting on board without Captain Wood knowing it. One of the crewmen recognized Heman from the day before. Telling Heman to stand down, he would give his Captain the message. After a few moments, Heman was led to what looked like a war room. He found Captain Wood agonizing over the route he should take to attempt an escape. "Come in, Captain. Are you fighting for the South today?"

"No, sir, just helping a friend out of a difficult situation."

The two captains shook hands. "I may need your help. You know this Harbour well, do you not?"

"Quite well, sir. What do you have here?" They both looked down at the marine charts before them. A detailed map of Halifax Harbour had dark markings upon it.

"I've decided to make a getaway through the Eastern Passage on the far side of McNab's Island." He jabbed his finger to the map.

"Never been done!" Heman was being honest with Cook. "Too shallow; you would be grounded in no time."

"But wait a minute, the moon should be full, or almost full this evening. That means the tide will be higher than normal. You just might be able to do it, but you can't do it alone. No way, you need to have someone who knows that part like the back of his hand. You need Jock Flemming.[81] He is from Eastern Passage. Jock is a local Harbour pilot and he knows this body of water. There are several small islands and he knows them well."

"Can we get him, and can he be trusted?"

"A friend he is, and he likes a good challenge and Irish whiskey. That's your man all right." Heman was practically talking to himself. He looked out the porthole towards the wharf. "Low tide – good. High tide will be another eight hours." Heman looked up at Cook, "I will have him here at high tide."

Heman did not want attention brought to himself, so he had Moses take the ferry to Eastern Passage. He had a message for his friend Jock Flemming. When Jock heard there was excitement brewing and it had to do with his friend Captain Kenney, he was on the next ferry towards Halifax.

It was 9 o'clock, August 20, 1864, Captain Wood took on a local Harbour pilot Jock Flemming. After explaining his plan, he said to Flemming, "You just find me the water, and with the twin-screws, I can turn her like a ruler."

Somewhat reassured, Flemming replied, "Captain, I'll find you the water where the only thing you'll feel under the keel is eelgrass."

And so over the next hour, Wood and Flemming began their harrowing task. She left the Woodside wharf steaming past

Georges Island to the Westward, she passed over to the Eastern Passage. The lights were extinguished on the *Tallahassee*, but those on the Eastern Passage mainland could see the dark hull and hear the throbbing of the engines. When she reached the narrow channel just opposite the sandy beach at York's Corner, Wood sent a crew member ahead in a small boat with a hand light to signal when to turn. Flemming guided the *Tallahassee* carefully through the crooked channel, where at high tide, there would only be a few feet of water under the keel. She passed Devil's Island at Midnight. Painstakingly they eased past Lawlor's Island to where the ship would be in open water. At this point, the Captain and the pilot bade their farewells.[82]

"Give Captain Kenney a message. Tell him I will see him after the war. Halifax is a nice place, and I think I will come back and live here."

"Sure will, Captain, good luck." Flemming got into his rowboat and started to pull towards shore. As Wood began to steer a course south, he looked back across the water, and in the distance, he could see the lights of the two unsuspecting Union ships, as they lay in wait for him. At dawn the next day, the Union vessels were still sitting at the mouth of the Harbour long after their elusive enemy had vanished.

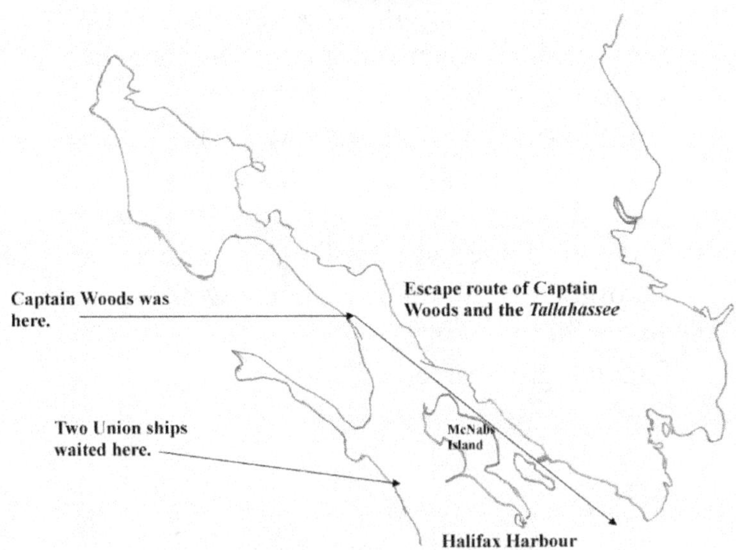

Author's Drawing of Captain Woods' Escape

On the next evening, Heman was back in the Finley parlour. Elizabeth was reading the newspaper. "The *Tallahassee* Escapes. Like a Ghost, she disappears in the night. But, how? Word has it through the shallow channel of Eastern Passage. Never before had so large a steamer gone through that shallow channel. Down to Lawlor's Island, the water is deep enough to float the largest ship in the world, but between it and the mainland, it is shallow. This was so difficult to traverse that no watch was kept for vessels coming out that way."[83]

"Isn't that amazing, Heman?"

"Amazing, Elizabeth."

"Did you have anything to do with this?"

"What makes you think I had anything to do with it?" He grinned at her.

"Where were you last night?"

"On *Lady Catherine*, with my crew."

"Are you sure? You said you wanted to help your new friend Captain Wood?"

"That I did. Captain Wood is an interesting man, and I believe our paths will cross again. Maybe you will even get to meet him someday, my sweet Elizabeth."

"With you Heman, I am sure I will."

* * * * *

April 1, 1865, all telegraph receivers were urgently tapping out messages in all the telegraph offices in Nova Scotia. In no time at all the employees in those offices were spilling out into the streets to spread the word.

The telegram received was:

The news did not take long to reach the Queen's Wharf. Heman was taking his early walk with *Lady Catherine*. He watched along the wharf as a wave of activity spread, and it was coming in his direction. As the word spread, the men stopped their work and a cheer would break out, and it continued on the wave. Heman turned to his 1st mate. "Henry, find out what all the excitement is and report back to me."

"Aye, Aye, sir."

Heman watched as Henry crossed the gangplank to the Queen's Wharf. The wave of cheers had reached the *Lady Catherine*. The cheering was loud and clear.

It wasn't long before Henry was back standing in front of his captain. "Good news, sir! The Confederacy has collapsed, Lee has surrendered, all slaves are free. The war is over!"

"Hear that *Lady Catherine*!?" The Captain was speaking to the schooner again. "The war is over. Yes, we must thank God for that, and, yes, the slaves are free! Thank God, *Lady Catherine*, Thank God!"

* * * * *

Elizabeth was reading to Heman, as they sat in the familiar parlour of the Finley's home. "By 1864 long-term Union advantages in geography, manpower, industry, finance, political organization and transportation were overwhelming the Confederacy. Grant fought a bloody series of battles with Lee in Virginia in summer 1864."

"How terrible Heman; War is madness, isn't it?

"Yes, Elizabeth, war is madness. What else does the paper say?"

Elizabeth continued; "Lee won in a tactical sense, but lost strategically, as he could not replace his casualties and was forced to retreat into trenches around his capital, Richmond, Virginia. Meanwhile, William T. Sherman captured Atlanta and marched to the sea, destroying a wide swath of Georgia. On April 1, 1865, the Confederacy collapsed as Lee surrendered and all the slaves were freed."

"How awful, those poor people in Georgia."

"Well, it's all over now, Elizabeth, now the United States can begin to heal. It is going to take a long time, but at least it has started. Look, I have my own telegram. It's from William in Boston: He says, there is dancing in the streets. Duncan and William are happily willing to help put the country back together again."

"Just like William, Elizabeth. Looks like my little brother has found more work to do."

August 1865

Dear Captain Kenney,

War has ended. Nasty thing war. I am tired of the conflict. I have done my duty for Jefferson Davis. I am weary and this body feels my age. I long for peace and quiet. In the back of my mind, I remember a place that could fill that bill very nicely. Halifax has fond memories, I have shared my feelings with my dear wife and have almost convinced her to pick up our lives from the throngs of people here and make a new life there.

New friends await me. I include you as that, sir, and also Jock Flemming. For without the assistance from both of you, I would not have my life today. There are no words that can be found that express my indebtedness. (To this day the Yankees can't figure out how it was done. I have also heard many have tried but failed.) When questioned about that great night, I just respond with a smile.

I look forward to seeing you in person in the near future. Also, have interest in seeing your schooner. Have you ever thought of racing her? We can have that discussion later.

Until that time.

I am yours truly,

John Taylor Woods

CHAPTER THIRTEEN

Romance, Sweet Romance

Elizabeth sailed through the double doors of the Irish Coffee Company in Halifax. "Good morning, Moses." Elizabeth was in front of the counter before the bell on the door stopped ringing.

"Good morning, Miss Elizabeth." It never failed to amaze Moses how this young woman could cause so much interest by just entering a room. Moses nodded his head. "Good morning, Mrs. Finley." Wherever Elizabeth went, you were sure to see her mother just a few steps behind.

"Is Heman here?" Elizabeth's eyes always lit up when she said his name.

"Yes, Elizabeth, he is in a meeting with Henry and John Charles. They are planning the next trade trip. Do you want me to summon him?"

"Of course not." Mrs. Finley looked at her daughter. "Elizabeth and I will wait until the meeting is over."

"No, Moses, don't disturb Heman. Mother and I will see if you need any more of my bonnets to sell." Mother and daughter headed towards the back of the store. Here was a special corner delicately decorated to display Elizabeth's work. She not only had bonnets, but had her own line of ladies' clothing. It was a very popular spot for ladies. They not only bought the dresses but exchanged news of the Social Society of Halifax.

Moses gave the ladies plenty of room. He didn't serve the women but waited for them to come to the counter for assistance. Moses never dreamed he would be a merchant. All he ever wanted to be was a sailor. It was just after the war began between the North and the South in the States, that Heman decided to open a new store in Halifax. The crew knew it was just a matter of time. Heman wanted to be in Halifax. The crew decided to follow; they didn't have anything else to do.

John Charles and Henry led the way out of the meeting room. Heman was right behind. Heman thought they had a very productive meeting. The next trade trip was planned for the 10th of June to New York. It was just another regular trade trip, except for one thing: Heman wasn't going. Henry would be in charge, and Heman knew, with the help of his crew, the trip would be successful.

As for Heman, he had other business to attend to – his Elizabeth, Sweet Elizabeth. He couldn't imagine loving her more, but he did. And he knew Elizabeth loved him. He didn't understand it, but he knew it and could feel it. Both their loves matured as Elizabeth matured. Now it was time to take his love one more step. He was preparing to ask for her hand in marriage. Not that he hadn't been preparing all these years, but now the preparing was over. He had established a successful trading business in Halifax. He had much to offer Elizabeth, and she deserved only the best. Now it was time to make it an official engagement. It wasn't that Elizabeth and he hadn't discussed the future, for they had. How could they love one another and not speak of the future? Heman didn't want to make another trade trip. He didn't have time. He wanted the engagement to begin now and a wedding to follow in the beginning of the New Year 1866. He was happy that today's meeting had gone well.

Moses got Heman's attention. "Captain, Elizabeth and her mother are awaiting your presence." Moses gestured towards the back of the store.

Heman quickly turned to see Elizabeth helping a young lady select a dress from her collection. His heart jumped, and a hot feeling struck him like lightning. He was used to it now, for it happened every time he saw her. He had learned to enjoy these feelings in a more controlled way. "You should have told me she was here." He was chiding Moses.

"Mrs. Finley and Elizabeth insisted that I wait until you finished your meeting."

"I understand, Moses." Heman knew it was Elizabeth's mother's idea. Soon, he wouldn't have to go through Elizabeth's mother to see Sweet Elizabeth.

Elizabeth, seeing Heman approaching, excused herself from helping a young woman with blond hair. "Heman, I thought your meeting would never end." Elizabeth loved to be with Heman and didn't care if the whole world knew it.

"Elizabeth, Heman's a working man and doesn't have time . . ."

"Oh, but Mrs. Finley, I have all the time in the world for Elizabeth. I should have been told you were here."

Elizabeth smiled, and Heman wished he could pick her up and take her away. That time would come but not soon enough.

"Do you have plans for this evening?" Elizabeth questioned.

"No, Elizabeth, what would you like for us to do? Name it and I will make it happen."

"There is a poetry reading at the Governor General's Mansion tonight."

"Then let's go." What time should I pick you up?"

"Yes, Heman, I do believe I can go." It was Mrs. Finley.

Heman replied, "How kind." But inside he was thinking, "You really don't have to go."

Elizabeth smiled.

Heman's heart was telling him it didn't matter who was there. All he would see was Elizabeth.

Two days later Heman decided he would do it. He would make an appointment to meet James, Elizabeth's father. He sent a message that read:

May 23, 1865
Dear Mr. Finley,
I request a meeting with you. Could you meet on my schooner, the Lady Catherine, Tuesday of this week at 7:00 p.m.?
Sincerely,

Captain Heman Kenney

Heman had everything ready. On his desk was a bottle of the finest Irish Whiskey. Two lead crystal glasses stood in their place waiting for Heman's guest to arrive. Heman did not think he would be nervous, but he was. After all, he had many meetings with James Finley and he never was nervous before. He held out his hand in front of him. It was shaking, and he could feel it in his knees. *Get a hold of yourself*, he told himself. He looked at his pocket watch. 6:15 p.m. *I have time to walk the deck; that will calm me down,* he thought.

The sunset was beautiful. Spring could be cool in Nova Scotia, but it reminded him of Ireland. How long had it been? More than eight years? "*Lady Catherine*, do you miss Ireland? Maybe we need to make a trip back. That's a great idea, *Lady Catherine*, a honeymoon trip to Ireland. My parents need to meet Sweet Elizabeth. Yes, I will work on that. But meantime, Mr. Finley . . ." He heard the whistle sound. "Mr. Finley himself. Wish me luck, *Lady Catherine*. My life is about to change forever. Thank you, it will be a good life."

Henry was by his side. "Captain, Mr. Finley is in your cabin."

"Thank you, Henry."

"Good luck, Captain."

Heman looked up at Henry. He knew, and Heman had tried to keep it a secret. That was impossible around here. "Thank you, Henry." Without delay, he entered his cabin.

"Thank you for coming," Heman spoke to James Finley as the two men shook hands in greeting each other.

"Heman, I hear your schooner is leaving for a trade trip soon."

"Yes it is, sir, but business can wait for another time. This meeting is personal." Heman poured the whiskey into the crystal glasses, placing one in front of his guest. Heman took two large swallows of the whiskey. It burned as it went down. "More than three years ago we had a meeting. I asked your permission to court your daughter Elizabeth. At the time you warned me that you would not allow me to take her away from you. I knew you were serious. I have spent the last few years building up a successful trade business. You and I have done business together. I love your daughter, Mr. Finley. I have from the first time I saw her. That was the day you and your family sailed on The *Lady Catherine*. I have invited you here this evening to ask for the hand of your daughter in marriage."

James Finley finished his drink while listening to the Captain's speech. He knew this was coming, but Heman had managed to surprise him with the timing. He lifted his empty glass and noticed Heman's handshake a little as he refilled it. "How does Elizabeth feel about this?" James thought it was a crazy question; he already knew the answer.

"James, I feel she loves me as well. And, yes, we have talked about our future. However, before I ask her to marry me, I wanted to talk with you first."

"I appreciate that, Heman. When we received the letter from Tom in New York several years ago, he said you were a fine man. You have lived up to that reputation since I have known you. But before I give you my blessings, I ask you what is your plan?"

Heman was eager to reply. "I want the marriage to take place the end of the year or the beginning of '. Then I want to take Elizabeth on a honeymoon trip to Ireland. My family has the right to meet their new daughter-in-law."

"How long would you stay?"

"Six months or so. Don't worry; I will bring her back to you."

James smiled. "I believe you." He handed Heman his empty glass. "Another, Heman, I need another. It's not every day a father gives his daughter away. I'm not sure I'm happy or sad, but this will help the pain. I know my daughter is now a grown woman and has a life of her own."

Heman filled up James' glass. The men drank until the bottle was empty. They left the cabin holding onto one another. They were going to walk the bridge, that is if one could call it walking. Neither man was accustomed to drinking. The Irish Whiskey had taken a toll, and as they walked, they slurred the words of the song, "Farewell to Nova Scotia, the sea-bound coast . . ."

Henry and Moses watched the two men. Henry was glad the meeting had gone well. Moses had tears in his eyes as he made the sign of the cross.

* * * * *

Heman opened his eyes and saw the familiar rays of the sunshine enter the porthole. It was morning. He closed his eyes for his head hurt. There was a knock at the door. With his eyes still closed, Heman managed to say, "Enter."

"Good morning, Captain. I have just the thing for you, sir."

Heman opened his eyes slightly. It was Dick. Heman moaned and closed his eyes again.

"Three fresh eggs, cow's milk, vanilla, a spoonful of sugar, and a dash of a secret ingredient." Dick was stirring the drink.

288

"What are you talking about, Dick? Can't you see I need to be alone?"

"No, sir, that is the worst thing you can do. Come, sit up and drink this." Heman didn't have a choice. Dick was yanking him up to a sitting position.

"You can't do this to a Captain. I can fire you, did you know that?"

"Yes, sir, you can fire me all you want, but first drink this."

"What's the secret ingredient?"

"The what, sir?"

"You said there was a secret ingredient. What is it?"

"Sir, it wouldn't be a secret if I told you."

Heman passed a look to Dick that made him come to attention.

"You sure you want to know?"

"Yes, Dick."

"Sir, it's whiskey and mineral oil. Drink up, sir; it will fix what ails you."

"Are you sure?"

"Have I ever steered you wrong, Captain?"

Heman had to agree; Dick's remedies usually worked. Heman drank the mixture. *It wasn't so bad. It must have been the whiskey,* he thought.

"Now you rest, sir."

"Where's Mr. Finley?"

"We have him bunked in William's old room. I'm taking care of him. We didn't want to send him home last night. Might scare his wife and Elizabeth. We sent word that his meeting would run late, and he would stay aboard The *Lady Catherine.* We will see that he is delivered home by noon."

"Thank you, Dick." Heman laid his head back down on his pillow.

"Not at all, Captain. Glad to be of service."

As Dick closed the Captain's door, Heman tried to remember the meeting between James and him the night before. He only remembered the first half. And what troubled him most: he couldn't remember whether James said, "Yes," that he could marry Elizabeth. He decided to go on the assumption that James gave a blessing to the union of his daughter and him. He also decided that the events that took place last night would stay between James and him. There was no reason for anyone else to know. They were beginning a new chapter in their lives, and it should start with a clean slate.

It was late in the morning when Heman had a chance to meet with James. They shook hands and, as their eyes met, the men knew words were not necessary. The events of the night before sealed a bond between them that would last a long time.

"Before I left for the Textile Factory, I wanted you to know that two weeks from Saturday I would like to have a special family dinner. I would like to make the announcement of your engagement to Elizabeth at that time. Is that satisfactory to you, Heman?"

"Yes, James, I look forward to it. That will give me time to ask Elizabeth. If you would, please keep this between you and me for a week."

"Agreed, but I will have my fatherly talk with Elizabeth one week before the announcement."

Heman walked with James towards the gangplank. James stopped and was serious for a moment. "I look forward to having you for my son-in-law. I will have many daughters-in-law but only one son-in-law. I am glad it will be you, but, one more thing as a father I must say: I expect you to take good care of my daughter. If I hear that she is unhappy in any way, you will have me to deal with."

"I assure you, James, that I will spend the rest of my life making Elizabeth happy." With that, James walked the gangplank to the Queen's Wharf, and Heman returned to his cabin. How was he going to propose to Elizabeth? He only had a week to prepare. He had to do it right, and he knew just what he was going to do.

* * * * *

It was the first of June, 1865. The sun was shining and the sky clear and blue. John Charles announced to the Captain that it was 71°F., a wonderful spring day in Nova Scotia.

"Good," replied Heman, "everything's going as planned. Does the crew know what to do?"

"Yes, sir, they are all dressed in their best."

Heman wanted everything to be perfect. He even hired a lady from the Public Gardens. She was dressing *Lady Catherine* for a special occasion. Tulips of every colour were everywhere. Yellow Daffodils looked like they were growing out of every corner of the deck. And flags –*Lady Catherine* had new flags, including the Blue Cross of Nova Scotia.

Elizabeth would be there any moment. What a surprise he had for her. She believed it was the first sail of the season. Her mother was looking forward to it as well. What they didn't know was that there were to be two kidnappings that day. He was to kidnap Elizabeth, and James was to kidnap Janet, his wife. The plan was all worked out. Elizabeth was to sail with him; James and his wife were going back home.

The whistle sounded. Elizabeth was on the Queen's Wharf. Good timing – she was making her way across the gangplank. Out of the corner of his eye, Heman could see James putting Janet back into the carriage. It was working. Heman was there as Elizabeth stepped aboard. In plain view of her parents, he picked her up into his arms. A squeal of delight came from Elizabeth. Heman could hear her mother protesting, "What is he doing?" as the carriage carried her away.

"Cast ho," Heman ordered as he carried Elizabeth to the Upper Deck. "Don't worry, darling. I have permission to kidnap you for the day, just the two of us together."

Elizabeth buried her head into his shoulder. She was willing to be taken anywhere, as long as Heman was with her. He

291

finally put her down on her feet. She wasn't in a hurry; she liked being in his strong arms.

"Oh, Heman, how beautiful. *Lady Catherine* looks like a spring flower garden. My favourite flowers, daffodils, and tulips."

"And roses." Heman handed her a long-stemmed pink rose.

"Where did you find roses this time of year?" She placed the rose at the bottom of her nose and inhaled the sweet fragrance. "It smells wonderful. Where did you find it? Tell me, Heman."

"Delivered all the way from Boston. All I have to do is make a request, and William can find anything."

"What a wonderful brother. I would like to meet him."

"One day you will, darling."

"Well, if you have kidnapped me, where do you plan to take me?"

"We will sail past the mouth of the Harbour, and then I have found a secret place for us."

"A secret place? How romantic."

"Now, come to the bow and sit with me. It is a good day for sailing, and we will see *Lady Catherine* at her best. Would you like me to carry you?"

Elizabeth smiled, "I do believe I can walk."

Heman had a place prepared for them to sit – two chairs close together with flowers tied down everywhere. It was a perfect place to watch the ocean spray and the coastline pass as they sailed out of the Harbour. "Are you cold?" The air was still cool as the sea breeze picked up. Heman was prepared. He picked up a royal blue cape that he had also ordered from Boston. "This will keep you warm." He placed it on her shoulders, and then put his arm around her and brought her closer to him.

"How did you ever manage to do this without Mother being here?"

"Your father helped."

"He did?" Elizabeth's eyes opened wide. She looked into Heman's eyes. Heman took the opportunity of her closeness and placed his lips on hers. She did not withdraw, and the kiss was sweet and warm on her lips. It ended and Heman put his arms around her. "Do it again, Heman. Kiss me again."

Heman smiled at her; how could he refuse? Holding her in his arms he pledged, "I love you, Elizabeth. I always have. You complete me. I am only half alive when you are not with me."

Elizabeth had tears in her eyes.

Heman was concerned. "What is it, Elizabeth? Are you not happy?"

"No, silly, I am very happy, the happiest I have been all my life. I love you, too, Heman."

"Oh, Elizabeth, that is what my heart needed to hear. Elizabeth, will you marry me? Will you spend the rest of your life with me? I will do my best to make you happy. Will you marry me?"

Elizabeth placed her hand on Heman's face. "I don't ever want to be away from you. I want to spend the rest of my life by your side. Yes, Heman, I will marry you." They kissed again, a beginning of a lifetime of kisses.

They sailed along, Heman holding Elizabeth in his arms. He couldn't help looking up and seeing *Lady Catherine*'s sails full of wind. It was like she was smiling upon them both. They didn't move, and they didn't talk; they enjoyed the sound of the waves hitting the sides of the schooner as they sailed on.

Henry was at the wheel. He knew exactly when to turn *Lady Catherine* into the wind and then back into the Harbour. The plan was working; everyone knew his part and was executing it well.

Elizabeth exclaimed, "We are headed back. Oh, Heman, I don't want this to end." She wiggled loose from his arms.

"Don't worry, darling, it's not over yet."

"What else is planned?" Elizabeth's eyes were sparkling with excitement.

Lady Catherine tacked to the right.

"McNab's Island – we are getting close to the Island." Elizabeth jumped up out of her chair to take a closer look over the side of the schooner.

"I found a small inlet on the south side of the island. It will be protection from the wind. I plan to cast the anchor there."

"How pretty! We are here all by ourselves." Elizabeth sat back down in her chair. They heard loud marching steps coming their way. Moses came to attention before them.

"Miss Elizabeth, for you." He handed her another long-stemmed pink rose.

"How wonderful." She smelled the soft petals. "Now I have two." She smiled back at Moses. She had never seen him so dressed up. He was wearing a green vest and jacket and canvas-colored trousers and a neckcloth that matched the ribbon on his vest. Embroidered on the ribbon were the words *"Lady Catherine."*

He turned towards Heman. "Captain, sir."

"Yes, Moses."

"Lunch is being served in the dining room, sir."

"Thank you, Moses."

"Will you join me?" Heman took Elizabeth's hand to guide her. As they walked towards the main hatch, he put his hand around her small waist and drew her close.

Patrick was standing guard at the main hatch leading to below deck. He was dressed the same as Moses. He bowed and said, "For you, my lady," as he handed her a long-stemmed pink rose.

"Another rose? How delightful!" as she added it to the other two.

"May I hold them for you?" Heman asked. "Be careful going down the ladder."

"Yes, you may." She handed over her three roses. I've gone down this ladder many a time." She quickly turned around and was out of sight.

Dick was discreetly at the bottom watching to assist Elizabeth. When Heman was by her side, Dick presented Elizabeth with her fourth pink rose. Heman passed the collection to her to carry.

"Thank you, Dick."

"My pleasure, my lady. Captain, sir, will you please follow me?" He guided them to the small dining room.

"Oh, how pretty!" Elizabeth exclaimed. The dining room had been transformed into a beautiful garden with a round wood table set for two. Flowers and candles decorated the small room. Heman took her hand and placed her at the table, then he took his own seat. He again reached out across the table to find her hand. "Heman, this is just wonderful. How did you do this? You did all this for me?"

"Just for you, darling." There was a small box wrapped in gold material. It was fastened with gold ribbon. Heman placed it in front of Elizabeth. "For you, my love."

Elizabeth carefully untied the ribbon and opened the material. She looked at Heman before opening the top.

"Well, go ahead; look inside," Heman encouraged.

Lying inside was the tiny ring. The diamonds caught the sunlight coming in from the porthole and glistened like small stars. Elizabeth gasped as the sight took her breath away. She had never seen such a beautiful ring. "Heman, oh Heman, how beautiful!"

Heman smiled and was relieved. He was worried that she might not like it. "Pick it up, Elizabeth, and let me place it on your finger. This ring will seal our engagement."

She picked up the delicate ring, handing it to Heman. Heman pushed back his chair and got to his feet. He walked the four steps that separated them and bent down on one knee. Taking her left hand, he questioned her, "Elizabeth, will you marry me? Will you be my wife?"

"Yes, Heman, I will be your wife forevermore."

"Then let this ring be a symbol of my love for you." He slipped the ring on the ring finger of her left hand. Then he kissed her on her tiny lips.

Elizabeth flung her arms around his neck, placing him off balance. He almost fell to the ground with her attached to his neck. With all his might he fought it and managed to save both of them from an embarrassing moment.

"How delightful, Heman! I feel like I am in a fairy tale."

"Not a fairy tale, my love; this is very real. Your father will be announcing our engagement in a week's time."

"So that is how you got Father to allow you to kidnap me?"

"And your mother, remember he kidnapped her."

"How long has he known?"

"A week now."

"He surely kept a good secret. Thank you, Heman. I will remember this for the rest of my life."

"The rest of our lives you mean," added Heman.

"Yes, for the rest of our lives. It's been so wonderful; I don't want it to end."

"It's not ending yet." Heman took his seat. He clapped his hands twice, and magically Henry and John Charles, dressed as fine waiters, entered the room carrying wonderful food for them both. Not that they ate much, all they wanted was to hold hands and look into each other's eyes.

They heard the whistle and Henry giving the order, "Cat the anchor." *Lady Catherine* was leaving the inlet.

"Elizabeth, come with me." He led her to the main deck.

Elizabeth couldn't believe it. "More, Heman, there's more?"

"Yes, my love, just for you. As we sail back to the Queen's Wharf, we will sit here and listen to your favourite music." A music ensemble was set up on the upper deck. A harp, two violins, and a cello sent sweet music in their direction. Heman held her close to him.

Elizabeth noticed they weren't quite alone. The Harbour was filled with leisure boats, and the ferry was passing to Dartmouth right in front of them. They were making quite a scene, for the sound of the music floated over the water of the Harbour. "Should you be holding me, Heman?"

"Yes, sweet Elizabeth, I want the world to know that you are mine. But you are right, there will be a lifetime to hold you." Heman sat up straight, causing a slight space between them. "Let me see your hand. No, the other one. I want to see the ring on your finger."

"I must not wear it until the announcement is made."

"I never thought of that." Heman thought he might have miscalculated giving her the ring too early.

"Don't worry, my dear. I think it is wonderful that only you and I will know for one week."

"You and I and your father, and don't forget the crew."

"The secret will be safe with them. I will wear this ring on a ribbon around my neck, close to my heart."

"Thank you, Elizabeth, for loving me, and you will always be close to my heart."

The day was over. All good things must come to an end. Life goes on. Heman delivered Elizabeth with a dozen pink roses to her home. Her mother wasn't talking to him.

Heman returned to *Lady Catherine*. The first thing he did was thank his crew. "A job well done."

Moses looked around and asked the Captain, "What are you going to do with all these flowers? The wharf rat and the other workers are going to talk if they see us living with tulips for long."

Heman smiled. "We will collect them in the morning and then deliver the flowers to the orphanage on Windsor Street. The children will enjoy them."

* * * * *

Heman wasn't very happy the next week. He didn't see Elizabeth, except at the Irish Coffee Company for a few minutes.

Elizabeth's mother was still mad at Heman, and she was making him pay.

Since *Lady Catherine* set sail Tuesday, June 10, he didn't have any place to live. Therefore, Heman set up a room upstairs at the Irish Coffee Company.

An invitation arrived for Heman to attend a family dinner Saturday evening at the Finley's home. Heman thought it was strange to get a written invitation to the dinner in which his engagement was to be announced. James must be keeping a great secret. He wondered whether Mrs. Finley was still mad at him. One thing he learned: there were consequences to pay if someone crossed her.

Heman knocked on the front door and was happy to see Elizabeth there waiting for him. "How I have missed you, Heman."

Heman wanted to hold her in his arms but knew that would not be a good idea. He had to be patient. "Is your mother still mad at me?" he questioned her.

"Not as much as she was. Father had to speak to her twice. She is just happy to have the whole family here. Did you know Tom and Emily and little Susanna are here all the way from New York? Father surprised Mother and the rest of us. They arrived yesterday by ship."

"Elizabeth, who are you talking to? If it is Heman, don't keep him standing at the front door; invite him into the parlour."

"Yes, Mother. Come in, Heman."

"Good morning, Mrs. Finley. Thank you for the invitation." In return, she gave him a half smile.

"Hello, Heman, welcome," James reassured him. "Come this way. James, Charles, George, and Tom are in the parlour." Heman was guided in that direction.

So much for seeing Elizabeth, he thought. He saw her mother taking her back to the kitchen.

"Elizabeth, I need your help in the kitchen. Emily is feeding Susanna her dinner."

Tom was the first to greet Heman with a handshake. "Happy to see you again, Captain. It pleases me to see you here with my family."

"Thank you, Tom. It's been a long time. How is New York treating you?"

"I could have sworn I saw your schooner pass by our ship on our journey to Halifax."

"Could have been. She sailed almost a week ago, heading for Boston and then New York."

"Sailed without her Captain?"

"This time she did."

Heman greeted the other brothers. They knew each other well.

"Word has it you opened the sailing season with a bang?" George questioned Heman. "The whole city is talking about it."

"Really?" Heman replied. "All I had was music on deck for all the Harbour to hear. Everyone had a good time."

The men enjoyed their conversation, while the women worked on the last preparations in the kitchen. Finally, James announced that dinner was served. There were eight sitting at the dining table. Heman and Elizabeth sat together to the left of James. Janet sat to the right of her husband. Tom and Emily sat beside her. The rest of the brothers filled the empty chairs. Little Susanna was being entertained by the maid, who would put her to bed shortly.

Heman managed to find Elizabeth's hand under the tablecloth, and Elizabeth tried not to show her surprise but held tight to his hand. It was clear to Heman the strong bond this family had for each other. It made him think of his parents and the family meals they had together back in Ireland.

Most of the conversation was directed to Tom and his wife Emily. They were bringing them up to date with how they lived their lives in New York.

After the dessert was served, James stood up at the head of the table and began to speak. "You don't know how happy I am to stand before you this evening. My family is together; it doesn't happen very often. Tom and Emily, we miss you, and we always enjoy when you can come home to visit. Of course, this visit is special, because you brought us my granddaughter Susanna, such a beautiful child."

"But your being here is not the only special thing that is taking place this evening. Heman is our guest and has been in our home on many occasions. But tonight is a special occasion for him, not just for him, but also for our daughter, your sister, Elizabeth. At this time will you take your wine glass in hand, stand, and I would like to make a toast."

James waited until everyone was on their feet. The secret had remained that – a secret. As he looked around, he could tell everyone was waiting in anticipation for the news he was about to make. Heman and Elizabeth were also on their feet, wine glasses in hand, looking into each other's eyes. They didn't know what else to do. They couldn't help smiling at each other.

Everyone else was looking at James. He continued, "I would like to toast and give my blessing to the engagement of Heman and Elizabeth. May God bless them both."

There was complete silence. No one expected this announcement.

"Go ahead, toast this wonderful couple."

James, Charles, and George cheered, "Welcome to the family, Heman."

Tom commented to Elizabeth, "Just think, I introduced you two." He hugged his sister. "I am so happy for you."

Janet was sitting in her seat. She was in a state of shock. No one seemed to notice, but James. He went to her, took her hand, and led her away to the parlour. With all the celebrating, no one noticed their departure.

"James, why was I the last to know?"

"You aren't the last; you are one of the first. I wanted the family to know together."

"But I've been so mean to him."

"I noticed, but don't worry; he will get over it."

"But how will Elizabeth get along without me? She needs to be taken care of."

"Our job is done, my love. Elizabeth is now a woman, and it will be Heman who will take care of her."

"But what will I do?"

"Visit your granddaughter Susanna in New York. And don't worry, I'm sure it won't be long before little ones will be running around closer to home."

"Are you happy about this, James?"

"I believe I am. Heman will be a good husband to Elizabeth; he promises to take care of her."

"And you, are you happy about this?"

"It's hard for me to say right now."

"Now, Janet."

"At least let me get used to it for a while."

"You have five minutes. Then we will rejoin our children in the dining room. There we will celebrate together. But first, come, let me hold you." Janet slid into James' arms, a place where she found comfort all these years.

"Are you ready?"

"Yes, I am ready. Let's go celebrate with our children."

Janet went straight towards Elizabeth and gathered her into her arms. "Elizabeth, my daughter, I knew this was going to happen, but I didn't know it would happen this evening."

"Are you happy for me, Mother? Are you still angry with Heman? I love him, Mother. I want my marriage to be like yours and Father's. Please be happy, Mother."

"No, I am not angry at Heman. How could I be when you love him so? I will always be happy for you, dear."

"Come and speak to Heman. He is worried you are still angry." Elizabeth, taking her mother's arm, guided her to Heman. He was still surrounded by his new brothers-in-law to be. When he saw Elizabeth heading his direction with her mother, he excused himself and met them halfway.

"Let's step into the kitchen, Elizabeth. It may be a little quieter in there." Heman looked towards Elizabeth's mother. "I am sorry I have made you cross with me. I apologize. That was never my intention. Just like I asked your husband James for permission to wed his daughter, I would now like to ask for your permission and your blessing." Heman held Elizabeth close to him. "I love your daughter and wish to take care of her forever."

Janet smiled and pointed in Heman's direction. "Just as long as you promise never to do anything behind my back again."

"That I promise."

"Well then, let's celebrate this evening, for tomorrow we begin to plan a wedding. When is the wedding?"

"I want a Christmas wedding," Elizabeth announced.

"And you, Heman?"

"Whatever Elizabeth wants. I plan to take her to Ireland for a honeymoon."

Elizabeth threw her arms around his neck. "Ireland? How wonderful! I will meet your parents."

"Yes, Elizabeth, you will meet my parents, and they will meet you."

"Can I wear it now, Heman?"

"I don't see why not."

Elizabeth squealed and pulled a white ribbon from her neck and bosom. "Here, put it on my finger."

"How long have you had that?" Janet smiled at her daughter. "It's a beautiful ring."

"Since the day he kidnapped me! Isn't it beautiful, Mother? Come, Heman, let's show the rest of the family." At that, they left the kitchen and continued the celebration.

* * * * *

The *Lady Catherine* returned to Halifax on July 23. Henry was happy to report a successful trade trip. Not only did they restock the Irish Coffee Company in Boston, they had plenty to sell in Irish Coffee Company II in Halifax.

Heman, Elizabeth, and, of course, her mother were busy making preparations for a December wedding. They chose December 18 as the wedding date. Three days later, December 21, they would set sail for Ireland. Christmas would be celebrated on the *Lady Catherine*. The news spread throughout Halifax High Society. There was excitement in the air. Everyone who was anyone wanted an invitation to the wedding.

Heman quickly learned his role in preparing for this wedding: nod his head in agreement, otherwise keep very quiet. He didn't mind; just watching Elizabeth's enthusiasm was entertaining enough for him. Besides, Heman was busy himself getting *Lady Catherine* ready for the honeymoon cruise. He took the best part of the cargo hold and turned it into a bedroom suite. There was no holding back, only the best for Elizabeth.

* * * * *

Boston, August 1, 1865, William had a spring in his step as he walked to the Irish Coffee Company. A telegram had just been delivered to him personally. He was in a hurry to share the news with Duncan, Peggy, and Faye. They were working at the Irish Coffee Company, and that is where he was headed. He swung both doors open as he entered through the double doors. The bell above the door rang loudly as he passed through. "He did it! He did it! Big brother has finally done it."

All three looked up and heard William's statement loud and clear. But it was Peggy, who asked, "Heman, what has he done?" She was eager to hear.

William was eager to tell. "He asked Elizabeth to marry him. The engagement has been announced, and preparations have begun for a wedding."

"How exciting!" Faye was thrilled for their good friend, Heman. "When will the wedding be?"

"A Christmas affair, I'm told."

"How romantic!" Faye exclaimed.

"Yes, Faye, and he wants us to be there – all of us. I'm to deliver invitations to Captain Freeman and his wife Marie and Charles and Madam Caroline."

"How can that happen?" Duncan was always the serious and practical one. "He doesn't live across town."

Heman is asking Captain Freeman to sail the *Alma* to Halifax. We are all to be aboard."

"Tell me more." Peggy finally found her way into the conversation.

"The wedding is to be December 18. December 21 the married couple will sail to Ireland on the *Lady Catherine* for their honeymoon. My parents get to meet the daughter-in-law."

July 1865

My Darling Elizabeth,

I must write down in words and on paper how my heart feels. Lady Catherine thinks my buttons on my uniform are ready to bust loose. I believe she is right. And all because of you. My heart beats for two and has for a long time now, but since I have asked for your hand and you have accepted, my heart inside my chest has doubled or tripled in size.

To see the sun shining like diamonds on the blue water, I think of the small diamond you wear on your hand. To watch a proud seagull march up and down the wharf, dressed in his black and white best, makes me think how I also will be proudly waiting for you, dressed in black and white. I can picture it now, in the front of St. Paul's church watching you and your father walking arm in arm coming closer to me. My dream comes true.

I ask myself, "How can one man be so happy? What have I done to deserve you? God is good. Just ask Moses, whenever our paths meet he raises his head and makes the sign of the cross. I too thank God for you daily.

I promise you, Elizabeth, I will make you happy. That will be more important than any trade trip I will ever make. Whatever you ask, I will search the world over to provide it.

Thank you, Elizabeth, for allowing me to share your life. Without you, I would have no life. I look forward to being your husband.

Until that day
I love you always,
Heman

CHAPTER FOURTEEN

Do You, Heman Godfrey Kenney, Take Elizabeth Janet to Be Your Lawful Wedded Wife . . . ? I do

Back in Ireland, Jeremiah Darby was sitting in a hard wooden chair, directly across the desk of Captain Seiber. It was rare indeed to find himself upon a schooner, but here he was in the Captain's cabin. Daniel, since he was a captain, usually took care of this part of the business they shared together. Jeremiah's job was the cargo, and Daniel found the captains and their schooners to transport the cargo. But today Daniel had appointments with four captains.

"Impossible," he stated to Jeremiah that morning. "Impossible. Can't be in four different places in one day. Impossible."

That is how Jeremiah found himself sitting across from Captain Seiber. "How long will this trade trip take?"

Seiber raised his pen from the paper. "How long you say?"

"Yes, how long?"

Seiber returned to writing his order. Drawing in a deep breath, he tried to calm himself. He disliked working with land lubbers. Now if Captain Daniel was here, the question would not have been asked. It was a good thing he took a liking to Daniel, or he wouldn't even try to be patient with this man.

"Long enough," he finally fired an answer to the question. He handed the written order over the desk towards Jeremiah. "Everything is in order – give this to Captain Daniel."

Jeremiah pushed his chair back and began to rise.

"Oh, and one more thing." Seiber turned to a shelf with doors. He pulled the ivory handle and inside were letters tied with string. "These are for Daniel from America."

"Thank you, I will make sure he gets them this very day." The business arrangement was sealed by a bone-crushing handshake. Jeremiah was escorted off the schooner and into his waiting carriage. Before closing the door, he instructed his driver to take him back to his office.

Jeremiah was glad that was over. He removed his top hat and rubbed the back of his hand across his tired eyes. He closed his eyes and tried to clear his mind. All he could hear was the rhythm of the horses' hoofs as they hit the stone-cobbled road. Slowly opening his eyes, the letters tied with string came into view. Picking them up he could read a familiar name in the top left corner. Heman Kenney, Halifax, N.S.

"Oh, yes, our partner in this company. What good is a partner if he lives on the other side of the Atlantic?" He didn't mean to be bitter, but having Heman here would make it a lot easier for him and his father. He flicked his thumb to the other letter. "Good old William. Daniel has letters from both sons. Bridget will be happy this day."

Jeremiah placed the letters on Daniel's desk and headed for his own office. He had work to do. Some time had passed when the clatter of a chair falling, the bang of a door slamming shut, and someone running to his door caused Jeremiah to raise his head from his work. All of a sudden his door flew open, with Daniel crashing through.

"I can't believe he did it!" Daniel was waving the letter like a sword in the air. He was laughing and his eyes were filled with excitement.

"Look for yourself!" He stabbed the letter towards Jeremiah.

"Well, it can't be bad news," Jeremiah replied, "Just tell me."

"He's getting married!"

"Who?" Jeremiah didn't know which letter Daniel was reading.

"My son, he's getting married."

Jeremiah was on his feet celebrating with his partner. "But who?" His partner hadn't gotten to the answer of his question.

"Heman!"

"You gotta be kidding me. Heman? I would have thought William, but Heman you say."

"Yes, Heman. It says so right here." Daniel was swinging the letter in front of Jeremiah again.

"And not just that, he's coming home. I mean after the wedding and all. Jeremiah, my son is coming home and bringing a wife."

"I got to go home!"

"Bridget, I mean, we have to make plans." And with that Daniel ran out of the office, down the stairs running for the stables.

Days later, Jeremiah heard all the details of the excitement that went on at the Kenney Mansion that day. Oh, yes, he heard what William wrote too, details about a big Christmas Wedding in Halifax and everyone was going.

* * * * *

Heman was sitting in the parlour with the Finley family. Elizabeth was sitting on a footstool at his feet.

"It won't be long now." James was addressing Heman. "A little more than three weeks."

"Oh dear, I do hope everything is done," interrupted Janet. "Only three weeks you say, James? Time has gotten away."

"Don't worry, Mother, everything has been ordered. The RSVP's are beginning to come in, and Heman, we received our first wedding gift today." Elizabeth's eyes were full of excitement.

"We did?!

"Yes, Heman, come into the dining room and see." Elizabeth was on her feet tugging Heman's arm. "Mother has made a special table for the gifts for everyone to view. Come see."

Heman saw a mantle clock sitting on a table with a white lace tablecloth. "Who is it from?"

"My grandmother. She likes to be early for everything."

"Well, it is a very lovely clock," Heman said to Elizabeth as they returned to the living room.

"You know this is the Sunday to 'bid the banns,'[84] Heman," James stated.

"Yes, you will need to be with us at church Sunday morning, Heman," Elizabeth added.

Heman gave one of his smiles. "I'll be there."

"When do your brother and guests arrive?" Janet asked.

"December 15 the *Alma* will arrive. I have made plans for her to dock beside *Lady Catherine* at the Queen's Wharf. Captain Freeman has invited the whole Finley family to a dinner December 16. Will, Tom, and Emily be here then?"

"Yes, they will all be here December 15," Janet answered.

"You all will enjoy seeing the *Alma*. She is three times larger than *Lady Catherine* and a very beautiful ship."

James with business always on his mind, "Is she sailing from Boston to Halifax with an empty cargo hold?"

"No, sir, Charles Drew is bringing more of his tools, and I believe shoes and boots. If I know Captain Freeman, he will have something for you and your Textile Factory. We will just have to wait and see."

Janet was still worrying whether everything had been taken care of. "Elizabeth, did you talk to the baker?"

"Yes, Mother, he will deliver the three-tiered wedding cake the morning of the wedding. The first tier will be white cake. The second tier, the groom's cake, which is, of course, fruitcake."

"What's the third tier?" Heman was curious.

"It is also fruitcake. But it is not eaten at the wedding."

"Then what's it for?" He was even more curious.

"For the christening,"[85] Janet informed.

"What christening? We don't have a new ship to christen," Heman stated.

Elizabeth, Janet, and James laughed out loud. This made Heman a little uncomfortable. He wasn't used to being the brunt of the joke.

"Babies, silly, christening our first baby."

"Really?" Heman now understood why they laughed. "I guess I am used to christening ships," and he joined in on their laughter.

"Getting back to the cake. . ." Janet brought them back to subject. "Is the baker wrapping cake for the ladies?"

"Ladies get wrapped cake?" Heman was learning more than one thing about wedding cake.

"Yes, dear, they take the cake home and place it under their pillow that night.[86] They will dream of the man they will marry someday?"

"Did you dream of me, Elizabeth?"

"More than once, dear."

Janet was still fussing. "James, what if it snows? We have already had two snow storms. What if it snows?"

"Don't worry, dear, if it snows we will hire more sleighs. It will just add to the beauty of the wedding. Don't forget, it is the holiday season and people want snow. By the way, when will we see decorations around here? It is Christmas you know."

"I have hired decorators to come three days before the wedding."

"But you always do it yourself. I mean you and Elizabeth."

"Not this time, dear. We will be busy preparing for the wedding. Anyway, this year I want the house to have a special look. You wait and see."

Janet's worry about snow was soon a reality. It began snowing December 10th and didn't stop until the 12th. Twenty-four inches of new snow now blanketed the city of Halifax. It took the crew a full day to remove the snow from the deck of *Lady Catherine*. The snow didn't bother Heman at all. A new coal heater added below deck kept him and his crew warm. The really cold weather wouldn't start until January. Heman planned to be in Ireland by then.

Three days later, just after breakfast, Henry, John Charles, Moses and the Captain were enjoying their second cup of coffee, when they heard a great commotion on the Wharf. "What was that?" Henry asked as the *Lady Catherine* rocked up and down.

"Not here, no ship can dock here!" Heman worried. "I reserved that birth for the *Alma*. She will be here tomorrow. Get your coats. Let's see what is going on."

Heman was the first on deck. He couldn't believe what he saw. The *Alma* was being tied down, and her crew was running around her deck making sure she was secure.

"Happy Holidays!" It was Captain Freeman yelling as he supervised his crew.

"Welcome to Halifax," Heman cried back. "Wasn't expecting you until tomorrow."

"Thought we would sneak in port between storms," replied Freeman.

Between the dinner on the *Alma* and the wedding rehearsal dinner, both families got to know each other well. They were making lasting memories. Elizabeth and William were instant friends. Heman was proud to introduce Elizabeth to his brother and friends. They all knew about Elizabeth and were delighted to finally meet her. And, of course, they all approved of Heman's choice of a bride.

It wasn't until late the night before the wedding that Heman got to sit down and have a brother to brother visit with William. Everything was in place for the wedding the next day at 3:00 p.m.

"Heman, big brother, you look happy enough."

" How could I not be happy? The woman I love becomes mine tomorrow, my brother is here, and all the people I care about in this world are here, all except Father and Mother that is. And they, too, will be a part of this, when we see them on our honeymoon. So to answer your question, little brother, yes, I am very happy. What do you think of her?"

"Who?"

"Elizabeth, of course."

"Just kidding you, brother. For not knowing much about women, you surely know how to pick them. She lights up the room when she enters it."

"She's strong, not like some women who just sit around all day doing nothing. I can't believe she is to be mine."

They sat in silence for a time just drinking their Irish Coffee.

"I'm coming, Heman."

"What did you say? I don't think I understood." Heman was giving William his attention.

"I'm coming with you to Ireland. I want to go home. Now don't worry; I will make sure you don't see much of me, it being your honeymoon and all. But I will keep company with the crew. I can stay in your cabin since you won't be using it. I want to come with you, Heman."

Heman didn't have any words to speak for a long time. He allowed his brother to do all the talking. He could see that William was very serious. Finally, Heman asked, "What about Boston, the Irish Coffee Company, and your business? Are you just going to leave it?"

"I've made all the money I need for a lifetime. When I received your telegram, and you told us you were going to

Ireland, I became really homesick. I didn't know I was homesick until then. Sure, Duncan, Peggy, and Faye are like family, but they aren't family like you. I found myself alone in Boston."

"But what about them, William, do they know you want to return to Ireland?"

"I took it upon myself to speak to Duncan. I made him a deal he couldn't refuse. He will take over my company and still oversee the Irish Coffee Company. Peggy and Faye practically run that themselves. Duncan has worked hard for me. He is a smart man; he will do well. I will tell Peggy and Faye before we sail."

"Heman, I need to return to Ireland; it is time. And, besides, Mother and Father need one son to live close to them."

"I have taken you away for eight years. Mother will be happy to have you back. You left a boy and you return a great man. You have done well, William. Father and Mother will be proud."

"That's enough about me. We need to get you married tomorrow, big brother. Are you nervous?"

"I don't know. All I think about is Elizabeth. The day is finally here that she will be mine."

* * * * *

It didn't snow, instead, the sun was shining. It was a beautiful, brisk winter day in Nova Scotia. The date was December 18, 1865, and Heman was to be married that very day. Heman, his best man, and groomsmen were to be at St. Paul's Church by 2:30 p.m. William, the best man, was performing his duties well. He and the groomsmen, Henry, John Charles, Moses, Patrick, and Dick, had a breakfast together. Their wedding suits, made specially by the Finley Textile Co., had arrived the evening before, and they were figuring out how to wear them. Sailors weren't used to High Society, but they felt honoured when their Captain asked them to be his groomsmen.

St. Paul's Church was warm when the men arrived, thanks to the coal-burning furnace. The stained glass windows shimmered as the sun shone through, telling the story of the Gospel of Christ. The gold cross sat in the middle of the altar. Heman and William took their places in a room at the front. His crew began escorting the lady guests to their pews. The church was filled with family and friends, who were eager to see the bride and groom.

The organ sounded, the cue for Heman and William to step to the front. The crew escorted the bridesmaids down the aisle to their places. The music changed to "The Bridal March." The congregation stood and the doors to the sanctuary opened. There stood Elizabeth and her father James.

Heman had never seen anything so beautiful. Elizabeth looked better than a princess, better than a queen. Words could not describe how lovely she was. He watched as she walked closer to him. Her wedding gown[87] was ivory velvet sprinkled with pearls. It had flowing sleeves with a gathered full skirt both trimmed with white fur. The same fur trimmed her veil, which flowed down the back of her gown and formed a train. Her hands were inside a fur muff. Hanging from the muff were long strands of white and blue[88] ribbon.

James delivered her to Heman. *What a gift to receive,* he thought. Their eyes met through her white veil. They exchanged a smile and then turned towards the minister. Heman felt like he was in a dream, a good dream. He answered the minister, "I do."

He heard her voice, "I do."

"You may now kiss your bride." He carefully removed her veil from her face and placed his lips on hers.

The minister turned to the congregation. "I would now like to present to you for the first time, Captain and Mrs. Heman Kenney."

They now walked back down the aisle towards the great doors. For an instant, they were alone. He took her in his arms and whispered, "I love you."

She kissed him and replied, "I love you too."

A receiving line was formed, and best wishes were given from family and friends to the bride and groom. William then approached them, "Heman and Elizabeth, your sleigh awaits." Elizabeth was using the navy blue cape Heman gave her the day of their engagement while sailing on the *Lady Catherine*. He had his fur coat. They both stepped out of St. Paul's Church heading for their sleigh. A handsome pair of black horses awaited to take them to the Finley home. There they would join their guests for the wedding reception. Darkness was falling upon them as the beautiful pair of black horses pulled the sleigh up Barrington St. The silver harness, mixed with silver bells, made music as they passed the lamplighters lighting the street lamps. The lighters lifted their torches in a salute as the sleigh passed by.

Heman held Elizabeth close. "Are you happy, my love?"

"As happy as I can be, my husband."

The horses made a right turn onto Prince Street and then a left onto Argyle. Luminaries lit up the way 50 yards from the Finley driveway. Friends and family were there to welcome the newly married couple.

The Finley house looked like a mansion. Luminaries lit up the whole yard. Balsam fir boughs with white bows surrounded the door and windows. A great Balsam fir Christmas tree stood in the foyer. Decorations of white bows, beaded cranberries, and sugar plums hung on the boughs of the tree. Candles also were placed on the tree, but no one minded when they were not lit.

A rope of fir boughs was strung on the stair banister. It was covered with red and white flowers made from tissue paper. Another Christmas tree was in the living room by the fireplace. Small coloured envelopes were in a Christmas bowl, ready for the guests to fill with money and hang on the tree, a gift for the newlyweds.

James didn't have to worry about Christmas decorations; Janet had filled the whole house. Their dining room sparkled with crystal and candles. The table was filled with food set for a banquet.

The bride and groom spent their time mingling with their guests. They finally found the time to be in the parlour, where Duncan, Faye, Peggy, and William were sitting visiting with Captain Freeman and his wife Marie and the Drews.

"Here's the busy couple." William stood, "Congratulations, and may we toast you, big brother?"

"Don't forget Elizabeth, little brother."

"You I can forget, but never dear Elizabeth. To you both."

Everyone was on their feet, raising their crystal glasses. "God bless you in your life together."

"Thank you."

"You are such a beautiful bride." Faye timidly reached out to touch the beautiful wedding gown.

"Thank you, Faye. And I am so glad you could come and be at our wedding."

"You must be tired?" Peggy asked.

"Oh, no, Peggy, I want this night to go on forever."

Heman smiled at Elizabeth. "I do believe my wife likes to party." His arm already around Elizabeth, he brought her closer to him.

"No, not the party, Heman," as she looked into his eyes. "The celebration of your being my husband, I don't want it to end."

"The celebration will never end, my love." Everyone in the room believed it.

It was after midnight when the last farewells were given to their guests. Now, only the Finley family was left to reminisce about the day. James and Janet had prepared Elizabeth's room for the married couple.

One by one they said good night, and Heman and Elizabeth were left alone by the fireplace. The logs were burned to red coals, which still reflected light towards the Christmas tree. Heman picked Elizabeth up and placed her on his lap. "It's been a great day, a day I have been dreaming about for several years. You are the most beautiful bride that any man could ever have."

"I love you, Heman."

He looked down and her eyes were closing. She opened them again. "I love you." Her eyes were too heavy and they closed.

Heman smiled down at her. He sat there watching her sleep for some time. He picked her up and carried her towards the stairs. He was going to put his wife to bed.

* * * * *

"Happy New Year!" Heman raised his crystal goblet towards Elizabeth.

"Happy New Year, husband!" Elizabeth's goblet gently hit the side of Heman's. "1866 – I wonder what it will bring?" she asked.

As she thought of what 1866 would bring, her mind wondered back just a few weeks before. A wonderful wedding, all the family, and friends that were around them. The day they sailed was bitter cold. Heman insisted they say their goodbyes at her parents' house. It may have been for the best, for her mother cried through breakfast and lunch before they said goodbye. Elizabeth remained in the honeymoon suite safe and warm, as they sailed out of the Harbour. It didn't take long for Heman to join her, and they remained together wrapped in the heart of *Lady Catherine* for three days. Christmas Day brought them out of their warm cocoon. Heman wearing his fur coat, and she the velvet cape, they strolled the upper deck, breathing in the freezing air. Christmas on a schooner, sailing across the Atlantic, watching ice burgs tower in the distance. My how her life had changed.

"The new year will bring happiness, of course," replied Heman. "Having you makes my life happy."

Elizabeth's thoughts returned to the present. She held her goblet high in the air, "Happiness, of course, 1866 will be happy for us. Can we stay here forever?"

"You like the *Lady Catherine*, don't you?"

"From the first time I was aboard her. Yes, I love The *Lady Catherine*. And this room, fit for a queen. Can we stay here forever?"

"Why would you want to stay here forever?"

"Because I don't have to share you with anyone else. Just you and me."

"You wouldn't get tired of me?"

"Never, and never." She put her arms around his neck and kissed him.

"The crew has been taking good care of us, haven't they?"

"Yes, and sometimes I think we are all alone on this great schooner."

"Oh, but we are not. Without John Charles, we might end up in Timbuktu."

"I like your crew."

"There is someone else onboard you like as well."

Elizabeth sat up straight. "Who?"

"William."

"William, your brother, William?"

"Little brother himself."

"But why?"

"He's homesick and wants to see his mother."

"How wonderful! You mean we have been on this ship almost two weeks and we haven't seen William?"

"Well, under the circumstances, he didn't want to get in the way. Remember you just said you didn't want to share me with anyone."

"Yes, but I didn't mean your brother." Heman laughed and drew his wife closer to him.

"Let's have dinner with him; he must be lonely."

"Don't worry; he has the crew. He's not lonely. Let's wait a few more days. I'm not ready to share you with anyone else."

It was a few days later that Heman and Elizabeth had dinner with William. It was not just William but all the officers. It was sort of a coming-out party.

* * * * *

January 1866 – Heman, Elizabeth, and William were top deck when they approached Cork Harbour. William pointed across to an inlet, where houses could be seen in the distance. "Right over there, Elizabeth, that's where the Kenney mansion is. I bet you Ada is outside the kitchen door waving her white towel. We can't see her, but she can see us."

"Heman, I do hope they like me."

"Don't worry," William spoke for Heman. "They have always wanted a daughter around the house. You will be the center of attention."

"He's right, Elizabeth. They can't help liking you. Don't worry." Heman took her hand to reassure her.

"I just hope there is not a Union Jack to go under."

"Very funny, big brother. Very funny." Nothing could spoil William's mood. He was glad to be home.

"A Union Jack in Ireland?" questioned Elizabeth.

"I will tell you all about it later, my love."

"Don't believe a word he says, Elizabeth."

Elizabeth didn't know what they were talking about, so she changed the subject. "How long will it be now, Heman?"

Elizabeth could see the excitement written on both men's faces. They were coming home. And she --she was to meet her new family.

She put her arm around her husband. Heman looked down at her and drew her close. "It won't be long now, my love. It won't be long."

Do You, Heman Godfrey Kenney, Take Elizabeth Janet to Be Your Lawful Wedded Wife . . . ? I do

Lincoln Wharf

Boston

January 1866

Dear Heman and Elizabeth,

Thank you for inviting Marie and me to witness such a beautiful wedding. I'm not into weddings myself; however, it was most enjoyable if I do say so. That is all the ladies talked about on our trip back to Boston.

The news of Duncan taking over William's company here in Boston was celebrated. Everyone in Boston is shocked by his return to Ireland. He will be greatly missed. William made a name for himself around these parts.

Halifax is quite the city. A little on the cold side. I would love to see it in summer. Maybe Marie and I will make a trip someday. I can see why you like it, and, of course, the reason for you settling there. Elizabeth, you are wonderful and your family very hospitable. Mr. Finley and I enjoyed talking business.

May you both enjoy your visit to Ireland. Our paths will cross again, I am certain of it, And until then;

A Fellow Seaman

Reuben Freeman

CHAPTER FIFTEEN

Cork, Ireland 1866

Daniel lowered his spyglass. "They're coming. *Lady Catherine* just entered the mouth of the river. I would recognize her anywhere." He wasn't used to having his wife at the shipyard, but Bridget had been there for the last two days watching and waiting for her son to return.

"Are you sure, Daniel? Are you sure?"

She raised the spyglass to her eye and searched the distance. "All I see is fishing boats."

"Look, farther over to your right." He pointed towards the direction in which he saw *Lady Catherine*.

"Is that her? I see a schooner. She only has one sail up."

"Full sail would bring her into the river too quickly. She is a fast ship, Bridget. Can you see anyone on board?"

Bridget continued to search. "I see people running around the ship, but I can't tell who they are."

"Here, let me take a look."

"Surely you have another spyglass." Bridget was reluctant to part with hers.

Daniel walked into his partner's office. "I need your spyglass, Jeremiah. I believe *Lady Catherine* is on her way up the river."

"I thought you had a spyglass?" questioned Jeremiah.

"I do, but my wife has taken it over."

Jeremiah laughed. "I will be there to greet them when they dock," Jeremiah spoke as Daniel returned to Bridget.

"Now I can look too." He smiled at his wife. "They are tacking around the bend. We will be able to see better soon."

"I see Heman!" Bridget cried. "Look, Daniel!"

"Saints preserve us! Can it be?" Daniel couldn't believe what he was seeing.

"What is it, Daniel?" Bridget turned her spyglass in search of what her husband was seeing.

"I see a man standing beside a young lady. Up on the bow, Bridget. Can it be? Look, can you see?"

"I'm trying, Daniel," as she maneuvered her spyglass back and forth to view the deck of the schooner. "I see the young lady, but the gentleman beside her is facing the other way."

"Oh, she is beautiful, Daniel. Look at our daughter-in-law."

"You should take a better look at the gentleman standing beside her."

"Who is he? I can't tell. Wait a minute. He is turning. William! It's William. Can it be, Daniel? Both of our sons are coming home. They held each other. "It's been so long, Daniel."

Jeremiah entered the room. "They must be getting close. Can you see anything?"

"William is with them. Heman is bringing William home."

"I thought he was bringing a wife?"

"He has brought both," Bridget answered, as she lifted her spyglass to her eye.

Thirty minutes later, they were on the Wharf waving as the schooner came closer to the dock. Daniel, Bridget, and Jeremiah were doing their best to welcome the *Lady Catherine* home. Mahoney joined them. He had just heard the news that Heman was bringing William home. A day did not pass without his thinking of the Kenney brothers. How many years had it been? He had no idea when they left that it would take so long for them to come back home.

Mahoney caught one of the ropes tossed ashore and tied the *Lady Catherine* to the Wharf. The gangplank now connected the schooner to the Wharf. Daniel and Bridget didn't wait for the whistle. They were onboard the deck heading towards their children.

Heman had given control of the *Lady Catherine* to Henry. He put his arm around Elizabeth and looked down at her. "Well, here they come." She smiled back.

The crew was not surprised how quickly the family came together. They allowed their Captain this time of reunion. Their job was to make sure *Lady Catherine* was settled.

William was holding his mother. Heman was shaking his father's hand. Elizabeth just watched the reunion and could feel the joy that filled the air. After Heman embraced his mother, he stood back and put his arm around Elizabeth. "This is Elizabeth, my wife, and your daughter-in-law."

Bridget reached out to Elizabeth and put her arm around her. "Welcome to this family. If Heman loves you, we will love you also. I've always wanted a daughter, and now I have one." Elizabeth noticed tears in the corner of Bridget's eyes.

Daniel said, "Now it's my turn." He took Elizabeth's hand into his. "Heman has chosen well. Welcome to our family. Heman has not only brought us a daughter but has brought his younger brother home too."

"You didn't tell us, Heman," Bridget added.

"He didn't know until the night before his wedding," William informed his mother. "I just wanted to come home to you and to Ireland."

"Does that mean you are going stay?" His mother questioned her son.

"Yes, Mother, that means I'm going to stay."

"That's wonderful, son." Daniel was genuinely grateful to have a son close by. "You can tell us all the details later, but first there are a few people on the Wharf that want to welcome you and your brother home." Daniel guided them down the gangplank. The whistle sounded. The Captain was leaving his ship.

Mahoney thought he was going to have tears in his eyes. He wiped them away quickly. He felt like his sons were home. He watched them grow as boys, and now they return as men, one with a wife. All of a sudden he felt old.

"Good to see you, Mahoney." William looked around at the familiar surroundings. He fought the urge to drop to his knees and kiss the ground. This was Ireland. William wasn't the same feisty kid that left years past. He remembered that awful night when Mahoney stuck him in the cargo bay of the *Lady Catherine. Straw for a bed, cold and very seasick,* he shivered at the thought.

"So good to see you, lad." Mahoney stuck out his hand to shake the hand of a man, not a lad.

"The feeling is mutual." William followed the handshake with a bear hug.

Heman was busy introducing his bride. William took in the scene in slow motion. There was a lump in his throat, and if he wasn't careful, tears would be flowing like a river. He was home, and glad to be there.

After a time of getting reacquainted, Jeremiah made an announcement to them all: "Welcome home boys, or should I say, gentlemen? Boys doesn't seem to fit. We all have been looking forward to this day for some time now." Gesturing towards Elizabeth, "Welcome to Ireland, my dear. Heman is a very lucky man to have you. May your visit to Ireland be a long and happy one. I am sure we will see each other soon, but for now, Daniel, take your family home. Enjoy them while you have them."

Mahoney had two carriages ready. It didn't take long for luggage to be packed, and they climbed aboard the carriages. William rode with his mother, and Daniel accompanied the newlyweds.

"Are you sure you don't want to be alone? I can ride in the other carriage."

"Oh, no, Mr. Kenney. We have been alone for several weeks. I mean . . ." Both Heman and Daniel laughed.

"I believe Elizabeth means we would be privileged to have you in our company as we travel home." Heman was teasing his wife. She smiled with gratitude.

Heman enjoyed seeing the familiar view as the carriage made its way to Carragline. In between conversation with his father, he was able to point out historical landmarks to Elizabeth. They continued up Churchill Road, turning onto Rose Hill and through the gates and down the great driveway to the Kenney Mansion. "How beautiful!" Elizabeth's eyes took in the mansion and surrounding gardens.

Doors of the mansion were opening, as the whole household gathered at the front drive to welcome the eldest son home. O'Sullivan and George held the bridles of the horses, as they tried to get a glance at the family as they exited the carriages. William was the first to jump out of the carriage. Everyone gasped in delight.

"William, it's William! What in the world?" Ada was crying and fanning herself with the edge of her white apron, for she was afraid she was going to faint. "My prayers have been answered." Ada looked to the sky, "Thank you, Lord, thank you, Lord, He is finally home. Now, look what you've gone and done." She wiped the tears out of her eyes. "Made an old lady cry." By that time, William was giving her a bear hug.

"This is the welcome that I have dreamed of. I am so glad to be back home in Ireland. Shhh, now Ada, I am not the most important arrival. You must meet Elizabeth."

Daniel was standing among his beloved household. "As you can see, both sons are home. How grateful Bridget and I are for this day. But, not just our sons, we have a new member of the family. I will let you, Heman, do the honors of introducing your fine wife to the other members of this family." Daniel smiled at both Heman and his new daughter.

"Thank you, sir, I would be delighted." He took Elizabeth by the hand. "Come with me, my dear. I have some friends I want you to meet." Everyone was happy, for the Kenney family was back together again.

Ada had a fine dinner planned. She had started cooking from the moment they saw the *Lady Catherine* enter the Harbour. Until it was ready, Heman and William were showing Elizabeth around. The first stop was the stables, where William was already waiting for them.

"Well, it looks like Father has lost interest in breeding horses for the hunt." It was more of a statement rather than a question.

"There are more horses here than I have ever seen." Elizabeth gave oats to a black beauty. He was watching her from his stall.

"Any horse that comes into the Kenney stables has a life better than some people." O'Sullivan had just arrived with a load of hay. "You can believe me when I tell you so. Welcome home, boys, and an Irish welcome to you, lassie."

"Thank you. You are very kind." Elizabeth found a chestnut with dark brown sleepy eyes wanting attention. She scratched him right between the eyes.

"Elizabeth, O'Sullivan and George are the keepers of the stable."

"Nicest Stable I have ever been in." Elizabeth wandered to the next stall, visiting a tall red horse.

"That's the only one left." O'Sullivan was informing William. Remember the new colts bought just before you left?

"Yes, I do. I thought they had great potential in racing or, for that matter, the fox hunt."

"Well, after you were gone, your father lost interest. Oh, it wasn't right away, but less and less he came to the stable. I guess he missed you, William. Your father rode this one in several fox hunts, but he lost interest in that as well. The other colt was sold, and now this one is old enough to be but a pet."

"I'm sure that now William is home to stay, things will pick up around here. I couldn't turn him into a sailor, so you and George will have to put up with him."

"Not like he didn't try. I prefer my legs being on solid ground, thank you."

"How sweet it will be having you here. It will be like the good old days, just like the good old days." O'Sullivan repeated the words over and over. They echoed throughout the stable as he went about his duties.

* * * * *

"Are you sure you won't miss all this?" Elizabeth tucked her hand into the crook of Heman's arm. They were strolling through the moors. The wind was blowing in from the Irish Sea. With her free hand, she brought her hood closer to her face.

"Are you cold?" Heman drew her closer to him. "Should we go back?"

"No, I love walking the moors. Are you sure you won't miss this?"

"Miss what, Elizabeth?"

"Ireland, Heman, I feel I am taking you away from Ireland and your family. Won't you miss it?"

"Elizabeth, you have not taken me away from Ireland. That happened years ago. I'm enjoying my visit, but it's no longer home. Home is with you. Nova Scotia is now my home. Now, don't worry yourself. Look, I have something for you – a gift."

"A gift for me?" Elizabeth's eyes lit up. "What is it?"

Heman gave her a small box from his pocket. "This is for you to wear while you are in Ireland."

Elizabeth opened the box. A ring, a very special ring was sitting on blue velvet. "What is it, Heman?" She took the ring out and looked at it closely. "Your mother wears one."

"It's a Claddagh ring."[89]

"A what?"

"A Claddagh ring. In Ireland, this ring is worn like a sign. Worn on the right hand with the heart pointing out means that the heart is uncommitted. Worn on the same hand with the heart pointing in means that the heart is taken. Worn on the left hand with the heart pointing in means, 'Let Love and Friendship reign forever, never to be separated.' " Heman took her left hand, removed her diamond wedding ring, and placed it on her right hand for safe keeping. He then placed the Claddagh ring on her finger and said, "While you are in Ireland, I want people to know that our love reigns forever, and it will never be separated from us."

Elizabeth looked down at her finger. The heart was pointing in towards her heart. "Tell me more about the ring. There must be a story to tell."

"According to 16th Century Irish folklore, a fishing boat from the Village of Claddagh was captured by Algerian pirates, and the crew was sold into slavery. One of the crew was a young man by the name of Richard Joyce, who was to be married the same week he was captured. Instead, Richard found himself far away from his love and his homeland. He was sold to a wealthy Moorish goldsmith, who taught him the trade and, eventually, he became skilled enough to design a ring of special significance. The hands were for friendship, the crown was for loyalty, and the heart was for love."[90]

"How sad, Heman, I feel like weeping?"

"No, wait, before you weep," he smiled at her, "hear the rest of the story."

"Years went by, but Richard never forgot his sweetheart. Somehow, he managed to escape and make his way home to Ireland. When he arrived back in Claddagh, he discovered that his girl had never married. They were wed immediately, and the ring he gave her was the one he had designed and made while he was a slave."

Elizabeth had tears in her eyes. "Elizabeth, why do you weep?"

"Oh, Heman, happy tears." She wiped them from her eyes. "True love is so wonderful. Go on, tell me more."

"Over the years, the design became extremely popular as a betrothal or wedding ring. While you are in Ireland, would you wear this ring?"

"Of course I will. Every time I look at it I will be reminded of our true love." She tightened her grip on his arm and walked along silently enjoying being together.

* * * * *

"Are you nervous, my love?" Heman took Elizabeth into his arms.

"Very nervous," Elizabeth responded. "I think your mother has invited all of Ireland. Please don't leave me, Heman."

"I will never leave you, my love."

"I mean tonight, Heman, don't leave me alone tonight."

"You are troubled."

"I don't know anyone. I want them to like me. I want to make you proud."

"You already make me proud. But I tell you what, if I have to leave your side, I will make sure William takes my place. Is that a deal?"

"Deal." Elizabeth left his arms. "I must get ready."

Heman was relieved to see Elizabeth's mood change. "Well then, I will go see if George or O'Sullivan needs any help. Mother has had them working for a week now."

"Don't forget to come and get me when it starts."

"How can I forget you? You are the love of my life." With that, he closed the door and headed for the stairs. He glanced into the parlour on his way to the kitchen. A large picture of his mother hanging above the fireplace smiled back at him. His father had placed it there shortly after Heman was born. Everything seemed to be in place for the great reception taking place that evening. His father and mother wanted to show off their new daughter-in-law. Everyone wanted to meet the wife from America.

Heman entered the kitchen. It was like a beehive. Everyone was rushing around making sure the food was perfect. Ada took a moment from the stove and greeted Heman. "How is the Bride holding up?"

Just like Ada to think of Elizabeth. "A little nervous, but I think she will hold up well."

"Well, you make sure you take good care of her tonight. With all these people coming to gawk at her, it would make anyone nervous."

"I plan to have William help me. That way we will make sure she is never alone."

"That's a good idea."

"Where is William?"

"Where else but the stable? He's been there since he came back home." Ada's eyes misted. "Thank you, Heman, for bringing him home. I hear he did a good job in America."

"Yes, Ada, William has proven himself over and over. He just had some growing up to do when he left here."

"Well, I need to get back to cooking. There is some kind of party going on here tonight." She smiled at Heman.

"That there is, and I need to find William."

Ada was correct. William was working a pair of red Hunters. They would soon be trained and ready to be harnessed to a carriage. Heman just watched for a time. "William, you seem happy enough."

William grinned at his brother. "I didn't realize how much I missed it, until I returned home."

"Ada says you are sleeping out here."

"No, I missed my bed almost as much as the stable. It's good to be home, big brother."

"I have a favour to ask you, William."

"Name it. Anything you want, brother." William let the horses run free and walked towards Heman.

"I need you to help take care of Elizabeth this evening."

"You not man enough to take care of your wife this evening?"

"Very funny. You know what it will be like – people milling around trying to get close to Elizabeth. I don't want her to be alone at all. If I am required to speak to the Captains, I want you to be with her."

"I will be delighted to take care of my sister-in-law. Don't worry. She will be in good hands."

"I knew I could count on you."

George and O'Sullivan entered the stable's double doors, pushing wheelbarrows. "What do you have there, George?"

Before he could answer, O'Sullivan, greeted the brothers. "Just the ones we were looking for. You can help us put all these in their places."

"He's talking about these pots of shamrocks,"[91] George replied.

Heman noticed the wheelbarrows were filled with pots of green shamrocks. "Where did you get them?" Heman knew it was too early for shamrocks to be growing.

"We have been growing these since we got word you were coming for your honeymoon," O'Sullivan added. "And there is a lot more in the greenhouse."

"What are you going to do with them?" William just knew it sounded like work.

"Your mother wants them placed on the steps in front of the mansion."

"And along the driveway," George informed them. "Like O'Sullivan said, we need your help."

"What's with all the shamrocks anyway?" William wanted to know.

"It's luck, my boy. Shamrocks are used in many weddings. The guests get to take them home, especially those looking for a mate. Before you know it, they will have a wedding."

"But we already had a wedding." Heman wasn't sure he was ready to go through another one.

"Tell your mother that." George was smiling.

"It is officially called 'A Coming Out Ball' my Misses keeps telling me," O'Sullivan informed. "I just do what I am told."

"I guess that is all we can do." Heman had learned that quickly.

The men were hard at work placing potted shamrocks in a colourful display. Ada came to inspect their work more than once. Even Bridget came to encourage their work. They were not surprised when another person approached to make sure the pots were perfectly placed. It was Vicar McCarthy pointing his cane, directing the placement of the pots. "Nice to see you again,

Heman. I was honoured when your parents asked me to come and bless the newlyweds."

"You are?" Heman hadn't been told. *I think I'd best inform Elizabeth,* thought Heman.

"It won't be a big ceremony or anything – just a few prayers and such. How do you like America? Not like Ireland, I suppose. I don't think I could leave. I think my bones will be buried right out there on the moors." The Vicar really didn't expect an answer. The men just finished their work.

* * * * *

Bridget lightly knocked on Elizabeth's bedroom door.

"Come in."

Bridget opened the door, and there sitting in front of her mirror was Elizabeth. "Hello, Mother Kenney." Elizabeth was trying to fix a dark curl that would not be controlled.

"Here, let me help." Bridget took the comb and quickly had the curl in place. "There, Elizabeth, stand up and let me take a look at you. How beautiful you are!" She turned her around to see every side. "Your dress is gorgeous." Bridget placed her hand on the soft, white material.

"It's my wedding dress. I thought I would surprise Heman. Of course, I wouldn't wear the veil. Do you think it is okay?"

"Of course, my daughter, you honor us all by wearing your wedding dress. I only wish I could have been there." Bridget dabbed a tear from her eye with her lace hanky. "But I'm not going to cry; you are here now and I will only think of tonight. I have a gift for you." Elizabeth opened a box. "It's a 'magic hanky,' "[92] Bridget continued. "All Irish brides carry one. I would like you to carry this tonight."

Elizabeth held up the delicate hanky. "How is it magic?"

"In time you fold it like this and stitch here and here, and it turns into a christening bonnet for your first baby. And then with a couple snips, it can be turned back into a hanky that your daughter can carry on her wedding day. I didn't have a daughter.

My mother gave this to me on my wedding day. Now I give it to you."

"Oh, Mother Kenney, how wonderful. I will always remember this moment."

Bridget took her into her arms and thought, *Yes, we will both remember this for the rest of our lives.*

* * * * *

Heman was pleased when he saw Elizabeth in her wedding dress. Her beauty took his breath away, the same as it did two months before. "Are you ready?" All they had to do was open the door, walk along the landing, and down the main staircase. "Everyone is waiting. Father is waiting at the top of the staircase to announce us. He is going to use a fog horn to get the guests' attention."

Elizabeth laughed. "Heman, don't make me laugh. I won't be able to stop. This is serious."

"Not too serious, my love."

"Is he really using a foghorn?"

"I've persuaded him to use another method – bells.[93] When we hear the bells, we are to make our way to the staircase. You see, the chime of bells is thought to keep evil spirits away. Also, they are to remind a couple of their wedding vows. Oh, yes, and to restore harmony if a couple is fighting."

"Amazing! Bells do all that? Heman, are there evil spirits around here?"

"I grew up around here. I've not seen an evil spirit yet."

They both heard the chime of a bell. "Is that our cue, Heman? I just heard one bell. You said 'bells.'"

"I thought 'bells,' but I guess one bell is going to have to do."

"Don't make me laugh, Elizabeth, this is serious business."

Elizabeth, holding tightly to Heman's arm, walked together with him to the top of the staircase. The sounds of delight reached them from below.

Daniel stepped close to Elizabeth and whispered in her ear. "You look beautiful, my daughter." Elizabeth answered with a smile.

Daniel met Heman's eyes. No words were necessary. He turned back to Elizabeth, "Are you ready?" He didn't wait for an answer.

Daniel rang his bell once, even though it wasn't necessary. All the guests had his undivided attention. All eyes were on Heman and his bride Elizabeth. "This evening I have the pleasure of introducing to you, my guests and friends, Heman's bride." Daniel had a lump in his throat. "As you can see, a beautiful bride, she is. May I introduce to you, Captain Heman and Mrs. Elizabeth Kenney?"

As Heman carefully lead his wife down the step, a symphony of bells rose up to them, for everyone had a bell to ring. Heman turned closely to her ear. "More than one bell, my dear." They both smiled as they descended the grand staircase.

Vicar McCarthy stepped forward, and when the blessing for the married couple was complete, Heman began to speak.

Elizabeth looked into his eyes, for she did not know what he was about to say. "I've made my wedding vows to Elizabeth back at her home in Nova Scotia. I plan to keep those vows forever. But now being back in Ireland, I would like to add another vow for all of you to witness."

Heman turned towards Elizabeth and took her hands into his and said these words:

"By the power that Christ brought from heaven, mayst thou love me.

As the sun follows its course, mayst thou follow me.

As light to the eye, as bread to the hungry, as joy to the heart,

May thy presence be with me, oh one that I love? ,

Till death comes to part us asunder."[94]

Silence hung over the room. Vicar McCarthy shuffled forward, "Amen."

The guests replied, "Amen."

"You may now kiss your bride." Vicar McCarthy thought it would be a good way to end the ceremony.

Heman placed his lips upon Elizabeth's. A cheer arose from all in the room.

"May the dancing begin," William cheered.

Heman and William didn't have to worry about Elizabeth. The new bride learned the Irish Jig, and there was no stopping her. When Heman finally got his turn, she cried. "You didn't tell me you could dance."

"Only the Irish Jig, my dear. Only the Irish Jig."

* * * * *

"Our first Fox Hunt since my return." William was sitting in one of the winged back chairs. "Are you ready, Father?"

"I am. Everyone in Cork is talking about it," Daniel replied as he made himself comfortable in his favourite lounging chair. He picked up his pipe and stuffed it with tobacco.

"Fox Hunts have only been in my dreams, the last several years that is." William rested his head on the back of his chair. Closing his eyes, he continued speaking. "To watch the day breaking from purple to dazzling gold while trotting up a deep-rutted lane; to inhale the early freshness when on the sheep-cropped uplands; to stare back at the low country with its cock-crowing farms and mist-coiled waterways; thus to be riding out with a sense of spacious discovery. . ."

"Well look at that, Elizabeth," Heman gestured towards his wife. "You don't even have to go to the Hunt, just close your eyes and. . ."

"Oh, Heman, you broke the spell. William, go on I could see everything you said."

"I'm grateful someone was with me," William smiled, "but you are right the spell is broken." He sat up straight in his chair. "Why don't you come?"

"On the Fox Hunt?" Heman was sitting on the chesterfield and Elizabeth was sitting at his feet. "I think I want my young wife to remain in one piece, thank you."

"I'm afraid I don't ride horses," Elizabeth informed William.

William was on his feet. "But she doesn't have to. She could watch all the action up on the ridge on the highlands. You could take her there and view the whole hunt."

"I would love to. Can we Heman?!" Elizabeth's excitement filled the whole room.

"Do you know how early we would have to be there? I'm still fast asleep at that time of the morning."

"I will personally kick you out of bed," William replied. "It's settled." He took Elizabeth's hands, lifted her up, and swung her around the room. She squealed with delight as she fell on the leather chesterfield beside Heman.

William turned to his mother. "And you?!"

"Don't touch me, William! You will mess up my needlepoint." She smiled at her son. She was satisfied sitting in her high back chair watching her children. Life had returned to the Kenney mansion.

"You are going, aren't you?" William asked.

"I wouldn't miss it for the world."

"Mother Kenney, you are going on the Fox Hunt?" Elizabeth was amazed.

"Of course, my daughter, everyone will be there."

Daniel added, "Yes, everyone will be there as he smiled and smoked his pipe."

* * * * *

William did not have to worry about Heman staying in bed. Elizabeth was up two hours before sunup. Not that Heman wanted to be awake. His wife made it impossible for him to sleep. "It's the middle of the night, Elizabeth. Go back to sleep."

"No, it is not. I heard the Grandfather clock strike the hour."

"Yes, so did I and it only struck four times. Go back to sleep."

"But I can't!" She jumped out of bed and ran to the window. The sun is going to be up, and I don't want to miss anything."

"It is 4 a.m., Elizabeth, you are going to wake the whole house."

Elizabeth reluctantly returned to their bed and drew closer to Heman. "I bet William is already up."

* * * * *

The sky was so blue, so pure, and grass so green it looked like a painted picture. "It doesn't seem real!" Elizabeth exclaimed, practically standing in the carriage.

"You had better hang on." Heman was actually enjoying the moment. Not because he liked Fox Hunts or horses for that matter. But looking through Elizabeth's eyes made it very exciting. They had been up since 4:30 a.m. and walking into the kitchen a short time after, he had been surprised to see Ada and her kitchen buzzing with activity.

"Good morning, lassie!" Of course, Ada's attention went straight to Elizabeth. Heman smiled even if he did feel invisible. "Come, sit yourself right here, Elizabeth, you need to eat before you leave."

"Can I sit beside her?" Heman turned and smiled at his wife.

"I don't want to stay long." Elizabeth was anxious. "I don't want to be late and miss anything."

"Don't worry, lassie, you will not miss a thing. William has it all planned. Your carriage is ready and George will be your driver. I also have prepared a basket of food."

"You have taken good care of us." Heman was drinking his steaming coffee.

Ada's only reply was, "Heman, you take care of Elizabeth today. Nothing is to happen to her."

"Do not worry, Ada. I promise to do my duty and make sure my wife stays safe. I will make sure no fox gets near her." Heman winked at Ada. "Where is William?" Heman noticed there was no sign of his brother.

"He has left already. He has been in the barn all night."

"See, I told you! Do finish your coffee, Heman. It is past time." Elizabeth was on her feet and with a swish of her black skirt, she was out the door heading for the stable.

Heman took a last gulp of his coffee, burning his tongue in the process. Raising his hand in a farewell gesture to Ada, "She may be harder to keep safe than I thought." He was out the door trying to catch up to Elizabeth.

Lanterns lit up the stable area and driveway. The sun would not be up for another hour. George and O'Sullivan were busy preparing the horses. "William and your father have taken their mounts but thirty minutes ago. Your mother's horse is ready and O'Sullivan will ride with her to the O'Flaherty's farm. There she will meet the Darby's. You and your lassie will ride with me in the open carriage. We plan to visit the O'Flaherty's farm before heading to the ridge upon the highlands.

Elizabeth pulled her black Melton jacket down over her black skirt. Her hat reminded her of a man's derby, and she pulled it down over her dark curls. "How do I look?"

Heman quickly replied, "Best bonnet I have ever seen!"

Elizabeth's laugh rang out in the darkness. "Oh, you are so silly."

"Are we ready?" George questioned.

Elizabeth's answer was to jump into the carriage, startling the two chestnut horses. It was a good thing O'Sullivan was holding their bridles.

It didn't take long to arrive at the farm. Carriages were drawn up on the side of the road. Horses were clustered on each side of a brook, the hounds sat stately on their haunches, for they knew the excitement wouldn't start until the sun rose from the horizon. Elizabeth could hear the hum of merry voices and see men in their red coats, and the sheen of the ladies' black hunting coats. There was an atmosphere of business and amusement all wrapped up together. "There he is! William, I see him!" Elizabeth was waving a riding stick she would never use.

"Welcome to the Fox Hunt. You are early!"

"I would have been here two hours ago, but . ."

"Don't worry, I understand. You couldn't get my brother out of bed!"

Heman just smiled and ignored his brother's comment. "Is Father here?"

"Yes, he is in the house with Jeremiah. The last I saw them they could not decide whether to talk business or fox hunting."

"How many are going to be here?" Elizabeth looked around in the darkness.

"Maybe a hundred or more."

Heman couldn't help but add, "They have all come for the chance to run after a fox, for a chance against which the odds are more than two to one of even seeing one. I had rather be in bed, he finished with a yawn." Elizabeth poked him in the ribs with her riding stick. "Okay, okay, I will be on my best behavior."

George interrupted the jostling. "We better leave if we are going to be on the ridge before sunrise."

"Enjoy yourself, Elizabeth. I will tie a red scarf to my riding stick. I will raise it to honor you. Look for it."

"The sun is coming up!" cried Elizabeth, as a big fiery ball poked its head up on the horizon. Streams of red, yellow and purple light flew across the grey-blue sky. Now for sure, they were in the middle of a painted picture.

"Listen! Can you hear that!"

"Yes, I can, it is the hounds. They know it is going to begin, don't they?"

Heman, Elizabeth, and George could see laid out before them like a carpet, horses, and hounds ready to begin. Elizabeth watched earnestly, for she did not know what was going to happen next.

"Now it begins!" Heman pointed. In a solemn procession, the red and black mass made their way to the centre of the pasture to the waiting Vicar McCarthy. He was garbed in white vestments that fluttered in the gentle breeze.

"What is Vicar McCarthy going to do?"

"Pray for the fox!"

"Pray for the fox?!" Echoed Elizabeth. "The poor fox. I hope he has gone away for this day."

Heman laughed.

"Everything is so pretty. The red coats. Why don't the ladies wear red?" She looked down at her black jacket.

"Pink, my dear. The men, only the men, wear the pink coats."

"Looks like red to me."

"So be it. Fox Hunting truly is a spectacular event, rich in protocol and steeped in ancient time-honored tradition. It is very regimented, with strictly enforced rules. Everything has to be in order. The Master of Foxhounds lines up first. He leads with the hounds. Then at a respectful distance behind comes the Huntsman and Whips. Behind him comes the Field Master, kind of the patrol boy, who keeps 'order', then the field members with colours. That is where William and Father will be, followed by field members without colours. Mother and Mrs. Darby and their friends will be here. Last to go are the Juniors. You were a Junior until 18, it didn't matter how well you could ride. Back of the field period."

They could hear a horn. The Master of the Foxhounds tooted his horn lightly and they started stately across the pasture, heading for the woods. The Field kept its proper distance and maintained its decorum.

"Look!" Elizabeth pointed. The ponies at the very back of the field were rioting, prancing around and giving their little riders a hard time. "There he is!" Elizabeth was standing again.

Heman was trying to hold onto her delicate waist. "I see the red scarf, it is William!"

The Field had barely gotten out of a walk when a hound gave a cry peculiar to his breed. The rest of the hounds picked up on him and rooted deeply in the dew-drenched soil.

"Tally ho!" Shouted the scarlet horsemen, standing in their stirrups and jesting with their caps.

"Gone Away!"– came the shrill call from the horn directing the hounds onto the line. The Field closed ranks and fell into line behind them.

Then horses galloped straight ahead. Some with more control than others. Most of them gracefully sailed over the biggest ditches. Elizabeth watched as a few cat jumped the ditches, unseating the rider and galloping away. They watched as the mass of horseflesh challenged a six bar gate. Most went over, but there were some horses that changed their minds at the last second, too late to stop the rider sailing over the horses drooped shoulders and into the gate.

Those riding in the rear, when they reached the ditches and banks, would often be torn up before they got there. They would slip in the mud and one fell. "Is she alright?" Elizabeth did not want to look.

Heman holding up his spyglass answered, "She is fine. She is getting up, the horse did not hurt her. She is full of mud but walking around.

*****

William was having the time of his life. He was a little rusty, but as the hunt continued he and his horse began to read each other, to communicate with heels and thighs. Her ears began to flick back towards him, giving him her attention. Oh, how he loved hunting! He had forgotten how much he loved everything about it. He loved the cold frosty air, the dappled woods, the smell of sweet grass, the fear, the adrenaline as he approached a fearsome jump. He lived for the headlong gallops, when he could rest his hands on either side of her fiery neck. He could stand in his stirrups and let her have her head, hearing the whoops and "hi-yahs" as her great haunches powered him past one rider after another. He loved the way she would rear slightly when he held her back and then plunge headlong down a hill. He knew if he fell at that speed both of them would be killed. Neither of them cared. His horse leaped walls with abandon, charged up headlands, splashed through freezing streams. They leaped banks and tore off again without a moment's hesitation. They were torn up, filthy, bloody and exhausted. They were alive, free, and they were as one. Everything was dandy until hedges came up in front of them. There were gaps in the hedges that William feared they would not fit through. He was right, for it felt like he ran right into a wall and then everything went black.

The excitement of the Fox Hunt was drawing to a close. Elizabeth and Heman were eating cucumber sandwiches while sitting in their carriage. "Do you think they caught the fox?" Elizabeth sounded concerned. "I do not know, but maybe it is better we don't know. The horn has gone quiet and we cannot hear the hounds. Maybe the fox got away this time."

"I do hope so."

They continued their lunch watching over the lowlands, which spread before them. A horse galloping towards them gained their attention.

George, sitting out on the ridge of rock, for he was trying to give the young married couple some privacy, was on his feet quickly. He recognized the rider at some distance. It was O'Sullivan. Why was he riding up here?

Heman and George met the horse and rider as they came to a halt. The horse was frothing at the bit and sweat glistened on its brown body as it was reflected by the sunlight. "Heman, it is William. There has been an accident. He has fallen from his horse."

"How bad is it!?"

"Don't know, he is on his way to the hospital."

* * * * *

Elizabeth held Heman's arm tightly as they quickly went up the steps to the hospital. As they entered the building, it was like going into a different world. The dark wood floors echoed every step they took as they walked towards the nurses' station. The lanterns hanging from the ceiling cast long yellow shadows down the darkened hallways.

Nurses quietly went about their duties, their white starched uniforms, causing a rustling sound breaking the silence. The rustling sound reminded Elizabeth of walking through fallen leaves in the park at Autumn time.

"William Kenney. We were told he is here?" questioned Heman.

"Yes, he is here. The doctors are attending him this very moment. You may wait in the public waiting room. Down this hallway and turn right." The nurse pointed the way.

Heman and Elizabeth stopped at the doorway of a large room. Elizabeth was relieved to see windows lining one side, which let natural light in. Wooden chairs were lined up to form squares. There were several square formations in the room. Their eyes searched each square for a familiar person. In the far right corner, Heman saw his father

"This way, Elizabeth. Father is over here."

"Your Mother too."

Elizabeth hugged Bridget; Heman his father. "How is he?"

"Come sit down." His father directed Elizabeth to a wooden chair.

Heman turned around, Jeremiah and Eileen were sitting in the other two chairs that made up their square. After acknowledgments, Heman repeated his question. "How is he?"

"The doctor is treating him now," Daniel answered.

"We don't know anything." Bridget was wringing her hands.

"William and his beloved horses." Heman was shaking his head.

"No more dangerous than your schooners, son." It was Jeremiah.

"You are probably right, sir, probably right."

A nurse and doctor entered the waiting room. "Kenney family?" The nurse was looking for them.

Daniel raised his hand. Heman and Jeremiah stood as they came closer to their square. "How do you do? I am Dr. Barclay. I have been tending. . ." He looked down at his chart. ". . .William Kenney."

"Yes, our son," Bridget informed the doctor.

"Yes, I see. Now, I believe he was riding in a Fox Hunt. Hate those things, I do. Have more patients here just for that reason. Where was I. Well, he is one lucky lad. He is going to be fine. We put him back together, fixed a broken leg, cuts, and bruises mainly. But his bump on his head is worrisome. He will have to stay in bed for a while. But, I believe a full recovery. Yes, a full recovery will be made."

"Thank God," Daniel said. Everyone hugged each other in celebration. William would heal.

"Can we see him?" Bridget was still ringing her hands.

"Yes, but two at a time. Parents first."

When it was Heman and Elizabeth's turn, they entered a room with six beds. There in the second bed lay poor William. His head was bandaged, he had a cut under one eye and his leg was in a cast on a pulley system, holding it up high above the bed. The cast ran from his hip to his foot.

The patient in the first bed pointed to William. "You must be here to see him. Fell off his horse, so I hear."

"Yes, thank you."

Elizabeth, without any fear went straight to William's bedside. She took his hand into hers and spoke softly. "William, we are here."

William opened his eyes. "Elizabeth, I thought it was your voice. For a moment I thought I was dreaming. Did you enjoy the Fox Hunt?" Then he closed his eyes again.

* * * * *

It was June 1866. Ireland was green and spring flowers bloomed everywhere. Heman and Elizabeth were sitting in the back garden, watching the sailboats in the distance coming in and out of Cork Harbour. Heman was staring towards the water.

"What is it, Heman? What is that look in your eyes?"

Heman smiled down at Elizabeth. "Nothing to trouble you, my dear."

"But it's something, Heman, tell me what you are thinking."

"Do you know me so well, so soon? I can't keep anything from you."

"No, and I don't want you to keep anything from me."

"It's just the sea, Elizabeth. She calls me. The sea is calling me even now. But it's okay. You know it's time, don't you? I promised your father I would take you back."

"Heman, I thought I would be homesick, but I haven't been. Even reading letters from home haven't made me homesick. I believe it is because of you, dear husband. Whenever I am with you, I can't be homesick, for I am at home."

"Sweet Elizabeth," Heman put his arm around her and drew her near, "How can I love you any more? But I do. I love you more and more every day." They were both content sitting close together enjoying each other's company.

"It's time, Elizabeth. It's time to say our goodbyes. It's time for *Lady Catherine* to take us home."

"Your poor mother and father."

"Don't worry; they will be fine. William will take care of them."

"He's still in bed and will be for a while."

"He won't be in bed forever. Why just yesterday Ada caught him out of bed. He had a crutch and he was headed for the stable. Of course, Ada took the crutch and threatened to whack him with it if he didn't get back in bed."

Elizabeth laughed. "When do we leave, Heman?"

348

"A week's time, Elizabeth. I will start preparing tomorrow."

Halifax
March 1866

My dearest daughter Elizabeth,
I miss you terribly. When is that brute going to bring you home? He made a promise you know to your father. He is bringing you home, isn't he? I don't know if I can trust him. You aren't going to stay in Ireland, are you? It would not be good for your health, nor mine. Your father says I am being silly, maybe I am. Write me and assure me you will be home soon.

Your brothers say they miss you and will be glad to have you home. I must admit, I tend to mother them more since your absence.

The Kenneys have been treating you well, have they not? You speak of a fox hunt. Surely you are not on the back of a horse.? Much less you jumping over some tree trunk, you will break your neck, and all because of some wild fox. High Society is one thing, but doing a crazy thing like that is not on the top of my list.

You are missed at the factory. Father even complains how long it takes to pass around one of your letters.

Please forgive me for I love you and just want you home.
Until I see you again.
Your loving mother

CHAPTER SIXTEEN

The Hated Cholera

The first week aboard the *Lady Catherine* was a little sad for Elizabeth. She loved being with Heman in their suite, but saying goodbye to Mother Kenney and the Captain was more difficult than she thought. And William, she shed more than one tear saying goodbye. It felt so strange that he wasn't coming, too.

Heman took back his duty as Captain. This left Elizabeth alone more, but she understood and tried to keep herself busy. The crew was kind to her, but she didn't want to be in their way. She found her a favorite place on deck and would read. She also watched the great schooner sail. The *Lady Catherine* seemed to be watching over her.

John Charles didn't mind having her around at all. He loved to talk navigation, and now he had a new student. At the end of each day, Elizabeth would tell Heman what she learned.

"You are learning better than William," he laughed.

"William?"

"Yes, William was John Charles' last student."

"I want to know all about William. I know there is a story to tell. I can feel it. Tell me, Heman?"

And he did. Every evening he told Elizabeth another story about the adventures with William. Heman made sure that one story was never told – the story of the slaves. That was between him and William and God. Not even his wife could know, at least not yet.

* * * * *

"Land Ho!" Henry was in the crow's nest. "Land Ho."

Elizabeth was soon on deck. "Nova Scotia right on the horizon," he yelled to Elizabeth. "We should be there by nightfall."

And they were. As the *Lady Catherine* crept close to Halifax Harbour on a warm starry night in July, Heman and Elizabeth were standing on the bow. "I've kept my promise. I've brought you home."

"Not to my home, dear husband, but to ours."

"How right you are. To our home, Elizabeth."

"Where will we live, Heman?"

"With all the plans I have made, I must confess I have no plan. Where would you like to live, Elizabeth?"

"Don't worry, husband, we can live on the *Lady Catherine* until we decide."

He liked the way his wife thought. "Yes, we will live on the *Lady Catherine* until we decide."

* * * * *

A whistle sounded. The same whistle that sounded when the Captain came aboard or departed his ship. This time it had a different message. The hair was raising on the back of Heman's neck again. All four of his major senses were on high alert. His eyes and his ears were the first to take over. His ears told him the sound of the whistle was coming from the crow's nest. His eyes turned upward to *Lady Catherine*'s high mast.

"What is it, Heman?" Elizabeth sensed the urgency in the warning the whistle sounded.

Heman didn't even hear the question. His mind was in danger mode and he always faced danger head-on, totally focused.

"Captain! " The message traveled loud and clear through the still night. "There is a ship anchored at the mouth of the Harbour. The colours she is flying don't look good." Elizabeth watched as Heman and Moses's words flew back and forth from the crow's nest. "She's flying the crossbones. Either she's a pirate ship or cholera, sir!"

"Pirates!" Elizabeth exclaimed.

"Pirates are past history," Heman assured Elizabeth, then quickly turned back to Moses.

"You're right, sir, I believe it's cholera. Sir, I see the yellow flag." It didn't take long for Moses to descend to the main deck.

Heman turned to his first mate Henry, "Make a wide berth around her. Upwind. We don't want *Lady Catherine* near her!"

"Those poor people, Heman, what are they doing out here in the middle of the Harbour?"

"I don't know, Elizabeth, but if they have cholera on board, the Harbour Master, and, for that matter every citizen in Halifax, will not allow them to come ashore."

As the *Lady Catherine* slowly crept by the ghostly ship, they could see the *S.S. England* in black letters written on her side. Elizabeth turned her head and stepped closer to Heman to escape the horror her eyes saw. Heman wrapped his arms around her, as they both could see the deck was heaped with coffins.

Lady Catherine continued her journey in silence. There was no sound except her bow cutting softly through the dark water. The host of stars and the full moon reflected and sent streams of light before them, making navigating around the stricken ship easy for first mate Henry. The crew went about their task without uttering a word. The silence was eerie and deafening, broken only by the sounds made in making more coffins. It hurt your ears.

"Look, McNab's Island!" Elizabeth's high voice split the silence like a knife. She didn't have to announce her findings for everyone on board could see a dozen or more bonfires burning just off the shoreline of Meagher's beach. "What ship is that?" Elizabeth was asking Heman. An old ship was anchored just off the beach.

"I don't know."

Elizabeth lowered her eyes. She thought Heman knew every ship that was afloat in these parts.

Moses intervened, "I believe it is the old *Pyranus*. She has been out of commission and rotting away for years, at least since I have been around the Harbour. They must have towed her over here."

"It looks to me," the Captain continued, "that a quarantine station has been set up. And by looks of things, it's been here a while. See the schooner? A guard schooner to make sure no one goes ashore and no one leaves."

The curtain of silence fell over them again. "How different the <u>cove</u> looks," Elizabeth whispered to Heman. "Not very long ago, it was so romantic we were right there with *Lady Catherine* and now look at it. A cloud of death hangs over the whole island." She was happy to see the Queen's Wharf coming into view. *Lady Catherine* slowly entered her berth.

"Go below to our suite, Elizabeth. I will join you soon." After delivering orders to his wife, he left the scene, for he had many more orders to deliver before the night was over. The Captain had to make sure *Lady Catherine*, his crew, and his precious wife would be safe. As he began his duties, he looked up to the main mast of *Lady Catherine*. "I know, I promised James Finley I would take care of his daughter, and I intend to do just that."

"Are you sure, Heman? I do not want to leave you. It's the middle of the night!"

"Yes, I am sure, Elizabeth, and it can't be helped if it is the middle of the night! You are not staying here in the Harbour!"

"But we just agreed we would live on the *Lady Catherine*." Elizabeth was confused.

"I'm sorry, that has changed for the foreseeable future."

"Is it that bad?" She had never seen her husband so serious. He always gave her anything she asked. "But I want to stay with you!"

"Elizabeth, I want you to stay, but I don't know how dangerous this cholera situation is, and until I know, you must leave and stay with your parents. I have a carriage waiting for you on the dock. You have fifteen minutes to choose what to take with you. Choose well, my dear. There is a chance you will have nothing to come back to."

Tears welled up in Elizabeth's eyes. "I don't understand."

Heman not only saw tears, but fear could be seen in her eyes. He took her into his arms. "I'm sorry I am such a brute. I forget you are not my crew and are not used to taking orders. But I know you are a strong woman, Elizabeth. I've seen it. Be strong, Elizabeth. Be strong for you and for me." He cupped his hand under her chin and raised her head to meet his eyes. "You are beautiful, Elizabeth, and I love you more than anything in this world. But all this I speak of is necessary."

Elizabeth wiped the tears from her eyes with the back of her hand. "I will be strong for you, my husband." Standing firmly on her two feet, she placed her hands on her hips and began to take a survey of their wedding suite. "I need 30 minutes."

Heman smiled.

"And the use of your cabin boy." Elizabeth didn't even wait for his reply. She was opening cupboards and began rearranging their precious belongings.

* * * * *

Janet sat straight up in her bed. "What was that?" She looked over at James. He was snoring softly in a deep sleep. His blankets were discarded on this warm late summer night. The window was open, the curtains danced a light jig as the breeze found its way through.

Bang! Bang! And a dog answered with a protective growl.

Could that be someone at the door? Surely not! Janet thought, *It is the middle of the night.* Janet tiptoed to the open window. A cool breeze welcomed her as she looked down below. She could see the front yard and the driveway. The moonlight lit up her view and a carriage was sitting there. Sure enough, there was a man standing at their front door.

Bang! Bang! And the dog was growling again.

What a racket, thought Janet. *He will wake up the whole neighborhood.* She turned back towards her bed. James was still snoring. It would take more than this racket to wake him. "James! James! Do wake up!" She was pressing on his shoulders, causing him to bounce up and down on the bed. James wasn't the easiest person to wake from a deep sleep. "James, wake up!" She bounced him harder.

Finally, he too sat straight up in bed. He wasn't sure if he was in a bad dream or not. It couldn't be a dream. Janet was lighting a lamp. "What is it, Janet? What are you doing?"

"There is someone banging on the front door. Not that you would ever hear them!"

James jumped out of bed. He may not have heard the banging but he heard that voice.

"Mother, Father."

James and Janet looked at each other. Could it be?

"Elizabeth!" They both cried at the same moment. And both arrived at the opened window at the same time. James raised the sash higher.

"Mother, Father, can you hear me?"

"Elizabeth!" Janet called. "Is that you?"

Yes, Mother, I am home."

"For pity's sake, Elizabeth, it's the middle of the night. Where is Heman?"

"At the Harbour, Mother. Let me in and I will explain."

"Of course, Janet, why are we talking through the bedroom window? I must open the door." James turned to look for his robe. He was thankful Janet had lit a lamp. Picking it up, he headed for the stairway.

"Your slippers, James, you need your slippers."

Looking down at his feet, he agreed with his wife. He may need to go farther than the front door. He fumbled for his slippers as he headed out into the hall. Janet was right behind him.

"Now don't fall down the stairs. Do be careful with that lamp; don't drop it. We don't want to burn the house down."

"Janet, I am not going to burn the house down. All I am going to do is open the front door."

"What's going on?" George and his brothers were standing at the bottom of the steps in their nightshirts.

"Seems like we are having a family reunion," answered his father.

"In the middle of the night?" Charles rubbed his eyes from the glare of the lamp.

"Don't mind your father. Elizabeth is home. Open the door for her." Janet was the first through the doorway.

"Now! Elizabeth is home now?" James Jr. turned to Charles, "Where's Heman?"

"My sweet, daughter!" Janet had her little girl in her arms. Tears flowed down her face. "I have missed you so! How could Heman leave you alone in the middle of the night? That brute!"

Exactly what Heman said, thought Elizabeth. *What am I doing by myself in the middle of the night?* She shook her head to clear her mind. *I am to be strong. That's what he said, so that is what I will be, strong.*

"Mother, stop crying. I am fine. I need help to unload the carriage."

Before her father and brothers could welcome her home, she was running back to the carriage. What they saw before their eyes made them become wide awake. The carriage was overloaded with trunks and bags of every size.

"Are you running away from home, little sister?" George asked. He never saw so much luggage.

"No, silly, help me get all this inside."

Janet had stopped crying. She just stood there watching trunk after trunk, bag after bag pass by her and pile up in her parlour.

James quickly turned to Janet, "Quickly, I need my money clip. It is on the table beside our bed. We need to pay the carriage."

"It's been taken care of, Father. Heman has paid him well for the inconvenient time of night." Elizabeth turned to the driver. "Thank you kindly for taking such good care of me."

"My pleasure, My lady. A lady like yourself shouldn't be anywhere near the Harbour. Not these days."

"Farewell." He was addressing James and the young men. He tipped his cap towards Janet. "Take care of your daughter." He was paid well to keep Elizabeth safe, and he wanted to make sure his job was done.

Janet's motherly instinct kicked in. She hurried towards Elizabeth and put her arm around her. "Come quickly, we need to get you in from this cool air. You must be worn out. Come in and I will make hot tea. That will warm you."

The family sat together around the kitchen table, while Elizabeth sipped her tea from a flowered teacup. What a sight they made. Everyone in night clothes, all except Elizabeth.

"We came right by the *S.S. England*."

Janet gasped and put her knuckles to her teeth.

"Don't worry, Mother, Heman made sure Henry took a wide berth and we were upwind."

Janet was not sure that made her feel any better. She did not understand a word of what Elizabeth had just said.

"When we landed at the Queen's Wharf, Heman told me I had 15 minutes to pack and leave. He had a carriage waiting. I argued and received 30 minutes."

"You did all that packing in 30 minutes?" James Jr. was amazed.

"Well, 45 minutes at the most."

"Heman thought there was a great possibility I wouldn't see anything I left behind again, so I brought everything I could."

"How awful it was, Mother, to see that ghostly ship. There were so many coffins."

"Now, now, dear," Janet interrupted. "I'm sure it was. You have had enough for one day. I need to get you settled for what's left of the night. You need rest."

"Oh, Mother, we want to hear more," James Jr. complained. "Where is Heman?"

"What will happen to *Lady Catherine*?" Charles added.

"Never you mind. Tomorrow is time enough for all your answers to your questions. It's time to go back to bed." Janet looked towards James.

James had seen that look many times. It was a signal. Janet wanted him to take over. He stood up and took charge. "Your mother's right. Off to bed with you. Looks like there will be lots to do tomorrow. You need some sleep before sunup."

That ended the family reunion.

* * * * *

Elizabeth was sitting again at the kitchen table. This time she was sipping more than tea. It was late morning, and her mother insisted she eat a good breakfast. She was hungry and appreciated her mother making her favourite things. There by her plate stood two rabbit egg cups holding her eggs.

"Five-minute eggs just the way you like them. Cut them open quickly or they will be hard-boiled." Janet was enjoying cooking breakfast for Elizabeth. "Maple cured bacon and homemade yeast rolls. Do you want porridge with brown sugar?"

Oh, how she had missed her little girl, but there was something different about her, she had grown into a beautiful woman.

"No, thank you," Elizabeth answered, "but I would like some of your rhubarb to put on these rolls. They taste wonderful."

Janet passed her the rhubarb and filled a glass with cold cow's milk.

"Thank you, Mother, it is good to be back home and eating breakfast in this kitchen." Elizabeth looked, around and fond memories flooded her mind. She had great memories growing up in this kitchen, in this house.

"My little girl is home," Janet smiled.

"That little girl is grown up. Here I am a woman." Elizabeth reached over and hugged her mother.

"Well, you will always be my little girl, and that is just the way it is." Janet stood and walked to the stove. "Can I get you any more?"

"Mother, I cannot eat another bite." Elizabeth pushed her plate away. "Where are Father and my brothers?" She always referred to her brothers as a group.

"Your Father is at the factory. And as you call them, your brothers are with him. I had to kick them out of the house this morning. They wanted to wake you to hear more stories of your travels. I told them this evening would be soon enough. We will gather on the veranda and you can tell us all about Cork Ireland."

"Mother, I had a wonderful time. Heman's parents are such nice people and they treated me as a daughter. I wish you could meet them. I'm looking forward to sharing everything we did. But, Mother, I am worried about Heman and this cholera. Tell me about it."

"It's been terrible. Everyone is scared to death it will spread to the mainland. We have had to deal with this since the first of April."

"Heman was correct," Elizabeth interrupted, "As we passed by the bonfires on McNab's Island and saw the campsites, he said it wasn't something that happened just yesterday."

"The doctor died."

"What doctor, Mother?" Elizabeth was anxiously waiting for her mother's reply.

"Dr. Slayter.[95]

"The steamer came here from England. They were on their way to New York. The captain and all the engineers were sick and couldn't go on, so they came here and the whole works were placed in quarantine."

"Dr. Garvie volunteered first."

"Wasn't he the doctor who went to Bermuda when yellow fever raged there?" Elizabeth knew she recognized his name.

"Yes, that's the one. The Halifax City Council accepted his offer, with compliments referring to his courage, humanity, and sense of duty. However, it was just too much for him. Too many people were sick. So Dr. Garvie and Dr. Gossip and some of their students had volunteered and joined him on the island. Not two weeks later, Dr. Slayter died after being sick only six hours. He left a wife and five children, he did." Janet was wringing her hands.

"The heroes of this tragedy were the Roman Catholics. Bless their souls. No one else would go. But that Archbishop Connelly went down to the Harbour every day to see what could be done to make those poor people more comfortable. And three Sisters of Charity went to the hospital ship 'Pyramus' to attend the sick."

"Poor Dr. Slayter's family." Elizabeth was taking everything her mother said right to her heart.

"That's what everyone said. It turns out the Assembly, the local government here in Halifax met and unanimously voted $2000 to his widow.[96]

"How many died?"

Janet was her hands again. "I heard 200 after they arrived in Halifax. But they already had lost at least 40 at sea. But they say the worst of it is over now. The Halifax Gazette just yesterday printed there haven't been any deaths since the end of May. But we can't let our guard down yet. Just the end of April, a case of Cholera was found at Freshwater Ridge, Halifax."

"Then Cholera did spread to the mainland!" Elizabeth's eyes were large with concern.

"One case. They picked up bedding that washed up onshore. You can't wash out Cholera; you have to burn everything. The Board of Health ordered men and boats to examine the waters and shores and burn or bury all infected articles found."

"So, Mother, there hasn't been a death you say for two months."

"A little more than that, I believe."

Elizabeth sighed with relief. The worry, she had for Heman diminished, if only slightly. She wanted to see her husband. Only then could she stamp out her worry. She had to see him for herself.

* * * * *

Heman arrived just before supper. She met him in the driveway. Heman took her into his arms and Elizabeth felt safe once more. She had survived their first separation, even though it was a short one. She did not look forward when the sea took him away from her for long periods of time. She knew that time was coming and she promised herself she would be strong. She would live in the present and tonight Heman was with her.

The Finley family was together sitting on the veranda. It was a summer evening in Nova Scotia. The hollyhocks and snapdragons were in full bloom. Looking up Argyle Street, you could see every other family enjoying sitting outside as well. Neighbours waved greetings. News had spread that Captain Heman and Elizabeth had returned from their wedding trip.

The family was catching up on everything that happened while the honeymooners were in Ireland. The conversation hadn't gotten to Cork, Ireland yet. Heman and Elizabeth couldn't get enough news about the Cholera Ship *S.S. England.* Heman assured James he had taken all precautions with his crew and *Lady Catherine.* "I have a code or model that I live by." Heman shared with everyone. "To be safe, rather than be sorry. My crew and I worked all night fumigating everything on board. A couple hours after sunup, my crew assured me everything was done that could be done. They urged me to join my bride." Heman brought his arm around Elizabeth and drew her closer. "You have raised a strong woman, for even the crew was impressed how Elizabeth worked to pack and leave the Harbour. Moses said you even gave him orders. He complained he didn't know his job was to take orders from the Captain's wife." The laughter from the Finley family carried down the street in the gentle breeze.

"I do hope he is not angry with me!" Elizabeth questioning eyes looked up at her husband.

"Not at all, my dear. I will make a Captain of you before long."

"I don't think I want my daughter to be a Captain." Janet had genuine worry as she spoke. "How can a lady be a Captain? That will not do."

"You are right, Mrs. Finley, I would not like my wife to be a Captain. I enjoy her being a lady. Have no fear, the crew will continue to treat Elizabeth as the lady she is."

"When can we return to *Lady Catherine?*

"Elizabeth, you can't go back down there!" Janet was concerned again.

George stopped the porch swing. "She's right, Elizabeth, before the Captain of the *England* died, he claimed that 100 escaped from the island. And did you know the pilot who brought the *England* into port died? Two of his children also died."

"Now, George." James stopped his son. "You know some of what you say are rumors."

"Well, Father, everyone is talking about it."

"That's the problem, James, you can't tell what is truth and what isn't," Janet added.

Heman answered his wife. "Elizabeth, I spent the day making my way up and down the Harbour. I spoke with captains, stevedores, and anyone else that would talk. Anyone who spent their lives on the Harbour. They have all lived in fear for several months. But they tell me they feel safe now. However, I myself have not been convinced. So if your parents agree, we should stay here."

Janet's worried look was melting away.

"How long, Heman? For how long? I want to go back to our suite."

"How long you ask? At least until the quarantine camps are closed down."

Elizabeth was about to argue but bit softly down on her lip. Heman wanted her to be strong. And strong she would be.

* * * * *

The Finley family was glad to have Elizabeth and Heman home. Elizabeth spent the summer evenings sharing stories of Ireland with her mother. It was also time for Heman to go back to work. He had already been on two trade trips – a short trip to New York and a longer one to Bermuda. When he returned from Bermuda, he had the wedding suite ready for Elizabeth to move back into.

Heman and Elizabeth's life turned into a routine. When *Lady Catherine* was in port, they lived in their honeymoon suite. But on the occasion when Heman was away on a trade run, he always felt assured that Elizabeth was being well-taken care of. That is because she was at her parents' house. Elizabeth didn't mind; she was being strong and knew being married to a Captain meant months of separation. Letters were their only mode of communication at that time. Both wrote daily.

Elizabeth enjoyed the summer evenings sitting on lawn chairs with her parents. There were times one or more of her brothers would join them. This particular evening, Tom and Emily and Susanna were visiting from New York. Everyone was enjoying watching the little girl explore the big world, the backyard. Susanna wasn't afraid of anything. More than once her father had to rescue her from a bumblebee.

"Elizabeth, how long are you and Heman going to live on the *Lady Catherine*?" James had a hard time giving up the role of taking care of his daughter.

"It doesn't seem dignified to me," Janet added to the question.

"Oh, I love living on the *Lady Catherine*."

"Well, the dock is not a suitable place for a lady to live. Isn't that right, Tom? Janet was hoping to get support from her older son.

"All I know is that Captain Heman will make sure his wife is well-taken care of. Seems to me she has the whole crew watching over her. It's not like she has any children to worry about. That is, whether they fall overboard or not." Tom looked at his sister.

"No, brother, there are no children in the near future that I know about." Elizabeth's cheeks turned a darker shade of pink.

Janet didn't notice any change in Elizabeth's colouring. "Well, I thought at least you would be on my side, Tom," his mother pouted.

"I can find them a place close to us in New York City. The place is booming."

"No, you won't, son," James quickly intervened. "But your mother is right, Elizabeth. It's time you and Heman looked for a place to call home."

"I don't see why everyone is so worried. I only stay on the *Lady Catherine* when she is in port. Then I am here. Do you not want me here? Or rather, do you want me to stay by myself in a flat or house or something?"

"You can still come here when Heman is away," assured her father. "All I'm asking is for you to start thinking about where you want to live."

"Heman will be home in a week. I will discuss it with him then."

"Look, Tom, Susanna is headed for the rose garden," Elizabeth shouted. Tom, James, and Janet were after her at the same moment. Elizabeth was glad to have a few minutes to herself. Maybe it was time to find a place for Heman and her to live. She could bring her wedding gifts out of storage. But she hated to give up her honeymoon suite.

* * * * *

Heman didn't use the suite when he was on a trade trip. He went back to the Captain's Cabin. There was more than one reason for this. One thing: he missed Elizabeth so much that he couldn't stay there without her. The other: he didn't want the crew to think he was soft. He realized a time was coming when he would have to move his bride to a more permanent dwelling. He knew it was not going to be easy. Elizabeth loved the *Lady Catherine*, and to tell her she couldn't live here any longer was something he dreaded. But he needed the suite dismantled and put back to a cargo hold. He needed more space for cargo. So the first thing he would have to discuss with Elizabeth was where to live.

* * * * *

It was late fall 1866. Heman and Elizabeth were getting settled into their first home on Barrington Street, a flat on the second floor. Their door with the stained glass window opened from the sidewalk. Climbing more than a dozen steps, one came to a landing circled with a wood banister. The room to the right of the landing was a kitchen. It was interesting to watch Elizabeth unpack wedding gifts and place them in her kitchen cupboards.

"There, everything is ready. Heman, doesn't everything look wonderful?"

Heman had to agree that it did. A wooden kitchen table with four chairs was in front of a window that went from the ceiling to the floor. There was a view of the backyard where someone had attempted a flower garden. Thank goodness for the three maple trees, for their beauty made up for the neglected garden. Elizabeth had made curtains that gave the kitchen a homey feeling. The same material was used as a tablecloth, and in the middle of the table was a flower arrangement.

"Where did you find the flowers? Heman asked.

"Out there." Elizabeth pointed out the window.

"In that flower garden?" Heman was amazed.

"Don't worry. Come spring I will make that flower garden sing."

"I'm sure you will." He kissed Elizabeth on her forehead and placed her dark curl back in its place.

"What do you think, Heman? Isn't it wonderful? Mother has been helping me."

Heman walked around the kitchen opening and closing cupboards. "What's this?" as he opened an upright white chest.

"An icebox. The iceman delivers ice every week."

Sure enough, ice was slowly melting inside the chest. He closed the door. "Everything seems really nice, Elizabeth, but I think you have forgotten something."

Elizabeth looked around. "I don't think so. A table, chairs, rocking chair by the stove. Cupboards, drawers filled with all our wedding gifts. Even a braided rug on the floor. Heman, what else would you want?"

"Food would be nice. What about the food, Elizabeth?"

Elizabeth sat down with a huff in the rocking chair. "It doesn't matter, Heman, if we have food or not. I can't cook."

Heman crouched down before her. "It's okay, Elizabeth, we will learn together."

"Are you sure, Heman? I'm not a very good wife; I can't even cook." She left the rocking chair, and Heman gathered her in his arms.

"We will learn together, dear. I wasn't hungry anyway. Show me the rest of the house."

Elizabeth's joyful spirit returned. Taking his hand and with a smile and a twinkle in her eyes, "Follow me and see what we have done." The next room off the landing was a dining room. A coal-burning fireplace was on the inner wall. Two large windows matching the ones in the kitchen were on the opposite wall of the fireplace. They also had a view of the backyard.

Heman smiled at Elizabeth. "Someone's been at the Irish Coffee Company II."

"Yes, James, Charles, and George helped us get everything here."

"Your brothers are very kind to you."

"Well, Moses wasn't here to help. He was with you and the *Lady Catherine*."

"I'm sure he was glad he was, looking at all the work that's been done."

"You don't know Moses at all. He would have been helping me if he were here."

"You have him bewitched," he laughed at his wife. "He could never say 'no' to you. But you forgot he is a sailor. He knows the ocean like the back of his hand. And your brothers are bewitched too, by the looks of things."

Heman picked Elizabeth up and swung her around. "Me too, love. I'm bewitched too. I'm so happy you are mine."

Elizabeth squealed.

He placed her on the floor. "Now, show me more. I love the mahogany table and chairs. Do you know where I found them? Bermuda. And our mantle clock, a wedding gift from your grandmother. Looks wonderful on the mantle."

The dining room had another doorway, which entered into the next room. "Show me what is in there. Would you like me to carry you through the threshold?"

Elizabeth swiveled around and quickly took two steps away from him. She composed herself. "I can walk, thank you." As she led him into the living room.

Like the former room, this room was filled with items Heman had brought back on trade trips. Heman stepped closer to Elizabeth. "Is there anything left at the Coffee Company?" He put his arm around her waist.

"Of course there is. Anyway, didn't you bring more things to sell? Remember, you just got back this morning." She looked into his eyes; she so much wanted his approval.

"Don't worry, my dear. It looks like I got home just in time. *Lady Catherine* is full of beautiful things to sell. You have done a wonderful job of making our first home."

"I'm not finished yet." She led him out of the living room and onto the landing. The final room was to their left, the bedroom. Elizabeth had chosen a large four-poster bed. She had made a blue velvet canopy over it. The blue velvet also covered the two windows that looked over Barrington Street. Elizabeth looked into Heman's eyes and could see that he approved.

"And what's through that door? he asked.

"Our privacy closet."

Heman looked in and saw a water closet and a bathtub, sitting on its claw feet. Over the sink was a beveled mirror. Two wicker stools stood in place at a long dressing table.

"What do you think, Heman?"

"Well, I don't know if it will be the same as living on the *Lady Catherine*."

Elizabeth's lip drooped. She had tried so hard to make it perfect.

"We both agreed that the honeymoon suite was very good." He took the three steps towards Elizabeth that were separating them. He picked her up. She buried her head into his shoulder. Heman continued, "But the more I see it, and if you promise to bring food into the kitchen..."

She lifted her head to face him. "I promise to learn to cook.."

Heman laughed, "My dear, I could care less if you can cook. I love you just the way you are. I don't care if I have food.

I love this place, Elizabeth. I love it because this is our home. When I open the door and climb those stairs, I will be looking for you. So, yes, Elizabeth, this is even better than the honeymoon suite on the *Lady Catherine*. And do you know what? I think *Lady Catherine* knows it too."

Cork, Ireland
November 1866

Dear daughter, Elizabeth,

I enjoy receiving your letters. Both Daniel and I were very concerned about the cholera outbreak of which you write. Daniel assures me, Heman has experience and knows what to do to keep both you and his crew safe. But do be careful.

William has won his first big race. It didn't take him long to get back into the business of horse racing. Buying and breeding stock, and working the horses as if they were his own children. There is a lot more activity going on here at the mansion than ever before. O'Sullivan and George seem to enjoy their work more than ever. And Daniel walks taller and has a certain spring in his step. He even spends more time at home, even though it is spent in the stables. I am happy for him.

I enjoy having William home. Heman has given us such a gift, bringing his brother home. Not that I don't miss Heman for I do. But the sea has taken my eldest son, and I have learned to live with that.

I remember the day that Daniel gave up the sea and settled into his company. The long separations were over. So, my dear, I know what it is like to have one's husband away for long periods of time on trade trips. Be brave, and do not worry whether he will come back. For I see the great love my son has burning in his heart. He will always return. His Lady Catherine will keep him safe and sail him right back to you.

How I enjoyed your visit. I have wonderful memories for a lifetime. Maybe we will get to visit one another again. Until then we will continue writing.

Until the next time I pick up my pen:
Love
Mother Kenney

CHAPTER SEVENTEEN

A Seagull . . . Or a Stork?
Spring 1867

Heman was walking up Barrington Street. This was the same journey he took every morning. It took him fifteen minutes to walk from his place to The Irish Coffee Co. II He noticed a haze in the air. *How could that be?* he thought. This sunny spring morning there shouldn't be haze, but there was. There was a change in Halifax. Most people called it progress. Heman wasn't sure progress was good for him. The coal industry was booming. Everyone used coal. He did and so did all the factories. It was easier to heat homes and factories with coal than wood. Every home, including his, had a coal bin. The coal was delivered once a week. Heman shook his head, even *Lady Catherine* had a coal bin. Progress. The skyline of Halifax had smokestacks rising along the shores of the Harbour.

Heman couldn't believe the change. It was only seven years ago that the *Lady Catherine* made her way into Halifax Harbour for the first time. That day he knew that special things would happen here and they did. He also remembered the beauty of the Harbour. The blue water reflected from the blue sky. But today you could hardly see the blue sky and no blue water. It looked dark green to him. What happened to the beautiful

Harbour he loved? There were days worse than today. Today was only hazy, but other days, early morning until late at night, black smoke billowed over the city. Foggy days were the worse; black soot fell over everything. Heman prayed for offshore breezes. He was tired of spending his evenings with his head under a tea towel breathing in the hot steam. Just the past week he spent two evenings trying to clear out his lungs. His asthma was becoming an un-welcomed visitor that was taking over his life. Elizabeth took good care of him. Dick had taught her all he knew. She made sure the stove was ready to boil water day or night. Unfortunately, the only time he could breathe freely was when he was at sea. He would sit on the bow and breathe clean salt air into his lungs. Heman wished he could bring some back to Halifax. He didn't know how long he could go on like this. Elizabeth made it worthwhile. That is why he could go on. *Why just a few hours ago I was smiling at Elizabeth,* he thought. His mind wandered back.

* * * * *

. . . "Pass the eggs and bacon, please." He had just finished a bowl of porridge. This was his favourite time of the day. He was eating breakfast with Elizabeth. "What are your plans for this beautiful spring day?"

Elizabeth was spreading strawberry preserves onto her toast. "Just the usual. Father has plenty for me to do at the factory."

"You aren't working too hard, are you?" questioned Heman. He had worry lines forming on his forehead. She looked tired, and were they dark circles under her eyes? "It's not that you have to work you know."

"I know, my husband, but I like to work. If I didn't work, I would be at the Irish Coffee Company. making Moses nervous. Anyway, Mother and I work together. It is fun."

Sally entered the dining room, coming from the kitchen. In her quiet voice, she asked, "Can I get you anything else for breakfast? There are more eggs and, Ms. Elizabeth, I have more

376

preserves. My Mother gave me a jar of raspberries just for you to try."

Elizabeth showed a warm smile to Sally. "I believe I would like to try your Mother's raspberry preserves tomorrow morning."

"Well, ladies, I must be about my morning business. I have a meeting with my crew at The Coffee Company. You both have a good day." Heman lowered himself to his sitting wife and kissed her gently on the lips. "See you at dinner at six."

Elizabeth accepted his farewell kiss. This time the farewell would be but a few hours, not like some farewell kisses that took him away for months at a time. "You have a good day and yes, I will see you at six." Elizabeth turned to Sally, "Do we need to discuss dinner?"

"I have it all under control," Sally continued, "My Frank told me a fresh catch of Halibut came in late afternoon, yesterday. I stopped at the fish market this morning and purchased two steaks. I thought the Captain would like them for dinner."

"How right you are. Heman will be thrilled. How would I ever get along without you?" She gave her a hug. "I must be going. I will be late."

* * * * *

Heman was still walking up Barrington Street. Life was good. Just thinking about the breakfast with Elizabeth had lifted his spirits. He headed closer to the Coffee Company. He didn't seem to be in a hurry to get to his meeting. Instead, he sat on a park bench. He was taking in the nice spring day and continued to evaluate his life. He agreed with himself. Life was good. Elizabeth and he had just completed their first winter as newlyweds. He was comfortable in their flat on Barrington Street. Lazily he thought back.

* * * * *

The winter had been a cold one. Many times the temperature fell below zero. The fireplaces were kept supplied with coal. They weren't the only thing that kept them warm from the cold. It was their love for one another. There were no trade trips. Heman couldn't tear himself away. He was happy to have the excuse that the Harbour froze over. But he knew deep inside, he wouldn't have left no matter what. He had made sure the storage space for the Coffee Co. was filled to capacity from the last trade trip the previous fall. Many times he had heard Moses make a comment to the crew that the Captain is hibernating with Elizabeth for the Winter. Moses was right.

The first thing Heman did was to hire a cook. After a few attempts of teaching Elizabeth to cook, he decided her talent was making clothes. He asked for Elizabeth's mother's help, and she was more than willing. Janet was thankful that Elizabeth no longer lived on the *Lady Catherine*. Janet and Heman interviewed many ladies for the job. Old ladies, fat ladies, skinny ladies and even cranky ladies. Heman was wise enough to allow Elizabeth to have the last word. Elizabeth chose Sally.

Sally was a happy-go-lucky girl, just a few years younger than Elizabeth. Sally had a husband and a young child. Her husband Frank worked at the docks. He was a hard worker and a family man. Frank loved Sally and his son John. Times were hard in Halifax, and they were very grateful that Sally could work for Elizabeth and the Captain.

Heman was grateful as well. Sally was a good cook and work came naturally to her. She took care of whatever needed to be done. But her main job was to see that the young Kenney family was well fed.

* * * * *

Heman's mind came back to the present with a jolt. He had heard a splat and he looked down at his white splattered shoes and up in the tree above him. A robin was singing. "Thanks a lot, Sir Robin. Are you trying to tell me something? I know it's time for my meeting." Heman thought, *I not only talk to schooners; I seem to talk to birds as well.* He chuckled to himself as he walked along the street.

The bell sounded as Heman walked through the familiar double doors of The Coffee Co. Moses was at the counter reading the Halifax Gazette News. "Good morning, Captain."

"Good Morning, Moses. Anything interesting in the newspaper?"

"Well, let me see. Yeah, here is something that may interest you. Bears waking up from long winter hibernation. Spring is here!"

"Are you trying to tell me something, Moses?"

"No, sir, not me."

"Winter wasn't long enough for me. But you are right. Spring is here. It's time to get *Lady Catherine* seaworthy."

"Aye, Aye, sir! I've been waiting to hear those words. I will contact the crew. Paint – we need paint." Moses was headed for the storage room.

"Whoa! Before you search for those paint brushes. . ." Heman was taking his shoe off. "Can you see to it that this shoe gets cleaned?"

"Are you sure you don't want to paint the other one white?"

"No, Moses, a Robin was trying to tell me something."

"And tell me, did you understand what it was?"

"I believe I did. Moses, it's spring."

"That it is, Captain, that it is." Moses was about to disappear through the doorway.

"What about our meeting, Moses? We are to have a meeting this morning?"

"Yes, sir, I will make sure the crew will be here by 11 o'clock."

Heman looked at his pocket watch. He had an hour. Time to prepare for the next trade trip. His heart was beating faster. He glanced out the window towards the Harbour. "Yes, *Lady Catherine*, the sea is calling us again." He walked like a square wheel into the meeting room. "I need my shoe, Moses!"

"It's coming, sir."

Heman had a lot to do. *Life is good,* he thought. *Life is good.*

* * * * *

Sally's skirts rustled, as she quickly but carefully made the feather duster fly along the surface of the living room furniture. The living quarters on Barrington Street had been a quiet place for the last two months. Sally didn't have much to do. She and her son John came every day. She was thankful she was still employed.

"There," she smiled at her young son, "All I have to dust is the dining room and of course the bedroom. You sit here and play with your blocks."

John smiled back with two little teeth shining through.

"Kitchen is done." Sally was talking to herself. "It's been done for months." She walked into the bedroom. "What can I do in here? I know, I will take the bed canopy down and also the curtains. That will keep me busy for a day or even more." She figured if the Captain was paying her, she wanted to earn her keep.

Elizabeth had been by just the day before. She had news and she needed to share it with someone. Heman would be home in the next few weeks. Sally was happy for the good news, but she also noticed more good news only a woman would know. She remembered the question she asked. "Does Heman know?"

Elizabeth was so surprised with the question that she sat down on the chesterfield and asked, "How did you know?" Sally thought that was easy, Elizabeth was beaming. Sally was surprised that no one else knew. Not even Elizabeth's mother.

Sally took a moment to look out the window. How nice it will be to have a little one join the Kenney family here on Barrington Street. She looked to the sidewalk below. It was busy with people hurrying here and there. The carts and carriages and their horses that pulled them stirred up the coal dust. No matter how often Sally washed the windows, the dust would be back the very next day.

The bed canopy and curtains filled her arms as she walked out of the bedroom onto the landing. Without even thinking she checked on John before she entered the kitchen. She raised the kitchen window sash. The coal dust wasn't as bad in the backyard. The task of shaking the dust from the canopy began.

* * * * *

The May flowers were at their peak. The tiny white star flowers reached for the warm sun. "This is my favorite time of the year."

"It is nice, but I prefer the early fall myself." Elizabeth and her mother were sitting in the warm sunshine. "Do put your bonnet on, Elizabeth. The sun is not good for your skin."

"Mother, I am drinking in the sun. How can I do that with my bonnet covering my face?"

Janet watched her daughter who had her eyes closed as she looked skyward. Having Elizabeth here for the last two months was good for her. But she saw the loneliness written in Elizabeth's dark eyes. The sparkle was no longer there. But there was something different about Elizabeth, but she couldn't put her finger on it. "Has the mailed arrived?"

"Yes, Mother. No, I didn't get a letter." Elizabeth lowered her head from the sun. "But I got three yesterday. Heman will be home soon. Do you think it could be today? How I wish it would be today."

"I pray every day that he will return safely. It would be a good day if he arrived today." She took Elizabeth's hand in hers. "He will be home soon. Now tell me about his travels."

Elizabeth sat on the swing next to her mother. The twinkle was back in her eyes if only for a moment. "Are you feeling well, Elizabeth?"

"Feeling well? Of course, I feel well, Mother." Elizabeth was worried, *Oh dear, how long will I be able to keep my secret. I thought I could keep it just to myself, when only yesterday Sally knew. Should I feel guilty that I want to keep it in my heart? At least for now, at least until Heman knows? How can I tell him something like this in a letter? Please, Heman, come home soon.*

Janet wasn't convinced, but promised herself to keep a watch for anything out of the ordinary. "So, Elizabeth what news does Heman send?" Janet broke into her daughter's thoughts.

"He writes of Nova Scotia becoming a part of the United States." Elizabeth recovered quickly. "Do you think we will become a part of the United States?"

"I hope not. I'm not ready to give up the monarchy. I happen to like the King."

"Do we have any say in this matter?"

"Men won't let us vote, remember? If it was left up to us, we would solve all the problems of this world." Janet's smile was contagious. "I don't like politics. You will have to ask your father."

"Maybe I will." If Heman was interested in such things, she needed to be interested as well.

* * * * *

"I can't understand Heman's concern? You say he writes of the United States taking over Nova Scotia?" Elizabeth was alone with her father in the parlor.

"Only a paragraph or two. Let me get the letter." Elizabeth headed for the stairs. Halfway up, she suddenly stopped as she gasped and put her hand on her stomach. *What in the world,* she thought. Then again, she felt something kick her from the inside. "My dear baby, you are truly in there."

"Did you say something, Elizabeth?"

"No, Father." Elizabeth continued up the stairs. It wasn't long before she was back on the veranda carrying a blue box decorated with pink and blue ribbons. She opened the box and retrieved the most recent letter received from Heman. After reading the first page to herself, she found what she was looking for.

"Here it is." She began to read. "Word has it in Boston and New York that the United States Congress in Washington, D.C. presented a bill on July 2, 1866, for the Annexation of Nova Scotia."

"July 2nd last year you say."

"Yes, Father, that's what Heman writes. Not just for Nova Scotia but for New Brunswick, Canada East, and Canada West.[97] Word had it that it was shelved and would be presented again to Congress sometime this year."

"Very interesting," James smiled, "We are slightly ahead of them, we are."

"What do you mean, Father?" Elizabeth placed the letter back into the blue box and was tying the ribbons.

"We have had the Father's of Confederation meeting for three years now. First, they wanted a union between Nova Scotia, New Brunswick, and Prince Edward Island. But the province of Canada wants a larger union. They are working on us to become our own new country. I would think most people want to become a new country, not join with the United States. We have too many British traditions. The States would make us give them up. However, if we become a new country, but still remain a British Colony, then we don't have to give up anything."[98]

"Not even the King?" Janet entering the room wanted to make sure of that point.

"Not even the King," James answered his wife.

"Very interesting." James was still deep in thought. He was talking softly to himself. "So the States want us. Never! It will never happen."

* * * * *

Sally was happily cleaning the residence on Barrington Street. Not that it was dirty, that didn't matter. Everything was getting cleaned again. A messenger just stopped by the front door. The message was addressed to her. She had never received a message before. Not in her whole life. Quickly she signed for it and the messenger left.

Now she was happily cleaning. Heman was back. The Kenney family would return to the residence tomorrow. She would fix them a special dinner. She didn't know what yet, but she would come up with something very special.

Heman was glad to be home. Here he was sitting in his living room watching his Elizabeth knit. He remembered as a child watching his mother knit, and now he was watching his wife. He had missed her so. Now they were catching up on all the news. There seemed to be no shortage of words between them.

"You look so well, Captain." How has your asthma been?"

"Haven't seen him in months, nor have I missed him."

"Ocean breezes are good for you."

"Yes, that may be, but I would take you over ocean breezes any day." Heman couldn't stop smiling at his wife. "What are you making?

Elizabeth's happiness also showed through her smile. "A sweater." Elizabeth held up a tiny yellow garment with two tiny sleeves.

"It's kind of small, isn't it?

Elizabeth jumped. She placed her hand on her stomach, "It did it again."

Heman was at her side in an instant. "What is it, Elizabeth, are you not well? What did what again? Are you in pain?"

"No silly, I am perfectly well, or rather I should say, we are perfectly well."

Heman was down on his knee beside her chair. "I do not understand, Elizabeth. You hold your stomach in pain one minute, and then you say you are perfectly well the next minute."

"I did not hold my stomach in pain, but in amazement. Here, silly, place your hand here."

Heman allowed Elizabeth to guide his hand. "What in the world?" Heman cried

"Did you feel it? Amazing, isn't it?"

Fear raced through Heman's whole being. *What terrible thing is wrong with her?* "You must see a doctor at once. The best, only the best. Who is the best Doctor in Halifax?"

"Dr. Garvie, and we've seen him already." Elizabeth was smiling at Heman.

"You have? Who is 'we,' and why are you smiling?"

"We are going to be a 'we.' "

"A what?" Heman was completely out of control. *What is she talking about? Has she been sick while I was away? Why was I not informed?*

"Sit down, Captain, and I will explain."

What else could he do? Heman fell back into his chair. *I have to be strong. Whatever she tells me, I still will love her. I will take care of her.*

"Heman. . ." Elizabeth was trying to reach him through some kind of fog.

"Go on, Elizabeth, I am listening."

"That is why I am making this sweater." She held up the small yellow garment with tiny sleeves. I didn't know whether to make it pink or blue, so I choose yellow. Since we don't know if it will be a boy or girl. What would you like, Heman? A boy or girl?"

"Heman's eyes were glazed over. He did understand English, but for some reason, he had no idea what was being said. Something about a boy or girl. "A boy or girl what?" He managed to ask the question.

"A son or daughter, a boy or girl?" Elizabeth was still smiling at him.

She was so brave, thought Heman. *She had something terribly wrong with. . . wait. .a boy or girl, a son or daughter. Could it be?* "Elizabeth, what are you trying to tell me?"

"I didn't think it would be this hard." Elizabeth wondered how else she could possibly say the words. "Heman, you are going to be a Father. Now, do you understand? We are going to have a baby." She reached for him to come closer again. She took his hand and placed it on her stomach. "Our baby is in there."

Heman finally came out of his daze. "Are you sure?" How could he be so stupid? He was at her side once more. "Are you sure?"

"Dr. Garvie, the best Doctor in Halifax, told me."

"I am going to be a father?" The movement of Elizabeth's head indicated a yes. Heman picked his wife right up out of the chair. He twirled her around like they were riding a merry-go-round. Laughter could be heard throughout their residence, and if the windows had been opened, could have been heard down Barrington Street.

"Please let me down," she laughed, "I am dizzy."

"Of course I wasn't thinking." Heman placed her carefully on the chesterfield. "I haven't hurt you, have I?"

"Don't worry, I won't break."

"Who knows, Elizabeth? Am I the last to know?

"Only Sally."

"Sally!"

"I didn't really tell her, she just knew. But no one else knows. I wanted you to know first."

"How long have you known?"

"Shortly after you left on your trade trip. I wasn't feeling well, so I went to see Dr. Garvie. I thought it was the flu."

"Why didn't you tell me, why didn't you mention it in one of your letters?"

"And miss what we have shared together tonight? How could I tell you in a letter? It wouldn't have been the same. I wanted to see you. I wanted to be with you. I didn't want to share my news with anyone but you. I wanted to keep a piece of you close to my heart. I love you."

Heman picked her up again. Carefully walking across the room to his strong leather chair, he sat down with her in his arms. "I love you too." They sat together wound in each other's arms for a long time. They were enjoying the moment. Time could stand still. Nothing else mattered. They were together again and that was their whole world, at least for the night.

* * * * *

"When!? Janet exclaimed.

"What great news!" James was thrilled.

Now Sally wasn't the only one to know. There was great excitement throughout the Finley family as the news was told.

Heman had a hard time convincing Elizabeth that they needed to tell her parents. And they needed to send a message through the Trans-Atlantic cable to Ireland to inform his parents they were to be grandparents. He hadn't even told his crew. Elizabeth was quite content to keep their news to themselves. It was a good thing Sally knew, or she would be wondering why Elizabeth was eating everything in the kitchen.

It was the end of June and here they were eating Sunday dinner with the family. No better time than now to break the news.

"When?" Janet asked again.

"Sometime in September, Dr. Garvie tells us," Heman answered.

"September!" Janet looked at Elizabeth. "That means. .."

"Yes, Mother, that means I knew early spring when I was staying with you." Elizabeth was buttering her second dinner roll.

"I should have known." Janet dabbed her hanky to her eyes as the tears started to spill.

"It's okay, Mother, I didn't tell anyone, except Sally."

"Sally?" Janet showed her surprise.

"She guessed," Heman quickly added.

"I don't know how she knew," Elizabeth was biting into an apple. "I wanted to tell Heman first."

James put his arm around Janet. "Well, that's understandable, isn't it, Janet."

"Yes, I think so." Janet wiped away any remaining tears. "We don't have very much time to get prepared."

Heman's eyebrows raised to attention. "Prepared? Prepared for what?" This was the first time he felt he had no control over what was going to happen. Well, maybe the second time. How soon could he forget the spell he was under when he fell in love with Elizabeth?

"Don't worry, Heman. I'm sure Elizabeth's mother will take care of everything." James looked to Janet, "See, she is already planning everything."

Janet wasn't even listening; she was deep in thought. "The shower must take place soon."

"Shower?" Heman was back in his fog.

"Baby shower, dear. Mother is planning a baby shower."

He decided not to ask any more questions. That is, not until he was with Elizabeth in the carriage heading back to Barrington Street. "Elizabeth, are you sure we will know how to take care of a baby?"

"Don't worry, Captain, you will learn the ropes and the way the winds blow. Can I sit on your lap?"

"Here?"

His breath was knocked out of him as she landed hard on his knee. The carriage swayed dangerously.

"Everything all right down there?" The movement of the carriage alarmed the driver.

"Everything is fine." Heman managed to get his breath back.

Elizabeth giggled. "Is there room?" She spread out the blue material of her skirt.

Heman held on to her tightly. "There will always be room for you, my dear."

Elizabeth always felt safe gathered in his arms.

Cork, Ireland
August 1867

Dear Heman and Elizabeth;

Receiving your telegram stirred up a lot of excitement around here. Just the fact that a telegram was delivered was newsworthy, having it come all the way from Halifax, Nova Scotia. The town crier delivering it was excited as we were. Before we could even open it, he was thrilled to tell us the message was sent that very morning. Just think of that. Came from the other side of the Atlantic in the morning and we had it before dinner time that same day. Now that's progress.

Ada wasn't as impressed as the rest of us. She told me to open up the message. I was the one to read the news that caused the second round of excitement. A baby you say. Elizabeth is to have a baby. That means I will be an uncle.

Father brought out the campaign. The bubbly was poured into the best china goblets and the whole household toasted the health and well being of you, Elizabeth. Actually, I toasted you twice. Didn't want the bubbly to go to waste.

Mother cried. Good thing she gave you the magic handkerchief. Now you can change it to a christening baby bonnet. I am sure her letter of congratulations will arrive soon. She is very happy for you both.

Big brother to be a father. I am sure you will get great wisdom from Lady Catherine. You talk to her about everything else. However, I don't think you will get any advice from your crew. I believe you are on your own on this one. I could be worried, but you having Elizabeth by your side, makes me feel a whole lot better. Elizabeth, you will be a wonderful mother.

My congratulations to you both.

With love
William

CHAPTER EIGHTEEN

"Reuniting Again"

"Are you sure, Heman? Mother disapproves. Anyway, I look fat." Elizabeth was examining her reflection in their full-length mirror.

"Why should your mother disapprove?" Heman's voice was loud, but not from anger. He was shaving in front of the mirror in their privacy closet. He wanted his voice to carry into the bedroom. "And you're not fat."

"Mother said a woman is not to be seen in public in my condition." Elizabeth touched the roundness of her stomach.

"You are not going to be in public. We are going to eat dinner with Captain Woods."

"My dear, Captain, eating dinner at the Royal Halifax Yacht Club with Captain Woods is very public."

Heman entered the bedroom with white shaving cream on half of his face. Pointing the razor in her direction like a pointing stick he argued, "I can't very well go without you."

"Most husbands would."

"Not this husband. Anyway, I want you to meet Captain Woods. You will like him."

Elizabeth continued to study her reflection. "Maybe I can put a few more pleats in the waistband. A jacket might help."

"Whatever you wear you will always be beautiful." He was going to kiss her neck, but her squeal prevented him doing so.

"Your face, silly, you have shaving cream all over it."

He smiled, "See how you distract me." Wandering back to the privacy closet, he continued, "So, it's final. I will send a message accepting Captain Woods' invitation."

"Yes, I am tired of being a prisoner in my own house," she answered.

* * * * *

Sitting on the veranda of the Royal Halifax Yacht Club, Heman and Elizabeth were enjoying the view in front of them. A perfect place to be on this early summer day the end of June. Many sailboats were moored in the blue water of the Harbour. You could hear the gentle ringing of the rigging as it hit the masts. The ocean breeze caused them to sing. The cries of the white and grey gulls joined in on the music. They seemed to be celebrating the beautiful day along Halifax Harbour. Heman was enjoying himself. He took in deep breaths of the fresh salt air. The Yacht Club was closer to the mouth of the Harbour. The breeze off the ocean was taking the black smoke from the smokestacks further inland. The air in the city seemed cleaner than usual.

"Your breathing seems clearer, Captain."

"Much better than last night, isn't it?"

"Here comes Captain Woods now." Heman was on his feet and reaching out his right hand to greet the tall man with a dark beard. The handshake was firm though friendly.

"Good to see you again, Captain Kenney."

"Pleasure is all mine," Heman replied. "My wife Elizabeth."

Elizabeth raised her hand from where she was sitting. Captain was there quickly to take it into his own. "Captain, you are a lucky man to have such a beautiful wife." He looked into Elizabeth's eyes. "Happy to meet you! The last time I met your husband he was of great service to me."

"You will have to tell me all about it, Captain, for it seems my husband has a problem remembering details." Elizabeth looked towards Heman.

"Forgive me, Heman, if I have spoken out of turn."

"Not at all, Captain." He smiled at Elizabeth. "My wife knows of our friendship during the Civil War. Sometimes friends help friends when the need arises."

"Well then, let's leave it at that. Elizabeth, you have a good man here. I was happy to leave Halifax Harbour that evening."

Elizabeth would have liked to hear more, but it didn't look like the subject of that night was going to be continued. "Thank you, Captain, maybe you can share with me more at another time."

Heman was eager to change the subject. "How long has it been? When did you move to Halifax? I heard you were in the area; however, our paths have not crossed until now."

"You are correct. I have made my home here for more than a year. I made inquiries about you more than once. You are a busy man. I have seen the *Lady Catherine*, but only from a distance. She is a nice schooner. But she doesn't stay in the Harbour long."

"One has to make a living, and being a Captain yourself, you know one cannot make money sitting in port. We are kept busy with runs to Boston, New York and down to Bermuda."

"Just the other day I saw *Lady Catherine* enter the Harbour from where we are sitting right now. I had to ask who the Captain of such a great schooner was. I was delighted to hear your name come up in the answer. So here we are reunited again. On this occasion with happier times."

"What have you been doing with yourself now that you are in Halifax?"

"I guess you could say a little of everything. Trying to get my feet wet in the merchant business. Been hanging around the

Halifax Pilot Commission, and also the Boston Marine Insurance Company needs an agent."

"But the most fun I have found to do around here is the sailboat races!"

"I've seen some of those races on the way back from Boston. I see to it *Lady Catherine* gives them plenty of room."

"Yes, and we have raced as far as New York City. The *Bluenose* is the best schooner around. No one can beat her."

"I'm sure *Lady Catherine* could!" Elizabeth was tired of sitting there quietly.

"Do you think so?" Captain Woods noticed the sparks fly in Elizabeth's eyes.

"Of course she could. She is the fastest schooner I've ever seen. Plus her crew wouldn't let *Lady Catherine* lose."

"What do you think, Heman? Does *Lady Catherine* have what it takes to be a winner?"

"Maybe she could, but I'm not interested in racing."

Elizabeth turned to Heman. "William would! If William were here he would race *Lady Catherine*."

Heman laughed.

"Who is William?"

"My brother. He is in Ireland. Elizabeth is right, if William were here he would want to race. He would race anything, including a rowboat. But mostly he races horses. That is what he is best at."

Heman smiling at Elizabeth, "No, thank you, I am not interested in racing *Lady Catherine*."

"What a pity." Captain Woods' look returned to Elizabeth, "I guess we will never know, will we?"

The Captain retrieved his pocket watch and opened the gold face. "It's time. I have a room ready for dinner. My wife will join us. Elizabeth, you will not have to listen to two old captains talking of their many voyages. My wife will make sure we speak of other things."

They left the veranda. Captain Woods took Elizabeth by the arm. "Do you mind?" The question was directed at Heman.

"Not at all." Heman followed behind.

Elizabeth was happy to see the room they entered had large windows looking over the Harbour. Captain Woods escorted her to a table set for four. "Make yourselves comfortable; I will see to the whereabouts of my wife."

When they were alone Elizabeth hit Heman's arm. She came closer and whispered loudly in his ear. "I thought you did not have anything to do with his ship leaving the Harbour that night."

Heman smiled, "I don't remember saying whether I did or didn't."

"Can I sit in your lap?" Elizabeth smiled back at her husband.

"Don't you dare!" Heman moved back. "I'm going to tell your mother."

Elizabeth giggled again.

"Behave yourself. Here comes the Captain with his wife."

"It looks like you two are enjoying yourselves." Captain Woods turned to his wife. "Linda, let me introduce the newlyweds, Captain Kenney and Elizabeth."

Linda's friendly smile won Elizabeth's heart. "Come, dear, let me escort you to the ladies' room. It will allow you to refresh yourself and also take you away from these captains and their stories of the sea."

"I don't mind their stories, but I would like to freshen up before dining." Elizabeth followed Linda as they left the room.

The captains now had the opportunity to talk man to man. "What do you think of Nova Scotia becoming part of the United States, Heman?"

Heman was surprised by the direct question. Knowing the Captain was from the Southern States, he decided to choose his words carefully. "I'm not sure it will happen."

"Really!"

"I heard a "Bill" was introduced to the United States Congress, but that was over a year ago." Heman was still choosing his words carefully. "Have you heard any more?"

"Americans are giving the British Territories a good deal."

"I am not up on the details," replied Heman.

"I hear the offer is big money. For Canada West alone it is $36,500."

Heman whistled.

"What about Nova Scotia? It can't be worth that much to them?"

"$8,000."

"You seem well informed. "

"I have connections." He shrugged his shoulders. "I have taken an interest in the whole affair. What about you?"

"Definitely interested." Heman was also concerned; he didn't want Nova Scotia to become a part of the United States. All this information made him a little nervous.

Woods continued, "I'm told that Newfoundland will become a part of Canada East and Prince Edward Island a part of Nova Scotia."[99]

"Unless I am mistaken . . ." Heman wanted to make sure Captain Woods understood the British side. "I believe the Americans are too late. The Fathers of Confederation are meeting now to make all of what you speak of a new country."

"I hope they do it quickly," Woods added, "For I would hate to see the Americans swallow it up."

"It may happen any day now," Heman replied.

Captain Woods stood as he saw the ladies approaching their table. "I hope so, Heman, I hope so."

"Your arrival has perfect timing." He welcomed Elizabeth and his wife Linda. "Talking politics makes me hungry."

"Looks like these captains are solving the world's problems, Elizabeth. They didn't even notice we were gone."

"Come, sit down beside me, Linda." Captain Woods pulled out the chair for his wife to sit. He was careful to give her time to arrange her full skirt before pushing the chair closer to the table.

"Have you saved Nova Scotia from the Americans?" Linda questioned. She knew that was the subject on her husband's mind.

Heman helped Elizabeth settle in her chair. He bent down close to her ear. "Are you feeling well?" he asked.

"I'm ravished as usual. All I need is a good dinner," Elizabeth quietly answered. She turned to Captain Woods and asked, "Tell me, Captain Woods, does Nova Scotia need saving from the Americans?"

"I have fallen in love with Nova Scotia. I wouldn't want to see it change in any way. But enough talk about politics. Politics does not fill the stomach, and right now my stomach is calling for food." He picked up his silver teaspoon and tapped it lightly on his water goblet. A light musical ring brought the servers to attention. Two women with dark skin were waiting patiently to serve the dinner. Their skin shone like ebony in contrast to their white skirts and white blouses. White starched aprons crinkled as they moved forward.

A plate of Solomon Gundy[100] and a plate of Codfish balls[101] were placed on the table.

"Thank you." Captain Woods looked at the older woman as she served the food. "What is your name?"

"Ismary Istroyer."

A crash and sound of broken glass broke up the conversation between Ismary and Captain Woods. Heman had dropped his water goblet. The younger woman serving was quickly by his side. "I'm terribly sorry!" Heman's eyes met Ismary's. He was sure lightning and a crash of thunder could be heard. It was only a split second, but to Heman, everything was moving in slow motion. He realized that the thunder was from his heart. It was beating so hard he thought he may pass out. Quickly he dragged his eyes away from Ismary. Looking at the younger girl, a strained voice came out of him. "Can I help?"

"That's okay, sir. I will take care of it. Be careful you don't cut yourself. I will get you another water goblet."

"Are you all right?" Elizabeth's hand touched Heman's arm.

"Yes, of course."

"Ismary Istroyer." Captain Woods was continuing his conversation. "I've heard your name before." Wood's turned to Heman. "She has an establishment in Preston,[102] just outside of Dartmouth. What do you call it?" He was asking Ismary.

Ismary was recovering from the shock of seeing Captain Kenney. She willed herself to speak calmly. "Deer's Castle."[103]

"That's right great food, Heman. I believe it is also an Inn."

"A small one, sir. My people use it when they are in the area visiting." Ismary didn't dare look in the direction of Captain Kenney.

Heman was relieved to see how calm Ismary was. He wasn't doing as well. His nightmare was back and he wasn't even dreaming. Everything continued to be in slow motion around him. Captain Woods was speaking to him, but he had no idea what he was saying. Everything he heard was garbled. Scenes were flashing in front of his eyes. Those slaves in the bowels of his beloved *Lady Catherine*. Those dark haunted eyes. The two little bodies that went to the bottom of the ocean. He tried to give them a Christian burial. The smell, he could smell it now. The box of smelling salts given to him from that blasted slave captain. He couldn't take anymore. Heman began to choke. Then he was having problems breathing. Heman saw Elizabeth as if in a far distance. Linda was looking his way. Captain Woods stopped talking to Ismary. They both were looking at him.

"Excuse me, I must get some fresh air." He backed his chair away from the table.

Elizabeth took her napkin from her lap and placed it on the table. "I will come with you."

"No, Elizabeth, I will be fine. I will return in a few moments. You stay here and enjoy your dinner." Heman was surprised he could speak so calmly. Before he made a complete fool of himself, he left the room.

Heman headed for the veranda overlooking the marina. He looked back to make sure he wasn't visible by the Woods or Elizabeth. The windows of the dining room were on the other side. He went down the steps, leaving the veranda, slowly walking to a bench under a spruce tree. Only then did he allow his body to fall upon the bench and put his head down below his knees. He felt faint and he willed himself to keep his stomach intact. His blood was rushing to his face. How long he stayed bent over cradling his head in his hands he did not know. Pictures still flashed before his closed eyes. Pictures he thought were long gone from his memory. *"Oh, God, I know. I will never be free of what I have done. I've tried to make up for it. Isn't Ismary proof that I did something good for the wrong I did? You want more. What else can I do? I have tried to go on with my life. But you don't want me to forget, do you?"*

"Captain Kenney." He heard his name. Who was calling him?

"Captain Kenney, are you in need of assistance?"

He raised his head quickly and fought off his dizziness. Standing beside him was Ismary.

"Captain Kenney we meet again. Your friends did not notice that we had met before. They are concerned about you. The lady thinks you are having an asthma attack."

"My wife, Elizabeth." Heman thought he was in a dream talking to Ismary.

"She is a beautiful wife, and I see great love, also she is with child. I am happy for you, Captain Kenney."

"Ismary, it is so good to see you again." Heman was looking around to see if anyone could see them together.

"Don't worry, Captain Kenney, we have a few minutes to talk. I served the main course. Lobsters with Irish potatoes.[104]

Captain Woods ordered them especially for you. I told them I would come and see about you.”

“How are you, Ismary, and the others? What about the others?”

“Most of us are doing well, Captain. We never worked so hard, and the winters, not good for the rheumatiz.”[105]

“You miss the South? I’m sorry your life is harder. You don’t like it here?”

“Oh, but we do like it here, Captain Kenney. We are thankful you brought us to Freedom Land.”

“Why do you prefer Nova Scotia where you have to work even harder, to suffer so much from the cold and rheumatism and get so little for it?”

“Oh! The difference is that when I work here, I work for myself, and when I was working at home, I was working for other people. I have my own house. My man made it. Ten-acres is ours. We raise potatoes. The government is good to us when times are hard. We get beef, pork, and rice.”

“What do your men do?”

“They are being taught to hew logs, cut boards and make shingles for our roofs. Lakes and rivers are close by; they catch trout, gaspereaux, eels, and perch. No one goes hungry. Then every Saturday we go to Cheapside, where we sell our things.”

“What kind of things?” Heman was fascinated how these people made a new life for themselves.

“Our men make shingles, hoop poles, brooms, axe helves, oar rafters, and clapboard. You can buy and sell anything at Cheapside.”

“Then you are happy?”

“We work hard and we are happy. We are free. I will tell everyone I saw you today. No one ever forget Captain Kenney. Nobody.”

“Come now, Captain Kenney, you must go eat. Then I can tell my people I cooked for Captain Kenney.”

Heman smiled. The burden he carried seemed a little lighter. "Thank you, Ismary. Tell your people, I have not forgotten them. They will be in my heart forever."

* * * * *

Once again Elizabeth and Heman were alone in their bedroom. Elizabeth was lying on their four poster bed with her feet raised upon a white pillow.

"Are you well, Elizabeth. Maybe your mother was right. Going to dinner today was too much for you, even though I wanted you to meet Captain Woods. I think too much of myself."

"It is alright, Heman. A little swelling in my ankles, but if I keep them raised for a while, they will be back to normal by morning. Come, my husband, sit close to me."

Heman didn't need another invitation. He stretched his great form out beside his wife, placing two pillows behind his head. Today was almost too much for him. But here beside Elizabeth, he felt safe from surprises of the world.

"How is your breathing?"

Heman took in two deep breaths. "Fine, seems fine. I won't need the tea towel this evening."

"What happened?" Elizabeth's eyes were searching her husband. "What happened this afternoon, Heman? I have never seen you so distressed."

Heman jerked forward and then remained quiet.

"It wasn't your asthma, was it? I feel you are keeping something from me. Please, Heman, what has distressed you so?"

Heman began to panic, what was he going to do now? *God, help me! What would happen if she knew? How could she love such a monster? Am I a monster? God help me!* His breathing grew heavy and his chest began to heave.

"Heman, are you alright. Please, Heman, talk to me." Elizabeth never felt so closed out from her husband.

Heman could hear his name. It was Elizabeth calling him. Someone was telling him to answer her. In his heart he could hear the words, *"Everything will be fine, my son."* He heard these words over and over again. Air was reaching his lungs, the heaving from his chest diminished.

"Yes, Elizabeth, I hear you."

"What is it, Heman, what are you keeping from me. Is it so bad you can't trust me to know?"

"No one knows, Elizabeth. No one knows but William and my crew, Elizabeth. Oh yes, *Lady Catherine* knows, she won't let me forget. God knows. A great secret, a big black secret."

"Are you sure you want to know? You may not be able to forgive and then our love will be no more. I can't live without your love my, dear sweet Elizabeth."

"Look at me, my husband. You yourself tell me I am strong. Nothing can take away the love I have for you. Nothing. I don't care what you did in your past, I only care what we have now in the present."

"Oh, my sweet, sweet Elizabeth."

For the next two hours, Heman spilled everything from his heart. He left nothing out. God was helping him choose the words. The story ended with the encounter with Ismary at the Yacht Club that very day.

"Well, that explained your reaction this afternoon."

Heman was amazed how well Elizabeth received his agonizing story. His head was resting by her side. It seemed a huge anchor was lifted off his shoulders. Even his breathing seemed easier, he closed his eyes.

"You think God is still punishing you?" Elizabeth was in deep thought about everything Heman had told her.

"How can God be still punishing you? You have asked for forgiveness. You have gone out of your way to make it right. Helping those people come to Nova Scotia wasn't an easy thing to do. I don't think God is punishing you?"

"Then why do I suffer so greatly?"

"You are punishing yourself, Heman. You did not want to do it in the first place. You said it was William's plan."

"Yes, but I could have stopped it, and I did not. There are consequences to pay, Elizabeth."

"Yes, consequences, Heman, like your asthma, but God's forgiveness is there if you will reach out and accept it."

"But you don't understand, I can still see those poor people chained together. The fear in their dark eyes."

"Yes, you made a mistake, we all make mistakes, some larger than others. In God's eyes, your mistakes are not any different than those that lie or steal or cheat."

"Heman, what you need to do is remember the people you freed. Look into their dark eyes and see the excitement of freedom. Remember the shoes they carried to the freedom land. Your mistake has taught you to be good and to serve others and to make a difference in this world. Heman, can't you see the days of being haunted are over."

Heman closed his eyes again. He remained silent for a long time. Elizabeth knew he wasn't sleeping, but made no move to disturb his thinking. Her hand reached out and softly stroked his brow.

His eyes opened and he reached for her hand. "Thank you, Elizabeth, for saving me from myself. From this day forward when the nightmare of dark eyes filled with fear returns, I will then remember those eyes of joy. Never seen joy like that before, the pure joy of freedom. You are right, I need to reach out and accept the forgiveness that God has offered. I didn't think I was good enough for God to forgive me."

"But that doesn't leave me off the hook. I still need to help these people. Today Ismary mentioned the hardships of the people living in . . . what did they call it?"

"Preston," Elizabeth was quite familiar with the settlement where the Negro people lived. "That's right. Ismary, she is trying to run what she has called 'Deer's Castle'." Heman was on his feet walking up and down the room. "Elizabeth, I think I will help her. I think I will help them. I don't know exactly how, but I am going to look into it. *Lady Catherine* will be happy, I just know she will."

"Come, it is late, lie beside me. Rest. You are right, *Lady Catherine* will be happy."

Heman closed his eyes again. In the darkness, he asked her to promise one thing.

"Anything, my love."

"May this be a secret between you and me."

"Yes, this will be a secret between you and me."

Heman then went to sleep.

Deer's Castle
1867

Dear Captain,

The surprise I had when a messenger delivered your letter, was such, my people gathered around wondering it be good news or bad. Just days before, I told them about our meeting and now a letter.

It being very kind of you, wanting to help me and my man. My man says you have done enough, and wouldn't want word to get around that he be needing anything especially money.

God take care of you. You have a good life, maybe our paths will cross again. To me, I have been given enough. You bring us all to freedom land. You won't be forgotten, your name will be passed on down for generations to come.

Thank you again, Captain

Always beholding
Ismary

CHAPTER NINETEEN

Dominion Day 1867

"The news has come!" Heman was shouting as he opened the door and leaped up the staircase. "Elizabeth, the news has come!"

Elizabeth, put her knitting down on her lap, "In here, Heman. I'm in the living room. Come and tell me the news."

Heman was out of breath as he stooped down beside her. He placed a newspaper on her lap covering her knitting. "The Canada Gazette, a new newspaper, has just arrived. It is a few days old but it tells the news. There's a proclamation in it. I was right when we told Captain Woods that the Americans were too late. Look, Elizabeth." He quickly pointed to the printed page. "Tuesday, June 18, 1867, a proclamation uniting the provinces. Look, a list of new senators and look at this!" He pointed his finger. "A notice declaring July 1, 1867, as a day of rejoicing."

"We are a new Dominion!"

"What does that mean?" Elizabeth asked.

"A new country, Elizabeth; we are a new country! Look!" He pointed his finger again. "Ottawa, which had been made the Capital of the Province of Canada in 1857, is now the Capital of the new dominion."[106]

"What will be the name of our new country?" Elizabeth was catching Heman's excitement.

"It was picked from a list." Heman turned the page of the newspaper and pointed his finger for her to see.

Elizabeth read the list on the page before her:
"Victorialand
Borealia
Cabotia
Canada
Tuponia
Superior
Norland
Hochelaga

"Don't read any further!" Heman urged. "The Fathers of Confederation picked 'Canada'[107]Elizabeth, we have a Prime Minister. Sir John A. Macdonald was voted in. He was one of the Father's of Confederation.[108] There is going to be celebrating July 1st like you have never seen before."

"Heman, that's only a few days away. I hope it doesn't rain."

Heman laughed, "You sounded just like your mother. Come, you have been cooped up in this house much too long."

"I'm not allowed, remember?" She touched her stomach. "Where will we go? I don't want people staring at me."

"It's okay, Elizabeth, we will go to the *Lady Catherine*. How would you like to go sailing?"

"Oh, Heman, could we? It's been so long. I haven't been on the *Lady Catherine* for months."

"As long as you promise not to run around on deck. And no going up and down the ladders." Heman smiled.

"I will sit anywhere you put me."

* * * * *

Every newspaper in the land spued out headlines.

THE DOMINION OF CANADA.;
Inauguration of the Confederation
– A General Holiday–Lord Monck
Sworn in–Review of Troops.
The Celebration at Toronto, The Day
at Halifax.

July 2, 1867, Wednesday

This day has given birth to the political infant, the Dominion of Canada. At 12:05 o'clock last night its advent was hailed by a salute of 101 guns and a bonfire, also by the ringing of bells. The day dawned clearly and brightly on its nativity. And the capital was dressed with bunting to testify the public pleasure. . . . [109]

The Unionist, and Halifax Journal
Wednesday, July 3, 1867
Dominion Day

The Dominion was inaugurated on Monday, under the most favourable auspices. The day was delightfully fine for outdoor demonstrations--in fact, it was real Dominion weather. The greatest enthusiasm was evinced all over the city. The cordiality and enthusiasm evinced exceeded the most sanguine expectations of the friends of Union. Everywhere, with a few exceptions, the day was observed as a Public Holiday. Some few antis, who were of "no account," kept their shutters down and pretended to do business; but as the day wore on, many got ashamed of their opposition, and ere the torchlight procession moved off, they were found hurrahing vociferously for UNION and the NEW DOMINION! It is gratifying to know that every Union man behaved himself as Union men know how to do, and, altho' the antis were greatly afflicted all day, it is gratifying to know that they bore their affliction with becoming resignation, so that all the arrangements of the day were carried on without interruption. The booming of cannon announced the Birth of the New Dominion, and the ringing of church bells proclaimed the gladness.

At noon there was a Grand Display on the Common of the Military and Naval forces, in presence of His Excellency the Lieutenant Governor and the Officers of his Staff.[110]

* * * * *

"Hello, I'm back. Where are you?" Heman always voiced a greeting as he entered the flat from the sidewalk of Barrington Street.

"Here in the kitchen." Elizabeth could hear him climb the stairs to the main landing.

"What are you doing? Surely not cooking? Where is Sally?" He bent down and gave her an *I've come home kiss.*

"To the first question, I am reading several newspapers."

Heman could see many of them scattered over the surface of the kitchen table.

"To the second question, No, I am not cooking. And to the third question, Sally is not here today. Little John was not well this morning. I told her to stay home with him and not to worry. I would be fine for one day."

"Is John okay?"

"I'm sure he will be fine. 'Just cutting teeth,' Sally said."

"I wouldn't have left you so early this morning if I'd known you would be by yourself."

"Yes, I awoke and you were missing. I did get your note you left on the mirror." She smiled his way. "Thank you. What have you been up to?"

"A meeting with the crew."

"Does that mean you will be leaving again soon?"

"No, my dear, I will not leave you. Well, at least not until . . ." He touched her round stomach.

Heman sat down on a chair at the kitchen table. "I need to fill out paperwork, now that we are a new country 'Canada.'"

"That still sounds so strange to my ears," Elizabeth replied.

"It does sound funny, doesn't it? But we will get used to it. Before *Lady Catherine* leaves port, everything has to be put in order. I've got Henry working on it."

"Would you please hand me the scissors from the kitchen drawer?"

Heman walked to the other side of the kitchen. "What are you making?"

"I'm making a scrapbook. It's not every day one gets to see a new country born."

"What was your favorite part?" Elizabeth questioned Heman as he retrieved the scissors.

"You mean Dominion Day?"

"Yes, it was such a wonderful day. *Lady Catherine* gave me the opportunity to be right in the middle of all the festivities."

"Moses was still talking about it this morning. He thought it sounded like the beginning of a war. Over a hundred cannons were fired."

"I heard every one of them!" Elizabeth closed her eyes. "*Lady Catherine* with all her flags and banners."

"Does your head hurt?"

"No. Why?" She opened her eyes.

"Your eyes were closed," answered Heman.

"All I have to do is close my eyes, and I see pictures of the first Dominion Day. I will always remember the day spent with you aboard *Lady Catherine*. The fireworks. Oh, Heman, they took my breath away." She closed her eyes again. "As long as I live I will remember that day."

"Yes, just to think we were part of history." Heman closed his eyes. "It doesn't work; all I see is darkness. I think I had better keep my eyes open. At least one of us will know where they are going." He touched her nose. She squinted her face at him.

"Did Sally leave any food? I didn't eat breakfast." Heman opened the door to the icebox. "Leftovers! Do you want some?"

"Don't eat too much. Mother is expecting us for dinner."

"On Thursday?"

"I think she is feeling guilty not being with us on the *Lady Catherine* for Dominion Day. She had a better invitation. She and Father ate dinner with the Rev. Dr. M. Richey."

"The main speaker of the day."

"Not only him but His Worship the Mayor and all the other Honorable guests. They sat beside Hon. E. Kenney."

"E. Kenney?" Heman was making a ham and tomato sandwich. "Where is the cheese?"

"Bottom shelf. He didn't seem to think he was related to us."

"I'm sure all Kenney's are related back somewhere." He was drinking milk with his sandwich. "Do you want a bite?" He lifted the sandwich towards Elizabeth.

Elizabeth took more than just a little bite.

"Leave some for me!"

"It's a good thing we are going out for dinner. There is nothing to eat here. I don't think I will ever learn to cook." She had a troubled look.

"I wouldn't change you in any way, dear. We can always eat at your mother's place."

* * * * *

Heman couldn't take his eyes away from the small bundle that the nurse was holding up to the window of the baby nursery.

Ahead full of dark hair reflected light from the overhead lighting of the hospital nursery. The baby yawned and tried to stretch. The nurse had her swaddled in a white blanket so tightly she couldn't move. Her eyes opened as if to take a look at her new world but quickly closed them again at the bright lights. However, her eyes were opened long enough for Heman to see they looked just like Elizabeth's eyes. He looked at her little nose. Of course, it was smaller, but it was the same shape as Elizabeth's nose. Heman smiled and placed his hand on the window. The nurse placed her back in her little box of a bed. A small square sign was posted on the side. Kenney baby – girl – was written in small block letters.

Kenney – baby – girl wasn't the only baby in the nursery. There were dozens of little boxes filled with tiny babies. Some were crying and others were sleeping. Kenney – baby – girl was quietly looking around. *Just like Elizabeth,* Heman thought. *Interested in everything around her.* He stood silently watching his daughter for a long time, until another family opened the door and began looking through the window, searching for their baby.

"You must be a new father too?" The lady was still searching for her grandson.

"Yes, a new father too," Heman answered.

The spell was broken. He left the room on another mission. He wanted to see Elizabeth. The last 25 hours had been agony for Heman. *Had it been that long?* he questioned himself. *It seemed it would never end.* The waiting, the worry and the agony he felt knowing his Elizabeth was experiencing such pain. And he couldn't do anything about it. He kept telling himself Elizabeth was strong. She would come through this and she would be stronger still. The only thing that helped him, if only a little, was knowing she had the best of care. The best doctor, Dr. Harvie, and many nurses were with her. She wasn't alone. How he wanted to be with her, but he wasn't allowed. No place for a man, they say.

"This way, Captain Kenney. Down this hallway are our semi-private rooms." A young nurse was guiding him.

Heman was glad he made sure Elizabeth was not placed in the Ward. Each Ward had between six and ten beds and maybe more. Heman wanted Elizabeth in a private room, for only the best would do. But Elizabeth thought she would be too lonely and convinced him that a semi-private room would be perfect.

"Room 16, Mrs. Kenney is right down here." The nurse was leading Heman to Elizabeth. Looking quickly through the small square window, she opened the wooden door. This room had two beds. Elizabeth was in the bed by the window. She had a view of the Harbour. Janet was sitting in a chair by her bedside.

Heman walked to the opposite side of her bed. Elizabeth seemed to be resting quietly. She looked so small and fragile in between the white crisp linen. Janet was about to protest, but Heman paid no attention. He gently kissed his wife on her forehead. He placed the dark curl from her forehead back into its place.

Elizabeth opened her eyes. "Heman." She had a raspy voice. A smile formed on her dry, cracked lips.

"Rest, my love. I am here." He took her hand into his.

"The doctor just gave her something to make her rest." Janet was watching her daughter closely.

"Heman, I am sorry." Her voice was but a whisper.

"My love, why are you sorry? What troubles you?" Heman was alarmed. Whatever you need I will see that you have it. Tell me, Elizabeth, what troubles you?"

"I wanted to give you a son." Her words were weakly spoken. "Are you disappointed?"

"Elizabeth, sweet Elizabeth. My heart is bursting with the love I have for you, and now it is overflowing because God has given me another Elizabeth. I've seen her my love. She looks just like you. And for a boy, why would I want a boy when I can have two Elizabeths? You will just have to knit another tiny sweater. Not yellow this time but pink."

Elizabeth sighed and relaxed back into her white pillows. "She is beautiful, isn't she?"

"Beautiful, Elizabeth, our daughter is beautiful."

"Heman, what will we name her?"

We can't name her Elizabeth, can we? That would be so confusing. Heman was thinking to himself. He thought for another moment. "Mary Elizabeth."

"What do you think, my love?"

"Mary Elizabeth Kenney," Elizabeth liked the sound.

"Mary is a nice name." Janet was witness to everything that had been spoken. She could see the love that bound these two people together.

"Not Mary. I don't want to call her Mary. Janet, our daughter will be known as Mary Elizabeth."

"Sadie the head nurse entered the room. "It's time for visitors to leave. Time to feed the baby. You may stay." She was speaking to Heman. "But you must leave."

Janet protested, "But I am the grandmother!"

"Those are the rules. There will be no changing the orders. Heman could tell she was the captain of this ship. With Janet protesting, nurse Sadie led her down the hallway. "Visiting hours will be at 6 p.m."

* * * * *

Heman was holding Mary Elizabeth. It was feeding time, well just past feeding time. Feeding time in the hospital meant Elizabeth and he would be alone with Mary Elizabeth. Heman's favorite time and he made sure he didn't miss them. Elizabeth was getting stronger and Heman felt she was being well taken care of. Nurse Sadie made sure of that.

Visiting hours were 6 p.m. to 9 p.m. Elizabeth had many visitors. Just her brothers alone would fill the tiny room. Heman worried Elizabeth would be worn out from all the people around her. His worry was unfounded for nurse Sadie was in control. She only let two visitors in at one time and then only for 15 minutes. She had them all lined up in the waiting room.

Complaining was not allowed. If anyone complained, they didn't get to see Elizabeth at all. Mary Elizabeth had more visitors than her mother. They spent time at the window of the nursery waiting for nurse Sadie to tell them it was their turn to see Elizabeth.

Knowing Elizabeth was taken care of in the evenings, Heman spent that time catching up on work. But during the day Moses had a timer set. He would inform Heman it was feeding time for Mary Elizabeth. Everything would stop at the Irish Coffee Company, and Heman quickly headed for the hospital. This routine was going on for a week now.

"Good morning, Nurse Sadie."

"You know what to do, Captain." She was getting used to his coming and going several times a day, but she never failed to remind him that he must follow the rules.

"Yes, Nurse Sadie, I washed my hands up to my elbows with lye soap."

"How many times?" She made sure he always did it right.

"Three times. Soap, rinse, soap again and repeat. Nurse Sadie, I have the cleanest hands in town. My shipmates call me dishpan hands."

"Can't be helped–No germs around my patients. Don't forget the cap and gown."

"How can I forget?"

"We are going to charge you for laundry."

"Send me the bill," Heman answered as he made his way to room 16.

Elizabeth never failed to laugh as Heman entered her hospital room.

"See what I have to do to see my two favorite girls! Your mother doesn't even have to wear this." He looked down at the stiffly starched white gown.

"Yes, but Mother doesn't get to hold Mary Elizabeth."

"I will wear whatever they tell me to wear, as long as I get to see you."

"Today is Mary Elizabeth's birthday." Elizabeth held the baby up on her shoulder to burp her. "There, that's a good girl." Two little air bubbles could be heard.

Heman smiled at them both. He was still held in awe watching her feed their daughter. She was a natural mother. "Her birthday?"

"Yes, she is one week old today."

"Should we have a birthday party?

"Not until September 22, next year 1868. That is when she will be one."

"Dr. Harvie was in to see us early this morning. He wants me to get up and walk around today."

"Are you ready?" Are you sure you are strong enough?"

"Well, I am tired of staying in bed and I am tired of being in this hospital. The only thing I have to do is watch the boats going up and down the Harbour. And I can't even see *Lady Catherine* because that red brick building is blocking my view."

Elizabeth sighed and her mood changed. "I get to go to a class this afternoon."

"They have school here?" Heman knew the hospital was new, it was only opened a few months ago.[111]

"No, not a school, though the nurses have been talking about a medical school opening soon. Just a class. I am going to give Mary Elizabeth her first bath. Her umbilical cord hasn't fallen off yet, and I need to know how to take care of that when I get home."

Speaking of home, did Dr. Harvie mention when you and our daughter will get to come home?"

"I asked the very same question. He said let's see in a day or two."

"I have a surprise for you both when I get you home."

"A surprise!" Elizabeth loved surprises. "Tell me, Heman. I don't want to wait until I get home."

"You must, my dear." Heman touched her nose. "I must leave now. I have several meetings this afternoon. I may miss the next feeding for Mary Elizabeth, but I will be here before, your mother comes at visiting hours. Have fun at your class." He bent down closer to Mary Elizabeth. "And you, young lady, be good for your mother." The baby stopped nursing and looked at Heman. "See, she knows I am talking to her."

"Do you think I can teach her to sail? She will love *Lady Catherine*."

Elizabeth laughed. "Yes, Captain, I believe you will teach her to sail. But let's wait a few years. Do you agree?"

* * * * *

"Make sure you wash away from her eyes. Let me show you." Elizabeth took the tiny face cloth from Heman's big hands. "We start with the eyes and a clean face cloth." She rinsed it in water. "Start at the corner of her eye and move the face cloth away towards the side of her face." Mary Elizabeth lay quietly, and it looked like she was listening to her parents' voices as they laboured over bath time.

"This is more complicated than I thought."

"I tell you what. You take care of *Lady Catherine* and I will take care of Mary Elizabeth. At least until she grows a little."

"Look, she is watching us."

"Talk to her, while I finish her bath."

"What should I say?"

"Pretend she is a sailboat. You talk to them, do you not?"

"Only *Lady Catherine*. I've been telling her about Mary Elizabeth." Heman answered naturally as if it had been a normal thing to have conversations with a schooner.

"And, what has she said?" Elizabeth knew she had the only husband around that talked to boats."

"Very funny," Heman replied. "You know she doesn't speak. I know she is looking forward to one day having her play on her decks."

"Here, help me put her in a towel. Put her down on the counter, I will fold the diaper." She picked up two large pins.

"Don't poke her." Heman was alarmed.

"Scary, isn't it? Have no fear. See I put my finger in between the pin and Mary Elizabeth's skin. If you want to worry about someone it would be me. I have poked myself more than once. After she was freshly dressed in her white nightdress with the pink and blue embroidered stitching on the front, Elizabeth handed the baby to Heman. "You hold her while I clean up."

Heman sat in the rocking chair by the stove. It being the first of October, they had a fire going. The kitchen was a warm place for Mary Elizabeth's bath.

The young Kenney family had been home together in their Barrington Street flat for less than a week. Elizabeth's mother wanted her to come to her place, but Elizabeth would have none of that. "I want to go home with Heman" was the answer.

"But Heman doesn't know anything about babies. For that matter, Elizabeth, you are pretty new at it as well. When you were born I stayed with my mother a whole month."

"Yes, Mother, but I was born at grandmother's house. Heman and I will learn how to take care of Mary Elizabeth together. Besides, Sally will be there every day. She has the flat all prepared. Even the cradle you gave me is sitting at the foot of our bed."

"That cradle is the one you slept in at the foot of our bed." Janet dabbed the corner of her eyes with a lady's handkerchief.

Heman was happy Elizabeth wanted to be home with him on Barrington Street. They worked well together. Every time Mary Elizabeth cried, they always figured out what the problem was. Mainly all they had to do was feed her every three or four hours. Sally was here to help Elizabeth. She spoke of Elizabeth being a Jersey cow. "Blessed she is." Elizabeth was blessed and could have fed two babies.

Heman was still rocking his baby. He could feel her tiny breath on the side of his neck. She was sleeping peacefully, while he was singing his favourite Irish lullaby.

"Too-ra-loo-ra-loo-ral, Too-ra-loo-ra-li,
Too-ra-loo-ra-loo-ral, hush now, don't you cry!
Too-ra-loo-ra-loo-ral, Too-ra-loo-ra-li,
Too-ra-loo-ra-loo-ral, that's an Irish lullaby."[112]

Elizabeth came closer to look. "She is the only baby in Halifax to hear Irish lullabies and sung to her by her father. Come, we need to put her in her cradle. Mother said we must not spoil her."

"How can you spoil such a tiny thing. Just look how content she is."

"Yes, but you are not here all day to hold her. She must learn to be content in her bed. You can rock her later, like in the middle of the night."

"I don't mind. I will gladly rock her in the middle of the night."

Elizabeth knew Heman was true to his word. It made her job being a new mother a whole lot easier, knowing her husband was there at a moment's call. She was happy they shared the responsibilities of raising this little person together.

* * * * *

"I think you have forgotten something." Her statement was directed to Heman. She had settled Mary Elizabeth in her cradle and was closing the door of their bedroom.

"Forgotten, what have I forgotten?

"Come, let us go into the living room." She didn't want to disturb the baby's sleep.

"Should I carry you?" Heman smiled, he knew the answer.

"I do believe I can walk, thank you. I will say that I miss sitting in your lap."

"There is always room." He patted his knee inviting her.

"I think I will sit here in my chair. It is softer." She carefully arranged herself.

"What did you say I had forgotten? I tend to think that I am one who doesn't forget a thing."

420

"You have this time. If I remember correctly, and you can tell me if I am wrong, you said there was to be a surprise when we got home. We have been home almost a week. I have not seen anything wrapped laying around. No sign of a surprise."

Heman jumped up out of his chair. "I have been waiting for you to mention it. I've been very patient. With all the excitement with the baby, I was waiting for the right moment." He kissed her on her lips and informed her, "I will be right back."

"Where are you going? Don't wake up the baby."

"Have no fear. I am headed for the closet at the top of the stairs." Heman bounded back into the room. He was holding something behind his back. Pulling up the footstool, he sat closer to Elizabeth. "Now, before I show you I want to ask you a few questions."

"Go ahead!" Elizabeth was catching his enthusiasm.

"Do you love me?" He knew the answer and wasn't afraid to ask the question.

"Yes, of course, I love you. I will always love you."

"Do you trust me?" He so much wanted her to trust him.

"Trust you! What a question to ask?"

"Yes. Trust me to take care of you and now Mary Elizabeth. Do you know I will always want the best for you. The best for us?"

"I have no worries, Heman. You are the perfect husband. Our love grows more and more each day. Yes, this love comes in the form of trust. I trust you, Heman."

"Remember, I have done this for both of us. It's been very hard to keep it a secret. I don't like keeping anything from you. But, I didn't want you to worry while you sat home for the last several months. It was my job to provide for you and so I did so."

"Heman." Elizabeth was trying her best to be patient. "What does this have to do with your surprise? What are you holding behind your back?"

"Yes, of course, behind my back." He brought one hand in front of him. He handed a small scroll of white paper to Elizabeth.

"This is the surprise?" Elizabeth untied the string.

"Part of it." Heman was holding his breath.

She unrolled the paper. A moment of silence as she read the words to herself.

Heman thought his lungs would burst. *Breathe,* he commanded himself. *Breathe or you will be in the kitchen under a cup towel.* Finally, he heard her voice.

"100 acres in Watt Section, Eastern Shore, Halifax Co., Nova Scotia." She looked up at him.

He produced the other item he held behind his back. It was another rolled up scroll, but larger. He handed it to Elizabeth.

She placed the first scroll on her lap as she untied the string of the second scroll. She could see pages of some kind of drawings. It looked to be a house, a very large house. "What is all of this, Heman?"

"I am building a house for you. And me. And Mary Elizabeth."

"A house for me? Can it be?"

"Yes, Elizabeth."

"But where?"

"You know we have to leave Halifax. I can't breathe here any longer."

"Yes, I know, we have spoken about that. A change had to be made, but I didn't know how we could make a change."

"I needed cleaner air. Elizabeth, I found it. Well, my crew and I found it." Heman lifted the small scroll off her lap. "Right here, my love. We, you and I, own 100 acres in Watt Section."

"Watt Section? Where is Watt Section?"[113]

"It's a beautiful place, Elizabeth. It reminds me of Ireland."

"Watt Section is on the Sheet Harbour Passage, three miles east of Sheet Harbour. Four acres of our land has been cleared. It is cleared right down to the shoreline. The building of the house, our house began last spring. The builders hope to have the main structure completed before the first snow. Then the work can continue on the inside all winter."

Elizabeth picked up the scroll that had the blueprints of the house. "It is huge Heman!"

"I wanted to make the largest house in the area just for you!"

"It may be the largest house in Nova Scotia." Elizabeth continued to look at the prints before her. "When will it be finished?"

"I don't know. You never know how building something will go. Bad weather would certainly slow things down. Thankfully, we have had a good spring and summer. Construction is ahead of schedule. I've hired a large number of men from the area. Anyone who knew how to use a hammer. Patrick and John Charles have been leading the project. They say it is not only a good home for us but a great place for *Lady Catherine.*"

"To answer your question, I hope we can move in next summer. Maybe we can celebrate Mary Elizabeth's birthday in our new home."

"How far away from Halifax Heman?"

"I know it is 70-75 miles east of Dartmouth, that is by land. By sea, *Lady Catherine* can make it in a day. We will still have the Irish Coffee Company. We would visit your family often. Your mother could visit us." Heman hoped he sounded convincing.

"Father may not be happy."

"Elizabeth, I made a promise to your father a long time ago that I would not take you away. I haven't taken you out of Nova Scotia and I won't. Nova Scotia is my home now. Watt Section is where we will settle."

"Please, Elizabeth," Heman was begging. "Please say you will be happy. It won't make any difference if I build you the largest house in Canada, if you are not happy."

"It doesn't matter where we live as long as I am with you, Heman. Yes, we will settle in Watt Section. Do other people live there?"

"Patrick tells me there are about 130 people living there.[114]

"There is a wharf just west of our property. The fishermen come and go from there daily. Other schooners come to trade and travel west up Sheet Harbour Passage to trade at Sheet Harbour. Across on the opposite shore of the wharf is a shipbuilding yard. It is not very big, but it does employ several men from the area. That is where *Lady Catherine* was delivering her trade when I found out land was for sale. I was visiting with Simon Rutledge that day. He and John Low own most of the land there. Before I knew it, I bought all the land I could see from the other side of the passage and as far as the horizon. It was all forest. It came right down to the shore and along the rocky beach. That was early spring, Elizabeth. I wanted to rush home and tell you. But you had just told me the news of the baby coming. I didn't want you to worry. So I kept it in my heart, for you and me and our family to be. Now is the time to share with you my dreams for our future.

"Watt Section will be our future. Elizabeth, they have a church there![115] Moses has been in it. He said it is the prettiest little church he has ever seen. Just the other day in our meeting he commented he couldn't wait to show you."

"You make Watt Section sound wonderful, Heman."

"What about your crew? Where will they live?" Elizabeth was trying to see how all this was going to work.

"A plan has been drawn up. The crew will live in Halifax. They, not a one, has a problem breathing in the dust from the coal there. John Charles has found two sailors who live in Sheet Harbour who will help me sail to Halifax. There we will pick up the rest of the crew. Then from Halifax *Lady Catherine* will make her regular trade trips."

"You really have taken care of everything, haven't you?"

"I've tried, but I'm sure I've forgotten many things, that only you, Elizabeth, can take care of."

"What a surprise! You said you had a surprise, and what a surprise it is." Elizabeth picked up the larger scroll and began turning pages. "It is a beautiful house. Just look at the four columns holding up the large dormer with the half-moon window in the middle. The wrap-around veranda is breathtaking."

"It wraps around two sides of the house. Three sets of stairs to come and go as you like. You can sit on the back veranda in your rocking chair and watch for the *Lady Catherine* to return from her trade trips."

"That sounds so lonely." Elizabeth wasn't sure she liked the idea of her being alone for months at a time.

"You won't be alone, Elizabeth. All the other wives of the settlement are waiting for their husbands to return from the sea one time or another. You can help one another."

"That's just the outside of the house, Elizabeth." Heman tried to change the subject. The main floor has a dining room right off the large kitchen. A living room and a parlour, and upstairs are six rooms." He was showing her the blueprints.

"Have you seen it?"

"Not since they began the foundation. That was six months ago."

"When can I see it?"

Heman didn't have an answer to that question. He wasn't ready for Elizabeth to even ask it. "Well, this being October and Mary Elizabeth but a few weeks old, I do believe it would be wise to wait the winter before sailing to Watt Section."

"All winter!"

"I will keep you updated on any progress that is made. Communication may be harder to receive in the middle of winter."

"We will just have to make plans here. Can I have a meeting with Patrick and John Charles?"

"I'm sure that can be arranged. John Charles considers you one of his top students."

"That was navigation," Elizabeth replied. "Now I need to learn how to build a house."

Irish Coffee Co.
Boston
Oct. 1867

Dear Captain and Elizabeth,

We received the great news of Mary Elizabeth's birth with happiness and thanksgiving. Thank God both mother and baby are healthy and strong.

The O'Donovan's are truly thankful you chose to share your happiness with us, for we truly feel like family. We all miss William, but he continues to correspond often. Faye continues to enjoy his stories about his horses.

Lady Catherine's trade trips are exciting times for Faye and me. The wares she brings keep us busy filling the shelves of the Irish Coffee Co. John Charles keeps us up to date with you and Elizabeth. I must admit it is hard to get details, but Faye always asks the right questions.

Captain, you are missed too. I can understand why you would want to stay close to Elizabeth at this time. We will look forward to your first trade trip.

Duncan keeps the Irish labourers working. He has a great responsibility, which he takes very seriously. Sometimes I think the burden is too great, but he always says William started this and he plans to keep it going. So many families are counting on him. My Duncan is proud to be chosen for the task.

Now you live in Canada. Sounds much better than British territories. We read all about it in the newspapers here in Boston.

May you enjoy your precious daughter.

You always remain in our thoughts and prayers,

Peggy, Duncan, and Faye

CHAPTER TWENTY

Watt Section
1868

July 3, 1868, the sun was shining and big white fluffy clouds were sailing by in the bright blue sky. The ocean water was dancing with sparkling diamonds as the light reflected from the sun. Another great day for sailing. The *Lady Catherine* was in full sail, including the jib. She was flying at six knots and making good time and following closely to the eastern shoreline of Nova Scotia. The waves could be heard as they slapped against the rocky shore. Seagulls could be seen flying down on the small sandy strip of beach that laid between the many rocks. They picked up sea urchins, carried them high into the sky, then dropped them on the rocks below. As the shells broke open, the race was on to see which gull would get the tasty morsel.

A beautiful July day in Nova Scotia. The fog was held at bay just offshore. The warmth of the sun melted it away. However, the settlers from these parts knew the fog would be back most likely just after sunset. They didn't mind; they were used to it. It was a natural part of life, the same as the tides coming in and out. Dolphins came up and swam just before the wake of *Lady Catherine*'s bow. They could feel the excitement onboard. A journey was being made and they were leading the way.

"Watt Section, here we come!" Heman had several deck chairs set up on the upper deck. They now were occupied by family and friends. James and Janet and all the brothers were enjoying the trip. The whole crew was up on deck. Those who were on duty were making *Lady Catherine* do what she does best, fly. She flew across the water like a smooth stone skipping across the surface of a calm lake. But this wasn't a lake. This was the ocean and the ocean was alive with a will of her own.

The crew that was on "Stand down" were among the family. They were sitting watching the excitement unfold before them. They didn't want to miss a thing.

"How long, Heman?" Elizabeth was eagerly awaiting their arrival to Watt Section. She had never been there, but Heman had painted pictures of a beautiful place, and she had stored those in her heart.

"An hour, maybe less. Here, let me take her." He reached for Mary Elizabeth and scooped her up into his arms. She squealed with delight. This was her first time aboard *Lady Catherine* and the little girl showed no fear. Looking up to the top of the sails, Heman was heard saying, "See, *Lady Catherine*, I told you she would love sailing. No fear! Just like her mother."

Ten-month-old Mary Elizabeth was pulling herself up to her feet. She walked around holding on to any piece of furniture that was close to her. But she still preferred crawling when she was in a hurry to get from here to there. The last ten months they watched her grow. She had so many admirers, between family and the crew, Heman had to begin to teach her who the real captain of her ship was.

In those same ten months, Elizabeth built them a house. Well, on paper anyway. She and John Charles had many meetings and discussions. If there was a difference of opinion, Elizabeth always won. More than once John Charles came out of a meeting complaining to Heman. "She is the hardest woman I have ever seen! I tell her it can't be done and she turns around and asks, 'why not?' Then we have to go back to the drawing board. It's those eyes and sweet smile."

Heman never got in the middle. He was smarter than that. "She has you bewitched. Just ask Moses?!" he always replied. But to tell you the truth, Elizabeth was good at it. Her teacher had taught her well. She soon surpassed the knowledge of John Charles of house building. Heman knew his money was safe in the hands of Elizabeth. She didn't waste a cent. She organized each room, and the last time he checked, he was happy with what she had accomplished. *Lady Catherine* had made three trips with supplies and furniture. Of course, everything was tagged to make sure it was put in its right place.

Everything was done. All the plans were completed. Each time Heman returned from a trade trip, Elizabeth brought him up to date on the progress being made on the building of their house. She always had a list of things she might need.

7 - Washstands

7 - ceramic bowls for hand washing

7 - ceramic water pitchers, matching the ceramic bowls for hand washing

6 - chamber pots, matching the ceramic pitchers and bowls

3 - Franklin wood stoves

1 - large cook stove

"Why do we only need six chamber pots?" Heman was reading the list.

"You don't need a chamber pot in the kitchen, silly."

"Of course not," Heman replied.

"Three Franklin stoves, where do you plan to put them?"

"Since we have four fireplaces. One in the living room, one in our bedroom, which is right above the living room, one in the parlor, and one in the guest room right above that. The stoves will go in the foyer, the upstairs hall, and the children's playroom."

"They don't burn coal, do they?"

"Both wood and coal. But, no, we will not be burning coal. There should be plenty of wood to burn, don't you agree?"

"We will have to hire someone to split wood. That is until you give me a son who could do the job."

"I believe you had better hire someone, or do it yourself."

"Are you hinting that I may be on the lazy side?"

With a twinkle in her eye, she replied, "I can picture you with an axe in your hand now."

"You wait and see; I may surprise you how much I will do around our own land."

All the talking and dreaming and planning was done. The time came to pack up their flat on Barrington Street. This was hard for Elizabeth. Saying goodbye to Sally was even more difficult. But here they were today on *Lady Catherine* and heading for a new future.

"The mouth of the Sheet Harbour Passage is coming up," Heman informed the family.

"Port Ho!" Patrick called from the crow's nest. *Lady Catherine* bore towards the left and sailed up the passageway to her new home.

* * * * *

Dan Rood and his crew of men had been cutting cordwood, a mile down the road in the dense forest. They started at sunup, and he left the work site early for he had another job to do before this day ended. He called himself a fisherman, but he hadn't been offshore for some time now. The business of fishing was on a downside and had been for a couple years. Since the Civil War ended, New England fish markets dried up. The money they were willing to pay for his fish didn't even cover the cost of supplies and shipping. Lucky for him, he found work building a house for Captain Kenney. He had never met the man, but the whole community of Watt Section could talk nothing else but Captain Kenney and his family.

Dan didn't know they built houses that big. After all, he spent his whole life between Port Dufferin and Mushaboom. He did go to Ship Harbour once, but that had been awhile. His world wasn't very big, but it was big enough for him. Dan was a proud man; he thought he provided well for his wife and boys. He built them a house. It had four bedrooms, bigger than most houses around these parts. Certainly big enough for his brood. *Maude and him were doing just fine, they were,* he thought. Dan was grateful for the work building the great house. The other men in the surrounding area were grateful as well. Now the house was completed, except some outside work. The whole community had great pride in being part of it.

"What do you think they will be like?" Maude asked Dan.

"Who?"

"Well, the Kenney family, of course. You know we will be their closest neighbour."

"All we can do is be neighbourly; the rest is up to them," Dan replied.

"Elizabeth has a young girl."

"Elizabeth who?"

"Captain Kenney's wife. I hear her name is Elizabeth, and she has a young daughter named Mary Elizabeth."

"How do you know that?"

"You can't tell me you don't know. The men talk just as much as us women."

"Yes, I have heard the same, but the men talk mostly of the great schooner, they do. You've seen her here twice now."

"But not the Captain."

"No, Captain Kenney's first mate was in charge. Henry was his name. He spoke as if he were straight from Ireland, he did."

Dan and Maude continued to enjoy the conversation and the ocean breeze as they sat on their porch. Through the young maple trees, they could see the great house. Before the house was built, all they could see were trees. Clearing the four acres right to the shoreline gave them a different view. Now they could see the ocean right out to the mouth of Sheet Harbour Passage.

"It looks like a postcard doesn't it, Dan?" Maude couldn't get enough of the new view in front of her. "A beautiful house with the ocean right behind it."

"After all the tree stumps are gone and the fields are sown, it will be a right nice picture."

"They already named the house."

"Who?"

"Anyone who has seen it. Anyone from Port Dufferin to Ship Harbour. They all call it by the same name."

"You mean, 'The Show House?'"

"See, you've heard it too."

They sat in silence for a spell. The only sound was a snap, snap, bing. Maude was busy snapping beans. Her bowl was almost full.

"Garden's been good." He had a grateful sound to his voice. "Maybe it will make the coming winter a little easier."

"What will the Kenneys do? It's too late to plant a garden this year."

"They have bins set up in the cellar. But they were still empty the last time I looked. I wouldn't worry, Maude, I am sure they have thought that through."

The sound of snapping beans stopped. Dan looked over at his wife. She was straining her eyes to see something. "Are those sails, Dan? It's only a speck, but it's white against the blue of the ocean."

Dan joined the search. Off in the far distance amongst the blue ocean, a sail could be seen. "I see it too, Maude." They both watched as the sail became bigger as it made its way up Sheet Harbour Passage and closer to Watt Section. "She's flying! She will have to slow down before the sandbar. There she goes!" The schooner dropped her sails. All that remained was the jib. She continued her journey, slower now. "It's the Kenney's schooner!"

Maude was on her feet. Quickly carrying her bowl of beans, she headed for the kitchen door. "It's such a lovely afternoon; let's go meet her at the wharf. Can we, Dan?"

"I cannot see any reason we can't."

"Round up the boys. I'll comb my hair." Maude quickly untied the bow from the back of her apron, checked her image in the mirror by the washstand and pinched her cheeks. "That will just have to do," she said to herself and headed for the door.

Dan was already waiting by the maple trees. Eric and Cecil were jumping up and down watching the schooner come closer and closer. Cecil was the older, just over six, and Eric always right behind his big brother, was five. "Can we go?! Can we go?!"

"Yes, go!" Dan replied. The boys started off on a run. Dan took Maude's hand. "We'd better hurry. We will never catch up to them."

"You boys wait for us at the bend, do you hear me?" Maude yelled.

The bend turned right as the road followed the shoreline to the wharf. The boys were yelling and waving as the schooner was even with the bend of the road. "You're right; it is the Kenneys." Maude had her skirt hiked above her ankles as she ran after the boys.

"Looks like the whole family!" Dan was waving his cap towards the schooner. Those onboard were waving in return. "What a way to meet the new neighbours, Maude."

"Just keep waving, Dan. Keep waving!

* * * * *

Elizabeth had tears in her eyes. Heman had his arm around her, which wasn't an easy task with Mary Elizabeth in his arms. Heman would have tears in his eyes as well, but he reminded himself he was the Captain.

"What do you think?" John Charles was beside the Captain and his family.

"The house is beautiful!" Heman and Elizabeth answered in unison.

"You don't have to close your eyes anymore, Elizabeth. You can see it; we can see it with your eyes wide open." He drew Elizabeth closer to him. Mary Elizabeth squealed. She just wanted to get down and explore.

Patrick was there to the rescue. "Let me have her. You two can enjoy the rest of the journey to *Lady Catherine*'s home in peace. Mary Elizabeth didn't mind and neither did Heman and Elizabeth. They held onto each other as they looked at their new home together.

"Oh, it does remind you of Ireland, doesn't it Heman?"

"That it does, that it does."

"Look!" Elizabeth pointed to the road. Everyone saw them at the same time. Two young boys running and a young couple running after them.

"I recognize them." John Charles was the first to wave a greeting. "They are your neighbours, the Roods."

"At least she has neighbours," Janet whispered to James. She wasn't so sure about living in the wilderness, a large house or not.

James had over a year to get used to the idea of Elizabeth moving away from Halifax. But he was okay with it now, for she did have a family of her own. He was excited for them as he watched them look at their new home together. And for Janet, she too would get used to it.

Everyone was waving. *Lady Catherine* was waving too. Heman had told her this would be home. She slowly glided to a buoy that had been prepared for her by John Charles. *A perfect place,* she thought. *A perfect view of boats coming in from the ocean and from Sheet Harbour on their way to the ocean.* A small red dory was waiting, tied to the buoy.

Moses took the hook and fished the end of the buoy from the water. "Cat the anchor" was ordered. It didn't take long to firmly tether *Lady Catherine* and the crew stowed the jib and other sails.

"How are we going to get to the wharf?" Janet anxiously asked.

"The little red dory at your service," Moses replied.

"Not in a million years!" Janet exclaimed. "James," she called. "You know I don't like boats. You didn't tell me I would have to swim! Heman, surely you aren't going to put Mary Elizabeth in that little boat? No, not my granddaughter."

Both James and Heman were at her side. "Calm down, Janet." James was trying his best to console her.

"Janet!" Heman was drawing her eyes to his. "I am the Captain of this schooner, and I will personally make sure you get to the wharf safely. Breathe, Janet, that's right take deep breaths and sit down here. Do you trust me?" He was speaking with authority.

Janet seemed to be more relaxed, if only a little. "I guess I will have to." She was fanning herself with her hat.

"That's not good enough, Janet. I want you to trust me without any fear. You sit here and watch. I will come back and get you personally. James, looks like you need to stay with her."

Moses, Henry, and John Charles were already in the red dory rowing in the direction of the wharf. Their job was to pick up two more dories and return to the schooner. Heman was back beside Elizabeth. Mary Elizabeth threw out her arms ready to go to Heman. He was ready to oblige. "How's my girl?"

"She is doing remarkably well, considering she hasn't slept all day."

"She will be a great sailor one day." Heman looked into his daughter's eyes, "Won't you? Are you ready, Elizabeth? Our new home awaits."

"Maybe, I should wait here with Mother. Is she all right?"

"I have taken care of your mother. I promised I would be back to accompany her personally. I believe we need to go ashore together as a family and the first to meet our neighbours, for they have come to meet us. It would be bad manners to shun them."

"You are right. I do so want to meet Maude. Was that her name?"

"Yes, Maude and Dan, her husband. We will have to let them introduce their boys. Are you afraid to get aboard the dory?"

"No, not at all." Elizabeth took Moses' outstretched hand as he helped her aboard. The dory rocked with her movement, but she checked her balance as she sat on the bench. Heman handed Mary Elizabeth to Moses. He thought it would be safer, for Moses already had his balance in the small boat. Moses passed her to Elizabeth, where she held onto her tightly. Heman easily stepped into the dory, and with one motion, was sitting opposite of Elizabeth. Of course, Mary Elizabeth reached out for her father.

"I think I am going to like it here, Heman." They couldn't stop smiling at each other. Moses smiled too. If he wasn't busy rowing, he would have taken his hand and crossed himself.

Elizabeth held onto the side of the dory, then turned around to see *Lady Catherine*. She waved at her parents who were sitting watching everyone leave the schooner.

"Little Sister!" George was yelling. He and his brothers were in a yellow dory just behind them. "Do you want to race?" John Charles was rowing and the yellow dory was gaining on them.

Elizabeth laughed, "Sounds like William, doesn't it, Heman?!"

Heman laughed too. "Remember your mother is watching. We wouldn't want to make her any more nervous then she is. So behave yourself, Elizabeth, there will be no racing today." Mary Elizabeth squealed with delight, as she saw her uncles come beside their red dory. Heman gave one look towards John Charles and the race was over. John Charles was going to let the Captain win this one.

The wharf was fairly quiet. It would be another few hours before the fishermen would be back with their catch of the day. That didn't mean there was no welcoming party. The two young boys were jumping up and down again on the wharf. It didn't seem to faze the young couple at all. They didn't have any fear that someone might end up in the water. It was high tide, making it easier to get out of the dories. No climbing ladders was necessary. The dory floated right to the top of the wharf, where Moses held the dory to its side.

"You go first." Elizabeth wanted to make sure Mary Elizabeth was safely on the wharf. Heman passed Mary Elizabeth to Dan. Dan was surprised and quickly steadied the little girl in his arms. Heman was on the wharf with such a smooth motion he didn't even rock the dory.

Turning around, he stretched out his hand to Elizabeth. "My dear, it is your turn." She took his hand, and like a cat, she lightly landed on her feet. Moses pushed off and headed back to the schooner for another load. He knew this would be his job for the remainder of the day.

It was John Henry's turn to come close to the wharf. His passengers awkwardly tried to get out of the dory. The yellow dory rocked and rolled. John Henry was afraid someone would end up in the brink. He was relieved when Elizabeth's brothers were safely standing on the wharf. He tied the yellow dory and outstretched his hand to Dan. "Good to see you again, Mr. Rood." Dan was afraid to remove one hand from his duty of holding Mary Elizabeth.

Maude stepped forward and took her from Dan. She smiled at Maude. "What a sweet little girl." Mary Elizabeth didn't mind who took her.

After shaking Dan's hand, John Henry turned to his Captain and Elizabeth. "Captain, this is Mr. Rood and his wife, your neighbours."

"Just call me Dan, and this is my wife Maude." The two men were shaking hands.

"My wife Elizabeth and you have met our daughter, Mary Elizabeth."

"Would you like me to take her?" Elizabeth didn't want to burden Maude.

"I don't mind a bit. I'm sure you have many things on your mind. I will make sure she doesn't go over the edge. Welcome to Watt Section."

"Thank you. It is nice to know I have neighbours."

"Likewise, I have been dreaming of having a neighbour for a long time. And now I have one." Maude continued, "You and I are going to get on just fine."

"Elizabeth smiled towards Heman. *So far so good,* he thought.

"Elizabeth, I must return to the *Lady Catherine* and help your mother. I promised to bring her to shore personally. You stay here and visit; I will return shortly."

"Before you leave," James Jr. got Heman's attention, "Can we go on ahead and check the place out for ourselves?"

"Be my guest," Heman replied.

"Don't scare the cook." John Charles warned them.

"Nothing scares Marilyn Rutledge," Maude replied.

* * * * *

It was slow going but the red dory finally returned to the wharf. "Now don't rock it!"

"No, ma'am, I won't rock it." Moses would be glad when this journey was over. It took the Captain and James a good 15 minutes to get her to step into the dory.

"Mother, take my hand." Elizabeth was trying to help.

"No, you aren't strong enough. We will both end up swimming."

"Oh, Mother."

Dan could feel the tension in the air. He stepped closer to be of service. Heman was already on the wharf. James held her steady from the back, and Dan and Heman pulled her onto the wharf.

"Well, I'm glad that's over!" she straightened out her skirt.

Mother, are you all right?"

"I'm fine now." Janet was fanning herself with her hat again.

"Sit here until you catch your breath." Maude was moving over to make room on the wooden crate.

"It smells funny. Fish." Janet made a funny face. "I don't want to sit. I would rather walk. Dry land is what I need." As she spoke, she was on her way to the beach. Everyone else quickly was on their feet following her off the wharf. "Where is the carriage?"

"Janet, there is no carriage and you are going to walk!" James was tired of his wife's attitude. "If you don't change your mood, I will sit you down right here on that rock. You will stay there until your mood improves. You will not ruin Heman and Elizabeth's day by the way you are acting. Now sit down!"

"Well! I've never!" exclaimed Janet. She soon found herself sitting on a large white rock

"You young people go on. We will join you in good time." James planned to stay with Janet for as long as it took.

Elizabeth didn't know what to do.

Janet finally saw the folly of her ways. "Your father is right. Go ahead, dear, we will catch up to you shortly." She was still fanning herself.

Heman carrying Mary Elizabeth against his shoulder, used his free arm and placed it around Elizabeth. "It will be okay. We will walk slowly; they will catch up in no time."

Elizabeth looked towards Heman. She could see Mary Elizabeth was sound asleep.

"See, she is having her afternoon nap." Heman acted as if this was the way she napped every day. "Let's go." They walked slowly along the road.

The young boys were at the bend, jumping up and down again; "This way! This way!"

"They are so cute," Elizabeth turned to Maude. "How old are they? I don't believe I know their names."

"Cecil and Eric. They are six and five. Cute they may be; it takes both of us to keep up with them. They seem to be excited to have new neighbours too."

They rounded the bend and the big white house came into view. Elizabeth stopped and Heman was close by her side. "It's huge, Heman, that house is huge!"

"It looks like a postcard, doesn't it?" Maude could see Elizabeth wasn't high society. *We are going to get along just fine,* she thought.

"You worked on the house, didn't you?" Heman was making light conversation with Dan.

"Yes, sir. One of many around here. A great Show House."

"A what?" Heman stopped to hear.

"It's been named the Show House. I'm not sure you will be able to change it. Once people put a name on something it sticks."

"The Show House it will be. Pass the word; everyone is welcome to our Show House." Everyone was enjoying their walk along the dusty road, a good place to get to know one another.

"They are still working on this." Dan pointed right towards the rough looking laneway that led up to the stairs to the wrap around veranda. "As you can see, there are tree stumps to remove. To the left here, will be your barn."

"Barn! We are going to have a barn?" Elizabeth was in a state of amazement with what she saw before her.

"We have to have some place for the horses and cows."

Elizabeth thought silently for a moment then said aloud, "Sheep, can we have sheep?"

"If you want sheep, Elizabeth, I will buy you a whole herd."

"You mean flock!" Maude was amused.

"Say goodbye, boys, we need to leave the Kenneys to see their new home now."

"But, Father." The boys were not jumping up and down any longer.

"You're welcome to join us," Elizabeth invited.

"Dan's right, you don't need two boys running through your new house. I will give you a few days and then come by and see how you are doing." Maude hugged Elizabeth and was walking down the road towards her own house before Elizabeth could say another word.

Dan turned and waved his cap in farewell. "Looks like the rest of the family has caught up just in time."

James and Janet were almost to the entrance of the laneway. "It's so quiet here. All I hear are the calls of the crows and those gulls. Have you been inside?" Janet was back to her old self.

"No, Mother, we are waiting for you." Elizabeth took her hand and they started walking up the lane. "Mother, a barn is going to be right here," Elizabeth pointed.

"A barn!"

"Yes, a barn! Just think of that."

"Where should we start? Heman, it's like Christmas, you don't know what present to open first."

"Let's walk the veranda. Here sit down. Everyone sit down on a deck chair, and we will watch the ocean for a while." He sat down and rearranged his passenger. She was still sleeping peacefully.

* * * * *

"Here comes Mrs. Rood!" George announced loudly. This was a large house and he wanted everyone to be able to hear. For the last two days, everyone was exploring the new house inside and out. There was a holiday atmosphere. Elizabeth and her mother were getting to know the cook. Marilyn Rutledge wasn't a young woman when compared to Sally. She spent most of her life helping her parents take care of her siblings. Being ten of them, it didn't give her time to look around for a husband. As she watched her sisters and brothers marry one by one, she realized soon there wouldn't be anything for her to do. She heard that the Kenney family needed a live-in cook, so she decided that would be a perfect job for her.

Elizabeth's father and her brothers spent time at the wharf. There they met the men who fished for a living. Among them were Lloyd and Gerald. An invitation was given for them to join them and fish offshore for a day. James thought better of it; he knew they would just be in the way. Instead, the brothers spent hours having dory races to and from the *Lady Catherine.*

Janet was the first to answer the door. "Come in, Mrs. Rood, do come in."

"Maude, you can call me Maude. I'm not disturbing you, or the Captain. . . Is Elizabeth here?*"Of course, she would be here,* thought Maude. *What a silly thing to ask.* She was a little nervous; she hadn't visited new neighbours before.

"No, not at all, you are not disturbing us at all," Elizabeth announced as she walked into the foyer from the kitchen. The foyer was a large open space that welcomed one when he entered this great house. The dark, rich colour of the mahogany staircase was breathtaking. Mahogany continued to flow around the room under the creamed coloured molding of the chair rail. A golden colour continued upwards from the chair rails to the beams of mahogany that crossed the light ceiling. On the great wall opposite the staircase hung two large oval pictures with dark wooden frames. One of the *Lady Catherine* in full sail and beside her Captain Heman Godfrey Kenney. A new addition of a Franklin stove stood guard between two doorways. One doorway led to the kitchen; the other to the great dining room. The side of the mahogany staircase made a hallway that directed one to a parlour on the right, and then opened up into the living room. Elizabeth was holding Mary Elizabeth as she came into the foyer. "See, Mary Elizabeth, we have our first visitor." She placed her down on the floor and she walked slowly, like a little duck towards Maude.

"She can walk!" Maude exclaimed. She had her hands full. "Here, take the pie!" Mary Elizabeth walked right into her arms. Maude picked her up. "You smart little thing, you."

Janet stood holding a hot pie and watching Mary Elizabeth be hugged by the new neighbour. *Maybe James was correct; Elizabeth will be alright.* She was still thinking to herself.

"That pie smells delicious." Elizabeth's nose picked up the delightful smell.

Janet looked down at the pie.

"Blueberry, isn't it!?" Elizabeth continued.

"Yes, the blueberries are ready, just down by the shore. The boys and I have been picking." Maude put Mary Elizabeth back on the floor. She looked like a wind-up toy soldier as she walked along. "I've come to tell you, church is at 11 a.m. tomorrow."

"The church, Moses spoke of the church," Elizabeth remembered.

"St. Andrews, it's along the shore towards the point." Maude pointed in the direction of the wharf. "We, Dan and me, would like for you to come as our guests. We don't have a carriage. . ." She was looking at Janet. "But, Dan will be hitching up Minnie and Topsie to the buckboard wagon. There will be plenty of room for everyone."

"That would be wonderful!" Exclaimed Elizabeth. "We will look forward to that. Won't you come in and visit."

"Thanks, I can't this time. I've left the boys chasing butterflies and who else knows what. We will see you 10:30 tomorrow morning."

* * * * *

"What will I wear, Elizabeth? I didn't know I would be going to church in the wilderness."

"It's not the wilderness, Mother. I'm sure you can find something suitable in the trunk you brought from home."

When Heman heard the whole family was going to church, he decided to inform his crew that they were going as well.

"Will there be room on the buckboard?" Janet was trying to be positive.

"No problem; they will walk. All they have to do is follow the shoreline. My crew will be there before the buckboard even arrives."

* * * * *

"Four days of sunshine in a row, and no fog. It's got to be a record." Dan was making conversation as he willed Minnie and Topsie to a faster trot. He didn't want them to go any faster; he might lose a passenger, since the wagon was so full. The sea breeze coming off the water helped keep the dust from settling on the ladies. They were dressed in their finest, and Dan didn't want to get into trouble delivering them filled with yellow dust.

Their speed slowed considerably as they turned left, and the horses strained to pull the wagon up the first hill. "That's our cemetery there on the left." Dan was showing the new people the sights as they passed them. "The Lowe's live there to the right; they have eight kids. The Rutledges built that house and their brood is ten." The Kenneys heard there were McPhees, Bouiliers, Currys, and Hubleys that lived along the road before they turned left again onto Church Road. Here they met other wagons, and to Heman's surprise, most of them were as full as their buckboard was.

The wagons lined the road both east and west of the tiny Church. The Church was built of white clapboard and had a small steeple that housed a bell. The two large front doors were on the west side of the building. St. Andrews Church stood tall and strong looking out towards the sea.

Heman watched through the opened doors a young boy in a short white robe take the rope from the metal hook. The bell began to ring in its deep metallic tone, as the boy pulled the rope up and down. Mary Elizabeth clapped her hands in glee.

"Here they come!" James Jr. pointed.

Up from the shore came a line of men. Everyone stopped to watch as they walked across the road towards the church. What a sight they made. Their dress uniforms stood out in the crowd, but blended in with the green of the grass and large spruce trees.

Elizabeth couldn't help but be proud. She loved their green jackets and vests. They were a perfect contrast worn with their canvas coloured trousers. Their bandanas tied around their necks matched their short ribbons that hung from their vests. Embroidered on the ribbons were the words *Lady Catherine*.

Word spread throughout the congregation that the church was going to be filled to capacity. "Let the visitors sit first." Dan and Maude, holding her boys back from running, led their guests into the sanctuary. They walked up to the front and sat down on the first white pew to the right. Their guest followed. The group of more than 20 filled five of the pews. The fifteen pews left were quickly filled. There was standing room only. Everyone came to meet the new neighbours.

Reverend MacDonald was pleased to see the church filled with his flock. He looked out amongst them making eye contact with many whom he hadn't seen in several months. His church was the centre of the community. They gathered often, not only for worship, but fellowship in good times and bad. Many times they met to pray for those who didn't come back from the sea. Today was a good day; a new family would be added amongst them. There was a festive atmosphere, and he was glad of it.

After services ended, everyone was invited to stay for a dinner on the grounds. Sawhorses and old doors were set up for tables. The white starched tablecloths made it look like a feast for a King. "Oh dear," Elizabeth whispered to Maude. "We didn't bring food, and there is so many of us."

"No worry, my dear. Marilyn took care of everything."

Elizabeth looked over to where Marilyn her new cook was standing. She was unloading a cart that seemed to be filled with food.

"But, when did she do all of this?"

"Don't tell the Reverend, but she has been cooking all morning. She hoped no one would notice her absence. You will see her in church next Sunday," Maude smiled at Elizabeth.

The men were busy making a fire pit between the rocks on the shore. Mackerel was running; they had enough for everyone. The smell of it frying in butter was carried in the sea breeze towards the workers setting up tables. Everyone's vegetable gardens were just coming to life. You could see the results, for on the tables were yellow and green beans, sweet peas, and the first of the tomatoes, and new potatoes, so new they didn't need to be peeled. There were turnips and parsnips, boiling in pots over one of the open fires. A procession of men carrying large platters of fried fish crossed the road, and when they reached the tables, everyone was waiting for them.

The people: men, women, young and old. Children: boys and girls and even babies looked upon the tables filled with food. They were grateful for what was placed before them. No one had forgotten the hard winter that everyone had to endure, but now the bounty of summer was placed before them.

In the hush of the silence, Reverend MacDonald began his prayer. "Thank you, Father, for taking care of your children. For all of this food set before us may we be thankful. And for the fish of the Sea. Our cup runneth over; our plates be full."

The sound of feet shuffling in the gravel could be heard. Some brave soul, or was it a hungry soul, thought he would help the Reverend and loudly cried, "Amen!"

"Amen!" was echoed, and the food was passed up and down the table. It didn't matter to anyone that there were no chairs to sit on. A place in the shade under a tree or a rock by the shore made a good place to sit and eat when everyone was hungry.

Dan introduced the Captain to all the men who lived in the area. Many had been workers for him on his house. They were eager to meet Captain Kenney. Maude did the same for Elizabeth. The ladies warmly welcomed her and her mother to the community.

Time for dessert arrived. No one had touched a thing on the dessert table, not until it was time. Heman wasn't sure how they knew it was time, but they did. Everyone gathered around the table. All the deserts laid out on the table were admired. Each dessert was pointed out, and the woman who made it was acknowledged. There were rhubarb pies, blueberry grunt, strawberry upside down cake. Sugar was hard to come by. The ladies saved every grain. Desserts of this quality were only seen at times like today. When the community got together, they brought their best.

* * * * *

Everyone turned in early that night. The combination of full stomachs and cool salt air from the sea breeze coming in through the opened windows made it easy to go to sleep. Did you have a good day? Elizabeth asked her husband.

Heman was standing by the open window of their bedroom. He could hear the ocean, but it was too dark to see. He didn't hear her question, for he was deep in his own world. "Elizabeth, I believe there should be a lighthouse right out there. Someday there will be a lighthouse out there."

Elizabeth didn't mind having no answer to her question. "Don't you think you should build the barn first?" She was now standing beside him. "Come, sit in your chair." As he did so she climbed into his lap. What did you think of our day?" She repeated her question.

"It didn't take us long to meet everyone for miles around. They seemed to be willing to be friendly to us. You know, I found cargo for *Lady Catherine* to take back to Halifax."

"Today! You were working on the Sabbath?"

"I couldn't help it. The crew was on the beach and the men came and gathered around and before I knew it, I had cargo."

"What kind of cargo?"

"Fish for one."

"How are you going to keep it fresh?"

"They know how. If they had known they needed it, they said they would have kept ice."

"Ice. Can they keep ice?"

"They say they can, but I believe they are going to use salt for now. I made a deal with them. '50/50'. They get 50% if they bring it to *Lady Catherine*. I get 50% for taking it to Halifax. Also cordwood. Everyone is cutting cordwood. I gave them the same deal. '50/50.'"

"I thought Halifax was into coal?"

"People are getting tired of the coal dust. If they could get their hands on cordwood, they would use that as well."

"So, you are happy?"

"Yes, and you?"

"Do you like our room?"

It was just like Elizabeth to change the subject. Heman looked around. "I'm glad you brought our four poster bed, and your dresser and vanity. That captain's chest of drawers fits nicely on that wall. Yes, I do like our room. And we can look out at the ocean." He looked around the room again. "I miss our privacy closet."

"It was your idea to move to the country. I have chamber pots in every bedroom. You have visited our newly built outhouse, have you not?"

"Two seater."

"Top of the line and only the best. That's what you tell me, isn't it?"

"Yes, Elizabeth, you deserve the top of the line and only the best."

Halifax
August 1868

Dear Elizabeth,

How I miss you. You were just like a sister to me. Sometimes the way Little John acts, I believe he misses you too.

Each day it gets harder for Frank to work at the docks. I worried how he would be able to continue. I prayed to God he would send some kind of answer. That He did. Elizabeth, we will be moving too. Away from this dirty coal harbour. Frank met up with an old friend. Turns out he works at the canal in Shubenacadie. Frank took two days and went back to Shubenacadie with this friend. They were hiring and Frank got himself a new job. He is coming back for Little John and me the end of this month.

He writes of fresh air and open country. Just like you, it will be a new beginning for us. You called it a new chapter. I am excited to begin.

Take care of Mary Elizabeth and say hello to the Captain. I will write again when we get settled.

Until that time
Sally

CHAPTER TWENTY-ONE

"Fire!"

January 20, 1876, the snow was blowing and the wind was howling. Heman was frantic; it wasn't because of the weather. Of all the times a baby could decide to come, this was not a good one. Just this afternoon, Elizabeth and he were sitting by the fireplace watching the great storm brewing outside their windows. There was definitely a chill in the air, much more than a chill, it was downright cold. The Franklin stove in the foyer and the fireplace in the living room were trying to keep the house warm. He saw it when it happened. Elizabeth was telling him all about the school that was being built. Then her voice changed and her face turned white.

"I believe it is time, Heman." She was trying to keep calm, but fear could be read in her voice.

"Time, time for what?"

"You'd better call June Rutledge." Elizabeth was still trying to remain calm.

The name June Rutledge had Heman on his feet. "Not now, Elizabeth, please tell me not now? Heman asked frantically.

"Yes, now!" Elizabeth's eyes pierced Heman's begging him to help her.

"All right, everything is under control!" Heman forced himself to be calm. "Mary Elizabeth!" he yelled loudly.

"Please don't yell." Elizabeth was still trying to be calm.

"She's in the kitchen with Marilyn," Eliza answered.

"Eliza, fetch your sister, then gather Laura and Sarah and take them to the playroom. Don't stand there, just do it!"

Eliza didn't have to be told twice. "Yes, Father," and she ran towards the kitchen. A few moments passed before Mary Elizabeth and Marilyn were in the living room.

"Marilyn, help Elizabeth upstairs to our bedroom. Mary Elizabeth, you help Marilyn!" Marilyn, where is Wayne?"

"He went to the barn to check the animals."

Elizabeth met Marilyn's eyes. "It's time; we need June Rutledge."

"Oh, dear, on such a bad night?"

"Mother, are you alright?" Elizabeth went to her mother's side.

"Of course, your mother is alright. Come, Mary Elizabeth, help me take her upstairs." Marilyn and Mary Elizabeth helped Elizabeth slowly climb the stairs. In no time they had her settled in the four-poster bed. "Mary Elizabeth, you stay with your mother. Wayne is not here, I will light the fireplace, then I must go to the kitchen to boil water."

Mary Elizabeth pulled up a chair and sat close to her mother's side. She remembered when Sarah was born. She was seven at the time, but now she was ten. Maybe she can help. She went to the washstand and poured water from the ceramic pitcher to the matching bowl. The water was ice cold. Taking the face cloth that hung behind the washstand, she placed it in the water. Ringing the cloth, she returned to her mother's side. Gently she placed the cloth on her forehead. "Thank you, dear, that feels good." Her mother smiled at her oldest daughter.

* * * * *

Heman and Wayne were in the barn. It took both men to close the barn door, since the wind and snow blew so hard. "Let me go, Captain." Wayne was willing to do anything for this man and his family.

"I don't know, Wayne, . . . the storm and everything." Heman looked down at the empty sleeve of Wayne's coat.

"I can do it, Captain. I only need one hand. I've proven it to you before." Wayne really wanted to go.

"Okay, Wayne, but we need June Rutledge here as quickly as you can get her here."

Wayne was happy he had won that discussion. "Let's harness Beauty; she is the biggest and strongest." Heman's young daughters named the black horse with the white star on his forehead. He looked just like the horse in the book Black Beauty. "Put blinders on him; it will protect his eyes from the snow and wind." Wayne and Heman worked together to harness the horse to the sleigh.

Heman was always amazed how this one-armed man could do the work of any two men. He knew he was lucky to have him. He had peace of mind when he was away on trade trips, knowing Wayne was here to take care of things.

There was a crashing and banging on the barn door. Marilyn wrapped up in scarves and wearing a very large coat, came through the door. She was carrying a heavy roasting pan. "Wayne, take these." As she removed the cover, a stream of hot air escaped. Four red bricks were sitting at the bottom of the roasting pan. "Here, wrap them in these burlap bags." She never thought twice it would be Wayne who was going. "Put them at your feet. Bring June back as quickly as you can. These will help keep you both warm. Now hurry." She was gone out the barn door from which she came.

Beauty seemed to know the emergency. He pranced his hooves, and hot air turned to steam as it snorted out his nostrils. "Be safe!" Heman yelled as they started out the laneway. A quiet sound of sleigh bells could be heard through the roar of the wind.

As he watched the sleigh make a right turn onto the road, he couldn't help but think back. . .

More than eight years ago this place became home. He and Elizabeth had four lovely daughters, *and probably another one, before this night was over,* he thought. He smiled to himself, he didn't mind, he wouldn't trade them for anything. Marilyn and Wayne were part of their family as well. Marilyn just came with the package, but Wayne showed up one day, shortly after they moved into their new house. He was a thin scrawny young man with dark circles under his eyes. You could tell he was a desperate man. Heman found out later that the fishermen wouldn't take him fishing. The shipbuilding yard would have nothing to do with him, and he was turned down at the Sulphite Pulp Mill in Sheet Harbour. And to be a lumberjack, Wayne didn't even try. Heman remembers the first words he spoke.

"Before you say no, or you are not interested, let me tell you something. I can and will work harder than any two or three men that you have ever known. My right hand is strong and can do anything a man with two arms can do. You won't be sorry if you hire me."

Heman wasn't. His girls loved Wayne as an uncle. He taught them how to do their chores, and he made sure they were done well. Just the other day he told Sarah, as he carried her through the kitchen, "I have a job just right for you; starting spring I will teach you." Sarah, being two years old, Elizabeth and I were interested in what kind of job he had in mind. Turned out it was collecting eggs from the chickens. Wayne had great faith that Sarah wouldn't break an egg.

A blast of cold wind brought Heman back to the present. He shivered, even though he still wore his buffalo coat. Every time he put it on, he thought of Boston and Captain Freeman. The steps to the veranda were covered with snow. Holding on to the railing, he forced his way up the steps. Seeing the snow shovel standing by the door, he picked it up and headed back to the steps. After the steps were cleared, he let himself in through the front door. Marilyn had spread newspapers on the floor, and like an ink blotter, the melted snow became part of the paper.

Marilyn stopped before climbing the stairs. "Can I do anything for you, Captain?"

"How is Elizabeth?

"Moving along more quickly than I like. We are making her as comfortable as we can."

"You go take care of Elizabeth; I will look in on the children before I see how she is doing."

"There is hot coffee in the kitchen." Marilyn disappeared up the stairs.

"How are my girls?" Heman entered the playroom. Seven-year-old Eliza was entertaining Laura and Sarah. "Where is Mary Elizabeth?"

"She is in Mother's room. How come she can go in there and we can't?"

"Don't worry, I will send her to take care of you and your sister. You can help her. Do you think you could do that for me?" Eliza was completely under her father's spell. She would do anything for him. He hugged Laura and Sarah. "Be good girls and listen to Eliza and Mary Elizabeth." Heman slipped out of the room and down the hallway to his bedroom.

Marilyn met him at the door. "Captain, I believe your wife will be fine. We are just waiting for the midwife. I'm sure Wayne will be here shortly."

"Yes, I hope they will be here soon. But by the sound of that wind howling and the amount of snow coming down, it may take a while. In the meantime, you may need my help whether you want it or not."

Marilyn stepped aside and let the Captain pass through the doorway. After scanning his surroundings, Heman headed straight to the washstand. He remembered how to wash his hands. Soap three times with lye soap and rinse thoroughly.

"Where is the lye soap? Cold water will never do; we need hot water." Marilyn was onto it.

"Mary Elizabeth . . ." She looked at her father. "You doing okay?"

"Yes, Father, I want to help."

"You have been a great help, my dear. But I have to ask you to help in another way. You may not think it very important, but Mary Elizabeth, I have no one else but you that can do it. Are you willing?"

Mary Elizabeth knew her father well. She didn't think she was going to like what he had to say. "Yes, Father, what is it you want me to do?"

"I need you to take care of your sisters. Someone needs to get them ready for bed. As you can see, it can't be your mother, nor Marilyn, and it looks like I am going to be needed here. Do you understand, Mary Elizabeth?"

"Yes, I will." Mary Elizabeth resigned herself to the tedious task. "Father, will you send word when it happens? I mean when the baby has come?"

"I will send for you all." Mary Elizabeth wiped the perspiration drops from her mother's forehead. "See you soon, Mother."

Elizabeth opened her eyes. "Thank you, Mary Elizabeth."

Heman drew all of his attention to Elizabeth. "Elizabeth, my love?"

Again she opened her eyes, this time searching for Heman. "There is not going to be time!" Fear was written across her flushed face. "Heman, there is not going to be time."

Marilyn arrived with an iron kettle filled with boiling water. She emptied the cold water from the ceramic bowl into the chamber pot. She was about to pour the boiling water.

"Whoa!" Heman stopped her just in time. "You had better add a little cold first or you will break that pretty bowl."

"You're right. What am I thinking?" Marilyn was clearly nervous about what was taking place around her.

Heman began to wash his hands. Marilyn watched. "When I am finished, Marilyn, you do the same."

"Me, sir?"

Yes, Marilyn, you too.

"I'd better get the chamber pot from the guest room; we are going to need it."

"Do that before you wash, or you will have to do it again," answered Heman as he made his way to the side of the bed. "I'm ready, Elizabeth."

"Are you sure?"

"Elizabeth, I have been through hurricanes more than once. I can help you do this. God will help us." She sighed and laid back into her pillows as her body relaxed after a strong labour contraction. "Marilyn, I need thread; actually 'cat gut' would be better. We need more hot water and towels or linen, something like that." Marilyn was onto it again.

Heman was alone with Elizabeth. "Don't you worry; everything is going to be fine." He wiped her forehead with a hot face cloth.

"But, Heman, you have never even seen a baby being born?" Elizabeth was worried.

"That's another thing. How am I supposed to see a baby being born? No woman in this world is going to allow a man to even get close. But, don't worry, Elizabeth. Remember how Wayne and I helped that cow have her calf."

"Heman, you have got to be kidding!" Elizabeth was panicking as another strong contraction hit.

"Well, Elizabeth, it can't be much different. Here, take my hand." Elizabeth grabbed his hand so tightly he had to grit his teeth to not cry out. "Remember nurse Sadie?"

"Who?" Elizabeth really didn't have time to think.

"The nurse in Halifax when Mary Elizabeth was born. We will just follow her example, lots of lye soap."

"Okay, Marilyn, you hold the sheet, while I use the soap."

"It's coming! Oh, it's coming!" Elizabeth cried.

Heman quickly changed his position to the end of the bed. Before he knew it a baby's head was crowning. Thirty seconds later he was literally catching a baby. He jumped two feet when the baby cried.

"Scissors!"

Marilyn handed him the sewing sheers.

"Thread!" 'Cat gut' was placed into his hand. "A reef knot should do the trick. Towels, he cried. I need towels." Quickly he wrapped the baby in a towel.

"Congratulations, Captain, a son!" Marilyn took the towel-wrapped baby to the washstand.

"A son, it can't be!" He was expecting another girl. And he was too busy to notice one way or the other. Elizabeth had tears spilling from her eyes. Heman was too busy to be by her side to comfort her. "Be strong, my love; this is almost over."

"Marilyn, I need more hot water!" Without Marilyn, he would never have been able to do this. *I must give her a raise,* he thought. Finally, Heman had his wife resting comfortably in the four poster bed, fresh linen and all.

He drew up a chair to be closer to her. "How are you, my love? Elizabeth, you are so strong. I believe you could captain a schooner all by yourself."

Tears fell from her eyes once more.

"Are you in pain?" Heman thought he must do something else.

"No, my love." Elizabeth was finally able to speak. "You have been wonderful. Any other husband would have run away."

"Run away?" Heman looked out the ice-covered window. "Not in this storm, my dear." He took her hand. "I would never run from you."

Elizabeth smiled and tried to wet her dried lips. "I finally did it, Heman, I gave you a son." Marilyn came to the bedside holding a baby wrapped in a blue blanket. Heman reached for the tiny bundle. Holding the tiny baby close to Elizabeth, they admired their handy work.

"He's all dressed up." Heman looked at the beautiful baby before him. He had lots of dark hair, and Marilyn had formed a curl on the top of his head.

"What shall we name him?"

Heman laughed, "I only picked out two names, Doris and Alice."

Elizabeth laughed also, "Oh, don't make me laugh; it hurts." She held onto her stomach. They silently watched their son. The silence wasn't very silent with the howling of the wind and the snow beating against the frozen window pane.

"It seems to me he needs a famous name. One with history. We will remember this night for the rest of our lives. Elizabeth, if it wasn't for our special bond and for the trust we have for each other, then this night could have turned out badly."

"How about Alexander the Great?" That was the only strong famous name Elizabeth could think of.

"Alexander sounds like a good name. But, I'm not so sure about 'The Great.'"

"Alexander Hugh after my great-grandfather. Is that history enough for you?" Elizabeth liked that name.

"Alexander Hugh – I like the sound of it. 'Little One,'" He looked at the sleeping baby. "Looks like your name is to be Alexander Hugh Kenney. Do you think you can live up to a name like that? There's a big world out here. Are you ready to make your mark in it?"

* * * * *

Wayne and Beauty were having a hard go of it. They got stuck in three snow drifts. The first being in front of the Rood's house. Beauty was stuck fast. Wayne managed to get to the front door and began banging. Dan opened the door with Maude right behind him.

461

"I'm stuck, Dan, right out there." He pointed to the front of the house.

"Wayne, why are you out on such a night?" Maude asked.

"The Captain's . ... Elizabeth, is having her baby. I need to get June Rutledge."

"Oh, dear, not tonight." The back of Maude's hand covered her mouth. "Dan, I must go to her."

"No, Maude! Not in this storm." Dan turned to Wayne, "Are Marilyn and the Captain with her?"

"That's right, and they sent me for the midwife."

"Eric, Cecil, and I will go help Wayne." Maude, you stay here. There is no sense you going out in this storm, there's not."

With the wind blowing and the blinding snow, the men had a hard job digging Beauty out of the snow drift. Beauty spent a lot of energy jumping forward, over and over before he was freed. "You can't even see the road!" Dan really didn't have to tell Wayne.

"Let me go with him, Father?" Cecil asked. "There's not room for all of us to go."

"Take the shovel; you will be needing it." How right Dan was. After two more snow drifts, they finally were outside the house of June Rutledge. Both Wayne and Cecil were half frozen.

"Here, throw the blanket on Beauty," Wayne instructed Cecil. Then they were on the porch knocking on the door. As it opened Wayne and Cecil tumbled through, landing on the floor.

"Saints preserve us!" Doctor MacMillan exclaimed. "June, come quickly we have two frozen bodies to take care of."

Wayne managed to get to his feet first. "I'm sure glad to see you, Doc. Good evening, Mrs. Rutledge."

"What are you doing out on a night like this? Is that Cecil there with you?"

"Yes, we've come for you. Mrs. Kenney needs you. The Captain sent me."

"Tonight, she needs me tonight? God have mercy!" June turned to the doctor.

Yes, I know the baby is due. I guess our visit is over." Dr. MacMillan was speaking to June's husband Jack. "No use you going, June. Since I am here, I will go."

June was grateful; she did not want to venture out on such a night. "I'll let you do this one," she quickly agreed.

"How long has it been?" The doctor was waiting for an answer.

"I was in the barn tending the animals," Wayne replied. "Must have been just after 6 p.m."

"Dr. MacMillan retrieved his watch from his pocket and flipped it open to see the face. " Five minutes after eight, that's been over two hours."

"This is her fifth baby," June added. "Could go either way, but my guess is you don't have much time." The doctor agreed with June. She was good at what she did and had been doing it for years.

"You mean it took you two hours to get here?" Jack questioned the young men.

"Slow going out there, real slow. My horse is tired." Wayne was worried.

Jack reached for his coat. "Let's harness both my Tom and Red; they will get you there. They haven't let me down yet. Put your horse in the barn; he's done his job for the night."

Tom and Red worked well as a team, and going down cemetery hill was a lot easier than climbing up. Only one snow drift slowed them for a time. Having three men to shovel the snow freed the horses quickly.

The weary travelers turned right and could see the lantern burning brightly in the window of the Rood's house. "That's my mother!" Cecil yelled.

"You getting out here?" Wayne yelled above the wind of the storm.

"No, I'm going to see this through," replied Cecil.

The two strong horses, Tom and Red, made a left turn into the Kenney's laneway. Several lanterns were lit in the Kenney's windows, helping them find their way to the steps of the veranda. Dr. MacMillan jumped out, "Thanks, boys," and hurried up the snow-covered steps. Wayne and Cecil headed for the barn.

The doctor let himself in the front door. Standing on the newspapers, he removed his snow-covered boots and coat. The warmth from the Franklin stove was certainly welcoming, but the silence wasn't. That worried him. All he could hear was the ticking of the clock on the wall. If his eyes could read it right, it was 9:35 p.m. He took his glasses off and wiped them clean with his hanky and took a second look, 9:36 p.m.

Marilyn was hurrying out of the kitchen and heading for the staircase again. She jumped and almost spilled the water from the kettle. "For pity sake, is that you Dr. MacMillan? You scared me half to death, you did. Where is June?"

"I came in her place."

"You could have just stayed home. It's not a good night to be out in such a storm."

"Tell me about it," the doctor seemed confused. "Marilyn, are you telling me Mrs. Kenney is not having her baby?"

"No, Dr. MacMillan, I wouldn't be telling you that. You're too late!"

Fear ran up and down the doctor's back. He couldn't say a word.

"You should have been here!"

"I tried, we tried; we gave it our best," replied the tired doctor.

"You would have been proud of him, Doctor. Just amazing! it was."

"Proud! Proud of whom, Marilyn?"

"Why the Captain, of course. He delivered that baby all by himself, he did. Well, I helped some."

"Delivered the baby? When?

"Oh, about 30 minutes ago, give or take a few minutes. Everyone is fine. He delivered his own son. What do you make of that, Doctor? Soap and hot water, never saw anyone use so much lye soap and hot water. See, I've got more here." She looked down at the iron teakettle.

"Think I should go with you?"

Marilyn had a questionable look on her face.

"The new mother and baby, shouldn't I look in on them? Now that I am here, that is."

"Of course, of course, follow me. They were just naming the baby when I left for more hot water. Alexander Hugh, a great name for a boy isn't it, Doctor?"

"Yes, Marilyn sounds like a great name for a boy." The doctor entered the room and saw quite a picture in front of him – Elizabeth resting comfortably in her bed. Heman was sitting on a rocking chair beside the fireplace holding a baby. At his feet were four girls who were getting to know their little brother.

"Dr. MacMillan!" Heman's voice was filled with surprise. "We were expecting June."

"She didn't make it, and it looks like I'm rather late myself."

"No, you are a welcome sight." Heman placed the baby in the cradle.

"Girls, it's time for bed. Say goodnight to Mother. The doctor needs to take a look at your new brother. Say goodbye to the doctor."

"Goodbye, girls." The doctor shook hands with each one.

The door closed as the last of the girls left the room. "It looks like I could have stayed at June and Jack's house, close to their fireplace. "You do all this?" The question was directed to Heman.

"Well, Doctor, it was no worse than a hurricane. Everything happened quickly. Before you know it, I had a son. Hurricanes last longer than that. Now don't misunderstand me, it wasn't easy, but God was with us. I wouldn't change jobs with you for the world. Sailing is my business; delivering babies is yours."

"Let's take a look." Dr. MacMillan began to inspect Heman's work.

"Wait!" Heman's voice was back in command mode. "Your hands, you must wash your hands. Over at the washstand." Heman's hand was pointing across the room. "There is lots of lye soap and hot water."

The command in the Captain's voice wasn't just a request. The doctor quickly walked to the washstand.

"Three times, and rinse!"

"Heman, I'm sure the doctor knows what he is doing." Elizabeth was a little embarrassed.

"Where did he get his method?" The doctor was asking Elizabeth.

"Why, nurse Sadie of course," Heman answered.

"I would like to meet this nurse Sadie sometime. Now, may I examine my patients? Clean, very clean, good job, Captain. Elizabeth had passed the inspection and the doctor turned to the baby. Alexander Hugh cried as he was unfolded from his blanket. "Good lungs; I like that." The doctor continued, "If I didn't know better, this looks like 'cat gut,' and a reef knot."

"Correct on both accounts." Heman was actually proud of his accomplishments.

* * * * *

The bell was ringing. Mary Elizabeth allowed her younger sisters three rings each. This was the first trade trip their father was taking since Alexander was born. The month being March, the girls knew winter would end soon. The end of winter meant their father would be leaving home. Now today they said their first farewell as he and *Lady Catherine* headed east up Sheet Harbour Pass. They would watch and wave and ring the bell, until only a speck could be seen on the waves of the ocean.

The bell ringing ritual began several years ago. Heman brought it home from Bermuda. This was a special bell given to him by the Port of Hamilton. Every time the Captain heard it ring, he was to think of his friends, family, and loved ones. He hung it by the front door and told his children it was to be rung only when he was leaving, as a good luck farewell, or a welcome when coming home. Every time he heard it ring, he would think of them and their mother.

Captain Heman Kenney was doing well. Life was good. He and *Lady Catherine* were kept busy making trade trips to Maine and Massachusetts. He didn't make the long trip to Bermuda any longer; he didn't have too. Heman didn't have to go far for cargo. Sheet Harbour Pulp Mill kept him supplied with sulphite pulp. Sulphite pulp was a new commodity and was in great demand for making of paper. Who knew Sheet Harbour would have the first mill in Canada.[116] A William Chisholm, a lumber manufacturer of Halifax, tested out the Philadelphian discovery. He actually built the mill in the East River of Sheet Harbour for this purpose. Changing the sulphite process slightly here and there, made the Sheet Harbour Pulp Mill famous for its sulphite in Maine and other eastern states. In fact, several businessmen sent American workers from those states to the Sheet Harbour Mill to learn the art of lead-burning,[117] a necessary step for processing the sulphite. Heman heard William Chisholm[118] was in no hurry to share the process. He was interested in employing the men in Sheet Harbour area. Twenty-five men worked on a single twelve-hour shift. Unskilled labour received 7 to 10 cents per hour and skilled 15 cents.

Heman stood at the wheel. He was happy to know that *Lady Catherine*'s cargo bay was filled to capacity containing processed sulphite pulp. It was neatly stowed in bales weighing two hundred pounds each. Every bale was sewed up in burlap bags. They were on their way to Massachusetts via Halifax and all because of this Mr. Chisholm. Heman was not greedy; he always allowed space to be saved in his cargo hold for local men, his neighbours, to have a way to send their fish and cordwood to market. They were his friends, and Heman was well aware that they needed to be able to support their families. Heman filled his lungs with the cold salt air. He could no longer hear the bell, only the sound of the ocean. The ocean was calling Heman again.

** * * * **

"Quickly, children, it is time for chores." Elizabeth was the head of the house while Heman was at sea. "Meet me in the playroom when the clock strikes the hour of 9 a.m." She had turned the playroom into the most active room in the house. The left-hand corner of the large room was hers. A spinning wheel was in front of the window. She spent her mornings spinning, taking advantage of the morning light that streamed into the room. The wall to her left was enclosed in white cupboards with glass doors. Her multi-coloured wool made a neat display. All those years ago, she started with two sheep. Now she had a flock, which turned out to supply wool for her and all the other ladies in Watt Section. There was also plenty of room in the cupboards to store her quilting supplies. Wayne made her a quilting frame that was attached to a rope and pulley system. The days she and her girls were not quilting, the quilt could be hoisted up to the ceiling, and stored safely out of the way. Elizabeth had her own sewing machine, a gift from her father. The shiny machine stood in its place under the glass cupboards, with counter space that ran on both sides.

There was another window on the right side of this room. A large table was set up here for the girls to do their lessons. Heman was adamant his girls be educated and brought back many books and newspapers from his travels. He would personally question them on the affairs of the world. The collection of those books was carefully placed in the bookcases that stood on either side of the small Franklin stove. In the corner opposite the stove was a play area. A small circular braided rug, made by the girls, laid on the hardwood floor. Small chairs circled a child's table. A set of children's china dishes were set out, ready for a tea party. Baby dolls and stuffed bears sat on a low shelf, and a Captain's chest was filled with wooden blocks and other treasures. Hats, four of Elizabeth's homemade bonnets, and one Captain's hat hung on pegs, waiting for an imaginary adventure. Here Heman spent many hours playing with his girls.

The view when looking out the window was like a painted picture. In the not so far distance was the ocean. The ocean was always in movement, with the white caps of the waves swaying back and forth. Seagulls circled the lighthouse that was in the process of being built, which was up against the shore. Another of Heman's dreams was coming true. The field that led from the lighthouse to the main house would soon be green with new grass, and before you knew it, white daisies with yellow centers would be blowing in the summer breezes. More than one time, the girls saw *Lady Catherine* returning from the view of this window. Everything would stop, for they knew their father had returned. The girls would run to the bell, banging the screen door behind them, and take turns ringing it. The older two always went first, and when done, would fly down the stairs from the veranda, waving and yelling a welcome as they ran over the field towards the lighthouse. Elizabeth and the little ones followed waving their own welcome, as they watched the schooner come closer and closer.

Today, Elizabeth was standing at the window watching the ocean, which she did often when Heman was away. She prayed silently, "Be with him, God. And bring him home safely. Bring him soon." Alexander was sleeping in his cradle, which she had rolled into the room. She turned from the window and sat at the spinning wheel. This was work, but work that she loved. She needed to keep her hands busy; time passed more quickly that way.

Mary Elizabeth was the first one to meet in the playroom. Her mother glanced up at the clock on the wall, 10 minutes to 9. "You are early."

"I ran from the barn and up all those steps." Mary Elizabeth was panting.

"Why are you in such a hurry?" her mother asked.

"It's opening today; the new school is opening today! Wayne just told us. They are signing up students. Can we go?"

Elizabeth knew the school would be ready any day now. She did not know it would be today. "I don't see how, Mary Elizabeth?" She looked at Alexander sleeping.

"I can take Eliza; I will take good care of her."

"Me too!" Laura and Eliza just entered the playroom. "I want to go too." Laura couldn't believe she didn't hear her name mentioned.

"You're not old enough," Mary Elizabeth quickly informed her.

"Am too. Mother, am too!"

Elizabeth thought it was time to intervene. Laura, how old are you?

"Four," answered Laura proudly.

"Mary Elizabeth, how old do you have to be to go to school?" Elizabeth already knew the answer. She was hoping Laura would understand more fully once it was explained.

"Six," answered Mary Elizabeth.

"Laura, you will have to wait until you are six," Elizabeth explained. Laura's lip went out and tears were about to fall. "Don't worry, you and Sarah can have a special day together. Maybe Marilyn has cookies and milk we can have later on." Laura decided if she couldn't go to school, she would take second best. Elizabeth still didn't know how she was going to get Mary Elizabeth and Eliza to school.

"Wayne can take us." Mary Elizabeth had the answer. "I know he will." Beauty was hitched up to a small cart, and Heman's girls were among the first to go to the newly opened school.

* * * * *

Summer passed slowly. Heman was seldom home. Elizabeth was a good shepherd not only to her sheep but her flock of children. It had been a rainy summer and frost hit early. Everyone was worried about their gardens. The vegetable bins in the cellar were not adequately filled. Elizabeth was not alone; everyone worried about the approaching winter. One morning she called Wayne in to tell him she had to send a message to Heman. Wayne made a visit to a schooner, which was in Sheet Harbour. The captain would gladly take a message as far as Halifax and deliver it to the Coffee Company II. From there the message was relayed by telegram to Boston. The message caught up with Heman when visiting Peggy, Duncan, and Faye at the Irish Coffee Company. in Boston. He was concerned to hear there might be a food shortage for the coming winter. Heman set out to see what he could do about it.

In the meantime, back in Watt Section, fall was upon them. The magical time of the year, when deep reds, orange and yellow were all around them. Low tide at the wharf made work for the fishermen more difficult. The catch of the day had to be hoisted up the ladders from their boats to the wharf. Gerald and Lloyd were later than usual before they had the nets stowed and ready for the next day's trip offshore. "Won't be long now before winter will be showing herself." Lloyd wasn't sure he was ready for it. He wasn't as young as he used to be, and the cold seemed to settle deeper in his bones than it used to. "There was a hard frost this morning. I'm glad the last of the pumpkins were stored in the barn. We covered them up with hay, we did."

"Most of ours rotted in the field." Gerald was shaking his head.

"The frost got our potatoes early," Lloyd continued. They were only half grown, they were."

"I think we will be eating lots of salt cod this winter." Gerald didn't want to think about it. The ring of the Kenney's bell caused the men to look towards the half-built lighthouse. "Captain Kenney must have been sighted at the mouth of the passage." Gerald raised his hand to his eyes as he continued to search the waters.

"Here he comes now!" Lloyd sighted the tall spar of the schooner *Lady Catherine*. "She's low in the water. Must have a full cargo bay." Gerald and Lloyd decided to wait for her to sail into her home port. It never grew old to watch the graceful schooner glide into her place.

"Welcome ashore, Captain." Lloyd held his hand out as the Captain climbed the ladder to the wharf.

"How's fishing?" Heman took time to shake their hands.

"Fair, could be better, but fair, wouldn't you say, Gerald." Gerald just tipped his head; he wasn't much of a talker.

"Well, men, maybe things will pick up soon." Heman wanted to leave with an encouraging word. "Good night to ya now." He was in a hurry to get home. Being away for three months, and the sound of the bell increased his awareness of how much he missed his family. After walking a hundred yards or so, he turned around to deliver a forgotten message. "Gentlemen, would you spread the word, I need to meet with the men after church tomorrow." That done he resumed his walk but with a quicker pace than before. Rounding the bend in the road, his house welcomed his return.

* * * * *

Reverend MacDonald had a full church that Sunday. The word spread quickly that Captain Kenney had something to say. Heman decided to speak to the whole congregation, and the Reverend MacDonald didn't mind giving up his pulpit after the last prayer was completed.

Heman left his pew and started for the front. Many strong hands reached out and tapped his arm as he continued to the front. "Welcome home." "Nice to see you back" were lightly spoken before he reached the pulpit.

"Thank you, Reverend, for allowing me to borrow your pulpit."

472

"Don't mind at all." The Reverend was eager to hear what the Captain had to say. Heman wasn't used to public speaking, only giving orders to his crew. He cleared his throat as he looked out at all his neighbours. "It's good to be home," he started. His eyes searched for Elizabeth. "Thank you for watching over my family, for I know you do. This is a good community that watches over each other."

The Reverend agreed whole heartily, "Amen," he retorted.

Heman continued, "I received word while in Boston that many of our crops had failed. The fear of running out of food this winter was a real one." Soft murmurs traveled like a wave throughout the crowd of people. "Through the help of my dear friends in Boston; Duncan and Peggy O'Donovan, Charles and Madame Caroline Drew and Captain Freedman, we have come up with a solution to our problem. You, every one of you, would like these people, and maybe one day they will be able to come to visit Watt Section. But, in the meantime, they have sent you a gift of beans, flour, and rice for everyone. Peggy O'Donovan added an extra shipment for you ladies – sugar.

A quiet hush was heard throughout the pews. It took a few moments for the words to sink in. Then the sound of happy people spilled forth throughout the church. Reverend MacDonald began to sing;

"Praise God, from Whom all blessings flow;
Praise Him, all creatures here below;
Praise Him above, ye heavenly host;
Praise Father, Son, and Holy Ghost."[119]

Everyone joined in, for their hearts were no longer heavy. Maybe the winter would not be so difficult. Heman waited for the singing to die down. "And may I have your attention again?" Everyone looked towards the pulpit. "We, Elizabeth and I, would like to invite all the adults to a dinner of thanksgiving at the Kenney's home on Saturday, November 4." Heman was now finished and stepped down. He gathered his family towards him and led them down the aisle to the door.

Many handshakes were exchanged with 'Thank you's' to match. Heman received as many handshakes as the Reverend did that Sunday.

* * * * *

All the older children looked after the younger children in every house in Watt Section that special night. Those who didn't have older children to do the job, borrowed one from a family that did. Every adult headed for the Show House. Wayne carefully directed traffic in the laneway. He made sure every horse had a bag of oats to make them comfortable, for it would be a long night.

Heman's favorite room in the house was the great dining room. He and Elizabeth had designed it together. The light green walls with white-crowned molding and chair railing were the perfect background to show off the mahogany furniture. Recently, they added a small Franklin stove insert that sat in the white framed fireplace. Family portraits, large and small, were hung by gold frames. The curtains, made by Elizabeth, were of a darker green with light yellow flowers. These were hung from the two windows. A matching valance was lightly hung by strips of material over the black iron rods. These rods complemented the black iron Franklin stove.

The dark mahogany table stood stately in the middle of the room, with eighteen chairs standing at attention around it. Royal china and two crystal candelabras were set in their place on the white linen tablecloth. There was a story to tell about this table, and Dan loved to tell it to the children. Dan will always recall the day the table arrived on the *Lady Catherine*. Getting the table off the schooner was a miracle in itself. It took six men to put it in the wagon. After getting it up the stairs to the veranda, they found out to their amazement it would not fit through the front door. Dan had to dismantle it and rebuild it once they had it inside the dining room. Tonight, however, it was beautifully set for twenty people. Since they were expecting twice that many people, Elizabeth wondered where they would sit everyone. As usual, Heman took care of it, by borrowing the sawhorses and old doors from the church. He then sent Wayne from house to house, neighbour to neighbour to borrow chairs. A table was set in the foyer, living room and parlour. As the guests arrived, Mary Elizabeth escorted them to a place at a table, beginning with the great dining room.

Heman and Elizabeth did not sit amongst their guests. Tonight they were going to serve them. The whole Kenney family had worked hard in the kitchen that day. It took the help of Marilyn, Wayne, Heman, Mary Elizabeth, and even Elizabeth, with the careful eyes of Marilyn watching over her, to make this evening a success. Now it was time to serve. Heman carried a platter of spareribs with sauerkraut and beef pot roast. Wayne was right behind him with a tray with fish chowder and scallops held high in his right hand. They were heading towards the second table in the foyer when Marilyn entered the dining room with fricasseed potatoes, creamed cabbage, and cucumbers with sour cream. The serving didn't end there, for Elizabeth had the clam pie and apple bread. They saved Mary Elizabeth for the end, for she took care of dessert. She placed the baked Indian pudding and the molasses cookies in the middle of each table.[120]

These hard-working people would have an evening they would remember for a long time. They had never been fussed over and pampered so much in their whole lives. They were enjoying it and having a great time.

The meal ended with hot tea served in china teacups for the ladies and Irish coffee for the men. All who were there lingered, enjoying the fellowship with each other. They were in no hurry to return home. Tomorrow was another day of struggle, as they lived their lives on the Eastern Shore of Nova Scotia.

A flash of light drew their attention to the windows. A storm was brewing and thunder could be heard in the distance.

Rain was falling. It was another reason for them to stay longer at the Show House. Heman and Elizabeth were making their rounds, mingling with their guests. How blessed they were to have good friends and neighbours.

"I'll check the barn." Wayne was in the kitchen with Marilyn. "I will be back as quick as a flash."

"Watch that lightning." Marilyn hated thunderstorms.

The front door opened with a lunge. "Fire!" Wayne was crying with a loud voice, "Fire!" The people sitting around the table in the foyer were the first to get the message. But that kind of news traveled quickly throughout the house.

"Where?" Heman was at Wayne's side.

"Over towards the Point, through those trees! See the smoke?" Wayne was pointing through the front door.

The men were out on the veranda before the women could leave their seats. Lightning streaked across the dark sky, and a loud clap of thunder was right over their heads. Above the trees, smoke could be seen in the flashes of lightning. The sky lit up again, and this time there was no doubt what was on fire. They all could see it. The fire was leaping out of the church steeple. "The church," echoed throughout the group of spectators on the veranda.

"God, have mercy!" Reverend MacDonald was praying out loud.

The horses, wagons, and carts were all lined up in the laneway. Gerald's wagon was the closest to the road. He led the way, as a group of men ran through the rain and jumped upon his wagon. Heman and Wayne were among them.

"Wait!" Heman stopped the progress of the men. "We need buckets and ladders."

"There are buckets in the barn." Wayne was on his way inside the barn. Anything that would hold water was thrown in the wagon.

The women watched from the veranda as three wagons left the Kenney's laneway. "It was such a lovely evening, wasn't it?" Maude spoke for all of them. "Now, this has turned into a night from hell."

The lead wagon turned onto Church Road. The darkness of the night didn't hinder their progress. Out in front of them, a red glow of fire led their way. Just like Moses in the wilderness, but this time it wasn't God leading them, maybe the devil but not God.

The buckets and ladders remained in the wagon. All they could do was watch their beloved church burn to the ground.[121] The other two wagons arrived just in time to hear the mighty crash and dull ring as the bell hit the ground. It was all over; the storm had moved east. In its wake, it left devastation and sorrow. It was evident that lightning had struck the steeple and the bell.

If captains have tears, they hide them quickly. Not this night. Tears ran down Heman's face, and he didn't care who saw him. He knew this was a huge blow to this community. Watt Section would take a long time to recover. Heman wiped the tears away with the back of his hand. *This winter will be a long lonely one,* he thought.

"Fire!"

December 1876
Halifax

Dear Elizabeth,

I was informed just this morning of the devastating news from Watt Section. Captain told us there was nothing more they could do but watch that little church burn to the ground. I looked up and asked God why? That is all those people had, they didn't have much, but they had that little church. God answered me right away. It wasn't Him, He would be with you whether there was a church or not. I quickly said amen and crossed myself. If it wasn't God, then you know who was to blame. Satan himself. He has been making problems everywhere lately. Gardens failing, rainstorms and fog. Here in Halifax, you can't see across the Harbour for the dark black fog.

Thankfully I hear you will be meeting in the school. But one day, I just know it, the people of Watt Section will rebuild that church. I look forward to seeing it for myself.

Give my greetings to the children. They make this old sailor smile whenever I see them.

Looking for better days ahead for you and your neighbours in Watt Section.

Until that time,

Moses
P.S. See you in the Spring.

CHAPTER TWENTY-TWO

Why Punish William?

The sun was setting in the west. The seagulls were making their daily journey to roost on Hen Island. All the summer birds had gone. They flew to wherever summer birds fly for the winter. The birds knew when the time was right; they wanted to be gone before the first snow.

"Take deep breaths!" Heman was at the kitchen table with a cup towel over his head. Elizabeth added more boiling water to the metal bowl. "Is that better? Can you breathe without whistling?"

Heman took the towel from his head, "Very funny. I do not whistle."

"Sounds like a whistle to me. As soon as I hear it, I get the boiling water. You know, Heman, I've been getting the boiling water more often lately."

Heman looked towards Elizabeth. *Were those dark circles under her eyes?* he thought. She worked so hard, never stopped. Her days ended late and began again before sunup. She said she couldn't sleep. Many a night he held her, but it didn't help. She forced her eyes to stay open.

"We must talk, Elizabeth, you can't go on like this."

"I don't have time to talk, Heman." She busied herself clearing away the bowl of hot water and hanging the towel on the washstand by the window. "Anyway, how is talking going to help? My sweet William will still be up on that hill. We buried him there, don't you remember?"

"How could I forget?" Heman's breathing began to whistle again. "You can't sleep and I can't breathe. Did you notice that, Elizabeth?"

"You left me."

"I would never leave you, my love."

"You only stayed home three months and then you left. You knew my heart was broken and you left anyway."

"We had to go, Elizabeth. *Lady Catherine* doesn't make money sitting in this little Harbour. I didn't want to leave. Your mother was here, Elizabeth."

"How long will my heart be broken?" Elizabeth searched Heman's eyes.

"Your heart, our hearts, will mend a little more each day we live." Heman thought his heart might mend, but there would be a black scar so large his heart would never be the same.

That terrible night last January, the night he lost his second son. The young boy of three was fine, playing with his sisters and brother in the playroom. By supper time he was sick and feverish. By nine o'clock he was dead. The fever shot up quickly. Dr. McMillan couldn't get there in time. William, Heman's son, named after his brother, took his last breath in his father's arms. He and Elizabeth did everything they could. Dr. McMillian tried to take William from Heman's arms, but he didn't dare for Heman growled, "Don't touch him. Don't you dare touch him!" Heman summoned his children to his side. After their quiet farewells, Marilyn took the children away. Heman held William to his heart throughout the night. Elizabeth slept fitfully in the four-poster bed. Dr. McMillian had given her medication to calm her. Heman rocked his son and watched Elizabeth sleep.

"So I'm paying for it again! Is that right, God? I'm the one who sinned. Why punish my sweet Elizabeth? Why punish William? I know there are consequences for my actions. Is this the consequence?" Heman had carried his dark secret of slavery with him for years. Only his sweet Elizabeth knew. They never spoke of it. But what if he could only go back; if only he had said 'no" to his brother.

He had a hard time remembering that God had forgiven him a long time ago. Isn't that what Elizabeth told him? Deep down, he really knew God was not punishing Elizabeth, nor William. Life in this world has both happiness and sorrows. It was Heman who couldn't forgive himself. Each time life's struggles bore down upon him, he again thought God was reminding him of those dark faces and dark eyes. If only Heman could forgive himself, but this life struggle was too hard to bear. To lose a young son, and to watch Elizabeth suffer like she did, was too much. He wanted to fix it. He was supposed to take care of Elizabeth, wasn't he? Here they were in the kitchen, struggling to find the love they had between them.

"Elizabeth, come sit on my lap." It had been a long time since she sat on Heman's lap.

She almost accepted the invitation, but quickly turned away. "The children need me. I must see to it they are ready for bed."

"They are in the playroom. Marilyn is with them. Come, Elizabeth, sit on my lap. Let me hold you like I used to." Her hand went up to her heart. She could feel it. The icy cold that covered her heart was warming to her touch. The great love between Heman and Elizabeth was coming to the surface. "We must get through this together, Elizabeth. We have other children that need our love and care. Come sit." He tapped his knee.

Elizabeth was ready to love again. She was ready to live again. She slowly approached her husband. His arms were outstretched waiting for her. She settled herself close to Heman's heart. They sat quietly, listening to the wood crackling as it burned in the cook stove. It was soothing music to their ears. Elizabeth's eyes closed and she fell into a peaceful sleep. Marilyn opened the kitchen door. Heman put his finger up to his lips, "Sshhh." She quietly backed out the way she came. She was happy to see the Captain and Elizabeth were back together. *It is a good sign,* thought Marilyn. The Kenney family would be okay.

* * * * *

"You can have a nice visit with your family." Heman and Elizabeth were alone in their bedroom, a rarity when five children had to be cared for. "The children will enjoy it as well. The trade run to Maine won't take more than two weeks."

"Thanksgiving is coming up. It would be nice to spend it with my brothers." Elizabeth was thinking out loud, "Since they have married, we don't see one another at all."

"You can have a family reunion, with Turkey and all the dressing. It will be good for you to get away from here for a while." Heman continued, "This is October and soon the weather will be changing. You know what winters bring."

"Yes, ice and snow," Elizabeth said with a funny face, "and then we will be stuck here for months."

"Then it is settled. You and the children will spend Thanksgiving in Halifax with your family. I'll start making plans right away. We will wait for a good day for sailing, no use starting off in a storm."

* * * * *

"Can you hear the bell?" Alexander was watching his house go by as *Lady Catherine* slowly sailed towards the mouth of Sheet Harbour Passage. "There they are!" Alexander saw Wayne and Marilyn waving from the veranda. The children waved back in a farewell salute.

"Mary Elizabeth, take the wheel," Heman ordered.

She didn't have to be asked twice, for she loved sailing on *Lady Catherine*. Her father had taught her well.

484

"Is she old enough to do such a thing?" Elizabeth was surprised how quickly her oldest daughter answered Heman's call.

"Oh, our secret is out, girls! Mother, let me introduce you to two of my newest crew members." Heman bowed swinging his arm in front of him. "My new sailor, 14-year-old Mary Elizabeth Kenney. She was taught by the best and has passed her examination with flying colours. Step forward, sailor!"

"Aye, aye, sir." Mary Elizabeth stepped forward and curtsied.

"My new Junior sailor, 11-year-old Eliza Kenney. Has potential of being one of the greatest sailors ever to sail the seas. Step forward, sailor!"

"Aye, aye, sir." Eliza stepped forward and bowed.

"Eliza too!" Elizabeth was amazed. She smiled at Eliza, "Ladies do not bow, dear."

"I don't want to be a lady; I want to be a sailor!" Eliza insisted.

"Oh, dear," Heman looked to John Martin, "I believe we have created a problem here." John Martin and his friend Angus Behie were his crewmen who lived in Sheet Harbour.

"She can be a lady sailor," offered Angus.

"Eliza will not be a sailor, nor will Mary Elizabeth." Elizabeth was firm.

"Your mother's right. Just because I went to sea at the age of seventeen, I shouldn't think you would do the same."

"They will never go to sea, no matter how old they are," Elizabeth insisted.

"Only if you go with them." Heman put his hands around Elizabeth's slender waist.

"Heman, don't you lift me up!" Elizabeth knew that was about to happen.

He changed his mind and turned her loose. "Now listen while I tell you a story. Listen closely, Alexander the Great." He tipped Alexander's cap down over his eyes. "And, you too, my lovely daughters. There was once a time, not so very long ago, when a young lady with dark curls, frolicked across *Lady Catherine*'s decks. She jumped from deck to deck like a young deer. The crew's job was to see this young woman didn't fall overboard. They didn't mind. They stood in line, just for a chance to hold her delicate hand as they helped her down from her perch. So, my dear," Heman turning his attention to Elizabeth, "*Lady Catherine* is used to having ladies aboard."

"Who was the lady?" Laura and Sarah loved the story.

"Mother, of course," Mary Elizabeth answered.

"Yes, your mother, of course. Come, my dear, I have your seat ready." Heman couldn't join her at this time. He, John, and Angus, and his new sailors were busy sailing the *Lady Catherine* into the wind.

After lunch, for Marilyn had prepared food for everyone, Heman had time to sit and be with Elizabeth. The younger children were playing a card game on the table in the small room where his officers ate. His new sailors were helping John and Angus keep *Lady Catherine* on course.

"I haven't been sailing in a long time, Heman. I haven't done anything in a long time. Where has my life gone?" Elizabeth felt more relaxed than she had since the loss of her son.

"Your life is right here with me, my love, where it always will be. Are you so unhappy?"

"No, my happiness is returning, but it also makes me aware how much time has passed. It seems only yesterday I was that young girl, sailing on the *Lady Catherine* for the first time. I never felt so free before that day. I remember I thought we were flying."

"I have never tired of sailing with *Lady Catherine*," replied her husband. "It's been a lifetime. I experience it anew, when I see the excitement in our children's eyes, as they experience it for the first time. That day, your first day on *Lady Catherine*, your parents where here to watch over and guide you. Now, it is our turn. Just look at them, Elizabeth. If they were young men, their vocation would be to follow in my footsteps. Was I so wrong in teaching them what is so natural in my heart?"

"No, Heman." Elizabeth was sure of what she said. "It was not wrong to teach those girls to love the *Lady Catherine*, for I feel that love too. They are lucky to have a father to treat them equally. It doesn't matter whether they are a girl or boy. Don't worry. They will grow up, and one of these days you will have to let them go, just as my father did."

Heman had a chill run through him from his head to his feet. Until this very moment, he never once thought about that. "I don't think I can do it?"

"What, Heman?"

"We are the only ones who can ever take care of our children. It doesn't matter how old they become."

Elizabeth smiled at her husband. "You have done a great job raising them. A day will come, and you will step back and let them fly. You will proudly watch as they grow into caring, loving adults."

"I hope so. I hope that time doesn't come upon me too quickly."

"Halifax Harbour, just above the horizon," John yelled.

"Sit tight. We are almost there." Heman left her side. "Mary Elizabeth mate, I need to take the wheel."

Elizabeth and her children watched the Harbour Master okay their entry into the Harbour. He didn't even stay aboard. "You know your way, Captain Kenney. The Queen's Wharf awaits you."

Alexander watched the soldiers march back and forth behind the pointed cannon. "Alexander the Great!" Heman noticed his son's interest. "How would you like to visit Citadel Hill?"

"You mean the large fort up on that hill?" Alexander pointed with his hand.

"That's the one. Before I leave for Maine, we will go see them fire the noon gun."

"The cannon, Father?"

"Yes, the cannon, son."

"Me, too." Laura always thought she was being left out.

"No, Laura, Nana Finley will have plenty for you to do." Elizabeth had two daughters thinking they were sailors; she didn't need a soldier in the family.

"Will we see our cousins?" Laura asked.

"Yes, all the cousins, all your aunts, and uncles. Papa and Nana. We are going to have a wonderful Thanksgiving.

* * * * *

The Finley household was bustling with activity. James and Janet were happy to have the whole family together. That didn't happen very often, and for sure it was a family reunion. They couldn't believe they had nineteen grandchildren. Tom had two, James Jr had three, Charles four, George and Elizabeth had the same number of five. They would have had twenty, but, they didn't want to think of that now. This was a happy time and the sorrow of William would be felt at another time. James, the businessman that he was, had a meeting with all nineteen grandchildren. There had to be rules. He had a copy printed for all those who could read. "Since Nana and Papa decided to put each gender in separate rooms, the first rule is: No girls in the boys' room and no boys in the girls' room. The second rule is: no one in the kitchen, unless invited by Nana. The parlour is off limits to all, but the whole outdoors is all yours. When you hear the bell ring, that means food."

"Papa, you have a bell too?" Alexander asked.

"I bought one just for your visit," answered James.

The children had the freedom of the yard. Thankfully, the October days were sunny and warm. This gave the adults time to visit and catch up on each other's lives. Heman stayed as long as he could. The afternoon of Thanksgiving day he announced that *Lady Catherine* was sailing that evening at 6:00 p.m. He told Janet thanks to her, he didn't have to eat again until he reached Bangor, Maine.

"Walk with me." Heman took Elizabeth's hand. He led her out the front door and down Argyle Street. His arm went around her shoulders, "Are you cold?"

"Slightly, the air is getting colder at night, isn't it?"

Heman removed his jacket and placed it around Elizabeth. "Are you happy, my dear?"

"You were right; it was good for me to come. I have enjoyed the visit. The children, I hardly have seen them since we have been here. I hope they are not getting into trouble."

"They are fine, Elizabeth. Let your parents take care of them. I notice they have more of a spring to their steps."

"Who? Mother and Father or the children?"

Heman laughed. "Your parents. They are having a great time with their grandchildren."

"I think I am going to miss you." Elizabeth was not looking forward to Heman leaving.

"I will be back in two weeks, I promise," Heman assured her.

"I will be waiting."

* * * * *

Elizabeth didn't sail through the double doors of the Irish Coffee Company II. She stopped just outside. So many memories flooded her mind. She was still deep in thought when she heard.

"Excuse me."

Elizabeth jumped. "Oh, I am sorry."

"Are you alright? I just need to go inside. Saw the prettiest mahogany coffee table, just the other day. Told my husband all about it. Here I am today. I do hope no one bought it." A lady with a brown wool coat and matching bonnet proceeded through the double doors, leaving Elizabeth standing there. The bell rang loudly as the door closed again.

There are bells everywhere, thought Elizabeth. She collected herself and opened the door. The bell rang again. "Was that Moses?" She studied the man at the counter. Except for the graying hair and moustache, it certainly looked like Moses. The man raised his head and looked towards the door, a natural habit he had when hearing the bell ring.

"Elizabeth, why, Elizabeth, is that you?" Moses dropped everything he was doing.

"Moses?" Elizabeth replied.

"It is you!" Moses jumped over the counter. "Elizabeth, you are a sight for sore eyes. I heard you were in Halifax. Come, let me see you. You are as beautiful as ever. Always said the Captain got a great catch when he got you. A great blessing from God himself." Moses crossed himself.

Elizabeth laughed, "You haven't changed a bit!" she exclaimed.

"Don't know how many times I looked up at that door, wishing to see you step through it. Today is the day! Tell me, how are you doing? Your children?"

"They are happily staying with my parents," Elizabeth answered. Then it happened again; a great pain went through her. Every time she spoke of the children, the pain would remind her that one was missing. William would always be missing. She focused her blank eyes back to Moses.

"I'm sorry for your loss," Moses was quick to say.

"How did you know? Can you read my thoughts, Moses?" There was a hint of tears on Elizabeth's eyelashes.

"It's your eyes and your heart. God will heal you in time." He crossed himself again. "Come, today is a happy day!" Moses steered her throughout the store. Elizabeth allowed this man to guide her to a happier place. Her pain was leaving, but she knew it would return when she least expected it.

"How can I help you? Whatever you want, it is yours."

Elizabeth couldn't help smiling. "Do you give all the merchandise away to ladies that come to visit you? I will have to speak to the owner." She looked at him with that twinkle in her eye.

There's the look; that twinkle in her eyes gets me every time, thought Moses. "Only to you, dear lady, only to you," Moses answered.

* * * * *

Heman had been away for two weeks. Each day Elizabeth woke up thinking today he will be back from Maine. Elizabeth kept herself busy. That day she decided to visit the factory. To her delight, she found Linda still working on the third floor. They spent the day catching up with details of their lives. Elizabeth had a great time collecting material to take back to Watt Section. She couldn't wait to show Maude what she had picked out for her.

Two days passed, still no Heman. Elizabeth never worried when he would return, when she was in Watt Section. Maybe she worried because she wasn't home. That was it; she wanted to go home. Two more days passed before word reached her that the *Lady Catherine* had docked at the Queen's Wharf. Elizabeth greeted Heman at the door. She didn't have a bell to ring; she didn't need one. She threw herself into his arms, knocking his captain's cap right off his head.

"Go easy, my dear. I'm not as young as I once was." She had her arms around his neck.

"Welcome home, Captain, I have missed you so."

"You haven't called me Captain in a long time. I missed you too. Think I can pick up my cap and close the door? Or, would you like me to carry you into the parlour?"

She turned him loose, straightened her skirt and with her hands on her hips and a smile on her lips, turned in the direction of the parlour. "I can walk, thank you very much."

Heman quickly retrieved his cap and closed the door. He hung his coat and hat on the umbrella stand. "Where is everyone?" he asked as he joined her in the parlour. "It's unusually quiet around here. The children?"

491

Father and Mother have the whole crew at Point Pleasant Park. They announced to the children this morning they were going to make a day of it. No telling where else they ended up."

"And you didn't go? You are here by yourself?"

"That in itself is a holiday, just me. Anyway, someone had to be here when you got home."

"I'm glad you are here. It's the best homecoming I have had in years."

"Heman, let's go home," Elizabeth quickly stated.

"Right now? I just got here."

She got up from her chair. "Yes, I would like that. Right now!" She placed herself in his lap.

"Well, this is about as close to home as you are going to get for a few days," he replied.

She sighed, "Whatever you say, dear. I am ready when you are."

* * * * *

October 31, 1881, *Lady Catherine* had just lowered her sails as she sailed up Sheet Harbour Passage. The day was cloudy with a mist of rain. The fog was held at bay as the rain fell. The wind had failed three hours out of Halifax. It was painfully slow as *Lady Catherine* tried to fill her sails with any breath of wind. Elizabeth entertained the three youngest children below deck. The rest of the family, dressed in yellow slickers and boots, were on deck.

"Sarah Ellen, please shut the porthole. You are letting in cold damp air." They were playing 'Old Maid' at the small table. The lantern was swinging back and forth as *Lady Catherine* sailed up one wave and down the other.

"It's your turn, Sarah," Alexander told his sister.

"Looks like we will have to finish this game later," Elizabeth said. "Look out the porthole."

The three children tried to see out at the same time. "I can't see! Mother, tell Sarah to let me see," Laura whined.

"What about me?" Alexander put his elbow into Sarah's ribs.

"Ow! That hurt."

"Now, children." Elizabeth knew it had been a long day for them. "You will have to take turns. What did you see, Sarah?"

"Our house!"

"Now, let Laura and Alexander see."

"Who's that coming?" Laura placed her face against the glass.

"It's Indians!" yelled Alexander as he flung the porthole wide open. A blast of cold air reached Elizabeth, not just cold air, but the loud sound of whooping and hollering and yelling.

"There aren't any Indians." Laura thought she knew everything.

"There is too. Just look; them coming towards us." Alexander could see them. At the same moment, Laura saw what Alexander was talking about. She started screaming.

With one hand Elizabeth grabbed hold of Laura and with the other, she banged the porthole closed. "Stop screaming, Laura. Stop at once!"

"They're still coming!" Alexander's head was at the window.

"They are going to get us!" Laura screamed. "Maybe they will scalp us!" Sarah began to cry.

"For pity sake!" Elizabeth was trying to keep control.

"Duck your head!" Alexander quickly dropped his head below the porthole. Elizabeth couldn't believe her eyes. A canoe passed by the porthole with two men yelling to at the top of their lungs. They stopped paddling for a moment and waved a bottle in the air. Then they were gone.

Alexander dared to look. "Here comes another one. Duck your heads!" He dropped his head again.

Three men were in this canoe, and the one in the middle was waving two bottles in his hands. Eight canoes circled the *Lady Catherine* whooping and yelling.

"Are they going to scalp us?!" Laura asked, for she was still very worried.

"No, Father won't let them," Alexander assured her. "They're leaving, going west." He strained his neck to see more out the window.

Elizabeth was amazed that Alexander knew his directions. He was right. The whopping and hollering were going farther away.

"Let's go top deck!" Alexander wanted to see more.

"No, sir, you stay put. Your father will tell you when to go top deck. Wait until they have moored *Lady Catherine*." Elizabeth still couldn't believe what they had just witnessed. Maybe her mother was right. They did live in the wilderness, Indians and all. But, why now? They never bothered anyone before. "Quickly, children, put your slickers on. We will wait just below the hatch." They were ready when the dim light came shining in as their father opened the hatch.

"Everyone okay?" Heman was surprised to see them at the bottom of the ladder.

"Where are the Indians?" Laura questioned her father.

"Indians? How do you know they were Indians?"

"Alexander told us, "Sarah replied.

"Oh, I see. Come along. The dory is ready to take you ashore." The children were quickly up the ladder headed for the dory. "Slow down, children; don't run." When the Captain spoke, everyone listened. "I will be there momentarily to help you."

"Well, what kind of a welcome home was that?" Elizabeth asked Heman as he took her hand to help her off the ladder.

"Interesting, wasn't it? I don't know what is going on. All I know is someone gave those Indians liquor and lots of it. It's safe for now. They headed west towards Sheet Harbour. I'll be happier when you and the children are safe in the house. Then I will find out what's going on."

"Won't it be dangerous?" Elizabeth's amazement turned to worry.

"I don't think so. They don't have bows and arrows, nor guns for that matter."

"Laura, put your hood up and don't dawdle." There was a light rain as the Kenney family walked the road along the shore. Turning the bend in the road, their house came into view. They could see someone sitting on a deck chair on the veranda.

"It is Uncle Wayne!" cried Sarah. Like arrows shot from a bow, the children were off on a run. They took the shortcut through the field.

Elizabeth was about to yell an objection, when Heman interrupted, "Let them go, Elizabeth."

"But, Heman, it is so muddy."

"They have boots; let them be children while they can. It won't be very many years now. Like you said, they will be gone. Take my hand. We will walk up to the laneway."

By the time Heman and Elizabeth arrived on the veranda, the only sign of the children where boots lined up in a row at the door. Wayne was sitting there in the deck chair keeping watch. Along his lap, he was holding a shotgun.

"You hunting something? Porcupines or groundhogs been bothering you? I don't smell a skunk." The way Wayne was sitting there, Heman couldn't help think it was funny.

"Indians. I'm going to get me one, if they come back." Heman could tell that Wayne was quite serious. "Welcome home. You have been missed." Wayne didn't want them to think he was mad at them.

"Thank you, Wayne, we are glad to be home," Elizabeth answered.

"I'm surprised the children aren't here to help you hunt Indians," Heman stated.

"I didn't tell them, and the shotgun was under that slicker on the deck chair." He pointed to a chair three feet away.

"Well, I've had enough dealings with Indians for one day. I am going inside where it is warm and dry. Where is Marilyn?" Elizabeth asked.

"I'm sure she's in the kitchen with the children by now. She missed those children something awful, she did."

Elizabeth opened the door and Heman said, "I will be in shortly."

"Don't hurry," she replied. "It's not like you get to chase Indians every day."

"Very funny." He wasn't sure she heard him for the door closed quickly. Heman turned to Wayne. "Now, let's talk about those Indians. They certainly gave us a welcoming home party."

"I was watching them. They were here first. Running around the house whopping and hollering, enough to wake the dead, they were. I was just in time to stop Marilyn from going after them with the wooden rolling pin. Not that they didn't deserve it."

"Was this the first time?" Heman questioned.

"No, three times this week. The first time scared everyone in Watt Section. The third time Marilyn wasn't going to put up with it any longer."

"Let's go see Dan Rood. Maybe we can see what we can do about the situation. Wayne, you can leave your shotgun here. I've never seen a one-armed man shoot a shotgun." Before the words were finished, Wayne swung the gun up under his armpit with one movement of his right hand. It was held fast, and his hand quickly went to the trigger.

"Wowww!" Heman was impressed. "They could use you as a cowboy out west. But I don't think we will need the gun today."

Wayne just smiled and lowered the gun. "I'll put it away."

"Is that gun loaded?" Heman yelled.

Wayne was already halfway to the barn. "I'll unload it." He just kept on walking.

The rain was still lightly falling. Heman and Wayne were walking to the Rood's house. There on his porch, Dan was sitting guarding what belonged to him.

"Peace!" yelled Heman. "You got a shotgun too?"

"That I have. I'm going to get me an Indian before this day is over. My Maude and I watched what they did to you and your schooner, and your children were even on board. Welcome home. You've been missed." Dan reached out to shake his neighbour's hand.

"Thanks," Heman shook his hand firmly. "You are the second person I have come across hunting Indians today. Not going to be any Indians left in these parts."

"That's fine with me," Dan added.

"Is everyone stirred up because of the Indians?" Heman asked. "I've got a question for you, Dan. Who helped you cut cordwood last winter? I thought it was Peter Francis and Lennie Highblood, or was I mistaken?"

"Well, I guess there are some good Indians."

"Some?" Heman questioned. "You went with me to deliver the flour and beans, did you not? The Indians lost their crops too. I remember seeing a lot of good folks over there. What's going on over at Indian Passage? Do you know Dan? Does anyone know?"

"All I heard is some kind of Festival."

"Where did they get the liquor?" Heman questioned.

"You know about that, do you?"

"When they were waving liquor bottles in the air as they circled the *Lady Catherine*, it was hard not to notice."

"I heard the Boutliers have a still in Ecum Secum," Wayne commented. "They made some money, they did."

Heman heard all he needed to hear. "Are you coming?"

"Where are you going?" Dan wasn't committing himself to anything.

"Someone has to clean this mess up. I'm going to see Joseph Paul."

"The Chief!" Dan should have known Heman would start at the top. "It's dangerous over there. No white man has been in there for two weeks. But, I'm with you!" Dan was out of his seat.

"Leave the shotgun." Heman never did like guns.

"You want me to go to Indian Passage without a gun?"

"That's right. Come on, Wayne, help me harness up Beauty. Dan, be ready. We will pick you up on the way by."

Dan could tell it was a command. *I'm not even part of his crew,* thought Dan. He went into the kitchen. "Maude, I'm leaving for a spell. Don't know when I will be back."

"Where are you going? I'm not sure I want to be here alone!" Maude stopped stirring the baked beans and closed the oven door.

"Chasing Indians. The Captain has gathered a crew, and it looks like I've been ordered to be a member."

"What about us?" Maude had been on edge for a week now.

"Just lock the door. You will be fine."

* * * * *

Beauty pulled the wagon up Cemetery Hill. The rain had stopped, but it was damp and foggy. "Never thought I would be chasing Indians on a foggy night like this," Dan elbowed Wayne in his good arm.

"We are not chasing Indians," Heman informed them both.

"Look, there is Lloyd sitting guard on his porch." As he spoke, Wayne thought Lloyd looked a little funny sitting there holding his gun. "Hey, Lloyd," Wayne yelled as they slowed the wagon by his house. "We're chasing Indians; do you want to join us?"

That got Lloyd's attention, "It's about time someone is doing something about it. Count me in."

"We're not chasing Indians." Heman found it harder to control these men than he did his crew. "You can come, but leave your gun."

"My gun?" Lloyd looked at the gun. He felt secure when toting it.

"Yeah, that's the rule," Wayne informed him.

"The Captain is the leader," Dan added. "He said no guns. I hope he knows what he is talking about."

"I do," Heman insisted. "There will be no guns."

"If you say so. But, wait; Gerald will want to come." Lloyd jumped the white picket fence separating his yard from the neighbours. Before you knew it, Lloyd was dragging Gerald towards the wagon.

"Chasing Indians?" Gerald was putting his arm into his yellow slicker.

Heman rolled his eyes. He waited until his two new passengers were aboard and gave a command for Beauty to continue the journey. They made a left turn onto Church Road. There was complete silence as they passed the ruins of the church. The wagon continued through the foggy night. Waves slapped onto the rocky shore. The fog continued to roll in, and only Beauty seemed to be able to see where they were going on this road.

"It sure is a creepy night! Maybe we should come back tomorrow," Lloyd suggested.

"What, you getting cold feet!" Gerald confronted his friend.

"I finish what I start!" The Captain's voice was in command mode.

"See, that's why I never want to work for no captain," Lloyd whispered to Gerald. "They get mean."

Heman pretended he didn't hear that remark. He was wondering how he was going to negotiate with the Chief Joseph Paul. Beauty turned onto Indian Road.

"The Chief's house is a half-mile down the road." Wayne didn't want them to get lost.

The road was quiet. No Indians were out and about. Doors opened, then closed as the wagon slowly passed shack after shack. "There it is!" Heman brought Beauty to a stop. This too was a shack, but it seemed to be larger than the others they had passed. The door opened, and a low lit lantern hung from the bare rafters. A stocky man looked out into the foggy darkness.

"Joseph Paul," Heman called his name. "Captain Kenney to see you."

"Captain Kenney and who else?" the question was thrown back.

"Just a few neighbours; can we meet with you?"

"You bring food?"

"No, Chief, I have no food this time. But we need to talk." Heman wished he had thought of food or something else to offer.

"Come, Captain Kenney, bring your neighbours." The door was opened wide. The men entered and stood around until their eyes were accustomed to the light. The Chief had the advantage and searched the faces of the men. He recognized all of them. "Bring wood. You make a circle." Heman and Dan knew the ritual; they had been there before. By the old wood stove stood several wood logs. Heman picked one up, turning it on its edge, he sat on it. The other men did likewise. The Chief sat in his chair and his wife and children sat at a small table by the stove.

"You celebrating a Festival?" Heman asked. "When does the Festival end?"

"Not for another fortnight."

After a few moments of silence, the Chief asked; "Do you know the Festival, Captain Kenney?"

"No, I do not. Tell me."

"The Festival is honoring the great Glooscap." The Chief saw the blank looks on the faces of these white men sitting around him. He began to explain, "Glooscap is a great man-made from nothing. He was created out of a bolt of lightning in the sand. Glooscap has taught my people how to love, how to sing, and how to play. He has always guided the arrows of the great hunters in the past and will in the future. Our people gather at this time to sing and dance and to tell the many stories of Glooscap. Now, listen carefully."

The Chief told this story:[122] "Once long ago there were people living by the side of a river that had dried up. Even when the rain fell and the snow melted the river remained dry. So the council decided to send a man up the river to find the cause. What he saw made him gasp. A huge water monster was sitting in a lake. He had been the one to keep the water from flowing. The man said timidly, 'Kindly sir stop polluting the water and please let some water pass so our people can have water to drink.' The monster replied with a song. "It goes like this," and the Chief began to chant:

> " 'Do as you please
> Do as you please
> I don't care
>
> I don't care
>
> If you want water
> If you want water
> Go elsewhere!'"

The Chief talked quietly again. "The little man was very scared now. He said, 'Please can't you spare any for my people?' Again the monster replied with a song. It goes like this." The chief continued his chant.

> " 'I don't care.
> I don't care.
> Don't bother me
> Don't bother me

Go away
Go away
Or I'll swallow you up!'"

The chanting stopped, and the Chief continued. "The man was terrified and ran back to his people and told them what he'd seen. Glooscap saw what was happening and was upset. He painted himself and prepared himself for battle and then was off. On the way, he picked up a piece of mountain and turned it into a flint knife. When he finally found the water monster he demanded that the creature let the water go. But again he only sang:

'Ho! Ho!
Ho! Ho!
All the waters are mine.
All the waters are mine.
Go away
Go away
Or I'll kill you!'

"They fought and fought until at last Glooscap slit the belly of the monster, spilling all the water. Glooscap squeezed the monster dry until it's skin shriveled so much that it shrank into a bullfrog. When Glooscap returned to the village the people were still worried. One of them asked, 'Is there anything you cannot defeat?' Glooscap replied, 'Yes, there is only one thing I cannot defeat that is a baby.'

"He told them the story of little baby Wasis and how he had ignored him. Glooscap became so angry he yelled, but still, the baby ignored him. He was defeated. He says when a baby makes goo goo noises he is remembering the time Glooscap was defeated."

The men in the circle couldn't say a word. They had never heard anything like it. This story was new to them.

Heman thought the story was very interesting. "Glooscap seems like a great man, but like the rest of us, he wasn't perfect." Heman broke the spell. "Have you heard that your men are causing trouble?" Heman was direct.

Nothing like beating around the bush, thought Lloyd.

The Chief raised his eyebrows. He wasn't ready to tell this white man anything. "Liquor, what you might call 'firewater,' is the problem. Your young men have much firewater. It makes them do things that are not good. You know that, Joseph Paul?" The Chief was quiet. He lowered his eyes and looked at his boots.

Heman didn't say a word. Lloyd was about to say something. Heman quickly raised his hand to silence him. The silence went on and on. Heman kept his eyes on Joseph Paul; he willed him to raise his head and meet him eye to eye. The children stared at the white men but didn't say a word. Heman didn't move; he continued to stare at the Chief.

Finally, Joseph Paul raised his head and his dark eyes met Heman's. "I will see to your problem."

"Thank you, Chief." Heman was on his feet. "Thank you for seeing us." He held the door opened for the men to pass through. Before closing the door, he turned to the Chief. "I will bring cordwood, beans, and flour." Joseph Paul acknowledged the Captain by nodding his head. Heman closed the door and headed towards Beauty and the wagon. In complete silence, the men were seated and traveling back from where they came.

Lloyd was the first to break the silence. "Never saw anything like it, Captain."

"Like you spoke a silent language," Gerald added.

"Do you think it helped?" Dan asked.

"There will be no more trouble." Heman was convinced of that. The rest of the men took his word for it.

* * * * *

Heman entered the playroom with a grand entry. "Children, we have company." Eric and Cecil were right behind him. Mary

503

Elizabeth and the rest of her siblings gathered around their father. Eric's face was heating up. He was afraid he was turning red, and walked over towards the window, hoping no one would notice. This happened every time he was in the same room with Mary Elizabeth. He willed his face to return to normal.

"Why, hello!" Elizabeth left her spinning wheel. "Maude, Dan, what a surprise." All of a sudden there was a holiday atmosphere in the playroom.

"Did you catch those Indians?" Alexander couldn't wait to ask his father.

"No, Alexander, we didn't catch any Indians. But we did have a meeting with them. They were having a Festival. Did you know that, son? I figured if the Indians are having a Festival, we need to have one too. On the way home, we stopped at the Rood's house and picked up the rest of the family. You know what night this is, don't you?" Heman looked around to the younger and older children.

"Halloween Night," Mary Elizabeth answered.

"Right you are," Heman continued, "We can have our own Festival." Wayne and Marilyn came into the playroom. They had their arms filled carrying pumpkins. "Just in time!" Heman announced. "Pumpkins from our cellar." Four pumpkins were placed on the table. "The older ones can help the younger ones. Marilyn, do you have candles?"

"Right here," she answered. "Let's see who can make the scariest Jack-O-Lantern." While the children were busy at the table, the adults were able to visit. Elizabeth gave Maude the material she had chosen for her from her father's factory. Maude was speechless.

"It's just like Christmas," she finally found the words.

"Not Christmas, but Halloween," Heman laughed. Turning to the children, "Now, everyone come sit close; I want to tell you a story."

Alexander was right at his father's feet. He looked up and asked, "Will it be a scary story, Father?"

"Oh, yes, a scary story. You must be brave, my son. Is everyone ready? Turn the lanterns down low." As the light faded, the newly made Jack-O-Lanterns burned brightly. Their eyes watching the children gathered to hear the story. "This story is about a man named Jack. Jack was the meanest man in all of Ireland. He lived in a village not far from where I lived as a boy. If anyone ever dared to set foot on his land, he would catch them and put them in prison, where they would never see their families again. His neighbours knew he was a miserly, bad-tempered man, and stayed clear of him."

"Jack died and he stood outside the pearly gates. Saint Peter took one look at him and said, 'You cannot come into heaven. Mean, bad-tempered men are not welcomed here.' Then Jack stood by the gates of hell. Satan looked out at him. 'You are not welcome here. No one has ever tricked the devil, not until you. You have tricked me several times, and you are not good enough for hell. You are not welcome here.' "

"'What will I do?' Jack asked. 'If I'm not welcome in Heaven, and I am not welcomed in hell. What will I do?' "

"Satan answered; 'You will walk the earth forever with only a coal from hell to light your lantern.' But Jack didn't have a lantern. All he could see were the pumpkins ready to pick in the cold field. He took a pumpkin and hollowed its centre out. He cut eyes, nose and a mouth, then placed his coal from hell inside. The face shone through the pumpkin. A scary face it was. Jack, to this day, walks the earth, carrying his Jack-O-Lantern. On every October 31, children, to this very day, carve Jack-O-Lanterns to remind them never to be a miserly, bad-tempered man or woman." The younger children stared at the Jack-O-Lanterns that they had just made. Their funny faces stared back in the darkness. Heman clapped his hands, the children screamed, and Heman laughed. "Now, if we asked very nicely, I'm sure Marilyn may have cookies for you all."

The children looked at Marilyn. "If you're not bad-tempered children." The young ones shook their heads. Then, let's go to the kitchen." They jumped to their feet and opened the door.

"Walk!" Heman commanded. When Heman speaks, everyone listens.

Cork Ireland
February 1882

Dear Heman, Elizabeth, and children,
Our hearts broke as we shared your grief. Young William will be missed dearly by you and the whole family. Speaking with your father that very night the news arrived, my heart ached for a grandson I never got to meet. I pray your hearts will mend and happy times will find their way back into your lives.

The very next day, your brother William sensing my sorrow, says there was only one way for my heart to heal. Of course, I had to ask, "What way was that?"

"It's about time you and Father go to Canada and visit. I would go myself, but I can't leave my horses right now. Several are ready to foul, but you, Mother, need to go." That is what he said. And your father agreed.

To see my grandchildren, how wonderful that would be.
Your father has bought passage for us. We will see you before Easter.
A hug is waiting for all,

Until then,
Your Mother, or Grandmother Kenney

CHAPTER TWENTY-THREE

Time Comes Full Circle

A cold March day in Watt Section, Heman was making plans for his first trade trip of the season. Thanks to the gift of food from Boston, the winter of 1882 passed without too many difficulties. The snow still covered the burnt ruins of the little church by the sea, but now that spring was here, the scars reappeared through the melting snow. Reverend MacDonald made visits often to the families of his flock. He had made arrangements for Sunday Services to take place at the schoolhouse. Even though the community felt the loss of their church, they still continued their fellowship at the school. Even now a committee had been formed. The church would be rebuilt.

Christmas holidays had come and gone. Heman enjoyed the holidays through the eyes of his children. It certainly wouldn't be Christmas without them. Elizabeth's parents had surprised the family, when they arrived as passengers on the Steamer. There was great excitement in the Kenney's house the night a wagon delivered the children's Nana and Papa. They were just in time to help get ready for the holidays. A large fir tree was cut, and Beauty helped transport it from the woods to the front door of the Show House. The decorated tree stood in the living room. Every evening the family gathered there to enjoy its beauty and to tell stories of Christmases past. For Heman and Elizabeth, Christmas spent on the *Lady Catherine* was one that brought back fond memories.

Before you knew it, Janet and James were aboard the Steamer making their way through Sheet Harbour Passage. They were heading back to Halifax. All their grandchildren rang the bell and waved a farewell from the veranda.

January was the anniversary of such sorrow. William was gone. A year had passed without him. So many times Heman had forgotten and expected to see him run by with the rest of the children. But that wasn't ever going to happen again. Elizabeth suffered the most. He was relieved, thinking back, on that fall evening in the kitchen. Sweet Elizabeth had broken through her deep grief. Their love flowed between them again. Her family reunion helped in her recovery.

Here it was the beginning of March and he had to make plans to put *Lady Catherine* back to work.

"Will you go to Boston?" Elizabeth asked Heman.

"No, Bangor, Maine is our first destination. I hear there is a slowdown coming. They may even close the Sheet Harbour Mill."

"How is that?"

"They're building their own mills in Maine and Massachusetts. The government in the United States plans to place a duty on sulphite pulp. Sheet Harbour won't be able to compete, when they raise the cost of trading with them.[123]

"That won't be good for you?"

"No, Elizabeth, it won't be good for us. But don't you worry; I'll find other cargo for *Lady Catherine* to carry."

"The fishermen are back." Alexander was watching the fishing boats pass by the lighthouse. "They are low in the water."

"That's a sign of a good catch." They both laughed, for Alexander and his father said it at the same time. Heman then continued reading his papers, and Alexander watched out the window.

"When will Grandmother and Grandfather Kenney get here?" Alexander was caught up in the excitement ever since they received that letter from Ireland.

"I'm worried, Father, I have nothing to give. I don't even know them; how can I figure out what to give?"

"What makes you think you have to give them anything?" Heman folded his paper and placed it on the table by his chair.

"Well, all the girls are. Mother has them sewing doilies and table runners and who knows what else." Alexander wrung his hands together. "What am I to make for them?"

Heman could see his son was taking this very seriously. "Let me think about this." Heman put his chin in his hand and rested his elbow on his knee. You help too, Alexander. His son put his chin in his hand and rested his elbow on his knee, just like his father. They sat there for a very long time, at least that is what six-year-old Alexander thought. His elbow kept slipping off his knee.

"What are you doing?" Elizabeth had just walked into the playroom. "Looks like it is very serious business. Do my two favorite men have a problem?"

"Your son has a very big problem. He doesn't want to make doilies or table runners for Grandmother and Grandfather Kenney. What do you think, Mother? Do you have any ideas?"

She put her hand to her chin and her elbow on her knee and joined the men thinking. "I have it, I believe I have it! Do you want to hear it?

"Oh yes, Mother! What is it?"

"*Lady Catherine*. You can make a *Lady Catherine*."

"I can?" Alexander wasn't so sure. "She is pretty big you know?"

"That is a great idea!" Heman was out of his chair, walking up and down the room.

"It is?" Alexander didn't know what to think.

"Well, I won't be here to help you. I have to leave on a trade trip, Alexander. But I know just the person who can help, Wayne."

Heman, Alexander, and Wayne had their first meeting. Alexander felt a whole lot better when he found out that they were to build a small *Lady Catherine*, a very small one indeed.

* * * * *

A gale was blowing but without storm clouds. One of those late spring winds that seem to clean the air. The salt water sprayed as the high tide threw the waves up towards the shore. There were white caps on the blue water of Halifax Harbour. Flags came alive as the wind showed them in full glory. The sun was shining, but it took second place to the gale. Mountains of white clouds took turns racing across the sky and darted out of sight over the horizon. A flock of gulls, just for the joy of it, rode the wind up high in the sky and then glided back down close to the water.

Heman walked down Cornwallis Street towards the Harbour and Pier 2. He breathed in the cool fresh air as he picked up his pace. Fresh air in Halifax – amazing. He took his pocket watch from his pocket. *Won't be long now.* He could see the sign Pier 2 just to his right. The steamer *Argenteria* was docked, and people were mingling about. His eyes scanned the crowd, looking for anyone familiar. No one. Changing his focus towards the steamer, he again looked for those familiar.

"Heman, Heman! Over here."

A woman, holding onto her dark wide brim hat with one hand and waving with the other, was trying to get someone's attention. Beside her, a man began to wave his hand too.

Heman recognized him. "Father!" His hand went into the air waving back and forth. It didn't take long for him to fight his way through the throng of people.

Their reunion was a happy one though cut short. The throng of people surged forward, and they were caught up in the flow. "Come over here." Heman took his mother's bag as they

512

stepped out of the forward flow of the people around them. "Are you okay?" He was referring to his mother.

"Yes, I think so." She straightened her ruffled skirt and rearranged the direction of her hat. "This is a busy place, isn't it?"

Heman hugged his mother. "I am so glad you are here." Then he reached out his hand to his father. They shook hands man to man. "Welcome to Canada."

"It's good to be here, son, hard to believe, but it's good to be here."

"Heman, you look well. It is so good to see you." Mother and son hugged again.

"Come, let's find a place for you to sit, Mother, then Father and I will gather your luggage."Bridget didn't argue. She sat patiently watching the people coming and going, until their luggage was set before her.

"I have your accommodations ready. I know you asked for hotel reservations, but the Finleys would hear nothing of that. Elizabeth's parents have asked for you to be their guests while here in Halifax."

"I wouldn't want to intrude." Bridget didn't want anyone to go to any trouble for her.

"Mother, believe me, you are no trouble. I believe you will enjoy yourselves at the Finleys. Tomorrow we sail for Watt Section. Your grandchildren are excitedly awaiting your arrival."

"And we are excited to meet them," Daniel replied. Come, Bridget, let's go visit the Finleys. Where are you to be, Heman?"

"The Finleys, of course." Heman picked up luggage and headed for a waiting carriage. "The Finleys, of course."

* * * * *

Lady Catherine knew her way to Watt Section. She didn't need the help of her crew, but she wasn't going to tell them. She recognized the visitors onboard and felt a great honor for having them. She would introduce them to Heman's home.

513

"I tell you," Daniel was speaking to Heman. "You can have your steamers. Not like sailing on a great schooner like the *Lady Catherine*."

"And noise, it was enough to give you a headache," Bridget added. "Dirty too, that coal dust was everywhere."

Daniel was shaking his head. "But, Heman, it was fast, and you didn't have to worry if there was wind. You just kept going forward. We made the crossing in five days. It doesn't seem like we are that far away from you as I thought."

"It is called progress, Father. Everyone will be touched by it before long."

"I suppose you are right." Daniel was feeling his age.

"It's beautiful, Heman. Nova Scotia is very beautiful. I can see why you wanted to settle here."

"That I have, settled here I mean. Raising five little ones. That's hard to believe even for me. Elizabeth and I are very happy here. Life throws us ups and downs. We try to remember the high points rather than the lower. But last year, losing William almost broke both of us. We made it through with the help of God and by holding onto each other."

Bridget wiped the tears out of her eyes with a silk handkerchief. "Life can be hard, my son. How is Elizabeth?"

"Doing better, and she is so looking forward to your visit. That is all we have been preparing for since we received your letter, telling of your coming. She and the children have planned many surprises for you both."

* * * * *

"They are coming. I see them!" Alexander was jumping up and down. Standing at the window for the last hour had paid off. He was the first to see the top sail of *Lady Catherine*.

"Quickly, children, clean up. We want everything to be nice for Grandmother and Grandfather Kenney." She was a little nervous about her in-laws' visit. She wanted everything to be perfect.

Needlework and puzzles were back in their places, and the children were running down the main staircase. Boots and coats and colourful hats were hung just inside the back door. "Let me ring the bell. Let me ring the bell," Alexander shouted as he ran towards the front veranda. He being the youngest, had to fight for attention.

Mary Elizabeth took charge. "Okay, Alexander, you go first." Alexander rang it ten times, then hopped down and ran to the side veranda. He was the first on the path to the lighthouse. He had a disadvantage of having short legs. Two sisters passed him and one more was ahead. Mary Elizabeth slowed her pace and ran alongside her little brother. She took his hand and both ran faster through the worn pathway leading to the lighthouse. There they jumped up and down waving their hands. *Lady Catherine* could see their welcoming waves.

* * * * *

Heman took his place at the wheel as they sailed into Sheet Harbour Pass. He had a spyglass in his hand, looking towards the house. This was his routine every time he sailed home. This time his parents were with him. "Now, the fun begins." He looked over to his mother. "Come see, it won't be long until the game begins. Listen, do you hear that?"

In the distance over the sound of the wind and the splash of the sea hitting the bow of the schooner, the sound of a bell could lightly be heard. "It's a bell," said his mother.

"Yes, a bell," added Daniel. "It's getting louder."

Heman putting the spyglass to his eye, "Just about now. Here they come. Mother, look and see."

As Bridget looked through the spyglass, Heman continued, "*Lady Catherine* already sees them."

Bridget could see children running across the field. They were almost to the lighthouse. "The children are jumping up and down and waving. Take a look, Daniel." She passed the spyglass to him.

Daniel laughed, "Not just children, Bridget, but our grandchildren."

"How did you know to look?"

Heman replied, "They are always there when I return, or rather when we return. Isn't that right, *Lady Catherine*?"

* * * * *

The next two weeks were pure joy for Captain Daniel and Bridget. They got to share their lives with their family. The grandchildren got to know Grandmother and Grandfather Kenney. A special day was set aside just to exchange gifts. It was like Christmas, but without the Christmas tree. Alexander was very proud of his schooner named 'Little *Lady Catherine*'. His grandfather Kenney assured him there was a special place to display it back in Ireland. "Alexander, I will place her right beside the first '*Lady Catherine*' right on the mantle of the fireplace. Every time I pass by, I will think of you and of your father."

Of course, Bridget loved the beautiful doilies and table runners given her by her granddaughters. "I never had a daughter, but now I have five. What a gift my son has given me." She dabbed the tears away from the corner of her eyes.

Mary Elizabeth was by her side. "Don't cry, Grandmother Kenney," and gave her a hug. All her daughters waited their turn to hug this member of the family they were just getting to know.

Elizabeth gave the fifth hug. "I am so glad you are here, Mother Kenney." Bridget was glad she came.

* * * * *

It was a little over a week until Easter. Grandmother Kenney and the girls were busy sewing in the playroom. Actually, Grandmother didn't know how to sew, or at least not very well. Her granddaughters were teaching her. They were making Easter Bonnets.

Heman found out at breakfast the next day. "You are making bonnets?" He was asking his mother. "You may not know this, but you are in the company of bonnet experts."

"I am?" Grandmother was helping Alexander butter his toast. "I did not know that."

"Oh, but you are. Elizabeth makes the best bonnets I have ever seen. And now she teaches her daughters. Isn't that right, dear?"

"Don't listen to him, Mother Kenney, he is teasing me. When we first met, he took my bonnets back to Boston to sell. I was young at the time. I thought he must know a lot about bonnets. Turns out he would have sold my boots if I had asked."

Everyone laughed.

"Not fair, my love. Everyone was wearing your bonnets all over Boston. Just ask Peggy ODonovan."

"She did sell a lot of them, didn't she?"

All week the sewing projects continued. It wasn't hard for Marilyn to round up the family.

"Dinner's ready!" Marilyn yelled up the stairs.

Everyone was hungry. It didn't take them long to meet in the dining room.

"I have been admiring your table for weeks now." Daniel knew good wood when he saw it.

The mahogany table was made smaller by removing a centreboard. Now it was just the right size for a family of ten.

"It is a great table, isn't it. I found it in Bermuda many years ago. It took an army to get it aboard. When it arrived here, the local men had a time of it getting it from aboard the *Lady Catherine* to the house. And then it wouldn't fit through the door. Dan Rood had to take it apart first."

"What was that?" Alexander asked, as his mother buttered his roll.

"What, dear?"

"I think it is someone banging." Alexander took a bite of his roll. "There it is again. Someone is banging."

"And yelling," Laura added.

"Everyone stay put; I will see if there is a problem." Heman pushed his chair away from the table. He opened the door to the foyer; it was chilly there for the stove was not lit.

Bang! Bang! The door trembled with every bang. *The door is going to break, if they continue to bang like that*, thought Heman. He opened the door.

"Your house is on fire! Captain Kenney, your house is on fire!" Gerald was standing there yelling, "Fire!"

Heman felt the blood rush from his face. Then, as if he was hit over the head by a two-by-four, his brain took over and his control mode kicked in. Behind him stood the whole family, eyes wide with terror.

"Mary Elizabeth and Eliza, go to the kitchen. Anything that will hold water." Before he was finished, they were running to the kitchen. "Meet at the well!"

"Laura and Sarah, go with your mother and grandmother to the well!" As he yelled, he glanced at Elizabeth. There was fear in her eyes. "Be strong, Elizabeth." Alexander began to cry. "Be strong, my son; be a man. Help your Mother."

Heman turned to Gerald, "Show us!" Heman knew his father was right behind him.

"There!" Gerald pointed, as they ran around the house. "By the chimney!" Heman was horrified to see flames dancing in and out.

"We will need a ladder!" As they headed around the corner of the house, they ran into Lloyd and Wayne carrying a ladder. "There is water in the rain barrel!" Mary Elizabeth appeared carrying a bucket of water. "Keep the barrel filled." She turned and disappeared into the darkness as quickly as she had appeared.

Daniel steadied the ladder as Heman was quickly at the top. There the smoke stung his eyes and then he began to cough. *"Please, God, not now."* Heman was pleading with God himself. He threw bucket after bucket of water towards the flames. The bell was ringing. *Good for Elizabeth,* he thought, *she's calling for help.* He saw another ladder go up. His hopes were raised, but his eyes told him the fire was spreading. The road in every direction was full of horses and wagons, all coming his way. The neighbours were coming and Heman was grateful.

Sweat fell from Heman's face. His head turned upward to the stars above him in the black sky. *"God, are you paying me back. I thought I paid my debt in full when my son William died. Am I still paying for the sins I committed years ago? I tried to be a better man."*

The war against the fire was fought all night. Heman was coughing again. The smoke took a toll on his weakened lungs. Day was breaking, the flames still reached towards the heavens. The weary neighbours stood around watching the flames. The great Show House was being eaten up before their eyes. There wasn't a thing they could do. Their shoulders were stooped over; they had lost. The fire had won. As Heman coughed, one by one, his neighbours came up and touched him on the back. Joseph Paul didn't say a word, his dark eyes made contact with Heman, that was all the communication they needed. There were no words that could be spoken. Daniel put his arm around his son.

"Where is Elizabeth?"

Gerald answered; "She, the girls, your mother, and Alexander are at the Rood's house."

"How am I going to face her? How am I going to tell her we have lost everything?" Heman's coughing interrupted his talking.

"She already knows that, Captain. Women are funny; they act like they need us men to take care of them. But, when a man is down, then the good woman is by his side, stronger than before, this time taking care of the man. I'm sure it won't be any different with Elizabeth."

Heman felt a small hand in his. It was Mary Elizabeth. "Oh, Father, what are we going to do now?"

Heman put his arm around her and drew her close to his heart. "Everything will work out. We have to believe that, Mary Elizabeth. We have to be strong."

Daniel watched his son talk to his daughter, a tear rolled down his blackened face. He felt deep sorrow for them both.

Mary Elizabeth helped her father walk along the road to the Rood's house. The road was still full of people. They stared in silence as Heman and she passed by. Spells of coughing continued as they reached the Rood's porch. "Sit here, Father, while I get Mother." Heman was too tired to argue.

"Are you okay, son?" Daniel was greatly concerned.

"I don't know Father, I really don't know."

Elizabeth was by his side. "I'm sorry I couldn't save our home." Then his coughing began again, but worse.

"Put him in the rocking chair." Maude was taken aback when she took one look at Heman. Bridget frozen with terror, couldn't speak the words, "Heman, my son!"

"It's his asthma; we need to boil water!" There was always a pot boiling on Maude's stove. Heman quickly put his face over the hot steam, as Elizabeth put a cup towel over his head. He felt like he was breathing in cotton batton. A weariness was taking over his body. He could hear a voice far away. It was the voice of his sweet Elizabeth. She was saying something, something about putting him to bed.

Heman laughed a troubled laugh, "I don't have a bed. I have nothing." Heman barely remembered them leading him to a bed. *A bed – maybe all this was a dream. Maybe I do have a bed.* He practically fell into the bed. *This is not my bed. It is too small. This reminds me of a book I read to Alexander when he was a baby, Goldilocks and The Three Bears. I must be in the mother's bed,* he laughed and then coughed again. *Maybe I am inside a book. There is not room on this bed for Elizabeth. This is not my bed.* The fog from his mind partially cleared, if only for a minute. He remembered that his bed was gone. His bed burned in the fire. It wasn't a dream. His house burned down, his beautiful Show

House. *Falling, I am falling. Is the dream back? I am falling. Backwards, I am falling backwards. Falling, falling . . . Maybe I'm falling off the roof? No, I'm still falling. I'm so tired. God, help me.* With that Heman fell into unconsciousness.

Summer of 1882
Watt Section

Dear Grandmother and Grandfather Kenney,

Thank you for coming to visit us here in Nova Scotia. I think you are good grandparents. I love you a lot. I remember the happy days just before the fire. Then it got sad around here. I rang that bell as long as I could. Father thanked me, but it was no good, our house still burned right down to the ground. I am sorry you lost your things in the fire too. Especially "Little Lady Catherine". Wayne and I worked so hard making her. Sorry, you can't put her on your fireplace with the first Lady Catherine, I would like to see her someday.

Our new house is almost ready to move into. Mother loves it. I think it a little small, but she says I will grow to love it as much as the big house.

Father's health is much improved. He has been on a trade trip and will return soon. I hope you do not get seasick when going to your home in Ireland. I wished you lived closer, for I miss you already.

I start school this fall. That makes me almost grown up. Mary Elizabeth tells me I am growing taller every day.

Come back and visit us soon. I will let you sleep in my room. My bed may be too small for you, Grandfather, but I am sure Father will take care of that problem. He is good at taking care of problems.

Please remember me, I will not forget you.

Your loving Grandson
Alexander

CHAPTER TWENTY-FOUR

Beyond the Lighthouse

Heman sat up on the side of the bed. He had a hard time opening his eyes. *Maybe I had too much to drink last night? That's hard to believe, since I don't drink.* He couldn't even remember last night. Placing his hands on the top of his head, he hoped would take the throbbing pain away. It didn't help. He used his hands to feel for the lamp beside his bed. *Maybe if I can see better,* he thought. But his hands couldn't find the lamp. *That's funny; why would Elizabeth move my lamp?*

"Elizabeth," he spoke her name. He hated to disturb her sleep. Reaching to her side of the bed, he had two surprises. There was no Elizabeth and no other side of the bed.

Dawn was breaking. The sun was rising. Heman could see his surroundings, if only dimly. He had no idea where he was. All he knew for sure was this was not his bed and more frightening, no sign of Elizabeth. Closing his eyes tightly for a moment and shaking his head, he reopened them quickly hoping to see something familiar. Anything familiar, but it didn't work. Lying back on the small bed, he closed his eyes again. *"Déjà Vu,* he thought, *this can't be happening to me again.* Afraid to open his eyes, he just listened with all his might. He could hear wagons and horses and voices of men. They seemed to be gathering somewhere. The sound was coming from an opened window. Heman was afraid to look out. *Any moment now, the door is going to open and Dick is going to walk through with soup,* Heman thought.

Heman opened his eyes. The sun was now shining through the window, and he could hear birds singing. Another day was upon him, whether he was ready for it or not. Scanning the room he could now see there were two single beds. He was happy to see the other was empty. Two portraits hung on the wall. They looked   to Heman. His mind told him they were young versions of Eric and Cecil. *I must be at the Rood's house.* Heman had a glimmer of hope. He was beginning to put the puzzle together.

The door opened. "I knew it. I just knew it!" Heman groaned.

"Good morning, Captain. It's good to see you with your eyes opened. You've given us quite a scare. I thought you were a goner this time. But, I knew all we had to do was get your body back in balance, and we did it."

Heman fell back on his pillow and closed his eyes, taking a deep breath. Air went into his lungs and came back out without a whistle. "I can't believe it. What in the blazes are you doing here, Dick?"

"Taking care of you, sir. Soon as I heard, I was on the first steamship to Sheet Harbour. I knew I was the only one who could take care of you. Now, Dr. McMillian is a good man, but I do believe he took a disliking to me right from the start."

Heman was afraid to look. "Do I have frilly pajamas, Dick?"

"No, sir. Why would you have frilly pajamas? Breathe again for me, sir."

"Do you have soup?" Heman could see he was carrying something on a tray.

"No, sir. I have porridge. Maude said it would put hair on your chest."

"I don't need any more hair on my chest. Why am I sleeping in a bed at the Rood's house? Where is Elizabeth?"

"You don't remember anything, Captain?"

"Something has happened to Elizabeth!" Heman was sitting up on the side of the bed again.

"No, sir. Lay back down. Wouldn't want you to pass out, sir. You haven't had time to get your sea legs yet. Elizabeth is just fine. She's busy right now. I believe she was talking to a Joseph Paul and Lennie Highblood. Never met any Indians before; right nice people, they are."

"The Chief? Why?"

"They are building you a house. Well, not just the Indians; the whole community is out there. Looks like you are well liked around these parts, Captain."

"House! Oh, God!" Heman's memory was coming back like a rushing river. He began to shake and his breathing began to whistle.

"Captain, sir!" Dick had Heman on his feet. "Walk, sir." Dick pulled him along towards the open window. "Breathe, sir, deep breaths. That's right, now relax, sir. You can do it." Heman obeyed his crew member; Dick seemed to be in control. His breathing became calmer. "That's right, sir, now back to bed."

"It's all gone isn't, it Dick? I have nothing!" Heman managed to say, as he fell upon the bed.

"Well, sir, I wouldn't say nothing, sir. The barn is filled with furniture."

"How long have I been here?"

"Well, now," Dick was thinking. "I've been here a week now, so I would say at least two weeks."

"Two weeks! Is Elizabeth alright?"

"Yes, sir. You would be proud. She's building you a new house."

Heman smiled, "And the children? It seems awfully quiet around here."

"Henry took them to Halifax. They are safe and sound with Elizabeth's parents by now."

"What about my parents?"

"The Reverend Mc Donald, he and his Misses are taking very good care of them."

"Dick, if you are here where is Henry?" Heman was amazed so many people he knew were around.

"Well, Henry and Moses," Dick continued, "Closed up The Coffee Company II and caught the first steamer to Sheet Harbour. Henry left last week, took *Lady Catherine* on her first trade trip. Elizabeth filled him in on all the details."

"How come you didn't go?"

"Needed here, sir. Angus Behie and John Martin were happy to take my place. Work is slowing down at the Mill. They were happy to have work."

"How can I pay them? How can I pay you? I've lost everything."

"Not everything, sir. You still have *Lady Catherine* and the Irish Coffee Company II. You will come back, sir."

The door flew open as Elizabeth rushed through; "Heman!" She stopped at his bed, and pointing her finger at him, "If you ever scare me like that again, I'll, I'll. . ." She promptly burst into tears.

Heman opened his arms and she fell into them. "Easy, Elizabeth, I wouldn't want you to knock the breath out of me."

"Balanced, and glad to see it, Captain. I'll leave you alone now," Dick spoke as he left the room and closed the door.

* * * * *

Heman was sitting in the rocking chair by the cook stove in his own kitchen. Elizabeth dipped hot water from the reservoir on the top of the stove. Carrying it to the sink, she added it to the cold water in the dishpan. Washing dishes, she looked out the window above the sink. "Fishermen are back."

"Low or high in the water?" asked Heman.

"Looks pretty high to me."

"Maybe, they will have better luck tomorrow."

"Hope so."

"You miss Marilyn, don't you?" Heman asked.

"We all do. But I am glad she found work in Musquodoboit. With Mary Elisabeth's help, we won't starve." She tried to grin at Heman. He noticed that Elizabeth was stronger than ever. "Are we going to have to let Wayne go?" She walked into the pantry, placing the dishpan on a hook. Elizabeth sat at a table, which was in the middle of the kitchen.

"No, I don't think so. He may be able to take extra work; he mentioned rebuilding the church."

"We will be fine, Heman. The Kenney family is back together again, for this I am grateful and thank God for every day." Elizabeth took a look around her kitchen in the new house. "Turned out pretty good, a cottage by the sea, just as I planned it."

"It's kind of small; it may take some getting used to." Heman missed the Show House.

"I like it small. The other house was too big. Three bedrooms upstairs and one down here, and the living room and dining room is plenty of room for us."

"Alexander loves his room," Heman replied.

"The older girls in one room and the younger girls in the other. A perfect fit."

"And our bedroom. We still have a view of the ocean," Heman added. "I like the desk placed right under the window."

"Our home is here, Elizabeth said. "I wouldn't want to live anywhere else but Watt Section. We have fine neighbours. We take care of each other."

"Yes, Watt Section is our home. *Lady Catherine* likes it here too. Come, I have a surprise for you."

Heman opened the door to the covered porch, which led to the back entrance of the cottage. Windows were on one side, hooks on the other. Each family member had their own hook, and coats of many sizes and colours hung neatly in their place. Heman picked up a box and passed it to Elizabeth.

"Oh, it's heavy." Elizabeth held tightly to the box. "What is it?""

"Bring it into the kitchen and open it." Heman led the way back.

Elizabeth placed the heavy box onto the table and began opening it. "Heman, you found it!"

"Turned out it was never lost."

Elizabeth lifted a shiny bell from the bottom of the box. "But we couldn't find it."

"Dan did the day after the fire. He took it and cleaned it up. He gave it to me just this morning. He didn't want us to see it until he finished with it."

"I missed hearing it," Elizabeth added. "Now, when we see *Lady Catherine* coming just beyond the lighthouse, we can welcome her home again."

"That you can. the *Lady Catherine* will be bringing me home to you."

* * * * *

Elizabeth was in her bedroom on the first floor of the grey-blue shingled cottage. She was looking out at the lighthouse and then beyond to the sea, as she sat at her small desk, just below the window. Her shawl felt good, as she pulled it up on her shoulders. Early March brought cold winds making it difficult to keep the house warm. She sighed, "How long has it been?" She was thinking to herself. Looking down at the small calendar sitting on her desk, the year jumped out at her. "Could it really be 1917?" She adjusted her spectacles and wrote numbers on a piece of scrap paper. "Thirteen years," she sighed again. "Thirteen years without the Captain." She gazed eastward up Sheet Harbour Passage. There was just an empty spot, no *Lady Catherine*. But, all she had to do was close her eyes and then she could see her. *Lady Catherine* in full sail and Heman at the wheel, headed for the open Sea. For the Sea was always calling.

"Mother," Alexander tapped at her bedroom door. "Can I get anything for you?"

"Thank you, dear, I don't need a thing," Elizabeth answered. "Do come in!" Alexander was standing at the door. "How is the baby?" Baby Gerald was born two months before.

"Baby Gerald is doing fine; he's sleeping. Catherine is giving Hazel, Erna, and Elbridge their bedtime snack."

"What about Lloyd?" Elizabeth wondered.

"He's doing homework at the dining room table."

"Can I be of any help?" Elizabeth wanted to be useful.

"No, Mother, just checking on you. Seeing anything out that window yet?"

"Not yet, son, but this would be a good night for a visit."

"I will be in later to say goodnight." Alexander was gone.

Heman would be happy to know the house was filled with children again. He enjoyed his grandchildren. All his daughters saw to it that he had plenty. Mary Elizabeth married first. Eric Rood finally got up the nerve to ask Heman if he could court her. It was hard for Heman to let her go, but he had no choice. She was married a year later. Then, one after the other his daughters were gone. Alexander, however, was more than willing to stay at home. He found work at the sawmills and did logging in the winter. Heman worried about his son up until the day he died. But his worry was for nothing, because look at him today, a beautiful wife, Catherine and five children. It looks like a new one comes every two or three years or so.

The death of Alexander's father was very hard on him. Alexander spent all his free time sitting with his father those last years. When Heman was well enough, Alexander asked him to share stories of the adventures he had with *Lady Catherine.*

Elizabeth continued to look out the window at the lighthouse. As the years passed, the pain grew bearable. Now, as she thought back to that day, she knew Heman would smile just knowing how many people cared for him. She closed her eyes and her mind took her back . . . .

Two black horses with red feathered plumes fastened to their heads pulled the hearse carriage up the laneway. Swallows flew in and out of the doors of the barn as they passed by. The undertaker, Mr. Webb, brought them to a stop, between the well and the front door of the blue-gray-shingled cottage. The family was gathered in the kitchen and dining room area. Final goodbyes were completed.

"Are you ready?"Mr. Webb asked the question to a group of men sitting on one side of the dining room. Captain Kenney's crew was all present: Henry, Patrick, Moses, John Charles and Dick, dressed in their green jackets and green vests. This would be the last time they would honor their Captain.

Henry, being the first mate, stepped forward, "We are ready."

"Mrs. Kenney?"

"She is in with the Captain." Henry led the way to the small living room.

"Are you ready, Mrs. Kenney?" Mr. Webb was trying to do his job. Elizabeth looked up at the two men.

Elizabeth looks so frail, thought Henry.

"Where is Alexander?" she asked.

"He is in his room," answered Henry.

"Please summon him, Henry." She turned to Mr. Webb, "Please, I need a few more minutes."

"Certainly." The undertaker left her alone with Heman.

Alexander entered the room and sat in a chair. It was not close to his mother, nor was it close to his father. "Come beside me, Alexander."

"I'd rather not," Alexander replied.

Elizabeth looked upon her son; "Please, Alexander, do it for me."Alexander would do anything for his mother, but she was asking something of him that was hard to give.

"Be strong, Alexander."

"That's what Father always said," Alexander cried. "But I could never be as strong as he was." He raised himself to his feet and slowly walked to her side.

Elizabeth took his hand as if he were a child. "Your father loved you, Alexander."

"Mother, what will we do without him?" Finally, tears came to the surface of his eyes.

"I've asked the same thing, my son. You will be the leader of this family now. This will be your house. The Kenneys will continue to make some kind of mark in this community.

Mr. Webb was at the door, "Mrs. Kenney, I hate to interrupt, but it is time. Are you ready?"

Elizabeth looked towards Alexander. He nodded his head; he was ready. She then looked over towards Heman lying in the rough wooden coffin. She walked towards him, lifted his hand to her lips for a final farewell. She turned to Mr. Webb, "Yes, Heman is ready."

People were gathering at St. Andrew's Cemetery. One could see from this hill several schooners moored off the Watt Section Wharf. They seemed to be circled around *Lady Catherine*, consoling her, for she was in mourning. From the top of her spar flew black flags, and her bow had black banners hanging from the side. The afternoon breezes helped them wave a goodbye. *Lady Catherine* knew her Captain's heart was no longer beating. He no longer heard the call of the sea. She was mourning her loss.

The horses, dressed in their red feathered bridles, made their turn, rounding the well, as they headed back out the lane. Slowly, very slowly, they turned right unto the rocky road. Elizabeth wanted to walk. "Heman and I walked to the cemetery every evening when he was well. I want to walk." The whole family walked.

The procession stopped outside the Rood's gate. The Rood family was waiting. Mary Elizabeth, Eric, and their children joined the procession. Mary Elizabeth took her Mother's arm, and Alexander took her other. Together they followed the horse-drawn hearse, as it made a left-hand turn and began its slow climb up the dusty hill. As the road leveled off, they approached the cemetery, where horses and wagons were parked on both sides of the road. The iron gate was swung open. The horses slowly pulled its cargo to the top of cemetery hill. The congregation gathered at the open-air church and stood as the family walked up the hill.

Captain Kenney's crew, dressed in green, carried the wooden casket and placed it beside a freshly dug hole. The family settled in the section reserved for them. Many of the men had to stand, for the Kenney family numbered more than twenty.

Reverend McDonald was standing to the side, speaking quietly to a Captain. Captain Woods, standing by the Reverend was heard saying, "Are you ready? It is time to sail."

The old Reverend looked up to the old Captain, cleared his voice, "With God's help I am ready." He picked up the gold cross, held it high and proceeded to the front, his white robe swishing with each step he took.

A hush fell over the crowd. Word had spread throughout more than one community that the famous Civil War Captain had arrived the day before at Watt Section Wharf. After Reverend McDonald had finished with a prayer, Captain Woods approached the front.

"Today is a sad day for me. I have lost a great friend. My heart is heavy, but how can it compare to the breaking heart of Elizabeth, Heman's true love." He stopped for a moment looking over towards Elizabeth. She acknowledged Woods with a smile and a nod of her head. "And to Heman's children," Woods continued, "a day they have lost a great father." Soft crying could be heard. The children were not as strong as their Mother. Elizabeth knew her time of mourning would come. Today, she would honor her husband. ". . . . and you the community have lost a good neighbour."

Elizabeth didn't hear the rest of Captain Wood's speech. Her mind drifted off like fog rolling over the sea. She closed her eyes and saw a young girl running on *Lady Catherine*'s deck, then her engagement and the trip to Ireland. Her first-born, and then the move to the great Show House, the fire, and now this. She opened her eyes to see the white caps on the deep blue ocean. *The sea is calling, my love. Go on, for you are free to sail for eternity.* Elizabeth set his spirit free.

* * * * *

Elizabeth and Alexander lived in the little blue-gray shingled house. This was home for Elizabeth. She wouldn't want to live anywhere else. Henry took "*Lady Catherine* back to Halifax. For several years she continued her trade trips. Heman made sure a small income would always come to Elizabeth. That was all she needed. Even with *Lady Catherine*, the winds of change were blowing. The steamships took over the trade routes. Schooners were too slow. They had to rely on the wind; the steamships did not. The terrible day came when *Lady Catherine* was sold. Elizabeth didn't know to whom. She didn't want to know. Henry made sure she received her share. All Elizabeth had were memories. Closing her eyes, she could still see *Lady Catherine* coming home, bringing Heman with her. Two months later, word reached Halifax, that the *Lady Catherine* had vanished off the coast of Bermuda.

Life went on like life always does. It wasn't always sad, but happy times tried to cover the heartache that Elizabeth carried. Two years after Heman died, Alexander found the love of his life, Catherine Cook. Heman had his *Lady Catherine*. Now his son had his own Catherine. Alexander and Catherine were married, March 30, 1906, and set up housekeeping with Elizabeth. For as far as she was concerned, this house was now Alexander's home.

Elizabeth pulled her shawl closer around her shoulders. She continued to look out of her bedroom window. She did so every evening at this time. She watched the lighthouse and its light turn round and round, calling to those ships and schooners.

"Here she comes!" Elizabeth waves. She didn't have a bell to ring. She didn't need one. Heman knew she was watching, as he and *Lady Catherine* sailed west, beyond the lighthouse to the open sea.

"So don't you feel sad for Heman. Don't feel sad for me. Heman is sailing with *Lady Catherine* on the blue sea."

"Oh, you say it could never happen! I just don't believe."

Go and see for yourself. Sit by the shore by the lighthouse on a foggy night. Better still, just ask Alexander's wife, Catherine, for she has seen the *Lady Catherine* sail out of the fog. Or ask Lloyd or Gerald. Also, Joseph Paul and Lennie Highblood talk about seeing the Captain and his great schooner. The Roods, Dan and Maude, have tales to tell about what they have seen sitting on their porch.

But it doesn't matter whether you believe or not. I, Elizabeth, watch and wave every evening, as Heman and *Lady Catherine* sail beyond the lighthouse.

* * * * *

Spring 2009

Dear Readers,

Thank you for reading my book.

I grew to love Watt Section as a child. My summers were spent around Sheet Harbour and Watt Section. I always wondered how the Kenney family lived their lives in that small blue shingle cottage in Watt Section. I spent hours by my grandmother Catherine's (Alexander's wife) side, as she told me stories, many of which I have added to this book.

The story you have just read is fiction. Yes, there may be a sprinkle of family history, but just that a sprinkle. If you see a familiar name, they are names I heard as a child and thought it fitting to use them for characters. They are not real people.

Yes, Heman was a Captain and had a schooner, which was moored off the Watt Section Wharf. Yes, Heman had his sweet Elizabeth. They had six children, four girls, and two boys, and the youngest boy did die. Yes, there was a fire that destroyed the great 'Show House.' Yes, Alexander had Catherine his wife and eleven children, six boys and five girls. One boy died. The fourth child born was Elbridge Reginald, my father. Yes, there was a lighthouse, but it is no longer there today. You may have other questions. The End Notes may answer those.

I enjoyed the journey and I hope you did as well.

Yours, the Author,

Catherine Alice Kenney Wilcoxson

P.S. A website has been set up. You can visit it at any time. http://www.theladycatherinecompany.com Also if you send me email I will answer any questions that you may have. cawilcoxson@theladycatherinecompany.com. I look forward to hearing from you.

ENDNOTES —

Chapter One: *Lady Catherine*

* * * * *

Chapter Two: Cork, Ireland 1833 (49 years earlier)

[1] (Potato pancakes and raisin bread)

[2] Coffee with whisky

Chapter Three : "The Queer Mist From The Irish Sea"

[3] History of Wet Nursing/Cross Nursing Http://www. lalecheleague.org/llleaderweb/LV/LVJulAug95p53.html Wet nursing and cross nursing have been controversial since the beginning of recorded history. The oldest of written laws included rules for wet nursing. One of the rules stated that if a wet nurse had been feeding an infant who died for any reason, she was prohibited from taking on another infant to wet nurse. Fashionable women of the period wore corsets made of metal with stays of bone. Th e corsets not only broke ribs but also damaged breast tissue and nipples, making breast feeding impossible. Employing wet nurses was a sign of a family's high status in society, showing that the family had the resources to pay someone else to do any physical tasks.

[4] Mass Eviction During Famine. http://www.nde.state.ne.us/ss/irish/unit-3.html

[5] Irish Potato Famine and Trade (History) http://www.american.edu/TED/potato.htm.

[6] *Ibid.*

[7] Coffin ships were "wet, leaky holds" of timber ships returning to North America that were crammed in with as many as 900 [people], with barely room to stand." Approximately half of the

people died during the voyage and the other half arrived in North America unable to disembark without assistance, due to sickness and starvation. Irish Potato Faminehttp://www.irishpotatofamine.htm

[8] Mass Evictions During Famine. http://www.nde.state.ne.us/ss/irish/unit-3.html 913 people in 18 months were evicted from their land. Newspapers printed 478 were receiving public relief, 170 had emigrated, and 265 were dead or left to shift from place to place."

[9] *Ibid*

[10] "Starving in a Sea of Seafood" http://qcpages.qc.cuny.edu/ENGLISH/Projects/postcol/country/ireland/economy.html

[11] Famine Scenes (Th e Horror) http://www.nde.state.ne.us/SS/irish/unit_4.html.

Chapter Four: *The Lady Catherine* Has a Captain

[12] The Gruel Cauldron. http://www.geocities.com/willboyne/nosurrender/Gruel.html

[13] Http://www.esb.ie/main/about_esb/powerstations/marina/stationhistory/didyouknow3.jsp. The Marina (Navigational Walk) was built from mud and gravel dredged from the river. In 1843 Th e Cork Corporation leased 1000ft. Of the land by 100ft wide to build the Cork rail-line to Passage. The old Cork Park Racecourse came into being because of one city's development (Improvement Act) and went out of existence 524because of another (industrialization).

[14] http://www.offshore-radio.de/fleet/dixon.htm

[15] Mock Goose is composed of lamb shoulder, lamb kidneys, onions, bread crumbs and herbs. Bread crumbs with onion herbs, kidneys, and eggs. Stuff shoulder. Roll and secure with string. Serve with vegetables and gravy. Became known as "Colonial Mock Goose."

[16] Dublin Coddle consisted of pork sausages, bacon, potatoes, and onions.

[17] Ireland, http://www.reference.com/browse/wiki/Victoria_of_

the_United_Kingdom

18 The Great Famine http://www.humboldtl.com/~history/ lexiso/famine.htmlChapter Five: "Fugitive Onboard"

19 Slave trade – History Ireland Feature - Wadell Cunningham-FEATURE from Vol. 11 No. 1 Spring 2003. http://www. historyireland.com/magazine/features/11.1.feat.html.

20 http://rumskulls.org/dailylife.htm.

21 *Ibid.*

22 Http://rumskulls.org/food.html

23 *Ibid.*

24 Http://rumskull.org/navigation.htm.

25 1853 edition of Nathaniel Bowditch's *Th e New American Practical Navigator, Ibid.*

26 Http://rumskull.org/navigation.htm.

27 *Ibid.*

28 Http://rumskulls.org/sickness.htm. Treatment.

29 Http://www.friendsvinp.org/archie/Cinamon/cinmer34.htm.

30 Pram - a flat bottomed boat to transport cargo. Http:// rumskulls.org/dailylife.htm

31 Clothing, Food, and Shelter. http://rumskulls.org/Food.html.

32 Http://www.friendsvinp.org/archie/Cinamon/cinmer34.htm.

33 Source: Bathe, Basil an Alan J. Villiers. The Visual Encyclopedia of Nautical Terms Under Sail, New York City: Crown Publishers, Inc., 1978. (A knot equals one nautical mile per hour.)

34 Brig - A two-masted vessel, a large main stay sail; Frigate – a fast, fully rigged ship with a raised quarter deck and forecastle, usually 20 to 50 guns; Cutter- fast, single masted scout ship; Sloop - square-rigged sloops of three masts or two-masted Brigrigged sloops; Lighters - a vessel used for the purpose of re-supply for ships unable to enter the harbour; Prams- a flat bottomed boat to transport cargo.

35 Http://www.ghcaraibe.org/hist/hisfwil.html

Chapter Seven: The Irish Coffee Company

36 "The tradition of burial at sea is an ancient one. As far as

anyone knows this has been a practice as long as people
have gone to sea. In earlier times, the body was sewn into
a weighted shroud, usually sailcloth. The body was then
sent over the side, usually with an appropriate religious
ceremony." See http://www.history.navy.mil/faqs/faq85-1.
htm#anchor74610 or http://www.history.navy.mil/faqs/
faq85-1.htm#anchor74610 for further information. One
source makes this comment: *"The Doctor read the service as the
Captain was unwell. The little things were lowered gently down
in the water and sank in the deep blue sea quick out of sight."*
[37] Matthew 19:14 (King James Version).

[38] Matthew 6:9-13 (King James Version).

[39] Romans 12:19 (King James Version).

Chapter Seven: The Irish Coffee Company

[40] "Catting the anchor" or pulling up the anchor to lash it to the
hull, thereby preventing it from banging the whip while in
motion. Http://rumskulls.org/nagivation.html.

[41] The New Ship *Alma*, of Boston. www.bruzelius.info/Nautica/
News/BDA/BDA(1855-02-26).html

[42] Boston Daily Atlas, February 26, 1855. (Th e Maritime
History Virtual Archives). The Daily Atlas. Copyright
@1996Lars Bruzelius.

[43] "Wainscot >noun an area of wooden paneling on the lower
part of the walls of a room. >verb (wainscoted, wainscoting or
wainscotted, wainscotting) line (a room or wall) with wooden
paneling." Oxford University Press.

[44] A raised deck at the stern of a ship, especially a sailing ship.
Oxford University Press.

[45] King's Handbook of Boston. Cambridge, Mass. Moses
King Publisher. Harvard-Square copyright 1855.

Chapter Eight: The Irish Coffee Company

[46] Book of Boston 1920 by Robert Shackleton. Boston
The Penn. Publishing Company, Philadelphia 1920.

[47] The oldest continuously operating hotel in the United States,

the Parker House's original building opened in 1855 and counted Charles Dickens among its guests (his first reading of *A Christmas Carol* was in the Parker). http://www.fodors.com/miniguides/mgresults.cfm?destination=boston@33&cur_section=lod&property_id=51649.

[48] Pork sausages, bacon, potatoes, onion.

[49] King's Hand-Book of Boston. Cambridge, Mass. Moses King Publisher – Harvard-Square Copyright 1855.

[50] *Ibid.*

[51] *Ibid.*

[52] http://encarta.msn.com/text_761557136___5/Boston.html.

[53] McNabbs Island. http://everything2.com/index.pl?node=Halifax.

[54] http://www.herald.ns.ca/NovaScotian/516575.html.

[55] The Halifax Noon Day Gun http://www.timegun.org/halifax_noonday.html.

[56] *Ibid.*

[57] Whether there were wild horses on McNabs Island is to be debated. But there is a history of wild horses on Sable Island, which is located far off shore, approximately 160 km southeast of Canso, Nova Scotia. http://www.greenhorsesociety.com/Sable%20Island/sable_island.htm There is a romantic notion that Sable Island horses are descended from shipwreck survivors. http://www.greenhorsesociety.com/Horses/Horses. htm. The author of this book has taken liberties and has used the story of the wild horses to embellish her book.

[58] Officially opened in 1867 The Halifax Public Gardens have survived for more than a century. http://www.halifaxpublicgardens.ca/ In the 1860's another garden, tended by Richard Power, was under construction on the northern boundary. Around this time the Horticultural Society, experiencing fi nancial diffi culties, was obliged to sell it's garden to the City of Halifax. The task of bringing the two together to form the harmonious formal garden we see today

fell to Powers. http://www.halifaxpublicgardens.ca/history.
htm

[59] PointPleasant Park: A Symbol of Halifax

Point Pleasant Park lies on a rocky 75-hectare (185 acre) promontory jutting into the Atlantic Ocean at the eastern end of the Halifax peninsula, in Nova Scotia, Canada. This park has been a place of recreation for the citizens of Halifax since the city's founding in 1749. Before that, it was a hunting, fishing, and ceremonial area for the indigenous Mi'kmaq people. Until 1866, Point Pleasant was primarily a military bastion, but in that year it was leased to a newly formed commission for a public park. Trees were planted in its early years as a park and it soon became an urban forest where citizens could find an oasis of peace close to the bustling city.
http://www.pointpleasantpark.ca/inside.asp?cmPageID=91

[60] http://docsouth.unc.edu/jones/supportl.html

[61] William Lloyd Garrison (1805-1879) one of the most articulate and influential advocates of the abolitionist movement in the United Sates. Lived in Boston after 1826.
Http://www.cr.nps.gov/nr/travel/underground/ma2.htm

[62] The escaping slaves were called passengers; the homes where they were sheltered, stations; and those who guided them conductors. http://www.answers.com/topic/undergroundrailroad.
http://alpha.dickinson.edu/departments/hist/
NEHworkshops/NEH/resource/textbooks.htm

[63] Secret codes were used for communicating, along with coded spirituals, which conveyed signals for hiding, and danger. One song, for example "Steal Away", was an obvious invitation to the slave to stealway to freedom. Black slaves spoke of Canada as the "freedom land". UNDERGROUND RAILROAD Freedom Trail To Canada http://www.bccns.
com/history_underground.html http://www.pbs.org/wgbh/
amex/singers/sfeature/songs_steal_sheet.htm

[64] http://www.geocities.com/Heartland/Fields/8616/stpat/
blessings.html.

[65] Both the tune and lyrics are public domain, and therefore
many different Nova Scotian artists have released their own
recordings of 'Farewell to Nova Scotia'. Http://en.wikipedia.
org/wiki/FarewelltoNovaScotia

Chapter Ten: Elizabeth, My Sweet Elizabeth

[66] Irish Taffy. 1 C. Brown sugar, 1/4 C. Butter, 1 lb jar dark corn
syrup, 1 teasoon baking soda, 2 Tbsp. Apple cider vinegar. Melt
butter in a deep saucepan. Add sugar, syrup, and vinegar.
Stir constantly until all ingredients are blended and melted.
Then, without further stirring, allow it to come to boil.
Continue boiling until taffy is hard and brittle when placed
in icy water. Remove from heat and add baking powder
(mixture will foam up). Stir well. Pour in a greased or
waxed paperlined plate. When it has cooled enough to handle,
pull and stretch until it becomes pale yellow.
Cut into squares.

[67] Potatoes, leeks, cream, celery

[68] Pork sausage, bacon potatoes, onion.

[69] Green cabbage, potatoes, onions, mace. Haddock, cream,
milk, mustard.

Chapter Eleven: Steal Away, Steal Away To Jesus

[70] Escaped slave 1861
http://www.nyscss.orglresources/publications/
NYand Slavery/Chapter%20E/Narrative/JamesBanks.pdf

[71] Africaville. Until recently, the Underground Railroad into
Nova Scotia was Canada's best-kept secret. People living
in the communities of Preston, Upper Hammonds Plains,
Guysborough, Lincolnville, Tracadie, Milford Haven and
Boylston can trace their roots to the escape slaves of the
Underground Railroad "the road that led to freedom." Http://
www.bccns.com/history_underground.html. Http://imprint.
uwaterloo.ca/issues/021601/4Human/features02.shtml.

Chapter Twelve: The Great Escape

[72] "Northern Industry in the Civil

War." Http://www.civilwarhome.com/civilwarindustry.htm.

[73] *Ibid*

[74] David G. Surdam. Traders or Traitors: Northern Cotton Trading During the Civil War. Http://h-net.org/~business/ bhcweb/publications/BEHprint/v028n2/p0301-p0312.pdf

[75] *Ibid*

[76] http://www.benmautner.com/widerangle/westernunion.jpg

[77] *Ibid*

[78] http://ns1763.ca/hfxrm/woodtaylor.html Also http://www. militaryphotos.net/forums/showthread.php?t=63461

[79] "Propeller, device consisting of a hub with one or more blades that propels a craft to which it is attached by rotating its blades in a fluid such as air or water. In the latter part of the 1830s the Swedish-American engineer John Ericsson and the English inventor Sir Francis P. Smith independently patented screw propellers. Screw propellers have almost entirely replaced paddle wheels and a variety of other devices that were designed to propel waterborne vessels. In a single-screw ship the propeller is mounted on the end of a shaft immediately in front of the rudder; the shaft is connected to a transmission or directly to an engine, which turns it and the propeller. The thrust generated by the propeller is transmitted to the hull of the ship by a thrust bearing attached to the shaft. Twin-screw vessels were first introduced c.1860 in England. Located on either side of the rudder, the two propellers may be used to assist in steering; if one breaks down, the other can still propel the vessel." http://www.answers.com/topic/propeller See also Http://www.ahoy.tk-jk.net/Marauders/civilWar/csstallahassee.

[80] *Ibid*

[81] *Ibid*

[82] *Ibid*

[83] *Ibid*

Chapter Thirteen: Romance, Sweet Romance

Chapter Fourteen: Do You, Heman Godfrey Kenney, Take Elizabeth

Janet to Be Your Lawful Wedded Wife . . . ? I do

[84] As far back as the 12th Century, the traditional method for announcing an engagement in England was to proclaim or publish the news at the local church for three consecutive Sundays. Th is was called "bid the banns," – a standard practice in the 19th Century. It still goes on today. Th e point of this custom during early times was to insure that anyone who contested the wedding would come forward – or forever hold their peace. Http://save-the-date.invitesite.com/announce-history.html.

[85] The top layer of the cake was saved, and tradition has its roots in the late 19th Century when this top layer would be used for the christenings. It was assumed that the christening would occur soon after the wedding ceremony. Http://www.maisiefantasie.co.uk/history-of-wedding-cakes.html.

[86] *Ibid.* There was an unusual notion of sleeping with a piece of wedding cake underneath one's pillow, which dates back as far as the 17th Century. Legend has it that sleepers will dream of their future spouses if a piece of wedding cake is under their pillow.

[87] Http://www.vingage wedding.com/history.html.

[88] Brides who wore blue believed their husbands would always be true to them, so even if their gown itself was not blue, they would be sure to wear something blue about their person. This is another tradition that has survived to this day. Http://wwww.antiquedress.com/civilwarwedgownealchensmg.jpg

Chapter Fifteen: Cork Ireland 1866

[89] Http://www.irishcultureandcustoms.com/AEmblem/CladdaghRing.html *The hands are for friendship. The heart is for love. And the crown is for loyalty Held high above.*

[90] *Ibid*

[91] Http://www.seawear.com/irish-jewelry/bookstore.html

92 Http://www.chiff .com/a/wed-irish.htm.

93 *Ibid.* Http://www.chiff .com/a/wed-irish.htm.

94 Irish Wedding Vow. *Ibid.*

Chapter Sixteen: The Hated Cholera

95 Http://www.rootsweb.com/~nshalifa/ch6.html
HalifaxCountyNSGenWebPages-HewittHistories

96 *Ibid.*

Chapter Seventeen: A Seagull . . . Or a Stork? Spring 1867

97 Historical Collections for the US National Digital Library
http://memory.loc.gov/il/iihb/039/4300/43160008.gif.

98 History of Canadian Confederation 1867-Birth of Ca. . .
http://Canadaonline.about.com/od/confederation/Canadian-
Confederation.

Chapter Eighteen: Reuniting Again

99 United States Congress July 22 1866. Source Bill HR 754
page 8 Historical Collections for the U.S. National Digital
Library. http://memory.loc.gov/il/iihb/039/4300/43160008.
gif

100 Nightinggale, Marie: *Out of Old Nova Scotia Kitchens.*
Nimbus Publishing, Ltd., 1959. Nova Scotia, Canada, p. 40.

101 *Ibid,* p. 42.

102 *Ibid,* p. 23.

103 *Ibid,* p. 24.

104 *Ibid,* p. 73.

105 *Ibid,* p.24.

106 Th e Canada Gazette http://canadagazette.gc.ca/book/
pg11-e.html

107 The origin of the name Canada comes from the expedition
of explorer Jacques Cartier up the St. Lawrence River. The
Iroquois Indians pointed out the route to the village of
Stadacona, the future site of Quebec City, and used the
word "Kanata" the Huron-Iroquois word for village. Jacques
Cartier used the word Canada to refer to both the settlement
of Stadacona and the land surrounding it subject to Chief

Donnacona {How Canada Got It's Name – Origin Of The Name Canada} http://canadadaonline.about.com/od/history/a/namecanada.htm.

[108] History of Canadian Confederation 1867-Birth of Ca. . . http://canadaonline.about.com/od/confederation/Canadian_Confederation.htm

[109] The New York Times Archive http://select.nytimes.come/gst/abstract.html?res=F50817F137B93C0A9178CD85F43. . . NYTimes.com

[110] http://www.collectionscanada.ca/confederation/023001-503-e.html

[111] The City and Provincial Hospital opened May 1867. Http://www.gov.ns.ca/nsarm/virtual/halifax/into.asp On Queen Victoria's Golden Jubilee in 1887, the hospital became the Victoria General.

[112] **An Irish Lullaby (Too-ra-loo-ra-loo-ra)**

Over in Killarney

Many years ago,

Me Mither sang a song to me

In tones so sweet and low.

Just a simple little ditty,

In her good ould Irish way,

And I'd give the world if she could sing

That song to me this day.

Chorus:

Oft in dreams I wander

To that cot again,

I feel her arms a-huggin' me

As when she held me then.

And I hear her voice a -hummin'

To me as in days of yore,

When she used to rock me fast asleep

Outside the cabin door.

Chorus:

http://www.thebards.net/music/lyrics/An_Irish_
Lullaby.shtml " . . .the words are by J.R. Shannon in
the 1890s though I suspect the melody is much much
older...perhaps as old as the days of Yore?)
[113] Settlement located on the east side of Sheet Harbour. This
land was a part of a 5000 acre grant given to Chief Justice
Jonathan Helener in 1773. In 1814 William Watt bought
land here and the settlement was named after him. In the
early 19th century John Low and Simon Rutleldge were early
residents. They both owned large parcels of land in the village.
[Nova Scotia Canada Public Archives of Nova Scotia] http://
www.gov.ns.ca/nsarm/cap/places/page.asp?lD=712
[114] Population 1956 237. Author's guess is 130 in 1867. Nova
Scotia, Canada, Public Archives of Nova Scotia. http://www.
gov.ns.ca/nsarm/cap/places/page.asp?ID-712
[115] *Ibid.* St Andrew's Anglican Church constructed in 1856 and
consecrated in July 1859. Ibid.

Chapter Twenty: Watt Section 1868

* * * * *

Chapter Twenty-One: "Fire!"

[116] Sheet Harbour Pulp Mill was the first to test the sulphite
process discovered about 1866 by a Philadelphian chemist,
Brig. General Benjamin Chen Tilghman. http://
www.sheetharbour.ca/history/chapter2.htm.
[117] *Ibid*
[118] *Ibid.* Mr. Chisholm continued in the lumber business, played
an important part in the aff airs of his city Halifax and province.
1901 he was appointed Legislative Council of Nova Scotia.
In politics he was a Liberal, in religion a Catholic. He built the
convent in Halifax for the Sisters of the Good Shepherd. He was
also devoted to the improvement of Point Pleasant Park and
elected Chairman of Board of Directors.
[119] Words: Thomas Ken, 1674. These lyrics, sung as the Doxology

in many churches, are actually the last verse of a longer hymn,
Awake, My Soul, and with the Sun.
Music: Old 100th, Genevan Psalter, 1551, attributed to Louis
Bourgeois http://www.cyberhymnal.org/htm/p/r/praisegf.htm
[120]Nightingale, Marie. *Out Of Old Nova Scotia Kitchens.*
Nimbus Publishing, Limited. 1989.
[121] The date of the actual burning of St. Andrew's Anglican Church
was November 22, 1874, but the Author has taken liberty here to
make it fit her story. http://www.gov.ns.ca/
nsarm/cap/places/page.asp?ID=712

Chapter Twenty-Two: Why Punish William?

[122] http://www.internet-at-work.com/hos_mcgrane/creation/
csmytgl.html

Chapter Twenty-Three: Time Comes Full Circle

[123] In 1890 the United States duty on sulphite pulp was raised to
six dollars a ton, thereby making the price of the Canadian
product prohibitive below the boarder. http://www.
sheetharbour.ca/history/chapter2.htm

Chapter Twenty-Four: Beyond the Lighthouse